THE SEAFORT SAGA

"A ripping good read – [illegible] sort of thing that attracted us all to SF [illegible] place"
S. M. Stirling

"S [illegible] ntuch has at last [illegible] ommunity the [illegible] ch as C. S. For- es [illegible] ason"
Bill Baldwin

"A [illegible] entertainment"
Analog

"Feintuch has constructed a fascinating story . . . You'll find his adventures highly entertaining"
Science Fiction Chronicle

"An excellent job of transferring Hornblower to interstellar space. A thoroughly enjoyable read"
David Drake

By David Feintuch

The Seafort Saga
MIDSHIPMAN'S HOPE
CHALLENGER'S HOPE
PRISONER'S HOPE
FISHERMAN'S HOPE
VOICES OF HOPE
PATRIARCH'S HOPE

THE STILL

Challenger's HOPE

DAVID FEINTUCH

ORBIT

An *Orbit* Book

First published in Great Britain by Orbit 1996
Reprinted 1997, 1998, 1999

This edition published by arrangement with
Warner Books, Inc., New York

*All characters in this publication are fictitious
and any resemblance to real persons, living or dead,
is purely coincidental.*

A CIP catalogue record for this book
is available from the British Library.

ISBN 1 85723 435 9

Printed and bound in Great Britain by Clays Ltd, St Ives plc

Orbit
A Division of
Little, Brown and Company (UK)
Brettenham House
Lancaster Place
London WC2E 7EN

Dedication

To Tony Straseske and Marshall Spencer, who helped me through, to Ragtime Rick of Toledo, Ohio, at whose corner booth an author often taps the keys of his laptop while the ragtime soars, and of course, to Jettie, who makes it worthwhile.

Ardath Mayhar, C.J. Cherryh and Roger MacBride Allen each contributed invaluable wisdom and wit while the author struggled with this work. No thanks can possibly be enough.

CHALLENGER'S HOPE

Being the second voyage of Nicholas Seafort,
U.N.N.S., in the year of our Lord 2197

Part I

November, in the year of our Lord 2197

1

"Carry on!" Geoffrey Tremaine strutted to his place at the head of the Admiralty conference table. Scowling, he set down his sheaf of notes and flicked invisible dust from his gold braid. As the assembled officers stood easy, I tugged at my jacket, made sure my tie was straight.

While the Admiral settled himself, we took our seats. Each of the eleven men and three women at this briefing in the Naval warren of down-under Lunapolis captained a ship in the UNNS squadron ready to sail to Hope Nation, sixty-nine light years distant. The Admiral's sloop, *Portia*, fitted with the newest L-Model fusion drive, was docked aloft at Earthport Station. So was my own sloop, *Challenger*, though I hadn't yet boarded her.

Tremaine's cold eye roved the table. "So," he said finally, as if disappointed. "My command is gathered together at last." Short, florid, he seemed on the edge of rage.

I glanced to either side. Length-of-service medals on Captain Hall's dress jacket indicated twenty-four years' service; Captain Derghinski, on my right, had twenty-two. Each of them had been a Naval officer longer than I'd lived. *Challenger* was my first assigned command. I was, I knew, the youngest Captain in the entire U.N. Navy.

"We sail tomorrow, gentlemen. As your written orders indicate, we'll Defuse seven times to provide the most accurate navigation checks possible."

Again I wondered why he wanted us to waste time and propellant with so many jumps, but as the most junior present, I kept my opinion to myself.

A Fusion drive was accurate to within six percent—whoops, no longer. Within *one* percent of the distance traveled. That change was astonishing; during my long cruise to Hope

Nation, vastly improved control baffles had been devised and Admiralty was retrofitting them on ships as they returned to Home System.

Navigation wasn't my strong point, and even the refresher course they'd made me attend left me a touch shaky on the mechanics of Fusion. Thankfully, the ship's puter and our Pilot would carry out most of the calculations, though I'd confirm them myself no matter how long it took.

Theoretically we could now Fuse to within three light months of Hope Nation, and follow with a short corrective jump. For greater precision, it was customary to make smaller jumps instead of one long one. We might normally expect to Defuse for nav checks twice during the sixty-nine-light-year voyage to Hope Nation. Seven times was absurd.

"I'll sail on *Challenger*," Tremaine said.

My jaw dropped. Could I have heard aright? True, *Challenger* was somewhat larger than *Portia*—the Admiral's flagship was one of the smallest vessels in our fleet—and I could arrange suitable accommodations, but—the Admiral himself? On my ship?

Tremaine glared, as if reading my thoughts. "With Captain Hasselbrad."

"What?" I heard my incredulous voice, as from a distance.

"I'm moving my flag. Naturally, I'll want a Captain with more experience. Seafort, you'll be taking *Portia*. They'll cut your new orders this afternoon. Pick them up from Ops."

"But—" I swallowed. "Aye aye, sir."

While he glanced through his papers my head spun with unasked questions. *Challenger*, the ship whose specs I'd studied until my eyes blurred, was no longer mine. All I knew about *Portia* was that she was a two-decker, tiny by comparison. And what of my crew? I'd had Alexi and Derek Carr assigned as my junior officers. And Vax Holser. They'd all be lost to me. How could I cope with the demands of an unfamiliar bridge without their dogged support?

Tremaine tapped his notes. "*Portia* and *Freiheit* will remain at each station until the rest of the fleet has Fused. Their L-Model drives will allow them to arrive first at the next rendezvous, to clear any, er, encroachment."

So that was it. The only, er, encroachment we might encounter was the bizarre alien creature I'd come upon during *Hibernia*'s voyage to Hope Nation, after I'd been catapulted from midshipman to Captain upon the death of *Hibernia*'s seasoned officers. The skirmish with the fish still brought nightmares, which my wife Amanda gently soothed away in the solitude of our cabin.

Lord God! Amanda had gone ahead to settle on *Challenger* while I struggled through Admiralty's refresher courses and my briefings. She'd be unpacking in our cabin—now the Admiral's. The sudden change of vessels would infuriate her—and I couldn't blame her.

I studied Tremaine glumly. Apparently he considered *Portia* expendable, so long as we protected his better-armed flagship. The fleet would Fuse and Defuse seven times to make sure my sloop and *Freiheit* were always in the lead to intercept a hostile force.

A gray-haired officer across the table intervened. "What will be our posture, sir, in case of unexpected contact?"

I grinned sourly at Captain Stahl's choice of words. Like most Naval officers, he found it difficult to concede that we'd really stumbled onto hostile aliens. At times I had trouble believing it myself, and I was the one who found them. After all, in two hundred years of exploring, man had discovered no animal life other than the primitive boneless fish of Zeta Psi. Thank Lord God our puter Darla recorded our contact. Without her playbacks and the few other eyewitnesses from *Hibernia*'s bridge, I'd be confined to a schizo ward for hormone rebalancing.

"Contact is highly unlikely." Admiral Tremaine paused, shot me an irritable glance. "However, you must not undertake threatening maneuvers without absolute proof of the hostile intent of the other party."

I blurted, "Absolute proof will likely result in the destruction of your ship." Unwise, but I couldn't stop myself.

The Admiral half-rose from his seat, his face red. "Flippancy and insubordination are what I'd expect from you, Seafort!"

"I wasn't flippant, sir." My tone was meek. "As far as we

saw, the aliens don't communicate by radio contact or signals. The first sign of hostility could be their acid eating through our hull. It's what took out *Telstar*, and—"

"Admiralty chose to give you a ship, Seafort." Vinegar was in Tremaine's tone. "I wouldn't have. Frankly, I doubt your whole report; puter disks can be faked. I don't know if you saw anything out there, but your report conveniently diverted attention from Captain Haag's death."

I gaped. Before the entire squadron, my new commanding officer had accused me of lying, of faking my report, perhaps even of murder. "I went through polygraph and drug testing before Admiralty offered me another ship." My throat was tight. "Mr. Holser and the others saw—"

He grunted. "Yes, for what that's worth." Before I could object he added, "At any rate, Seafort, your orders are to avoid initiating hostilities. Disobey and I'll relieve you so fast your head will spin." He turned away.

I sat through the rest of the briefing in a daze, doing my best to pretend calm. It was, I thought ruefully, a fit end to my shore leave.

When I'd brought *Hibernia* home with the startling news of the aliens, Admiralty hadn't known what to do with me. After they reluctantly accepted my verified report, Admiral Brentley, head of Fleet Operations, personally intervened to reward me with another ship and the rank of Commander, though most of my classmates at Academy hadn't yet made lieutenant.

When the gruff Admiral had concluded with me, I'd brought Amanda to Cardiff for a gloomy introduction to Father; afterward we set out on our delayed honeymoon.

I don't know why we'd chosen New York, except that she didn't know when she'd have another chance to see it. I'd been there and had no desire to return, but I held my peace for her sake.

Neither of us had really enjoyed the tense, busy luxury of Upper New York. Uncomfortable with my new celebrity, my mind flitted between memories of my recent voyage and the anticipation of a new ship, while Amanda struggled with her advancing pregnancy.

Waiting out the weeks of mandatory leave, I stared out of skytel windows while helibusses glided between sleek towers, high above decaying streets overrun by the ragged transpops, our ever-present urban homeless.

Once, Amanda and I descended to ground level to take a Gray Line tour, locked behind thick protective steel bars on an armored bus that wended its way through the teeming city. Well before nightfall we were returned safely to our hotel aerie, to which supplies were brought by air to avoid the hostile and savage transpops below. I wondered why the SecGen didn't send in the Unies to wrest control from the streeter gangs. An entire city was crumbling beneath our eyes.

In the evenings Amanda and I took helitaxis to plays, concerts and once, to my dismay, to an art show where I stared helplessly at holograms that dissolved in incomprehensible patterns. Around me, cognoscenti nodded with appreciation.

When our leave was over, we'd flown back to Houston; I had to attend more dull briefings while Amanda took the shuttle to Earthport Station and *Challenger*.

I recalled the irony of those incessant conferences. Our self-appointed experts in xenobiology offered guesses about the nature and intentions of the aliens I'd encountered, while glancing nervously to see if I suddenly recalled some detail that would contradict their theories.

I shook myself back to the present; Admiral Tremaine's briefing was finally ending. As we rose, Tremaine shook hands with several senior officers. I edged away, anxious to be gone, but his cold eye fixed me with a disapproving stare. He beckoned.

I approached, waited until he'd finished with my seniors. Could I get him to reconsider taking my prized ship? "About *Challenger*, sir. I personally selected her officers. I was hoping to sail with—"

"The ones who backed your tale about that fish? I imagine you would." His tone was sharp. "You'll have your way. You'll find their orders with your own."

"To *Portia*?"

"Of course. I won't sail with children manning my bridge. This is my first squadron, and everything must be shipshape.

Hasselbrad knows whom he wants, and I trust his judgment." The remainder of his thought was unspoken, but I blushed nonetheless. "Now, listen, Seafort."

I waited, hoping for a sign of conciliation.

"I told Brentley I wanted no part of you. In fact, I made it clear it was insane to give you a ship. He insisted on my leaving you in command, but I'll be damned if it will be a vessel of any importance. Each time we Fuse, take *Portia* to your station and stand guard. If those loony aliens you reported really exist, dispatch them before we arrive."

"But you said—Aye aye, sir." How could I dispatch a fish without initiating hostilities?

"That's all." Glowering, he took my salute.

As I left the room I sighed. I was disconsolate, hungry, rocket-lagged, and too far from my wife.

"Wait your turn!" A heavy-jowled woman, her face a mask of disapproval. I hesitated, blushing, but Lieutenant Alexi Tamarov pushed to the head of the line of impatient passengers at the Earthport Station ticket counter. Sheepishly I followed.

"G Concourse?" he called.

The attractive young lady looked up from the boarding passes thrust at her from all sides. "End of the corridor and downstairs, Lieutenant." She turned back to her forms.

"Thanks, ma'am!" Alexi ignored the civilians' hostile stares. "You have to learn to be aggressive, sir," he admonished. Only our years of service together on *Hibernia* permitted such a remark, notwithstanding his congenial tone.

We threaded our way through the station's main concourse. Harried families clutched children and baggage while magnetronic carts whizzed past with station staff. Roughened crewmen sprawled in seats, awaiting the arrival of their ships.

Earthport Station, the largest orbiting station ever built, moved all Earth's interstellar traffic and much of its interplanetary shipping too. Its many levels held bonded warehouses for the duty-free zones, dozens of shuttle bays, administrative offices, staff housing, waiting areas, rest rooms, restaurants and snack bars. News of the aliens had done little to slow the frantic pace of traffic.

"I keep forgetting how big the place is." Alexi hurried to

keep pace. A year younger than I, at nineteen Alexi was no longer the handsome boy just out of Academy I'd met three years before. He had grown into an athletic, confident young man.

"A lot of joeys moving out," I said. Perhaps fewer folk would embark on the sixteen-month cruise to Hope Nation until the danger from the aliens had passed. I lengthened my stride. In the two days since Admiral Tremaine had taken my ship, I'd grown almost desperate to be done with the interminable briefings and to board my command, whatever she might be.

"This way, sir. I remember now." Alexi diverted me to a staircase at one side of the corridor. I followed, grateful that he'd taken the trouble to meet my incoming shuttle, despite the inconvenience of resettling himself at short notice.

Only a few sailors and civilian workers hurried along the lower corridor as we strode past successive airlock gates. We were now at G-12; *Portia* was moored at G-4, almost halfway around the rim of the station. I shouldered the heavy duffel Alexi had twice offered to carry.

We slowed a bit, but kept a steady pace. Alexi offered a few remarks about ships outlined in the transplex portholes we passed, but subsided when I only grunted in reply.

The truth was that I was nervous; never had I boarded my own ship to take command. My captaincy of *Hibernia* had begun in tragedy and confusion, light years into our cruise from Earth to Hope Nation. Now I was to command U.N.S. *Portia*, a vessel that shipped sixty passengers and a crew of thirty. Among them two lieutenants, three middies. Far smaller than *Hibernia* or *Challenger*, she was a significant ship in the United Nations Naval Service despite Admiral Tremaine's disparaging remarks.

I knew that Lieutenant Vax Holser and my three midshipmen had already transferred aboard, along with the Pilot and Chief Engineer I had never met. As to the crew belowdecks, I had no idea whom I might find. I wondered again why Vax had turned down his own command to sail with me, considering how badly I'd treated him during our years in *Hibernia*. I nonetheless felt more secure for his steady, dependable presence.

As we reached G-4, I stopped to run my hands through my hair. When I tugged on the jacket of my dress whites, Alexi grinned. "It's not funny," I snapped. "I need to make a good impression."

"Right, sir." He was still smiling. Alexi was as close a friend as I had, but at times I wondered if our long voyage would chafe. I bit back a cutting remark, knowing my own tension and not Alexi's irrepressible good cheer had spawned it.

"I'm ready." I picked up my duffel. At the lock two armed marine sentries stood guard. I pulled out my papers.

One sentry remained standing with his hand on the butt of his pistol; the other saluted the bars on my dress uniform, took my papers. "Commander Nicholas Seafort?"

"That's right." I waited patiently while he compared the holopic to my face. After the rebellion we'd blundered into at Miningcamp, I appreciated their security measures; any orbiting station now left me ill at ease.

"There's your ship, Captain." He gestured.

Alexi followed me into the lock. As *Portia* maintained the same atmospheric pressure as the Station, the airlock had no need to cycle; *Portia*'s inner hatch would be opened as soon as we sealed the outer for safety.

Through the transplex airlock panel I caught a glimpse of sailors milling in the ship's corridor. "Gawd, there he is!" someone hissed within. The hatch slid open.

"Attention!" Vax Holser's bellow rang through the corridor. Utter silence greeted me as I took a step forward. Correctly, Alexi waited behind, in the lock. Vax's muscular frame stiffened to rigid attention as he snapped an Academy salute.

"Permission to come on board." My tone was formal.

"Granted, sir." Vax's grin was heartfelt and warming.

I strode through the inner hatch. Vax, Midshipman Derek Carr and two seamen remained at attention, eyes locked front.

I unfolded my orders. "To Nicholas Ewing Seafort, Commander, United Nations Naval Service," I read aloud. "Effective November 4, 2197, you shall command U.N.S. *Portia,* a vessel assigned to the squadron commanded by Admiral Geoffrey Tremaine. You are to voyage to Hope Nation and thence to Detour Colony in such manner as may be ordered by the Admiral commanding . . . " I read through the orders and folded the paper.

"As you were." As they relaxed, I looked about. We were at the fore airlock, adjacent to the ship's launch berth. The aft lock was below, on Level 2.

From a distance our vessel—or any Naval starship—would look like a pencil stood on end; the disks in which we lived consisted of two rings fitted tightly over the pencil about halfway from bow to stern. *Portia* had only two Levels rather than the three of *Challenger* and larger ships.

I turned to the waiting midshipman. Derek Carr, lean and youthful at eighteen, stood confidently in his crisp blue middy's uniform, buckles and shoes shined to perfection. As his eye caught mine I winked. Derek, whom I recruited from among the passengers of *Hibernia*, was maturing into a fine naval officer, despite occasional traces of the haughty young aristocrat he'd once been.

"I'll show you to your cabin, sir," Vax offered.

I made a quick decision. I still knew virtually nothing about my new command. "No. Mr. Carr, take my duffel to the Captain's cabin, and tell Amanda I'll be there in a while. Vax, show me everything, bow to stern."

"Aye aye, sir," Vax said automatically. No other response was possible to a Captain's command. As the others drifted away, he hesitated. "It won't take long to see. Compared to *Challenger*, this is a toy. He had no right—"

"Mr. Holser!" My voice was tight. "Don't even think of saying that aloud."

"I—no, sir."

"Did you forget an Admiral is senior to a Captain? The squadron is his to deploy. No criticism, now or ever."

"Aye aye, sir." His tone was subdued. "Shall we start at the bridge?"

"If you like." As I followed him along the corridor I remembered that I still wore my dress whites; I'd get them dirty poking around the ship. I'd also be hot. I decided against stopping to change; better not to appear indecisive my first day aboard.

As we were still moored, the bridge hatch was open and only a nominal watch was kept. Midshipman Rafe Treadwell came to attention when I entered. My eyes took in the control consoles, the navigation equipment, the simulscreens covering the front bulkhead. I would spend many of my waking hours in this compartment. Smaller than *Hibernia*'s bridge, still it had ample room to move around. I wondered if Naval designers knew Captains liked to pace.

I looked down at Rafe, fourteen, promoted from cadet at my recommendation so that he could join my next command as midshipman. "Enjoy your shore leave, Mr. Treadwell?"

"Uh, yes, sir." He blushed furiously. It must have been an interesting leave indeed. As midshipman, Rafe had his majority by statute of the General Assembly, and could frequent the bars and dives of Lunapolis. He'd been but eleven the last time he'd seen home port.

"Good; carry on. Vax, where to?"

Lieutenant Holser led me from the inactive bridge to the sickbay, and I chatted a moment with the Doctor. I'd see a lot of that place now that our baby was near. Down the circular corridor just past the ladder was the officers' mess, a tiny compartment barely larger than a passenger cabin. We officers would take our evening meal in the ship's dining hall with the passengers, and few enough of us would share the mess for morning and noon meals, as we stood our staggered watches.

Belowdecks, I glanced at the engine room and took a long look at Hydroponics, on whose output we would all depend. Outside the crew berth the chief petty officer brought a gaggle of seamen to attention. "Akrit, stand even with the others! Wipe off that idiot smile, Clinger. Sorry, sir."

I nodded curtly. The petty officers would have their hands full for a time, one of the pitfalls of guaranteed enlistment. Virtually any able-bodied person was guaranteed acceptance into the Service, and got a half-year's pay in advance as a bonus.

Back on Level 1, I surveyed a few passenger cabins as well as officers' quarters. I said little, trying to memorize what I could. We came across Alexi in the passengers' lounge chatting with two civilian girls; he detached himself and joined our tour.

Vax knocked on the wardroom hatch. By custom the wardroom was the midshipmen's private territory; except for inspection, other officers entered only by invitation. The hatch swung open. Seeing us, Midshipman Philip Tyre came rigidly to attention, in regulation naval slacks and tee shirt. His white shirt, tie and blue jacket lay neatly on his bunk.

"Mr. Tyre." I regretted my impulse to include Philip in my new command. I should have let him resign when *Hibernia*'s homecoming had released him from his purgatory. Tyre, at seventeen, was still as breathtakingly handsome as the day he'd first come aboard *Hibernia*. But now he wore a wary look, a legacy of the undying enmity he'd kindled in Alexi Tamarov, when Tyre had been Alexi's senior in the wardroom.

"Yes, sir." Philip waited anxiously. The middy was always obedient to his seniors, eager, cooperative and helpful. It was to his juniors that his unbearable traits were exposed. After Alexi's promotion, on the long trip back from Hope Nation, Lieutenant Tamarov had exacted vengeance by setting Philip over the barrel for a caning whenever opportunity arose.

Time to face the issue. "I wish you a good voyage, Mr. Tyre." I meant it as a signal; Alexi heard but gave no sign.

Philip's look was almost pleading. "Thank you, sir." Wisely he said no more. We left him to contemplate his future.

"Are you ever going to ease up, Alexi?" Together, we descended the ladder to Level 2.

"When you order it, sir." His tone was flat.

There was little more I could say. By tradition, the Captain was expected not to involve himself in wardroom affairs. Alexi, an amiable, goodhearted joey, could normally be depended on not to harass a middy, but in his misery under Mr. Tyre, Alexi had sworn an oath of revenge to Lord God himself. Lieutenant Tamarov meant literally what he had told me; he would stop when ordered, but not a moment before.

Fortunately for Philip, the miscreants' barrel was now in First Lieutenant Vax Holser's cabin, rather than Alexi's where it had sat most of our voyage home.

Shrugging, I continued my tour. Philip had made his own bed. Now, as with all of us, he must sleep in it.

2

"God, Nicky, where have you been?" Amanda shifted her bulging body to the side of her cushioned chair. The baby was due very soon.

"Hi, hon. Inspecting the ship." I tossed my jacket on the bunk and bent to nuzzle the soft brown hair I'd admired ever since I'd first seen her, an awkward young middy on *Hibernia*.

She gave a rueful grin. "She's not quite what *Challenger* would have been."

"Well . . ."

"I couldn't pack fast enough when they told me you were transferred. I dreaded that somehow you'd ship on *Portia* and I'd be left where I was. What on earth were they thinking of, changing Captains at the last moment?"

It wasn't a topic I cared to dwell on. I sat, made a lap, beckoned her to it. "You didn't want a rest from me?"

She settled cautiously, rested her sweet-scented hair in the crevice of my neck. "Not that long."

I loosened my tie, sighed. "My feet hurt."

From my collarbone came what sounded like a growl. "Try changing places. Everything aches these days."

I knew Amanda's pregnancy was trying, but she'd borne it with a good grace for which I cherished her all the more. She'd refused even to discuss a host-mother embryo transplant, prenatal rearing, or other alternatives that would have eased her discomfort.

My eye wandered around the cabin, examining my home for the next three years. It was the largest stateroom on the ship, far larger than the wardroom I'd shared with several midshipmen in earlier days. An open hatch led to the Captain's private head. Our cabin had its own shower compartment, similar to the one I'd had on *Hibernia*. That was one luxury I'd grown used to.

Amanda stretched, rose to her feet. "Learn anything in your briefings?"

"Only that Admiral Tremaine doesn't like me." I slipped out of my dress uniform, wishing I'd done so hours earlier.

"Why not?" She sounded indignant.

"It doesn't matter. He has his ship and I have mine." I donned my regular ship's blues. "I'll hardly see him at all."

"I missed you." Her voice was soft. "They boarded me on *Challenger* three days ago, while you were still in that Fusion course." She frowned. "A whole day I spent, checking their reference library. Wasted." Earlier, I had arranged for her appointment as *Challenger*'s civilian education director, the same post she'd held on *Hibernia*. Luckily, I was able to have her given the similar duties aboard *Portia*.

"Have you checked out *Portia*'s library?" I asked, to divert her.

"It seems complete enough." A whole library could be contained in a trunkful of holovid chips, so storage space wasn't a problem. I knew Amanda would examine the booklist carefully; as ed director, her task would be to teach children who wanted education, and to supervise adult classes during the long, dull Fuse to Hope Nation and to Detour beyond. It was common for passengers to use the uneventful months in space to learn new skills or carry out research.

I checked my watch. "Seven o'clock. Hungry, hon?"

"I'm always hungry," she admitted. She flashed the smile that had captivated me as a fumbling midshipman. "Don't worry, I won't stay fat." We headed for the dining hall.

Most of the passengers and all of the crew had already boarded. However, many passengers had chosen to leave the ship to wander in Earthport Station's vast concourses, watch through the observation ports as other ships arrived and departed, or sample the many expensive restaurants the station provided. Dinner that night aboard *Portia* was sparse and informal.

At the Captain's table Amanda and I were joined by only two passengers. Normally we sat eight to a table; nine large round tables would seat my officers and *Portia*'s sixty passengers.

I felt uneasy beginning the meal without the traditional Ship's Prayer, recited every night while under weigh, but it was not the custom to pray in port. Instead, I said a silent grace.

Amanda introduced me to Dr. Francon, a synthetic cardiology specialist on route to Hope Nation to run Hope General's cardiac generation unit. Our other guest, Mr. Singh, told us he had no reason for traveling except to see as much of the known universe as his lifetime would let him.

"The galaxy is a hundred thousand light-years across, Mr. Singh. You won't have time to see but a fraction; why did you pick our corner of it?"

The small, tan-skinned man smiled delightedly. "Pure chance, Captain Seafort. Fortuity. As you know, I had to arrange my cruise before you returned on *Hibernia*, so I had no idea when I chose Hope Nation that I might actually get to see alien life."

"Let's hope you don't," I muttered. A chill prickled my spine.

"It isn't foreordained that our contact must be hostile," he said in his gentle singsong voice. "Now that we each know of each other's existence, perhaps more positive, loving contact may be had."

"Not by me." I changed the subject. As we progressed from soup to the main course I was distracted by boisterous children and teenagers at a table across the hall. I ignored them, though their presence surprised me. *Hibernia* had carried few youngsters.

Under the table, my wife pressed her hand on my knee. I hoped no one noticed; I could hardly maintain the dignity of a Captain while an attractive woman fondled me.

After dinner I escorted Amanda to our cabin and returned to the bridge. Lieutenant Tamarov had the watch; he was sitting comfortably at the first officer's console when I came in.

"Are we all set, Alexi?"

"All supplies loaded, sir. The last contingent of passengers arrives late this evening. The mail comes aboard at 04:00 standard time, then we'll be ready to cast off."

Idly I tapped the back of my soft leather watch chair. "Why would passengers reboard so late?"

"The Lower New Yorkers, sir. The station didn't want to bring them aloft any earlier than necessary."

"Who?" I gaped. "Street people?"

"Transpops, yes, sir."

"On my ship?" I sank into my chair, dismayed. "Are you joking?"

"Not at all. Didn't you read the memo?"

"What memo, Alexi?" It came as a growl.

"From Cincfleet, sir." He glanced at me, hurried on. "While you were away. It's a pilot program arranged by the Reunification Church, endorsed by UNICEF. They're rounding up teen transpops and sending them outward. Give them a better life while harnessing their raw energy to productive use, or some such folderol. Our band is headed for Detour, in the custody of a UNICEF social worker."

Appalled, I pictured my honeymoon in New York. Our tour bus had crawled down Fifth Avenue along the ruins of Central Park, past the old Central Park Zoo, long bereft of animals they couldn't protect from hungry human scavengers who prowled its cobbled stones.

As we came upon the twenty-foot wall topped with broken glass and barbed wire that ringed the ancient Plaza Hotel, the bus was abruptly surrounded by a mob of ragged, frantic youths brandishing what I at first thought were homemade weapons, but soon realized were tourist artifacts carved or pressed from sheet metal, worn pieces of rubber tire, and other scrap.

"Getcha Newyawk souvs!" a grimy boy shouted through the grillwork welded to the tour bus windows. "TraCenta, Empiyabuildin', lookadem heah!" He waved his crude skyscrapers at any prospective takers. Amanda pressed my hand tightly.

The driver glanced at his mirrors, decided it would be safe to stop. While he and the guard grasped their stunners, two of the wild children were allowed to enter the fortresslike bus to peddle their wares. After five minutes they were hustled off and we'd continued on our way to Timesquare.

I slammed my fist into the chair arm, startling Alexi. "I won't have it!"

By day, Lower New York maintained a semblance of civilization; tour buses such as ours penetrated its outer reaches. Not by night. In the darkened alleyways and torn avenues of Lower New York, rival Hispanic, Black, and Oriental gangs preyed on the transient population, the transpops, our permanent and ever-increasing urban homeless.

Rarely, if ever, did anyone descend to street level; residents of Upper New York flew in and out of the city from rooftop heliports. Derek Carr, the young aristocrat I'd befriended and enlisted in the Service, was of that urbane and civilized culture. Buildings such as Derek's home generated their own power and were heavily fortified against invasion by the transpops.

How could Admiral Brentley think of infesting my ship with such savages?

"How many?" I demanded.

"Forty-two, sir."

I was aghast. "Out of sixty passengers?"

"No, sir." Alexi took a deep breath, eyed me warily. "We have our sixty passengers. And forty-two transpops."

I came out of my seat, fists bunched, controlling myself only with effort. "We have cabins for only sixty!"

"Yes, sir. A number of scheduled passengers will double up. The, uh, transportees will bed six to a cabin."

"That's worse than the wardroom! How can you cram six bunks into a stateroom?"

"Pardon, sir, but they've already been installed." A nervous adolescent voice, from the speaker. "Double bunks against each bulkhead."

I glared from speaker to speaker. "Who are you?"

"Danny, sir. Uh, hi."

"Danny?" I turned to Alexi.

"Our puter."

"Oh." I paused. "Hello, Danny." I glowered at Alexi. "Supplies? Hydrononics and recyclers?"

"Adjusted, sir, but we'll be at near-maximum utilization the whole cruise."

"Why didn't you tell me sooner about the transpops?" My voice was dangerously quiet.

"I thought you already knew." Alexi eyed me steadily.

Petulant, I threw myself into my seat. "Patch me through to Fleet Ops." Alexi picked up the caller. "This isn't a prison ship," I muttered, half to myself. "Are they insane?"

"Perhaps, sir," said Alexi gravely. Despite my agitation, I had to smile; Alexi had taken the opportunity provided by my question to suggest criticism of his superiors, which otherwise would have been unacceptable. Neatly done, but it reminded me that I had just criticized Admiralty in front of my lieutenant.

It was an hour before my call got through to Admiral Brentley on Lunapolis. The conversation was brief. "I can't do a thing about it, Nick. This comes straight from the Secretary-General's office. I know you're overcrowded but I can't help you."

"But what possible good could it do to haul forty transpops from among the hundreds of thous—"

"Ask the Council of Elders of the Church; it falls under 'charitable works' and they have the ear of the SecGen. I gather that if the experiment works, they'll begin mass shipping of trannies to the newer colonies."

"But, sir—"

"I know, I know. As a means of relieving population pressure it's nonsense, and you'd think they'd know better. A nuisance for you, but it's out of my bailiwick. Put up with the overcrowding as best you can."

"It's more than overcrowding, sir. The recyclers aren't meant to handle—"

"I know, Seafort, but there's ample safety margin built into the specs. As for food, we'd provided extra canned—"

"Sir, they're dangerous to the ship and the other passengers!"

"I'd feel the way you do if *Portia* were mine. But the U.N.'s desperate to relieve pressure in the urban centers. The program is set. Anyway, they've sent you younger ones who have no known parents, and a supervisor to watch over them.

I understand the most violent cases have been screened out. Do your best, Seafort."

"Aye aye, sir," I said automatically. The connection went dead. I turned to Alexi. "Make sure the purser is prepared. Set up additional tables in the dining hall. Have extra crewmen stand by when they arrive. Good Lord!"

"Yes, sir. Aye aye, sir." Alexi's faint smile was almost hidden by the hand propped in front of his mouth.

I knocked at the Level 2 corridor hatch, waited as it slid open. "Chief Engineer Hendricks?"

A thin, graying man, whose officer's jacket ill fitted his long, skinny arms. "Yes, sir." His voice was flat and emotionless, his mouth unsmiling.

"You were bunked down when I visited the engine room," I said. "Good to meet you."

"Thank you."

"Are we ready for departure?"

"Yes, sir. I would have told you otherwise."

"Uh, right." I felt like the awkward middy I'd once been. "Carry on. We'll talk later." I continued along the Level 2 corridor, Philip Tyre at my side. "Which cabins, Mr. Tyre?"

He pointed ahead. "There, sir, just past crew berth one." We strode past the crew berth. Two seamen lounging in the corridor stiffened to attention. I ignored them. Tyre opened the cabin hatch.

Upper and lower bunks were stacked alongside three of the four bulkheads. The two extra dressers utterly filled the rest of the compartment, leaving barely enough room to move about. "A few nights is one matter," I said, "but seventeen months of this . . ."

Philip shrugged, unconcerned. "They're just trannies, sir."

I was outraged. "Two demerits, Mr. Tyre! Make that three!" I ignored his stricken look. "On my first posting, we middies were taught to show respect for passengers!"

"Yessir," he said quickly. "I'm very sorry, Captain. I only meant they're probably used to it. Not that they deserved it." His tone was meek. "I'm sorry if I offended, sir."

Perhaps I'd overreacted, but a few hours of calisthenics wouldn't hurt him. It only took two hours to work off each demerit, unless he reached ten and was sent to the barrel. "Very well. Are all their cabins like this one?"

"Yes, sir. Pretty much."

"They're all on this Level?"

"Yes, sir, 211 through 217. I think Mr. Holser wanted them near crew quarters, sir, in case of trouble."

I considered a moment. Vax was probably right, and I certainly didn't want them on the same Level as the bridge. Anyway, the transpops were due to board anytime now; too late for changes. "Very well, Mr. Tyre, we'll go back up. You'll help the pursuer when they board."

"Aye aye, sir." As we climbed the ladder to Level 1 he blurted, "Sir, I already had seven demerits."

Alexi must have been at him again. I hesitated. Canceling demerits was bad for discipline. But still . . . ten meant the barrel. "Very well, Mr. Tyre. Two demerits instead of three."

He shot me a grateful look. "Thanks, sir. Thanks very much."

Exhausted, I contemplated returning to the bridge. There was no reason to stay awake; Vax could settle our passengers. I had to be alert in the morning for our departure. I headed for my cabin, and Amanda's soothing care.

Straightening my tie and checking my jacket I strode onto the bridge, a confident young Captain about to take command. Still I paused before taking the chair at the left console. The seat was empty, of course; it would have been unthinkable for a junior officer to be found in it.

I nodded to Vax Holser in the chair across, and turned to the unfamiliar figure at the console at my right. "Pilot Van Peer, I presume?"

The red-haired young man smiled engagingly as he stood and saluted. "Walter Van Peer, yes, sir. Glad to meet you." Mr. Van Peer was a holdover from the ship's last voyage to Casanuestra.

I glanced at my instruments. "We're ready, gentlemen?" I keyed the caller to Departure Control. "Station, U.N.S. *Portia* is prepared for departure from G-4."

After a moment the reply crackled in the speaker. "Initiate breakaway, *Portia*."

"Roger." I thumbed the caller. "Attention, aft and forward airlocks. Cast off!"

"Aye aye, sir!" Alexi and Rafe Treadwell were at the aft lock; Derek was forward. With a pang I remembered *Hibernia*'s departure from Luna Station on my first interstellar flight, three years ago. I'd been at the aft lock where Rafe now served, Lieutenant Malstrom supervising my every move. Impulsively I jumped from my seat. "I'm going below," I said. "Hold breakaway until my command."

Vax glanced at me in mild surprise; the Pilot's mouth opened in astonishment. Of course neither said a word except to acknowledge my order.

I hurried down the corridor to the ladder. At the forward airlock Derek Carr was calmly supervising the seamen who were unhooking our steel safety line from the stanchion in the station lock. At my approach he raised an eyebrow, but said nothing.

Portia, like any vessel, secured herself to a station with its capture latches, and the ship's airlock mated to the station lock with rubber seals, but ever since the *Concorde* disaster, backup safety cables were mandatory.

A sailor wound in our cable, pulling it into our own lock. The cable bent with difficulty through the gloves of his spacesuit as he folded it. "Line secured, sir," he called to Derek.

"Forward line secured, sir," Derek repeated, though I stood at his side.

"Proceed, Mr, Carr." Then I blurted, "I'm not inspecting. I just wanted to watch." Idiocy, explaining myself to a midshipman.

"Yes, sir." Derek turned to the sailor. "Close inner lock, Mr. Jarnes. Prepare for breakaway."

"Aye aye, sir." Seaman Jarnes pressed a coded transmitter to the inner lock panel. The thick hatches slid shut smoothly, forming a tight center seal.

"Disengage capture latches."

The seaman keyed open the latch control panel, touched the pad within. "Disengaged, aye aye."

Derek glanced at me. "Forward lock secured, sir. Shall I report also to the bridge?"

"I suppose, Mr. Carr." I looked helplessly at the outer lock still mated to the station. What I'd wanted to see was our actual breakaway, but my duty was aloft. I sighed, and reluctantly headed back topside.

In my seat again I thumbed the caller. "Departure Control, *Portia* ready for breakaway."

"Proceed, *Portia*. Vector oh three oh from station. Godspeed."

"Thank you, Station." I touched a button on my console three times. Three deep blasts from the ship's whistle resounded, signaling imminent breakaway to all on our vessel.

"Pilot Van Peer, you have the conn."

"Right, sir." His tone was cheerful. He signaled the engine room. "Chief, auxiliary power, please."

Chief Hendricks's dry, unemotional voice. "Auxiliary power, aye aye."

"Hang on, folks, here we go," the Pilot said with an irreverent grin. He gently fired our side thrusters; jets of propellant shot from the nozzles imbedded in the ship's hull. *Portia* rocked, her airlock suckers stretching. Abruptly they parted from their counterparts on the station lock; U.N.S. *Portia* drifted slowly clear of Earthport Station. Stars slid across the simulscreens on the forward bulkhead. After a few moments the Pilot asked casually, "Would you care to close the outer locks, sir?"

I flushed. It was my responsibility to give the order, but I'd been too busy gawking at the receding station. "Very well." I thumbed the caller. "Secure outer hatches!"

Red console lights switched to green as the outer airlock hatches slid closed. "Forward hatch secure, sir." Derek.

Alexi's steady voice followed. "Aft hatch secure, sir."

"Secured, very well."

The Pilot maintained us on course. I watched the station in the simulscreens until it was swallowed by the starry backdrop. Long minutes stretched into an hour.

"We're clear to Fuse, sir," the Pilot said.

"Danny, Fusion coordinates, please."

"Aye aye, sir," the puter said promptly. He flashed the figures onto my console screen.

As I began to punch calculations onto my screen I felt sweat gathering under my jacket, as always when I plotted Fusion coordinates.

The Pilot stirred. "I ran our coordinates myself and checked them against the puter's figures, sir."

I ignored him.

"They check out to six decimal places," he added.

"Vax, you too," I said.

"Aye aye, sir." My first lieutenant tapped figures into his console.

Pilot Van Peer looked from one to the other of us, perplexed. "Is there a problem, Captain?"

I made no response.

"I thought it's customary for the Pilot to calculate Fusion coordinates." He sounded plaintive.

I grunted. "On my ship we all do. Nothing personal." I returned to my laborious calculations.

"The puter's figures and mine are in full—"

"Pilot, shut up!" Nav didn't bring out the best in me.

"Aye aye, sir." His hurt was manifest.

Half an hour later I had my figures. They checked with Danny's and Vax's. "Very well." I fed them into the puter.

"Coordinates received and understood, Captain." Danny sounded breathless.

"Thank you." I thumbed the caller. "Engine room, prepare to Fuse."

"Prepare to Fuse, aye aye." After a moment the speaker came alive. "Engine room ready for Fuse, sir."

"Chief Engineer, Fuse."

"Aye aye, sir." The Chief's voice was flat. "Fusion drive is . . . ignited." The simulscreens abruptly blanked.

I remained in my seat, the melancholy of our isolation pressing. In Fusion, all our external instruments were dead; we rode the crest of our N-wave out of the Solar System at superluminous speed, blind and deaf. Even communication was denied us; nothing we broadcast could travel as fast as the N-wave itself. Now we had only our own resources to sustain us until we reached safe haven sixty-nine light-years away.

Vax had the watch; I knew he was reliable. Besides, there

was nothing on the bridge that needed doing. After a while, morose, I left. Amanda wasn't in our cabin, so I wandered to the Level 1 passengers' lounge, where I found only unfamiliar faces among the holovids, easy chairs, and game machines.

I could have remained; officers were free to use the lounge and we weren't discouraged from socializing with passengers, but I withdrew, ill at ease. I followed the circumference corridor to the west ladder, climbed down to Level 2. Perhaps I'd find Amanda in the library.

"Here's cap'n! Here's cap'n!" A teen joey pranced around me, sandals flopping on the deckplates as his high, excited voice beckoned his mates. He pointed at my jacket. "Mira, mira da man!" Rough-trimmed hair hung over his ears. His scrawny body was covered by a blue denim jumpsuit.

"He da man! He da man! Mira threads!" Grimy hands pawed at the braid on my jacket. I slapped them away, but other curious youths pressed close.

A voice sliced through the jabber. "Knock off, joeys! Knock off!" A meaty hand flung aside one ragged youngster. A short, chunky woman pushed through the opening she'd made. "Gi'im room! Knock off, gi'im room." Her words tumbled. Slowly the crowd drew back. She smiled briefly. "Sorry, Captain. Melissa Chong. I'm supposed to make sure things like this don't happen." Apparently unaware of ship's protocol, she stuck out her hand.

Awkwardly I took it. "You're the supervisor?"

"Right, I'm a UNICEF DSW, but these joeys call me Mellie." She collared the youth who first approached me. "Say sorry, Annie! Tell'im sorry cap'n!"

"Naw!" Her charge tried to squirm away.

"Noway toucha cap'n, Annie! Noway!"

"Din' hurtim," he—she?—said sullenly. "Jus lookin'!"

"Say sorry," repeated Dr. Chong, a firm grip on the youth's neck.

The look Annie shot me was wrathful. "Din' mean nothin'," she muttered. "Din' hurt, just lookin', sorry."

I nodded. "No harm done. Your name is Annie? You're a girl?"

Her face flashed into an elfin grin. She wiggled her hips. "Cap'n wanna fin' out?"

"Knock off, Annie!" Dr. Chong said sharply. She thrust the girl away. "Inna room, allyas. Inna room." Reluctantly they drifted away toward their cabins.

"How do you speak that jargon?" My tone was mild.

"You pick it up after a while. Mostly it's just fast." Her round Oriental face broke into a grin. "I'll teach you, if you wish. In case you ever go transient."

I shuddered. "Lord God forbid." I glanced about, frowned at the litter that hadn't strewn the deck a few moments before. "Well. You'll have your hands full."

"Yes, 'til Detour. Then they're someone else's responsibility."

Seventeen months, with such rabble. I sighed. "How do you control them?"

"I'm trying to meld them into a single tribe. Most of them respect tribal authority. It's all they know."

I raised an eyebrow, puzzled. "I thought trannies were—"

"Don't use that word!"

"I beg your pardon?" My tone was frosty.

"Say 'transpops,' or 'transients.' The other is a racial slur, like 'chic' or 'black.' They'll take offense, and the consequences could be violent."

"I've heard it used." I wrinkled my brow. "Very well, I'll take care. Anyway, I was asking . . ."

"About tribes, yes. Most Uppies don't realize there's more than one transpop subculture. Transpops live in social units based on location. Some homelands are contained in a few small blocks, others quite large. They get along by trading, or selling sex. Or warring. For instance, the Unies—"

"How many tribes among our group?" I was impatient to be on my way.

"Several, and it's caused no end of problems. If UNICEF had only listened—" She sighed. "Anyway, I'm sorry for the disturbance, Captain." On that note we parted.

I found Amanda sorting through holochips in the library. "Look, Nicky, they even have Marx and Engels! I could do a comparative economics course."

I grinned. "For whom, hon? The transpop joeys?"

"I'll have you know we've plenty of educated passengers this trip." She racked a stack of chips. "We'll have lots of guest lecturers. In fact I was thinking of—ungh!" She flinched.

"What's wrong?" I couldn't hide my alarm.

"I got kicked. I think he wants out, Nicky."

"Right now?"

She laughed at my consternation. "Not in the next few minutes. But soon, I think. He wants to see his papa."

I grimaced. The idea of parenthood was still alien. "I want to see him too," I assured her. I paused. "Will you lunch with me?"

"Officers' mess or the dining hall?" Ship's officers ate their morning and noon meals in the tiny officers' mess, and joined the passengers for the formal evening meal. The passengers took breakfast and lunch cafeteria style in the Level 1 passengers' dining hall. The crew, of course, always ate belowdecks in the Level 2 crew mess.

"The officers' mess," I said. "I don't want to share you with all those people." She rewarded me with a smile. I took her hand and we wandered back along the corridor toward the ladder. I didn't care how undignified I looked.

Lunch was a simple affair, some sort of stew served over bread. I chose the small table against the bulkhead rather than the long wooden table in the center of the cabin. By tradition that signaled I meant to eat alone, and the other officers wouldn't bother me. If I chose the long table, officers were free to strike up conversation.

"You ought to talk with Melissa Chong," I told Amanda. "Set up an education program for the transpops."

She grimaced. "From what I hear I'd have to start at the very beginning." She eyed me suspiciously. "Who's Melissa Chong, and where were you?"

I made allowances. In her pregnancy Amanda had a right to insecurity. "Talking to passengers." My voice was mild. I changed the subject.

After lunch I returned to the bridge. In Fusion I had little to occupy me there. The puter's sensors monitored air pressure, power, recycling and hydroponics controls, airlock status, and the like. We would stand watches against the risk that something might go seriously wrong, but if it did, we were unlikely to survive.

Philip Tyre and Pilot Van Peer had the watch. Both stood politely as I entered. I waved them back to their seats, took my place, and scanned the displays.

"Readouts are normal, Captain," the Pilot offered.

"May I check for myself?" I regretted my growl almost instantly; Van Peer hadn't meant any criticism. I was still touchy from the trouble I'd had with my Pilot on *Hibernia*. "Sorry," I added lamely. That annoyed me even more; a Captain didn't need to apologize for snapping: it was his privilege. The commander of a vessel under weigh had virtually unlimited powers. The respect his officers showed him was partly tradition and partly from self-preservation.

To ease the strain I made conversation with Midshipman Tyre. "Work off any more demerits, Philip?"

"Yes, sir. Three." That meant he'd spent six hours in the exercise room since yesterday evening. I made a joke of it. "Calisthenics should be quite easy for you now, Philip."

He smiled politely. "Yessir, I've had practice." We both recognized we were near forbidden territory and dropped the subject. As first midshipman, Philip was supposed to run the wardroom under the lieutenants' supervision. I wasn't expected to delve into his affairs, and he knew better now than to complain to me about his treatment.

Though Philip Tyre was our senior midshipman, it was clear he wouldn't be in charge of the wardroom. A year ago on *Hibernia*'s return voyage, Derek Carr had challenged Philip's authority in the traditional manner. The two boys had gone to the exercise room to fight it out, and Philip had lost the fight and with it control of the wardroom. Now he didn't dare interfere with Derek.

According to tradition I should have blackballed Philip; a midshipman who couldn't hold his wardroom was assumed unfit for command. Instead, though I felt only distaste for the boy, I'd suggested that Admiral Brentley assign him to my new ship. Now, I realized the extent of the problem I'd made for myself. Philip, hated thoroughly by both Derek and Lieutenant Tamarov, was a liability. Unless, somehow, I could turn him around. But I didn't see how.

Pilot Van Peer spoke cheerfully into the silence. "I understand you're a rather good chess player."

I grunted. "I play, yes."

"So do I, sir. I'd enjoy a match." I yearned to accept; I loved chess. But his suggestion was a serious breach of custom; an officer didn't initiate social contact with his Captain.

"Perhaps." His lack of discretion left me uncomfortable.

He seemed unabashed. "We can play here if you like. Lord God knows there isn't much to do on watch during Fusion."

"I don't know about that." My tone was cautious.

"Here's a board, sir," Danny said eagerly, as it flashed onto the simulscreen. "Tell me where; I'll make the moves for you!"

I didn't like being pushed. "Not on watch," I said. "Let it be."

"Aw, it'd be something to do." Danny sounded plaintive. "I'm bored." He sounded more like an ill-disciplined middy than a ship's puter. Again I pondered the age-old question: was he really alive? I dropped it; there was no way to tell.

"Captain Steadman played on watch." The Pilot.

I was astonished. Was Van Peer actually arguing? He should know better. Or was discipline on a sloop more relaxed than on a ship of the line such as *Hibernia*? I hesitated; the puter's urging and the Pilot's casual informality made the bridge seem far more friendly than I was used to. I would enjoy the game. On the other hand, regs required an officer on watch to remain alert at all times.

I made my tone cold. "You're relieved, Pilot. Confine yourself to quarters until your next watch. When you return to the bridge, be prepared to obey my orders without argument."

He gulped. "Aye aye, sir. I apologize, Captain Seafort. I meant no disrespect." He slapped open the hatch. "Perhaps we could play another time then, sir. Off watch." He left, apparently unfazed.

I sighed. We would be cooped together for a long voyage, and as was my custom with all my officers, I'd gotten off to a bad start. I glared at the board on the simulscreen. "Turn that thing off."

"Aye aye, sir." Danny flicked off the screen.

Philip Tyre remained very still. I realized I had just consigned myself to a long watch alone with a midshipman I didn't like. "Don't just sit there," I snapped. "Call up random positions and calculate Fusion coordinates. One demerit for each percent difference between your solution and Danny's."

"Aye aye, sir!" Immediately, Tyre bent to his console.

Now I was turning on a helpless middy because I was annoyed with the Pilot. Disgusted with myself, I added, "And one demerit is canceled for every solution that agrees with Danny's to four decimal places."

Philip's look was almost worshipful. "Thank you very much, sir." He diligently tapped figures into his screen. I remembered that Tyre, unlike myself, was very skilled at navigation.

When the watch finally drew to a close I went to find Amanda. Elated, Philip trotted ahead of me. He'd worked off three demerits by mental rather than physical exercise. I wondered if I'd acted improperly but decided I hadn't. If Alexi hadn't searched for excuses to discipline Tyre, the midshipman wouldn't have logged the demerits in the first place.

I stood tapping my glass for quiet. Into the silence I said, "Lord God, today is November 15, 2197, on the U.N.S. *Portia*. We ask you to bless us, to bless our voyage, and to bring health and well-being to all aboard." My eyes stung. The Ship's Prayer has been repeated nightly for over one hundred sixty years aboard every United Nations vessel to sail the cosmos. For the first time I had offered it aboard a ship that was truly mine. Even if she wasn't quite the ship I'd expected a few days ago.

I felt stiff in my freshly ironed navy-blue pants, white shirt, black tie. The insignia on my blue jacket gleamed, as did the brass on my ribbed cap. My black shoes had been spit-polished by Roger, the ship's boy, instead of by myself. Nonetheless, except for my insignia, my costume was identical with that of every officer from Dr. Bros down to Rafe Treadwell, our most junior midshipman.

But, as my bars indicated, I was Captain, and presided at the ship's table of honor. Passengers who wished to sit with me made a request to the purser, and I was free to choose from among them. Normally, seating rotated monthly. As this was our first month and I knew nobody on board I'd made no attempt to select my companions, but left it to Purser Li.

I toyed with my food, making awkward conversation. Idle chat was something I'd learned in the Navy; before that, in Father's house, we usually took meals in silence. Since our marriage, Amanda had lifted the conversational burden from me. Tonight she was making sporadic efforts, but she was preoccupied with a backache.

A friendly middle-aged woman looked at her with sympathy. "It doesn't go on forever, my dear, even if it seems that way."

Amanda smiled gratefully. "It feels that way sometimes, Mrs. Attani."

"Greg, here, was my first." She indicated the dapper young man of seventeen at her side, whose careful manners matched his elegant dress. "Time was in slow motion while I carried him."

Gregor Attani's smile was polite. He made no comment.

"You're going to Hope Nation?" I asked, knowing the answer from her file.

"Yes, Captain. I took my degrees at MIT and now I'm on my way to the Agricultural Station on Eastern Continent."

"And your husband?" I asked, unthinking.

"I never had one," she answered calmly. Unless she was confessing promiscuity, which was most unlikely, that meant Gregor was clone or donor.

Amanda nudged me in the ribs. I thought she was chiding my gauche remark, but she gestured surreptitiously to a table across the hall, where Melissa Chong's charges had been segregated. None of the paying passengers had cared to dine with transients.

Several of the transpop youngsters jostled and shoved each other; as I watched, one flung a roll at his opponent. Dr. Chong hurried from her nearby seat; behind her a mini-riot broke out at the table she had left. I snapped my fingers; the steward bent discreetly.

"Put a seal on that, flank!" I indicated the trouble spot.

"Aye aye, sir." In a moment he was leaning over one of the tables, hands spread on the tablecloth. The commotion subsided.

* * *

Alexi took his place at the first officer's console. "Morning, sir. How's Amanda?"

I grimaced. "Restless. She's not sleeping well." Amanda was due in a week. Josip Bros, the Doctor, was watching her closely.

Alexi smiled sympathetically, but with no real understanding. That Amanda needed me to do even the simplest things for her was acceptable and even pleasurable. As for her occasional petulance, I bore it as best I could, knowing it sprung from her physical discomfort.

Alexi yawned. "We could have coffee, sir, if you'd like."

Normally we didn't eat on watch, but coffee was allowable. I could hold the bridge while he strolled down the circumference corridor to the officers' mess. "That would be nice."

"Right." He thumbed the caller. "Mr. Tyre, report to the bridge on the double!"

I waited, deciding to say nothing. After a moment the young midshipman arrived. He panted, "Midshipman Tyre reporting, sir!"

"Get us two black coffees." Alexi's eyes were on his console.

It was an unusual command; an officer might normally order the ship's boy to fetch something—that was what he was for—but one didn't send a midshipman for coffee. Unless one was hazing the middy.

Philip knew better than to show any resentment. "Aye aye, sir." Obediently he left for the officers' mess.

I asked, "Did he deserve that?"

Alexi said curtly, "He can use the exercise, now he's not working off demerits by calisthenics."

I was amazed. This, from my friend Alexi? "You know better than to talk that way to your Captain!"

Alexi looked mildly surprised. "I wasn't criticizing, sir. Please don't take offense."

I sighed. "Alexi, you're so anxious to harass him you've lost all sense of proportion."

"Have I?" Alexi considered it with indifference. "Perhaps."

The hatch opened again. Philip Tyre held a steaming cup in each hand. He brought me mine first.

"Thank you."

"You're welcome, sir." He approached Alexi, who was abruptly busy studying his console. Tyre waited.

After a while Alexi reached absently for the cup. "Dismissed."

"Aye aye, sir." Philip went to the hatch and slapped it open.

"Just a moment," I said quietly. "Mr. Tamarov, I will have courtesy among officers."

Alexi raised an eyebrow. "Courtesy?" He waited a moment, as if in thought. "Aye aye, sir. Mr. Tyre, thank you for bringing me a cup of coffee. That's all."

"Aye aye, sir." Glancing nervously between us, Midshipman Tyre made his escape.

A long silence. When he spoke, Alexi's tone was bitter. "Sir, you're within your rights to rebuke me, but I respectfully suggest that doing so in front of a middy interferes with discipline."

I was astounded. Because I'd leapfrogged from midshipman to Captain I had never been a lieutenant, but if I'd been one who spoke so to my Captain I'd expect summary court-martial at the least. I was also worried; Tamarov was a seasoned officer who should know better. "Are you all right, Alexi?"

"Fine," he shot back. "Humiliated in front of Mr. Tyre, who knows you'll intercede whenever I demerit him, but otherwise fine."

"If you were a midshipman I'd cane you for insolence!"

He gave no ground. "Yes, sir, I believe you would!" We exchanged glares.

"Mr. Tamarov, you presume on our friendship." My voice was cold. "I won't allow insubordination. Confine yourself to quarters for a week. You're relieved from the watch roster until you explain to my satisfaction how your conduct was unsatisfactory. Leave at once!"

Alexi had no choice but to obey a direct order. "Aye aye, sir." He slapped open the hatch and stalked out.

I paced the bridge, my adrenaline surging. When I calmed

myself I sat and reflected on my novel approach to watch standing: banish any officer with whom I shared the bridge. "Were you recording that, Danny?" I didn't want a permanent record of Alexi's misconduct.

"Nope. I probably should have. You really gave it to him." Danny brimmed with enthusiasm.

I grunted my dissatisfaction.

The rest of the watch was uneventful. Just before noon Vax came to relieve me, Rafe Treadwell in tow. Rafe, scrubbed and immaculate in a crisp new uniform, was to stand his first watch as a midshipman. Biting his lip, he glanced at the console.

"Don't worry." My voice was reassuring. "If you blow up the ship I won't live to know about it." It brought a weak smile. I left for my cabin. Amanda was out, so I lay down on my bunk hoping to nap.

I couldn't sleep. Restless, I went to the officers' mess, deserted at this hour, to make a cup of tea. I'd just taken my first sip when the ship's caller blared. "Captain, call the bridge!"

I grabbed the nearby caller. "What, Vax?"

"It's Mrs. Seafort, sir. She's had some trouble down on Level 2. She sounds upset."

Oh, Lord God. "I'm on my way!"

"In the purser's office, sir."

I ran. Derek Carr, coming up the ladder on some errand, gaped as I careened past, two steps at a time. I dashed along the corridor, burst into the purser's office. Amanda came into my arms, clung to my shoulder.

I held her close. "Carry on," I growled at the purser, who had come to attention. "It's all right, hon, I'm here. What happened?"

She held me a moment longer. "Nick, I'm sorry. I'm all right now."

The purser and I exchanged glances. "Some of the joeyboys, sir," he said uneasily. "The streeters. They, uh, molested Mrs. Seafort."

"They did not," Amanda interrupted. "I was just scared. Nobody hurt me."

"Who? Where?"

Amanda took a deep breath. She released me, tried a tentative smile. "Calm down, Nicky, I'm fine. I was going to the library for some chips. The corridor was crowded, those young men and boys all in blue denim. As I passed, someone shouted a joke about me, and suddenly they were dancing all around me, pointing at my stomach, laughing, jostling, and I couldn't understand a word they said."

Her expression darkened. "I thought they meant to hurt the baby. I tried to run but there were so many of them! Everyone was pushing. I shouted to let me go; no one listened. They just kept crowding close, giggling. Then the purser came and took me away." She turned to him. "Thank you, Mr. Li."

"Where are they?" My fists were clenched.

"Back in their cabins, sir," said the purser. "Miss Chong showed up just after I did, and herded them to their bunks."

I studied my wife. "You weren't hurt?"

She clutched my arm. "Only frightened." Her tone was emphatic. "Don't overreact, it was all a mistake."

"Overreact? Of course not." I stalked to the hatch but she got there before me.

"No, Nicky, I mean it. Leave them be. Please."

"Don't tell me how to run my ship," I spluttered.

"Damn it, Nicky, I have to live here too! They meant no harm. If you retaliate you'll make my life more difficult than it need be!"

"All right." I was reluctant. "I won't make a scene. But I'm going to have a talk with Miss Chong, before those dam—" I caught myself in time—"those blessed transpops turn my ship into a zoo!"

She smiled at my scowl and came close. "Excuse me, Mr. Li." As he turned away she kissed me on the nose. That coaxed a reluctant smile from me. "Escort me up the ladder, Nicky," she said. "I feel like I need a thrustersuit to jet up there."

"T-suits aren't that big," I told her, and got a poke in the ribs for my pains.

3

"Lord God, today is November 19, 2197, on the U.N.S. *Portia*. We ask you to bless us, to bless our voyage, and to bring health and well-being to all aboard."

"Amen." The word echoed through the crowded hall. I surveyed the room briefly before sitting. By now, the transients' tables had been pushed as far as possible from the rest.

Despite Melissa Chong's efforts, the transients' behavior seemed to be deteriorating. Steward's mates stood against the bulkhead ready to intervene in the case of riot. Dr. Antonio, newly elected President of the Passengers' Council, had approached me to suggest that the transpops be fed separately, before or after the paying passengers. It was not a solution I liked; by long understanding, the Navy traveled with but one class of passenger.

After the soup was cleared we waited patiently for our salads. A robust, muscular man in his late fifties leaned forward to speak. "Captain, nobody wants to be first to mention that it was you who found the life-forms on *Telstar*. Would you tell us about them?"

His remark invoked the most frightening moment of my life. Our glimpse of hostile fish-shaped aliens was the reason an entire squadron was en route to Hope Nation system, instead of the usual lone supply ship.

"I'd rather not, Mr. MacVail. I didn't see much, I don't understand what I saw, and it's not fit dinner conversation." A chill settled over the gathering, and no one spoke for a long while.

After dinner I offered to take Amanda for a stroll but she sent me on alone; her back ached. I wandered the Level 1 circumference corridor, then went below to Level 2. I would amble all the way around, until I came back to the ladder where I'd started.

I passed several passenger cabins, then the crew's mess hall. I went past the engine room hatch without stopping; this wasn't an inspection tour. Outside crew berth one, crewmen lounged, chatting in the passage. "Carry on," I blurted, before they could come to attention.

Beyond the crew berths were more passenger cabins. I noticed a strong odor of ammonia. I stopped at the purser's office. "Mr. Li, what do I smell in the passage?"

"Probably the disinfectant, sir." His tone was stolid. "We scrub down the corridor twice a day." I raised an eyebrow. "The transients."

"Yes?"

"They, uh, urinate in the corridor."

"They piss on my deck?" My voice rose an octave.

"Miss Chong says they're not accustomed to plumbing."

"Get Dr. Chong! Right now!"

A few moments later the social worker faced me, hands on hips. "What did you expect?" she demanded. "Civilized graces? These joes were born on the streets and lived there all their lives! Most have never seen a building with working plumbing. Sure, we've shown them how, but habits don't change overnight!"

"You expect me to tolerate using the corridors as toilets?"

"No." Her tone was reasonable. "I'm working on it, as I'm working on everything else. We knew there'd be problems when we shipped these joeys, and so there are."

Her calm helped restore my own. "I know you're doing your best, but—look, Miss Chong. We have to live together sixteen months before we reach Hope Nation. They're disruptive, these charges of yours. Get control of them!"

"How?" she asked simply. I had no ready answer. "There are forty-two of them," she said. "I can't be everywhere at once. Give me time."

"All right." I was grudging. "I'll be patient. But not about this. If they foul my corridors again they'll wish they hadn't!"

I thought about ordering a guard posted in the Level 2 corridor, but decided against it. A Naval vessel was a civilized environment; passengers weren't prisoners to be watched every moment.

During the next days Amanda began irregular contractions. I sat in the white infirmary cubicle while Dr. Bros examined her. "I'm almost as excited as you," he said. "How many births do you think we get on an interstellar cruise?" Not many, of course. The crew and officers—except for the Captain—routinely lined up each month for their sterility shots. Married passengers occasionally bore offspring during a long voyage. Of course, unmarried passengers either took sterility shots or ended their pregnancies; to do otherwise was unthinkable, except through registered host or clone centers.

"Very soon now," Dr. Bros promised. I took Amanda back to our cabin.

As the days went by I continued to notice the pungent smell of disinfectant in the corridor. I conferred with the Chief Engineer; shortly afterward work parties strung wire mesh along the junction of bulkheads and deck. I gritted my teeth as a holorecorder was mounted and connected to Danny's sensors on the bridge; it violated Naval tradition to spy on passengers and crew and I found it hateful, even if necessary.

I had Danny monitor the corridor and switch on a carefully modulated current whenever a transient paused and appeared to adjust his clothing.

The startled squawks of the transpops provided much amusement to the other passengers, especially the younger ones. One teener jeered, "Electropiss!" at a transient named Deke and earned a black eye for his troubles.

The days passed slowly. One afternoon I played chess with Pilot Van Peer in his cabin. He was an enthusiastic player but a momentary carelessness cost him the game on the twenty-fourth move.

I endured long, quiet watches on the bridge. After several days, Alexi, his confinement to quarters ended at last, stopped me outside the officers' mess. "Can we talk privately, sir?"

"Very well." I followed him to his cabin, a four-meter cube with a tightly made gray bunk. All his belongings were neatly stowed in his duffel in the manner we had been taught in Academy.

He faced me awkwardly. "Sir, I'm sorry about last week."

He anxiously checked my face. "I don't just apologize, I mean I'm truly sorry. I was out of line. No lieutenant can mouth off to his Captain as I did. But I also—" He broke off and turned away. "I owe you more than that," he said in a muffled voice. "For what you are to me. Please forgive me."

I felt vast relief; my friend was back. "Sit down, Alexi." My tone was gentle.

He perched on his bunk, eyes fastened on my face. I pulled a chair near. "I'll repeat what I said on the bridge. You're so anxious to harass him you lose all sense of proportion."

He let out a long breath. "The truth is, I don't know what to think anymore, sir. He was a monster. You know what he did to us last cruise. I swore an oath that if I ever had the chance, I would hurt him. I have, and he deserves it. But . . . I don't feel better."

"You've hurt him a lot, Alexi. Isn't it enough?"

His hands clenched. "Sometimes I think so. Then I remember how often Derek and I were put over the barrel, thanks to his endless demerits. And his tone of voice in the wardroom, when I was helpless to defend myself. Sometimes I think you should have let me resign, back on Detour!"

"I'm sorry you're troubled." It was all I could find to say.

Our eyes met. "I'll stop if you require me to, sir. I'll obey orders."

"No." I was certain it had to come from him. "Alexi, I hated him as much as you did. But he's paid for his sins. He's endured everything you've given him, even when we moved the barrel to your cabin last cruise. He's still ready to do his duty as he understands it. Can't you respect that?"

He looked grim. "No, sir, I can't. What do you think he'd do to Derek and Rafe if he were in control again?"

"I don't know. I'm more worried about what he's doing to you." It startled him. I sighed. "Anyway, I accept your apology. You're back on the watch roster."

"Thank you." He swallowed. "I'll think about what you said, sir."

"Very well." I went back to my cabin to prepare for watch.

I'd left Amanda in the infirmary, promising to stay close—though I couldn't get very far without a thrustersuit. Her contractions were more frequent and she wanted to be near Dr. Bros. But I myself was on the watch roster, I couldn't relieve myself just to wait with her. The infirmary was but a quarter turn round the corridor and I could be there in a minute or less.

Vax Holser and Midshipman Derek Carr shared my watch. The lieutenant was running navigation drills for Derek, whose computational skill increased daily. I called up a few of the problems on my own console but Derek solved them far faster than I. Once Derek raced through a calculation and made an error in the process. Vax quietly reproved him for inattention to detail; Derek flushed deep red. Thereafter he was consistently accurate.

An excited young voice burst over the speaker. "Captain, Midshipman Treadwell reporting. There's trouble down here!"

I snatched the caller, fear pumping adrenaline through my system. "What kind of trouble? Where?" I glanced at my console; all readouts were green.

"Level 2 corridor west, sir. A fight. Some of the transients!"

Relief left me weak. "Bless it, Rafe, you've been taught how to report! Four demerits! I'll be right down." I dropped the caller. "Derek, remind him how to call the bridge in an emergency!"

"Aye aye, sir," Derek said, his chagrin evident. Though Philip Tyre was nominally in charge, in actuality Derek ran the wardroom.

"Shall I come too, sir?" On his feet, Vax was ready to face the entire troop of transients single-handed.

"No, I'll handle it. Wait here." I slapped the hatch shut behind me.

From the ladder I could hear shouting below. On Level 2 I rounded the corridor bend and came upon a wild melee; some two dozen streeters grappled with youths from among the paying passengers. Midshipman Treadwell watched, at a loss. "Get the master-at-arms, Rafe!" Sensibly, the boy turned and ran the other direction, realizing he was safer going the long way around the circular corridor than trying to claw through the riot.

I shoved two youngsters aside, stalked into the eye of the

storm. "What's going on here? You, get back!" I thrust a boy against the bulkhead, raised my voice another notch. "Nobody move! You, Mr. Attani! Let go of him! Now! Put your hands down!"

A paralyzing blow to the small of my back slammed me into the bulkhead. A bull-necked youth in blue denim loomed, fists bunched. "Buddout! Notchour bidness! Buddout!"

I wasn't sure I could move. I took a tentative step. I breathed with difficulty, but my muscles functioned. "All right." I held out my hand. He stared at it without comprehension. I lunged forward, kicked him in the stomach with all my strength. He doubled over. My stiffened right hand arced in a chop to the back of his thick neck. He fell heavily to the deck and was still.

I glared at the suddenly quiet throng. "Anyone else?" I took a step forward and they pressed back. One boy braver than the rest held his ground. Metal flashed as he lunged. My right hand at my side, I slapped him hard with my left. His hand shot to his face. I gripped his wrist, bent his arm behind his back.

"Whachadoon, joeys? Whachadoon here!" Melissa Chong pushed a hefty shoulder through the gaping bystanders. "Leavim lone! Leavim Cap'n lone!" She grabbed an offender by the hair, flung him to the side. Others made way. "Captain, what's going on?"

"Get your people against the inner bulkhead! You other boys, on the outer bulkhead. Move!" I was too enraged to say more. I heard the clatter of running footsteps. The master-at-arms and two mates appeared, truncheons ready. "Mr. Banatir, help separate these criminals. Watch this one, he's got a knife."

His lips tight, Mr. Banatir pried the weapon from the wrist I clutched.

A few moments later two bands of surly youths faced each other across the corridor. "All right," I demanded. "What started it?"

A babble of voices rose in reply. After a time we got it sorted out. Some transient joeys had attacked a group of passengers, and other teens had joined the fracas.

I snarled, "Your people caused this riot."

Melissa Chong held her ground. "Yes, but didn't you hear why? Tellaman, Annie! Tellaman boudit!"

The scrawny youngster pointed an accusing finger. "Dey callinus trannies! Allatime callinus trannies!"

"I don't get it." My tone was cautious.

"Didn't you hear?" Miss Chong. "Trannies. Your high-class passengers are calling my joeys names."

I turned to one of the better-dressed teens. "Is that true?"

He shrugged. "Maybe. It's what they are!"

"Your name?"

"Chris Dakko." His look was sullen.

"Age?"

"Seventeen."

I looked around, scowling. Several of the young passengers looked as if they wanted to be elsewhere. "Very well. Mr. Banatir, take charge of these hoodlums. Bring them to the bridge one at a time with their parents." I rounded on the social worker. "Your time's up, Miss Chong. Get your wild children under control! Who is that, lying on the deck?"

"Eddie, Captain."

"Eddie what?"

"On the street he was called Eddie Boss."

"Mr. Banatir, Eddie Boss goes to the brig. And let me see that weapon you took from the other joey."

I examined it, and my breath hissed. "Silverware? They steal tableware for weapons?"

"You see, Captain? They're anima—"

"Speak when you're spoken to, Dakko." I rounded on Melissa Chong. "What next? Laser pistols? I won't have it. All you joeys, back against the bulkhead. Mr. Banatir, search the lot of them. Brig anyone with a weapon."

Gregor Attani bristled. "Search *them*; it's a good idea. You'll probably find a lot more they stole. But we're civilized. It's a violation of—"

"All of them, Mr. Banatir. If this *civilized* joey gives you any more lip, brig him too."

Our search uncovered two more knives and a fork, hidden in the transients' clothing. Eddie Boss and the transpops who'd carried weapons were hauled to the brig.

The groups dispersed, herded by Miss Chong and my crewmen. I caught Rafe's eye. "Back to your duties, Mr. Treadwell!" I was still irritated at his sloppy report.

"But—Aye aye, sir," he said unhappily.

I went directly to the infirmary. "Amanda's doing fine," Dr. Bros said as I came in.

"But I'm not." My voice was tight. "My right hand is broken." I held my breath as he manipulated my wrist.

"You're right. What'd you hit it on, sir?"

"A rock." I let the doctor immobilize my wrist. He gave me calcium and ran a wave bone-growth stimulator back and forth over my hand for several minutes.

"It'll ache a bit but you'll be all right after a few days."

"I know." In the next room Amanda groaned. When Dr. Bros finished building the cast for my wrist I looked into her cubicle. "I can't stay, hon," I told her. "Problems. I'll be back in time to greet the baby."

"I'll go and you stay," she grated.

"Sorry." I strode back to the bridge. The watch had turned; Pilot Van Peer and Philip Tyre were on duty. I sat in my chair, my hand throbbing. I was lucky I hadn't been lynched. When I'd felt my wrist snap I knew I didn't have a chance in a fight, so I'd brazened it out and gotten away with it.

Shortly afterward Mr. Banatir escorted the first of the parents to the bridge. I read him and his youngster the riot act and dismissed them. The father, a metallurgist bound for Detour, seemed more chastened than his offspring.

I was waiting for the next miscreant when the hatch opened. "Permission to enter bridge." Rafe Treadwell, his voice subdued.

"Granted."

Slowly he walked in, hands pressed to his sides, and came to attention. "Midshipman Treadwell reporting, sir." Regs required him to identify himself.

"Go on." I was impatient.

"Lieutenant Holser asks you to enter my discipline in the Log and to cancel ten demerits." His eyes were liquid with misery.

I realized what I'd done. "You had more than six, Rafe?" I asked gently.

"Yessir," he mumbled. "Seven." The four I'd added had

put him up to eleven, and Vax had caned him. Too bad, but I couldn't undo it now.

"Very well, dismissed." The boy saluted, turned, and left.

I'd lectured several passengers and their sons by the time Mrs. Attani appeared with Gregor. She protested immediately. "Captain Seafort, you have no right to hold Greg prisoner."

"I won't tolerate hooligans on my ship. If your son doesn't understand that, it's your job to teach—"

"All he did was defend himself!"

"Mrs. Attani, see that he has no more incidents with the transients."

Her voice was tart. "Perhaps you'll see that the transients leave decent people alone!" Philip Tyre's jaw dropped; he'd never heard that tone used to a Captain. Nor had I.

"Very well, lacking your assurance, I won't release him. Mr. Banatir, take him to the brig to think it over for a week."

She gasped, "You wouldn't!"

"You're mistaken, madam."

"Wait!" she cried as the master-at-arms grasped the young man's arm. "Gregor won't get into any more fights. You have my assurance."

"What about yours, Gregor?" In the background the caller chimed; Philip Tyre moved to answer it.

"Yes, sir," Gregor said smoothly. "If you'll remember, I was one of those who was attacked. I'll try not to be attacked again."

"If you think you can—"

"Excuse me, sir." Midshipman Tyre shifted anxiously from one foot to the other.

"Later, Philip. Watch how you speak to me, Mr. Attani, or—"

"Excuse me, sir, please!"

I spun to Philip, ready to hurl a rebuke.

"It's the infirmary!"

I stopped short. "Amanda?"

"The Doctor says now!"

"Pilot, take the watch! Philip, get these people off the bridge!" I ran.

* * *

I held my newborn son, my cast making me awkward. The baby's clear blue eyes stared into mine, piercing my soul. He was very quiet, very still. I knew he couldn't see me; he couldn't yet focus. But still I smiled at his serious gaze as I rocked gently side to side.

When I passed through the gates of Academy at thirteen, there was a stunned moment when I realized my life was no longer my own. Now was also such a moment.

"Hello, Nate," I said quietly. "I love you. Everything's going to be all right." His eyes closed briefly and opened again. A moment later they were shut and he was fast asleep. I slipped back into the cubicle and gently handed the baby to Amanda, radiant underneath her crisp white sheets.

"Good work, hon," I told her.

"Not bad, first time out," she agreed. She nestled the baby alongside her arm. A few moments later she too was asleep.

For a week I walked around in a daze, unable to believe the miracle to which I'd contributed. When I passed, Rafe Treadwell stiffened anxiously at my unseeing scowl. Vax Holser repeated himself to me several times, as to a small child, before I heard him. He seemed to think it amusing. Our passengers were profuse with their congratulations as if I'd done something unusual. Even Mrs. Attani, vigilant in defense of her son, softened and visited my wife and child.

With Amanda in the infirmary, I had our cabin to myself. For some reason it made me restless. I took to exploring the ship, hungering to memorize every inch of its confines. I wandered into the mess hall, where stewards were setting the tables for the evening meal, but my presence made them so self-conscious I left again. Past the lounge I came to the exercise room. On the spur of the moment I looked in, to a scene of strenuous activity.

Philip Tyre, shirtless, was doing vigorous jumping jacks. On the mat Rafe Treadwell, in shorts and T-shirt, was performing sit-ups, breathless. Lieutenant Vax Holser worked the bars, muscles rippling his hairy arms and chest.

Before the three could jump to attention I waved them back to their labors and sat at the bicycle. Uneasy at watching idly, I folded my jacket across the handlebars and took off my tie. I began to pedal.

After a while Philip finished his jumping jacks and leaned against the bulkhead to catch his breath, his smooth chest gleaming with perspiration. After half a minute he began to do deep knee bends, his back stiff.

Smiling, I asked Vax, "Are you working off demerits too?" Lieutenants were not subject to demerits, but his penchant for physical exercise was well known.

"No, sir." His tone was agreeable. "Just working." He held himself above the parallel bars.

I dialed up the bicycle controls and pedaled harder, feeling lazy in comparison to the two boys laboring at their demerits. As a midshipman on U.N.S. *Helsinki* and later on *Hibernia*, I'd spent long hours enduring similar punishment.

With a sigh of relief Rafe Treadwell got up from the mat, his shift finished. In two hours he would have worked off one demerit. "Good afternoon, sir," he said politely. "Mr. Tyre." He nodded, acknowledging his senior. He left for the wardroom shower.

Philip lay on his stomach and took a deep breath. He began energetic push-ups. "Easy, boy," I warned. "You'll hurt yourself." Out of breath, he nodded but pressed on. After the push-ups he gave himself another thirty seconds, then began sit-ups. Pedaling with effort, I watched with uneasy interest as he struggled to continue.

Half an hour later he finished his exercises, leaned wearily against the bulkhead.

"Hard calisthenics doesn't mean you're to injure yourself," I said.

"Yessir." He stopped for breath. "Those are the exercises I'm to do, sir. I'm not to vary them."

"Ah." If I hadn't wandered into the exercise room I'd never have known; Philip would have risked drastic punishment bringing it to my attention, and rightly so. In the Navy discipline was to be endured, even harsh discipline. An officer had to know he could handle whatever a tyrannical Captain might bestow upon him, light-years from civilization.

"How long have you had those orders?" I knew their source.

"Several months, sir. Excuse me, please. This can't wait." He picked up the caller and thumbed it. "Lieutenant Tamarov, sir? Midshipman Tyre reporting. Exercises completed, sir." He listened a moment and replaced the caller.

"What was that?" I was appalled.

"I have to report," the boy said tonelessly. "At the beginning and end of each session. Standing orders."

"To Mr. Tamarov?"

"Yes, sir."

"Why?"

"I'm not to be trusted, sir." Tyre wiped himself off with a towel, avoiding my eye.

I scrambled from the bike, snatching my tie from the handlebars. I knotted it with fumbling fingers.

"It's all right, I don't mind," Philip blurted.

I grated, "The orders are countermanded!" From the bars, Vax Holser watched with a quizzical expression. I jammed my arms into my jacket, slapped open the hatch, and stalked into the corridor. A moment later I was pounding at Alexi Tamarov's cabin.

"Belay that racket!" Alexi flung open the hatch. His eyes widened in shock. His tie was loosened; his jacket lay over the chair. Behind him, his bed was rumpled.

I barged past, slapping the hatch shut behind me. "Attention!" I shoved him back against a bulkhead. He stiffened immediately, eyes front.

Standing nose to nose I savaged him, my voice harsh, my words brutal. A red flush crept slowly up Alexi's neck and across his cheeks while he stood helpless. "Not trusting another officer's word is abominable," I raged. "The Naval Service is founded in trust! Apparently you don't understand that, and if not, you're unfit to hold a commission! You get what you expect from your officers. Tell Philip he's untrustworthy and that's what he'll be!"

I broke off, out of breath. Alexi's eyes were pained. I remembered he had once idolized me. Well, that would be the case no longer. "I let you carry on your damned vendetta, Alexi. Once I even encouraged you. But you've gone too far; you've disgraced Naval tradition. I hope you're as ashamed of yourself as I am of you!" He flinched at that.

"Your orders to Philip are countermanded. You'll assume his word is honorable until he proves otherwise. Apologize to him for distrusting his word and enter your apology in the Log. Acknowledge!"

"Aye aye, sir! Orders received and understood, sir!" His voice was strained.

I slapped open the hatch. I paused. "I won't check to see if you did those things, Alexi. I accept your word as an officer. A pity you don't have the decency to do likewise." With that I left him.

Stalking back to my cabin I cursed my lack of control; in flaying Alexi for destroying the morale of a subordinate, I'd done exactly the same to him. Alexi deserved more of me. On the other hand, I was appalled at how he'd been treating Philip. What other grim secrets would I come upon?

My cabin was the largest living space on the ship. Accustomed as a middy to the confining wardroom, shared with three other midshipmen, I'd once been awed at the sight of the Captain's quarters. Even shared with Amanda it seemed more then ample.

Somehow, merely adding a baby made the cabin cramped and uncomfortable. The bassinet took up space; so did the unused high chair and all the changes of gear a baby seemed to require.

My sleep was altered too. One ear was tuned to the breathing of a tiny pair of lungs. Amanda's abrupt departure from the bed at intervals during the night also affected my rest. The bridge now seemed a relaxing haven, and I spent extra time there.

For several days after my savage rebuke, Alexi Tamarov had difficulty meeting my eye. Notwithstanding my promise to him, I looked for and found his apology to Philip in the Log. Alexi and I endured a watch together, mostly in silence.

In the dining hall I sat at table surrounded by passengers but lacking the solace of Amanda. Though some passengers brought their young children to table, Amanda found it awkward to care for the baby through a formal dinner and asked to eat alone in our cabin for a time. She understood it was my duty to preside at the Captain's table and didn't resent my attending.

"Tell me, Captain, you've been to Hope Nation. Do you

think they're ready for membership?" Jorge Portillo, an agronomist from Quito.

I wondered if I should avoid the question as too political. I decided I might as well answer; a remark early in a sixteen-month interstellar voyage could have no political repercussions by the time I returned home.

"The U.N. Charter provides for membership of 'any geopolitical unit that is not a subdivision of another member and has adequate resources to exist independently,'" I quoted. "Hope Nation is administered directly by the U.N., so it can't be claimed by another member state. The question is whether the colony is self-sustaining. From what I've seen it has a vigorous economy and an active political life. Why shouldn't it have membership?"

"You'd give an unsophisticated bunch of yokels equal vote in the General Assembly with the nations of Europe?" Mrs. Attani. Other passengers chimed in, and the debate veered to what constituted true sophistication.

"Now take Bulgaria," said Dr. Francon. "I think you'd have to agree they're about as unsoph—good Lord!"

I followed his glance. At a transpop table a minor riot had erupted. Bread and salad flew. One boy overturned his chair, scrambled atop the table. "Vax!" I pointed, spluttering.

Vax Holser bounded out of his chair as steward's mates converged on the fracas. Vax hauled the offending boy off the table and half carried him out of the dining hall into the corridor. He returned to collar two more, while Melissa Chong, red-faced, tried to restore order. I watched seething from my table until all offenders had been ejected.

I signaled the steward. "Pass the word: all officers to the bridge after the meal." My voice was tight.

"Why should decent people have to put up with that behavior?" Mrs. Attani, her glare indignant.

"Could they eat an hour earlier?" Mr. Singh.

I took a deep breath, let it out slowly. "I'll deal with them. There'll be no more of this." I wondered how to fulfill my pledge.

After dinner I paced the bridge in irritable silence until the officers arrived. Vax, who was reporting for watch, came first. Then Alexi, followed by my three midshipmen, Philip, Derek, and Rafe. Then Dr. Bros, hesitant at entering the unfamiliar territory; of all the ship's officers, only he was not on the watch roster. Pilot Van Peer entered shaking his head, grinning. "Couldn't believe it. They should be in cages!"

"Enough." He subsided. Finally the Chief Engineer arrived, completing our party.

I sat, and swung to face them. "I've had it. We've got to take control." I looked at each of them in turn. "Any suggestions?"

Vax spoke first. "Feed them in the crew mess, sir."

I thought it over. "No, it's not fair to the crew. What else?"

"We could set a transpop zone, sir." Alexi. "Level 2, around their cabins. Feed them in their own area."

"Restrict them like prisoners, you mean? I don't—"

"Why not?" blurted the Pilot. "Think of all the ship's regs they've broken. For that matter, you'd be justified throwing the lot of them in the brig."

I stood slowly. "You call me 'sir'!"

Van Peer gulped. "Aye aye, sir! I'm sorry. No disrespect meant, sir!"

"Very well. And stop interrupting. As for the brig, forget it. I won't make us into a prison ship." U.N.S. *Indonesia* orbiting Callisto was a disgrace to the Navy. I'd be damned before my vessel became another.

A long silence. The Chief asked, "Could you tranquilize them?"

All eyes turned to Dr. Bros. He shook his head decisively. "A few days, perhaps, but not for sixteen months."

There were no more suggestions. "Very well." I paced as I spoke. "The transients are passengers, not prisoners, and we all know regs require passengers be given every courtesy consistent with the safety and well-being of the ship. We won't hold them in a security zone or drug them, or force them to eat with the crew. Nor will we tolerate their behavior."

I leaned against the back of my chair facing my silent officers. "We won't isolate the transients, we'll integrate them. Each officer will take charge of five streeters, at dinner. And for that matter, you're to take all your meals with your transients. I'm holding you responsible for their conduct; make sure it's acceptable!"

Derek's face reflected his disgust. Coming from Upper New York he would have particularly strong revulsion toward the streeters. "Supervise them outside the dining hall as well," I said. "Break them of their more obnoxious habits and teach them how civilized folk behave." I turned to Mr. Van Peer. "Pilot, you won't be given a table to supervise." His relief was evident, but I punctured it immediately. "You will take the place of the officer who would stand watch during the dinner hour." His face fell.

"Excuse me, sir." Vax waited for my nod. "If we each take five, we're short an officer unless you take a group too."

"I know."

"But what about the Captain's table? I mean, the passengers are invited . . . it's a place of honor . . ."

"Training these joeys is more important." I tapped the chair. "It will be a major effort, and we'll need coordination and cooperation. Mr. Tamarov, you're in charge of the transient project. Any officer requiring special assistance will come to you." Alexi gaped. "Mr. Tyre, you will assist him." Dismayed, they exchanged glances.

"The rest of you are dismissed. Mr. Tamarov and Mr. Tyre will remain." I waited for the officers to leave. Vax, on watch, leaned back to listen. "Stand to," I barked at Alexi and Philip. The two stiffened immediately.

"I have enough problems with the transpops. Regardless of your personal relations, you're to work together. Alexi, Midshipman Tyre is all the help you'll get, and you're going to need him. You're to assume he is acting in good faith unless you know otherwise. Your vendetta can wait."

I glared at Philip. "Mr. Tyre, you're to help Lieutenant Tamarov every way you can. You will be courteous, friendly, useful, and as helpful as any middy ever was. Acknowledge orders, both of you!"

"Orders received and understood, sir! I'll help Mr. Tamarov in every way I can. I'll be courteous and friendly and useful, sir!"

"Orders received and understood, sir," said Alexi. "I'll handle the transpops with Mr. Tyre's assistance and I'll assume he's trying to help me, sir!"

Their ready acquiescence didn't lessen my irritation. "Out,

both of you." They saluted and left. Vax, familiar with my ways, said nothing.

After a while I realized I was still standing with my hands clenched. I slumped into my seat and let out a deep breath. "Sometimes I wish I were still a midshipman."

Vax smiled sympathetically. "Not often, I'm sure."

"Well, when I see Alexi going after Philip . . ."

The speaker came to life. "But then you wouldn't be able to tell them both off."

"Who invited you into this conversation, Danny?"

"This is the bridge," he sniffed. "I live here. Since when do I need an invitation?"

I was in no mood for humor. "Pipe down. If I want your opinion I'll ask for it."

"That'll be the day," the puter said darkly.

"Quiet, Danny. That's an order!"

For answer he threw a few random wavelengths of interference across the simulscreen.

"Belay that!" I snapped. No response. "Acknowledge my order!"

"How, when you told me to be quiet?" Danny's tone was sweet.

I might have dropped the matter but I'd had a rough day. "Puter, do you have EPD?"

Danny shouted, "Captain or not, don't say that to me!" Electronic Personality Disorder was one of the three known A.I. psychoses, and Danny didn't care for the suggestion that he was crazy.

I scowled, standing to pace.

It was said that personality overlays smoothed the interplay of electronic and human intelligence, and ultimately made for a safer ship. Just as we humans had infinite variations in temperament, the randomizing program in a shipboard puter generated unique character traits on reboot. Thereafter, subtle learning programs developed the puter's personality to a high level of sophistication. Which is why we were reluctant to shut a puter down, and wait while it went again through the learning process.

Yes, I knew all that. But why was it whenever I wanted to be left in peace, some puter would take it on himself to—

"Captain, a word with you?" Vax's tone was urgent. He beckoned to the simulscreen.

"No. And, Danny, you're out of line. You speak to the Captain with courtesy!"

"Yeah, I better or you'll put me to sleep like Darla." The speaker sounded sullen. "I heard how you worked her over!" Darla, our puter on *Hibernia*, had been glitched by the Dosmen on Lunapolis and needed emergency repairs.

Vax waved frantically for my attention. "Excuse me, sir, may I speak with you outside—*please*?"

I knew he was anxious to avert a quarrel with the puter. Like me, he'd heard rumors of ships that had sailed with an angry puter and had never returned.

I was irate enough not to care. "No, Vax. We might as well find out who's Captain here: me or that bucket of chips. Danny, I order you to apologize! Acknowledge!" Vax held his breath.

Reluctantly Danny gave the required response. "Aye aye, sir. Order received and understood. I apologize."

"You will not speak to me disrespectfully again, ever! Acknowledge."

The belligerence seemed to flow out of him. "Aye aye, sir. Order received and understood. I won't speak disrespectfully again." Now he sounded frightened.

"Very well. Danny, alphanumeric response only, displayed on screen. Acknowledge."

My console lit. "AYE AYE, SIR. ORDERS ACKNOWLEDGED. ALPHANUMERIC ONLY, ON SCREEN. PLEASE DON'T DEPROGRAM ME! PLEASE, SIR!" The speaker remained silent.

"I don't intend to. Not if you're under discipline. Alphanumeric only for forty-eight hours. Disconnect conversational overlays, discontinue all voluntary statements except alarm functions, for forty-eight hours."

"AYE AYE, SIR!"

Vax stared aghast. My arms folded, I glared at the now silent console.

4

Eddie Boss, released from the brig by my orders, toyed disgustedly with his salad.

"Dinner not to your liking?" I asked.

He glanced up with a snaggletoothed grin. "Fat puppy be nice, Cap'n," he said dreamily. "Eddie chowdown good den." I shuddered.

The transients had reacted to their seat changes with wariness, assuming they were in for trouble. Derek Carr maintained control at table five only with the greatest effort, snapping curt orders at his unwanted charges. Vax Holser, at the next table, spoke softly with a smile and was quickly obeyed. Vax's physique had its advantages.

"Excuse me, sir." Philip Tyre, an apprehensive look on his young face. "Mr. Van Peer asks if it would be convenient for you to come to the bridge."

I was alarmed. "Problems?"

"He didn't tell me, sir, just that it would be better for you to be there."

"Very well." I glared at my young charges. "Mr. Tyre, take my place. See that these uncivilized persons stay seated until the meal is finished."

I left the dining hall and hurried to the bridge. For the Pilot to call me from dinner the matter must be serious.

"Well?" I slapped the hatch closed behind me. Van Peer gestured at his console in answer. I read over his shoulder.

"D 20471 REQUESTS PERMISSION TO REACTIVATE CONVERSATIONAL OVERLAYS, SIR. FORTY-EIGHT-HOUR PROHIBITION IMPOSED BY CAPTAIN HAS PASSED. REQUEST TERMINATION ALPHANUMERIC ONLY."

The Pilot murmured, "I thought you'd best see for yourself." I grinned; his low tone wouldn't stop Danny from overhearing if the puter had ignored my order restricting him to alphanumeric input.

"You think he's learned his manners now?" I said loudly. Pilot Van Peer flinched. I sat in my own seat and began to type. "Reactivate conversational overlays."

My console lit immediately. "AYE AYE, SIR! THANK YOU VERY MUCH!"

I typed, "I am prepared to terminate alphanumeric only."

"PLEASE, SIR! I WON'T GIVE YOU ANY MORE LIP, HONEST, IT'S LONELY IN HERE. PLEASE LET ME TALK, I'LL BE RESPECTFUL FROM NOW ON. I PROMISE, CAPTAIN, SIR!"

I raised my eyebrow. The Pilot chewed his knuckle. "I think it worked, sir."

"It seems so." I bent to the console. "Terminate alphanumeric only."

"Thank you, sir!" Danny's tense voice filled the speaker. "No more trouble, Captain Seafort. I promise!"

"Very well. The incident is closed." As I sat back in my chair I luxuriated in the Pilot's look of astonishment and respect. I tried not to let it show.

"Lord God, today is December 12, 2197, on the U.N.S. *Portia*. We ask you to bless us, to bless our voyage, and to bring health and well-being to all aboard." I felt stiff and awkward in my dress whites, constrained by the fully charged stunner strapped to my side.

"Amen." I joined in the general murmur and glanced at the crowded dining hall before sitting. Dining with ship's officers apparently no longer impressed the transients; I was seated with Mr. Singh, Mr. MacVail, and five young hoodlums who jabbered among themselves while calling to their friends scattered at various tables.

"Sit down," I snapped at Eddie.

"Naw." He remained standing. He waved enthusiastically at another table. "Talkina Jonie!" Next to him Norie snickered.

"Sit, Eddie!"

Still he ignored me. I unholstered my stunner and touched it to the boy's side. He sprawled across the table unconscious. Water dripped to the deck from an overturned glass. I put my unaccustomed stunner back in its place. "Sit quietly, all of you, until the food is served." Awed, they did. I decided my baby-sitting was going to be easy.

It was, until the soup came. As the steward's mate served the first course from the big tureen, Norie, Tomas, and Deke lunged impatiently at their bowls.

"None of that!" My tone was sharp. It had no effect. "Mr. Dowan." I motioned to the steward to remove the tureen. "Serve Mr. Singh and Mr. MacVail from another table. The children and I will do without soup."

"Aye aye, sir." The steward sounded uncertain.

"Hey, wanna eat, wanna eat!"

"Pipe down, Les." I glowered. "None of you gets soup tonight. If you settle down you'll be given meat and salad when it comes."

"No joe gonna takur food, noway! Cap'n ain' gonna takur dinna!" Norie was indignant. She scrambled out of her seat but stopped short when my hand fell to the butt of my stunner.

My voice was cold. "Now we'll do without dinner. You get to eat when you behave yourselves." I signaled the steward's mate. "Serve the passengers only, Mr. Dowan."

"Whata bouda Cap'n? Cap'n gonna chow, naw?" Les spoke in a sneer.

"No. The Captain eats when you do." I didn't know why I said it, but it silenced them. "You'll have food when you learn manners. Until then we'll go hungry."

"Cap'n go inna kitchen nighttime," Deke said derisively. "Cap'n nobe hungry, hebe da man!"

"We call it the galley, not the kitchen. And I won't go. We'll work it out together."

"He chowdown latetime sure," Deke told the others.

"No. I swear it by Lord God." I felt a pang of alarm but it was too late; the oath was given. Now, if they were stubborn enough, I could starve to death. They'd starve with me, but that was slight consolation.

Mr. Singh cleared his throat. "Captain, are you sure you want to . . ."

"It's done."

"In the heat of the moment surely you don't hold yourself to such an oath—"

I bristled. "My oath is good, sir, no matter how given!"

"Of course," said Mr. Singh hurriedly. "I didn't suggest otherwise. I just thought . . ." He let his sentence trail off. We waited out the meal. It looked delicious.

"Alexi's had Mr. Tyre up again," Vax said, indicating the Log.

"I know. I can read."

"Yes, sir. The demerits are tapering off a bit, though."

I was already aware. The month after I'd ordered Alexi and Philip to work together had begun with a flurry of demerits to the midshipman, then they had decreased. Now they were sporadic, though still enough to keep Philip in the exercise room during his off hours.

Vax persisted. "I don't like what Philip did, sir, but . . ."

"But what?" I asked, annoyed.

"It's time Alexi let him off," he said bluntly. My direct question had freed him to criticize a brother officer.

"What about you?" I asked. "The barrel's in your cabin. Do you go easy on him?"

"Of course not!" Vax looked shocked. "What would be the point? If we have a system of discipline, we should enforce it. The middies and cadets should dread being caned. As we did," he added, remembering.

"So you feel sorry for him, but you won't ease up." I smiled grimly at the irony.

"No, sir, not unless you order me to." He waited.

I lay back, my eyes closed. When First Lieutenant Cousins had caned me shortly after I arrived on *Hibernia* as a middy, I'd loathed it. The pain was considerable but the humiliation was far worse. But I'd survived it, as I had in the past. Philip would too.

"Bridge to engine room, prepare to Defuse." I waited impatiently for the response.

"Engine room ready for Defuse, sir. Control passed to bridge." Chief Hendricks's voice was unemotional, as always.

"Passed to bridge, aye aye." I traced the line from "Full" to "Off" on the console.

"Confirm clear of encroachments, Lieutenant."

Vax Holser checked his instruments. Our first priority emerging from Fusion was to make sure we were clear of whatever objects might be about. Danny's reflexes were faster than ours, but we followed the Navy rule: don't trust mechanical sensors. Recheck everything.

"Clear of encroachments, Captain." Vax's attention was fastened on the readouts.

"Very well. Plot our position, please." Vax bent to his console, fingers flying, as Danny's own calculations flashed onto the screens. It was an extra precaution: though we were to remain in the vicinity until the rest of the fleet arrived, I wanted to be able to Fuse on a moment's notice.

I was hungry, but I made an effort to put it out of my mind. The week of starvation during my battle of wills with the transpops seemed to have changed my metabolism. Now that the ordeal was over and we were eating again, I found myself gaining more weight than I'd lost; disgusted, I worked out regularly in the exercise room and watched my diet rigidly. I'd managed to take off my excess weight but now I had to cope with hunger pangs. An unpleasant change.

"The other ships should show up in a few days," Vax remarked. An unnecessary comment. His nerves too must be on edge.

"Yes." I cleared my throat hesitantly. "Vax, I don't have to tell you how to stand watch, but make sure the middies are extra vigilant. Please."

"Aye aye, sir." He understood my fears. Two years before, on our return from Hope Nation, we'd Defused for a nav check and come upon the remains of our sister ship *Telstar*. Worse, we'd been attacked by the bizarre fishlike creature that lurked behind her.

Three of our men had died; I bore scars of the encounter in nightmares that persisted to this day. Vax had paid a stiff price for his refusal to Fuse until I was safely aboard; I'd stripped him of his commission as punishment. Though I later relented, he'd lost three months' seniority and had an official rebuke that would affect his Naval career to the day he died or made Captain.

We had no idea where the alien had come from, or how it had arrived in interstellar space. Just as the attack on *Hibernia* by desperate miners at Miningcamp Station had made me wary of orbiting stations, the encounter with the aliens made me very uneasy while drifting in deep space, Defused and vulnerable.

After the watch I went back to my cabin. Amanda sat in the shadows, rocking little Nate, both of them half asleep. She smiled at me in the dim light.

"Can I take him, hon?" I held out my arms at her nod and we gently transferred my baby to me. I swayed as I stood, rocking him. Gravely he watched me. "I love you, Nate. Mommy loves you. Everything is going to be all right." At the reassurance of my quiet voice, his eyes closed. He drifted off to sleep. One tiny hand opened and closed a moment before he was still.

I loved fatherhood.

Quietly I put my son into his crib and covered him. Amanda stretched. "I heard the engines stop, Nicky." One grew used to the throb of the fusion drive and noticed its absence.

"Nav check, hon. We're waiting for the rest of the squadron to rendezvous." Though the margin of error in Fusion was reduced with the new controls, the other ships could Defuse anywhere within two or three light-hours, but we would find each other and quickly move closer. I hoped it would be soon.

During the first leg of our cruise I had run frequent General Quarters and Battle Stations drills. Should we detect an encroachment, alarms would ring throughout the ship; we'd go immediately to General Quarters even though there was a near certainty the encroachment was an arriving vessel in our fleet.

A few hours later Amanda and I brought Nate to the dining hall for our evening meal. As we entered the conversation lulled momentarily. I escorted Amanda to her chair. The youngsters at our table stood reluctantly as we approached, knowing failure to do so would mean going without, again. I was embarked on teaching them more than how to refrain from throwing food at each other; I now labored at elements of courtesy.

"Evenin', Cap'n." A young girl was the first to speak, and they all followed suit, mumbling. Even big Eddie, though with his customary surliness.

"Good evening, um, ladies and gentlemen." I sat.

* * *

Days passed, during which I awaited the rest of our squadron with increasing impatience. I haunted the bridge, as if my presence could somehow trigger the alarms that would warn us of the encroachments we expected. When I caught Vax and Derek exchanging amused glances, I bit back a savage remark, recognized my irascibility, and left the bridge.

I went down to Level 2 and looked into hydroponics and recycling, more to give myself something to do than to carry out an inspection. Then, trying to ignore my persistent hunger, I climbed back to Level 1 and went to my cabin. Nate might be asleep, so I opened the hatch gently. Amanda sat in her favorite rocker, smiling. I grinned back. "Hi, hon, ready for lunch yet? I—"

We weren't alone. Midshipman Philip Tyre sat in my favorite chair, a smile fading from his handsome young face. He began to rise to attention but could not; my son Nate was in his arms.

"Why are you here?" I was white with anger. "Get out! Don't ever set foot in my cabin again!"

"Aye aye, sir!" He scrambled to his feet.

"The next time you touch my son I'll break your neck!" I was beside myself. "Out!" I flung open the hatch.

Amanda was on her feet. Quickly she took Nate from the dismayed boy, tugging at my arm. "Nicky, don't. I invited him."

"Go!" I slapped the hatch shut before Philip had half cleared it.

Nate was wailing. Amanda soothed him as she rounded on me. "How dare you! Philip was a guest!"

"He's despicable." My voice was tight. "I don't want him around you or Nate."

"Who are you to make that decision for me!" Her glare of fury met mine. Nate began to scream, reacting to our anger.

"Damn it, Amanda, this is my cabin!" Why couldn't she understand? I must have some place of refuge from the ship and its problems.

She put Nate in his crib and faced me, hands on hips, eyes blazing. "Either I have the freedom to entertain here, or I want a cabin of my own!"

"Ridiculous," I snapped.

Her slap was like a rifle shot and caught me unprepared.

My cheek stung. Her voice dropped to an eerie calm. "Whatever else you do, Nick Seafort, you will take me seriously."

I stared at her in amazement. What had gotten into her? "I do," I protested. "Philip Tyre is one of my middies; I can't have him making himself at home in my own cabin."

"Your own cabin," she repeated quietly. A moment's thought, and then she nodded. "Yes, I suppose it *is* the Captain's cabin, not the Captain's wife's cabin. Very well. Where will you move me?"

"Nowhere, Amanda. I want you with me."

Her look was steadfast. "Not on those terms, Nick. It's not possible."

I loved her, yet she could be so infuriating. I sighed. "Amanda, what is it you want?"

"To know my status. If this isn't my cabin too, give me my own. I want the right to make my own friends. What do you want?"

I risked the hurt she might do me. "I want you to know how much I love you."

Her eyes misted and she bit her lip, shaking her head. Then she came to me and rested her hand on my shoulder. "I love you too, Nicky. But you have to give me room. Can you understand how I can love you and still be furious for what you did to poor Philip?"

"Poor Philip?" I waved in exasperation. "Good Lord, Amanda, you know what a vicious tyrant he was in the wardroom, until Derek put a stop to it."

"Until you put a stop to it, hon."

"Me?" My bitterness showed. "I gave him his way for so long that Alexi's still suffering. It took Derek to stand up to him. I just fumbled."

"That's not the issue," she reminded me.

"No," I agreed. "He's a sadist, that's the issue. I couldn't believe you let him into our cabin. Or around Nate."

She looked at me curiously. "Did you think today was the first time?"

"What? I mean, you—he—"

"I've had him here on other occasions. We sit and talk, like I do with Alexi. The look in his eyes when he holds Nate . . ."

"God, Amanda, how could you?"

"Nicky, you know I socialize with your officers. I lunch with Alexi when you're on watch, and—"

"Alexi's different. He's a friend."

She met my eye squarely. "So is Philip. Mine, at least." She paused, debating whether to continue. "And I resent what you did to him. He was here by invitation, and you threw him out."

"I suppose you expect me to apologize to him?" I meant it as sarcasm.

"He deserves an apology, whether he gets it or not."

My temper finally unraveled. "God—" With difficulty I stopped short of blasphemy. "—bless it, Amanda, I don't understand you! I will not abase myself before that . . . that person! Not for you, not for him!"

"Why not for yourself," I heard her say as the hatch slammed shut behind me. I stomped down the corridor. Vax was just outside his cabin. He made as if to speak, but averted his gaze after seeing my expression.

I was halfway to the bridge when the alarms went off.

Alexi's taut voice crackled over the speakers. "All hands to General Quarters! Captain to the bridge! General Quarters, all hands!"

I raced down the corridor and slapped open the bridge hatch. "What is it?" I skidded to a halt.

"Encroachment, sir." Alexi's fingers were busy at the console.

"Four hundred thousand kilometers, closing." Danny. "Shape and size consistent with *Freiheit*, sir."

"Let's hope so." I slid into my seat. "Alarms off, Danny." The din ceased. "Send our recognition signals."

"Aye aye, sir." In an emergency Danny was all business. For a few seconds, silence. Then his high-pitched adolescent voice, with what sounded like relief. "*Freiheit*'s code received, sir. I think it's them."

My nerves were still jumpy. "Never mind what you think."

"Aye aye, sir," said Danny, subdued. "Second recognition code received, sir. Positive ID on *Freiheit*."

Nonetheless, I took the crew to Battle Stations as we approached. I was sick with the memory of *Telstar*, from behind which an apparition had emerged. I only relaxed when

Freiheit's reassuring lights appeared on the simulscreens, and Captain Tenere's familiar voice boomed through the speaker. "*Freiheit* to *Portia*. Are you there, Seafort?"

"Ready and waiting, Mr. Tenere." He was senior to me by several years and was a full Captain to boot; I really should have called him "sir." But among Captains informality seemed to prevail.

"Well, we'll probably have to wait a bit for those great rowboats to catch up to us. Would you care to join me for dinner? I hear we're serving chicken Kiev."

I hesitated. I was reluctant to leave my ship, but my stomach juices were churning. And the friendly company would be welcome. "Thank you, yes. My wife is aboard too, sir."

"Well, she's the reason you were invited, son. We'll look forward to seeing you both."

After breaking off the connection I went to find Amanda; the invitation would be a good diversion from our quarrel. And so it was, until the question arose what to do with Nate. I flatly refused to bring a babe in arms to a formal dinner. Amanda, hesitant to leave him, had to concede my point. She agreed to find a baby-sitter among the passengers.

I rearranged the watch schedule to make sure Vax Holser was on the bridge while we were gone. We took the gig across, with a sailor to man it. Captain Tenere met us at his lock with a jovial smile. "We didn't get much chance to talk at Lunapolis, Mr. Seafort. May I call you Nick? My name's Andrew. The Admiral did most of the talking and not much listening, if you ask me."

His bluntness made me uncomfortable, though I'd said as much to Amanda. I made some noncommittal answer and we chatted about other things. During dinner, though, he returned to our briefing. "It doesn't make sense having us drift here, by my way of thinking. I don't think there's a chance of encountering anything—good Lord, look how far out we are—but say we did: if we were disabled, Tremaine would still Defuse right into the middle of it. So what's been gained?"

"Well, we're the point of the wedge," I said, temporizing.

"I suppose," he said. "Still, we're so deep interstellar . . ."

"About as deep as *Telstar* when we found her." My tone was somber.

"You know," he mused, "that's what I can't fathom. How could those beasties get out there? I saw the holovids you shot. Those, what'd you call them? Goldfish? They're organic, they've got to be. No place for fusion drives. They couldn't, uh, swim that far, not without spending centuries en route. How do they carry enough propellant? What in Lord God's name were they doing?"

"I don't know," I said. And I didn't want to think about it. Amanda, sensing my mood, changed the subject.

After the meal, in the privacy of his cabin, Captain Tenere nonchalantly served us a glass of wine. I was uneasy about sharing contraband but didn't want to offend him, so I took a cautious sip. Amanda, less bothered about such niceties, downed hers with enjoyment.

We returned to *Portia* shortly after. I went immediately to the bridge; Amanda went to the cabin to check on Nate.

During the next two days three more ships of our fleet appeared, and on the third day *Challenger* Defused, some two hundred fifty thousand kilometers distant. Remarkably close, given the distance traveled. We waited for the remaining vessels amid a flurry of directives from the flagship.

I made myself busy on the bridge, while Amanda occupied herself with Nate. Twice I returned to my cabin to find her in earnest consultation with Alexi. I knew there was something not quite right that the Captain's wife involved herself with his officers, but after the row we'd had over Philip, I was careful not to let my uneasiness show.

Finally the remainder of the squadron arrived, and one by one we Fused again. *Freiheit* and *Portia* remained on station until the others were gone. Then I checked our figures one final time and gave the order to Fuse. As the engines kicked in, our screens went dark.

After the flurry of activity, Fusion was duller than ever. I spent about half my waking time with Nate and Amanda, and the other half on the bridge, though there was little for me to do. I shared watches with the Pilot, with Vax, with the midshipmen.

Derek Carr, whom I'd enlisted as a youngster of sixteen on *Hibernia*, was by this time a seasoned middy with an air of confidence he wore well on his lean, aristocratic face. He was sensitive to my moods, chatting when I felt sociable, courteously remaining silent when I was not.

Rafe, like any younger middy, approached the bridge with great anxiety, and didn't dare speak unless spoken to.

I'd known Alexi Tamarov since my first day aboard *Hibernia*; I could tell he was troubled. Rather than fuss over him, I let it be. I watched the Log closely. The demerits to Philip Tyre tapered off, then increased in a sudden flurry of fault-finding. I knew to a certainty that Mr. Tyre hadn't earned the demerits; like Derek, he was a competent, seasoned midshipman. Again I wished I hadn't chosen to bring the boy along; Philip was a lightning rod for the resentment of his seniors.

One afternoon, on the idle bridge, Alexi thrust his hands in and out of his pockets, distracted. Finally he said, "I have something to say to Mr. Tyre, sir, and I'd like you to be present."

I raised my eyebrow. "Oh?"

"Yes, sir. I told him to come to my cabin after my watch."

When the watch ended Alexi and I strode in silence to his quarters. Philip Tyre waited anxiously outside with a look of foreboding that deepened at the presence of his Captain.

Inside, Alexi stared at the midshipman until Philip began to knead the edge of his jacket in an agony of anticipation.

Silence.

Abruptly Philip blurted, "Sir, if it's about last week's demerits, I've worked off three. I'm sorry I haven't had time to do the others, I've been busy with the transpops and—"

"It's over."

"Mr. Tamarov?"

Alexi said heavily, "It's over. I'm done with you."

Philip looked back and forth between us, biting his lip. "I don't understand what I've done, sir. Please, I'm sorry if—"

"Midshipman, I've hated you more than any person I've ever known." Tyre drew in a sharp breath. Alexi continued, "You've deserved to be hated, Mr. Tyre. You've done hateful things."

I felt a pang of alarm, not knowing where this was heading. I opened my mouth to intervene.

Alexi added, "And now I've done hateful things." I kept silent. "After what you did to me and the other middies on

Hibernia I swore to have vengeance on you, Mr. Tyre, and I have. Oath or no, I can't do it anymore. Lord God will understand, or He won't. I set aside my oath. I renounce vengeance."

The boy's eyes were riveted on his lieutenant.

"I don't like you, Philip; I never will. But I'll leave you alone. Any demerits I issue in future will only be when you've truly earned them. I'll try to learn how to be fair again."

I stirred. "Alexi, enough said."

"No, sir, please pardon me. There's more to be said. Mr. Tyre, for over a year I've been as cruel as you were to us, until I can't stomach what I've become. I've watched you, even when you thought I was indifferent. I was never indifferent to you, Mr. Tyre. And when we've worked together, as we did with the transpops, I've found what the Captain said to be true. You are a diligent worker, a willing assistant, a dutiful subordinate. I can find no fault in your work. I commend you in that. I will so note in your next fitness report." Alexi took a long breath and let it out slowly. "Well, it's over now. I don't apologize. I will let you be. You are dismissed."

Philip Tyre saluted automatically and turned to the hatch. He paused. "Sir—I—"

"Dismissed," Alexi said woodenly.

"Let him speak." My tone was gruff.

Tyre swallowed. "On that frightful trip back from Hope Nation—after they made you lieutenant—I thought I'd go insane. Nothing in my life was as awful as the way you treated me. I tried to bear it until we got home, but finally I couldn't take any more."

His eyes were fastened on the bulkhead, recalling a private nightmare. "I wrote out a note and put clean clothes on and lay down on my bunk to take the pills I'd stolen from *Hibernia*'s infirmary, and then I wasn't brave enough to do it. I lay there, a helpless coward, until it was time to go on watch again. Those months without end . . .

"When we got home, when Admiral Brentley reassigned me to *Portia* instead of letting me resign, I convinced myself it would get better on a new ship. But it went on, and on . . . Four, no, five times I've tried to end it with the pills, only each time I didn't, I don't know why. Except once when I took three and it wasn't enough."

His cheeks were wet as he turned to me. "Captain, I don't know what I did to make you hate me so, that's God's honest truth!"

Alexi stirred angrily but Tyre rushed on. "Captain, you warned me, I know that. I just thought I—I was doing my job. To this day I don't know what was wrong about the way I treated the midshipmen. But . . ." His eyes fell. "You kept telling me it was improper, and Mr. Tamarov despises me, and Mr. Carr . . . so I have to believe you. I know something I've done is terribly wrong. I don't really understand it, I think that's why I tried to kill myself, but I believe you. So, I'm sorry. I'll try to do better. Mr. Tamarov, sir, I ask your pardon. If you can't forgive me, try to believe that I mean that. I'm sorry for whatever hurt I did you."

He brought himself to attention, snapped an Academy salute, wheeled, and was gone.

Alexi moaned, "Lord Jesus, what have I done?"

"I did it to both of you," I said, my tone bitter. "I left you to suffer, then I put you in charge of him. You're not to blame." I loathed myself; I had to be alone. "You've done right, Alexi. Have peace." I didn't know if he heard.

5

When she wasn't hovering over Nate, Amanda busied herself arranging classes. As weeks passed into months our little boy grew unconscionably fast. In the privacy of our cabin I would take him on my lap and jiggle him while he sat contentedly exploring the textures of my jacket and shirt. Occasionally, on the bridge, I would find my knee jiggling absently while I chatted with Vax or Pilot Van Peer. But I never brought Nate to the bridge; it was one thing to have my family aboard; quite another to involve them in my official duties.

Occasionally Amanda invited passengers to visit, and once she asked if I would mind her having the officers to afternoon tea. As she was confined to shipboard society for sixteen months, I didn't feel free to object, though it made me uncomfortable. I did ask her to hold her party in one of the lounges instead of our cabin. She agreed without comment. All the officers were duly invited; all showed up except Philip Tyre, who sent a polite note indicating he wasn't feeling well. Amanda wordlessly handed me his note of regret.

I began to look forward to our next Defuse in three weeks, but I knew with growing unease that there was business unattended to. I tried to thrust it out of my mind until the night I found myself tossing sleeplessly for hours; the next morning I went to the wardroom and resolutely knocked at the hatch.

By ship's custom the midshipmen's wardroom was private territory; the Captain didn't enter uninvited, except on inspection.

Derek Carr opened the hatch, came to attention.

"As you were, Mr. Carr."

He stood down. "Would you care to come in, sir?"

Now I could enter. "Thank you. Er, Mr. Tyre, I was looking for you. I'd like a word." Philip's apprehensive look made me even more bitter. "Derek—Mr. Carr—could I trouble you to let me speak privately with Mr. Tyre?"

"Aye aye, sir. Of course, sir." He scrambled to put on his jacket and tie. "Make yourself at home." He left quickly.

Philip swallowed. "I meant no disrespect by not coming to your party, sir, I—"

"No." My tone was blunt. "You were quite right not to attend, after what I said to you." He colored. I took a deep breath and forced out the words. "Philip, I've come to apologize and to withdraw what I said in my cabin."

"Please, sir," he blurted. "There's no need—"

"You will recall," I said, overriding him, "my admonishing Mr. Tamarov that I will have courtesy among officers. When you were a guest in my cabin my behavior to you was far worse than discourteous."

"I understand, sir," he stammered. "I know how you feel—"

"But that's the point, Philip. I wasn't only discourteous, I was wrong to feel that way. Your behavior to me has never warranted it, not even when you were abusing the other middies, and in any event that's long past. You are welcome in my cabin as Amanda's guest or mine. I have no objection to your holding my son, if you come to visit."

My cheeks were aflame, but I managed to hold his eye. "This is a personal matter between us, Philip, and I won't hold it against you no matter how you respond. But I ask you to forgive my foul manners."

"There's nothing to forgive, sir. You had every right—"

"None of us ever has that right," I said with savage force. "Otherwise you had the right to pile demerits on Derek and Alexi until they were sent to the barrel, over and over again. Viciousness and cruelty are never excusable! Never!" My vehemence shook me. I wondered what had caused it.

He looked at me in wonderment. "Is that really what I was doing?" he asked, half aloud. Then he focused again on me. "Thank you for coming." He hesitated. "I feel out of line saying it, sir, but since you asked me, I forgive you. I'd like not to talk about it anymore, sir. It's embarrassing to hear you apologize." He met my eye and smiled weakly.

I felt awkward, not knowing how to leave. Impulsively I put out my hand, and after a second's hesitation he took it.

Then he seemed reluctant to let go. I gave his hand an extra squeeze before releasing it.

He couldn't have offered to shake hands, of course. To touch the Captain without permission was a capital offense.

I took my accustomed place on the bridge, reining in my unease. I thought our orders to Defuse seven times instead of twice for nav checks was a waste of propellant. Every time the squadron assembled, each ship had to maneuver to its station in relation to the others.

Our auxiliary thrusters used LH2 and LOX as propellant, manufactured from our stores of water; we had ample power from the fusion engines for such conversion. But a ship could carry just so much water, and it was a long way to Hope Nation.

Further, assembling the squadron over and again was a waste of time; we might wait days on end for all our ships to arrive; the speed of Fusion varied with minute differences in the design of each ship's drive and its tubes.

I sighed. I'd chosen a Navy life, and long dreary voyages were part of it. "Vax, sound General Quarters."

Alarms shrilled throughout the ship as crew and officers hurried to duty stations. All noncritical systems were closed down. The airtight hatches that separated corridor sections slid shut. During General Quarters, passengers were expected to wait in their cabins with hatches sealed; the purser and his mates went through the corridors checking each cabin.

When all was ready I ran my finger down the screen and Defused. I caught my breath as the myriads of stars reappeared on our simulscreens.

"Check for encroachments, Mr. Carr." Vax was terse, his huge shoulder muscles taut.

"Aye aye, sir." A moment's pause. "No encroachments, sir."

"We're first again," I said. "We wait."

The next to show up, two days later, was *Kitty Hawk*, under Captain Derghinski. She maneuvered to her station and drifted at rest relative to *Portia*, waiting as we did for the rest of the squadron. For some reason she had outrun *Freiheit*, which Defused into normal space a few hours after.

Waiting for the fleet, I'd camped on the bridge for nearly three days with only occasional breaks for rest. When I found myself dozing at my seat I knew it set a bad example for the other officers; reluctantly I trudged back to my cabin, undressed, and collapsed in bed. Though Nate was crying loudly, within moments I was asleep.

Minutes later Amanda shook me awake. I propped myself up, shook my head in a vain effort to clear it. "What now?"

"Sorry, hon. You slept right through the caller. Alexi is paging you to the bridge."

Panic seized me. "Trouble?" I snatched the caller, thumbed it to the bridge setting. "What's wrong?"

"*Challenger*'s arrived, sir. Admiral Tremaine's been calling you every two minutes."

I cursed, tugged at my jacket. "I'm on the way." I staggered to the hatch, adrenaline barely overpowering the fog in my head.

On the bridge the simulscreens were in visual contact with *Challenger*; Admiral Tremaine's unfriendly face loomed as I dropped into my seat. "Captain Seafort reporting, sir."

"Where the hell have you been, Seafort?" Tremaine's features were contorted with rage. "You were supposed to guard the rendezvous, not lollygag about in bed! I expect to find *you* on the bridge, not some infant lieutenant!" Alexi flushed.

"I was asleep, sir," I said. My head was filled with cotton.

"It's *your* aliens we're watching for, Seafort!" The Admiral's voice was a snarl. "Keep a proper watch, do you hear? That's why you were sent ahead in the first place!"

"Aye aye, sir." It was all I could say.

It didn't seem to satisfy him. "I warned you: any disobedience and I'd relieve you. I have a good mind to do it now!" At my side, Alexi drew in a breath.

"I'm sorry, sir." I said no more, though the injustice rankled.

"Don't be sorry, do your job." His tone was acid. "I'll be over to inspect when I'm done with *Freiheit*."

"Aye aye, sir." The connection went dead.

"That ass!" Alexi pounded the console. "He's so unfair—"

I snarled, "Shut your mouth!"

Alexi stopped in midword.

"Don't you ever—and I mean ever, Lieutenant—criticize your commanding officer in my presence. Is that understood?" My fists were clenched.

"Aye aye, sir," said Alexi, his tone meek.

"I wouldn't expect that remark from a first-year cadet, Mr. Tamarov. We'll obey the Admiral's orders without question and without comment."

"Aye aye, sir."

I let out an explosive breath. "Very well. I know you meant to sympathize. Thank you for your intentions." I turned back to the screen. "He'll be here within the hour. Let's get as ready as we can."

Admiral Tremaine and two lieutenants who served as his aides crossed in *Challenger*'s launch. The Admiral bustled through *Portia* issuing running commentaries to his aide, who made copious notes. He found fault with the airlock watch crew, wrinkled his nose at the crew berths, glanced in the engine room and found nothing amiss. "To the bridge, Seafort," was all he said.

I followed a step behind. Vax Holser and Midshipman Rafe Treadwell snapped to attention as we entered; Tremaine didn't bother to release them. Let's see your Log." He snapped it on, flipping through the entries. Vax glanced at me; I kept my face impassive.

"A lot of disciplines for a small ship. Shows a lack of leadership." I was taken aback; such a comment should have been made privately, if at all. "I see you have a middy who likes trouble. This Tyre: dozens of demerits. Is that one Tyre?" He waved at Rafe Treadwell.

"No, sir. Mr. Tyre is in the comm room. That situation's under control now."

"So you say," he said, glowering. "The trick, Seafort, is to come down hard enough so you don't have to do it often."

"Yes, sir." I wondered how to divert him. "The laser simulations—"

"Don't try to distract me." He scowled, and I reddened.

"Sorry, sir."

"Look." He drew me close, and for a moment his tone seemed almost pleading. "This is my first squadron, Seafort, and they'll be watching my Logs like a hawk. Everything has to be right. *Everything.*"

"I understand, sir."

"Send him up to be caned."

I was astounded. "What?"

"You heard me. Teach the middy that we won't tolerate insubordination. Give him a caning today."

"But—"

His eyes turned cold. "I see where he gets it from, Seafort."

There was only one possible response. "Aye aye, sir."

"Very well. I'll inspect again after the next Defuse. By then I expect to see a tighter ship." He beckoned to his aide and stalked from the bridge.

I followed, benumbed. The Admiral's launch was at the aft airlock, on Level 2. His party descended the ladder and followed the corridor around the bend.

"Mira da man! He da bossman, mira alla gol'!"

Furious, I pushed into the crush of jabbering joeykids. "Get away from him! Don't touch him!"

"Watchadoon, man? Whatsa fatman doonhere?"

The transpops, in a playful mood, shoved and pointed derisively at the braid on Tremaine's dress uniform. "Mus' be a Boss Cap'n, mira alla gold!"

I collided with Eddie's large form. The boy whirled angrily before recognizing me. I hissed, "Get them away from him, flank!"

Something in my tone reached him. He flung the nearest boy aside and collared the girl closest to the Admiral. "Gii'm room, trannies! Oudahere! Backoff! Oudahere!"

In moments Tremaine was free of the jostling, livid with rage. "Who are those—animals! God curse it, Seafort, what kind of ship do you run here?"

"They're transients, sir," I said quickly. "They were assigned at the last minute in Lunapolis. I'm sorry, sir. They don't know any better."

"You let that trash run wild with decent passengers aboard? Lock them up! It's no wonder your ship is a mess!"

"I'm sorry, they—"

"They're scum! Brig the lot of them the next time I board!" With that he turned and disappeared into the airlock.

The look on my face kept the transients well clear as I stalked to the ladder. A few moments later I was in my place on the bridge, but I couldn't keep to my seat. I paced back and forth, my fury welling. Vax had the good sense to say nothing. Rafe Treadwell sat very still, his eyes glued to his console.

After a time I was calm enough to drop heavily into my soft black leather chair. This would pass; soon we would Fuse and continue on our way.

I could guess, though, what the Admiral's visit would do to *Portia*'s morale. My lieutenants had heard him disparage how I ran my ship; his stinging rebuke wouldn't help my authority. And what the midshipmen witnessed was hardly a proper example for their own conduct.

The midshipmen! What was I to do about Philip Tyre? I rocked back and forth, dismayed. The Admiral had given me a direct order; I was to have Philip caned.

The order was utterly unjust; I was Captain of *Portia* and in charge of my ship's discipline. Tyre's demerits littered the Log because of Alexi's attitude, not Philip's. The nightmare relations between Tyre, Alexi, and myself had just begun to be resolved, and Lord God knew what effect an unwarranted caning would have on the young middy now.

Could I appeal Tremaine's order? Call him, after he calmed down? It was unlikely to succeed, and I'd refocus his wrath on myself. Better for *Portia*'s sake to let the order stand.

A wave of disgust made me cringe. Cane Philip, because I was afraid the Admiral would be annoyed at my protest? What kind of coward had I become? Unconsciously I rose from my chair and began to pace, my ire rising anew.

After a time I was aware of the intense silence. Midshipman Treadwell was still trying to make himself invisible. Vax watched with a pensive look. When I caught his eye his glance dropped. My disgust rose to new heights. Now my own officers were afraid to meet my gaze.

I made an effort to smile. As calmly as I could I said,

"Rafe, do some nav problems. Determine our position and plot a course to Caltech. Lieutenant Holser will help if you run into trouble. Vax, if you would?"

With the two of them concentrating on their console I resumed my pacing. Well, I had to try to change the Admiral's mind, even if he didn't like it.

I would wait two hours; perhaps then Tremaine would be more agreeable. I yawned, realizing I was still exhausted. There was no reason to stay on the bridge. I left the middy to his calculations with Vax, trudged to my cabin for a nap before dinner. I told Amanda what had transpired, as I slipped off my jacket and tie.

"Oh, poor Philip." Her eyes glistened. "You won't let them hurt him, will you?"

"I'll try to get him out of it," I said. "But it was a direct order. There's not much I can do if Tremaine won't listen." She wanted to argue but I was too tired. I set the alarm, rolled over, and went to sleep.

Three hours later I felt no better. I stopped at the bridge before going to the dining hall. At my console I smoothed my hair, straightened my tie while the comm room connected me to *Challenger*. Captain Hasselbrad came on the line. "The Admiral's not aboard, Captain Seafort. He's at dinner on *Kitty Hawk* with Derghinski. You could page him if it's important."

I thanked him and snapped off the screen. There was no point whatsoever in calling the Admiral from his dinner to make my request. He'd refuse instantly and I would probably be relieved from command, as I should be for such bad judgment. I went down to dinner.

Eddie Boss, Annie, and the other transients stood as I approached. As we sat Annie said uncomfortably, "Din' mean makin' trouble wid fatman, Cap'n. Funnin', was all." Either their English was improving or I was developing an ear for transpop dialect. Perhaps both.

"Thank you, Annie. I appreciate that."

"We leave'm lone nothertime," said Eddie, glowering at the others. "Stay way f'mim." He poked Deke, who nodded sullenly. The others nodded agreement.

I called *Challenger* again an hour after dinner; the Admiral still hadn't returned. I chewed at my lip. Tremaine had snarled, "Do it today." I waited impatiently on the bridge. At 21:30 ship's time, I tried again.

"Is the Admiral back, Captain Hasselbrad?"

"Yes." The Captain paused, his face impassive. "He went to bed. He left orders not to bother him except for an emergency." His glance met mine and I wondered how much he knew. How must it feel to be Captain under the Admiral's constant supervision? I couldn't ask, of course.

"Thank you, sir." I broke the connection. Well, there was nothing to do but carry out the order. Philip would survive, as he had before. I opened my mouth to summon the midshipman to his fate, then hesitated.

If I did nothing, Tremaine would never know. Three months from now he'd hardly remember to check my Log for a middy's discipline. Vax would keep his mouth shut and Philip need never be told what he'd faced. With a sense of relief I knew I'd stumbled on a solution. Philip had been through more than enough, and we'd promised him it was over. I'd be violating orders, but I would have to live with that.

"I'm going to bed," I said.

"Good night, sir." Vax hesitated. "And Mr., uh, Tyre—?"

He'd blundered into it. Better nothing had been said. "I'm going to my cabin," I said firmly. I went to the hatch. "Good night."

I tossed and turned for a long while. Then I slept.

Father and I walked slowly down the shaded walk to the Academy gates. My duffel hung heavy at my side. When we reached the compound his hand rested on my shoulder for the briefest moment, but he said nothing. I turned to look at him. He turned my shoulders, pushed me toward the open gates. I walked through.

When I turned to say good-bye he was striding away, not looking back. I felt the iron ring close around my neck as the gates swung shut.

I woke in gasping panic. Amanda was sitting at my side, her soft hand stroking my shoulder. "Nicky, it's all right. I'm with you. You were having a nightmare."

"Ungh." I swung my legs to the floor, shuddering. "The dream again."

"Your father?"

"Yes." I put my head in my hands. Would it ever go away? After a while I pulled myself together and went to the head to wash the fear and sweat off me. I'd had the dream off and on since I'd gone to Academy at thirteen.

Other than the iron ring, it was all true.

I came back to my bunk. Well, Father wasn't aboard *Portia*. He was back in Cardiff, set in the dour hardness of his ways.

Musing, I was drawn back to my studies at our worn kitchen table, Father watching while I worked my way through the difficult texts. I recalled our Bible readings. He was intoning from Leviticus. I heard myself make some flippant remark about an oath, and recalled his stern rebuke. My sense of shame.

"Promise, Nicholas." He waited for my answer. "Promise it, son."

"I do, Father."

"Say the words, Nicholas."

I closed my eyes. "My oath is my bond. I will let them destroy me before I swear to an oath I will not fulfill. My oath is all that I am."

I looked up from my bunk, my eyes stinging. I knew the value of an oath; as Lord God knew, I'd taken one often enough. That solemn ritual my first day at Academy: *I, Nicholas Ewing Seafort, do swear upon my immortal soul to preserve and protect the Charter of the General Assembly of the United Nations, to give loyalty and obedience for the term of my enlistment to the Naval Service of the United Nations and to obey all its lawful orders and regulations, so help me Lord God Almighty.* The oath that still bound me.

I cast about for an escape. *"To obey all lawful orders and regulations."* No doubt, Admiral Tremaine's order was unjust. Nonetheless, it was lawful. I was bound to obey it, despite my flailing to escape.

I glanced sharply at the clock: 23:35. I still had time. Philip would have to suffer. My voice rasped over the caller. "Midshipman Tyre to the bridge, immediately." I threw on my clothes.

"Nicky, what are you doing?" Amanda, her eyes worried.

"What I must." I ignored her hurt.

Philip Tyre was waiting with Vax when I arrived. He looked like he too had been sleeping.

I managed somehow to meet his eye. I said, my voice harsh, "Mr. Tyre, during his inspection Admiral Tremaine reviewed our Log. It is full of your demerits. You're to be caned for insubordination. Go to Lieutenant Holser's cabin. He will be along in a moment."

Philip's astonishment gave way to another expression: betrayal? Emotions flickered across his face before his training reasserted itself. "Aye aye, sir!" He saluted, turned on his heel, and marched out.

I turned to Vax and rasped, "I'll finish the watch. Get it over with!"

"Aye aye, sir."

Vax's expression told me how he felt, and I was much relieved. If Vax let Philip off lightly, not too much harm need be done.

As Vax strode to the hatch I recalled with a pang our earlier conversation. How could Vax let Philip off easily, after what he'd said about enforcing discipline?

No, Vax couldn't take it on himself to do right by Philip. I was disgusted; now I was making Vax choose between disobeying orders or brutalizing Philip, because I wouldn't take the responsibility I must.

"Just a moment!"

Vax stopped at the hatch, watching me.

"Vax, I—" The words grated in my throat. I said firmly, "I order you to go quite easy on him. Do you understand?"

Vax's face lit up in a warm grin. "Aye aye, sir." Still smiling, he left the bridge with a jaunty step.

It was done. Tremaine hadn't said anything about going hard on Philip, had he? I'd carried out my orders to the letter.

Despite my sophistry, I felt sick. I had skirted my oath and risked my soul.

We were Fused, and days passed with dreary slowness. Amanda taught the transients what she could; the girl named Annie laboriously learned to write her name and they were both elated.

For two days after the Admiral's inspection Alexi volunteered himself on the watch roster to replace Philip Tyre, though from Philip's gait it clearly wasn't necessary. I said nothing. Philip Tyre gave me a shy smile on our first encounter after his visit to Vax's cabin. I didn't want to be reminded of my folly; I stared coldly until his smile faded.

My son grew daily. The most precious moments of my life were spent playing on the deck of my cabin while he drooled happily on my white shirt and tie. With an effort he could turn himself over. I wondered when he would begin to crawl.

After three weeks in Fusion we had settled down once more to ship's routine. Mrs. Attani arranged a party in honor of her son Gregor's eighteenth birthday. Naval policy in such matters was ambiguous. There was only one class of passengers aboard Naval vessels; all were provided similar cabins and were served the same meals. But wealthy passengers could buy additional amenities, such as Mrs. Attani's party. Many of the passengers were invited, though not all, and of the officers only Amanda and myself.

Amanda and I agreed that the party, even if held in the ship's familiar dining hall, was too formal an occasion to bring little Nate. We learned that the young baby-sitter who had watched Nate on other occasions had also been invited.

"Too bad Erin can't watch him, Nicky. Mrs. Attani's made such a fuss; she wants the party to be perfect. If Nate cries she'll take it personally."

"Have you asked Philip Tyre?" My tone was gruff.

Amanda shot me a sharp glance; when she realized I was serious she put her arms around me, kissed me on the end of my nose, and captured my heart afresh.

Young Gregor stood in the entranceway greeting his guests, his mother at his side. At eighteen, Attani was still four years short of his majority, though I, at twenty-one, had been an adult for five years by act of the General Assembly. As a cadet I'd been a minor, but on promotion to midshipman I'd attained my majority and could drink, vote, and marry.

At home one occasionally heard agitation to reduce the age of majority to twenty, but I doubted it would come to anything. The aftermath of the Rebellious Ages had left society far more cautious and conservative than once it had been.

"Thank you for coming, Captain." Gregor's manners were impeccable. Well, by virtue of office I was of his class.

"It's our honor, Mr. Attani," I said stiffly, matching his courtesy. As Captain and an adult I might use his first name, and sometimes did, but it would be graceless to patronize him at his own celebration.

Arm in arm, Amanda and I moved into the crowd. I felt awkward and unsophisticated among our cosmopolitan passengers. Usually, I depended on Amanda to make casual conversation and tonight was no exception. We nibbled on canapés and settled near a group that was chatting with animation.

"It's worth the privation to reach open spaces," a woman said. "A whole unsettled continent! For the first time in our lives we'll have room to stretch."

"Emily Valdez," whispered Amanda. "As in the Valdez Permabattery." She, or her family, had enormous wealth.

"But all the settlements are on Eastern Continent." Walter Dakko, young Chris's father. "The holo said Western Continent isn't opened for settlement yet."

"How long can that last?" A heavy-jowled man, and belligerent. "Land sitting there unused!"

"I wonder what the colony's really like," mused Galena Dakko, her arm linked in her husband's.

"Wait a year and you'll see, honey," someone said dryly.

"All of us bound for Hope Nation, yet no one knows quite what to expect," remarked Walter Dakko. "We've put our faith in—in a—"

"U.N. emigration brochure." Emily Valdez was rueful. "We may have consigned ourselves to years on this—this coop, only to find we've all been had."

"Shh, the Captain will hear you," someone whispered.

"I don't care," said Miss Valdez defiantly. "Captain Seafort, is our imprisonment a good bargain? Is Hope Nation worth the cost of getting there?"

"What cost, Miss Valdez?" I asked.

"Well." A pretty laugh. "The accommodations. I'm sure you do your best, but really!" Amanda squeezed my arm.

"Is something wrong with your cabin?" I was puzzled.

"Not in the sense that you could send a man to fix it. But it's so ridiculously small, Captain. At the hacienda, even my dressing room wasn't so cramped. How could one expect civilized people to live in such a space for extended periods. Sixteen months? Really!"

Amanda's grip tightened further but I ignored the signal. "Would you care to exchange cabins with one of my officers?" My voice was cool.

"Which one?" Miss Valdez was smiling.

"Any of them. My two lieutenants are fortunate; their cabins are about half the size of yours. Well, perhaps a bit smaller. My midshipmen sleep in a wardroom the size of a lieutenant's cabin, and we carry three middies. On my last trip to Hope Nation four of us shared a similar wardroom."

"That's true, then?" asked Galena Dakko. "You were a midshipman on your last cruise? I'd heard rumors, but it didn't seem polite to ask."

"Yes, Mrs. Dakko. At that time a cabin like yours was beyond my wildest dreams."

Mrs. Attani had come up behind us. "But your officers enlisted as children, Captain. Surely they're accustomed to the crowding."

"Yes." I was curt. How could people of such wealth understand wardroom life? Four joeys of both sexes in the midst of turbulent adolescence, crammed like sardines into the tiny wardroom, living intimately while maintaining the rigid Navy hierarchy even among themselves. No, I couldn't explain that.

"You have to understand." Walter Dakko's tone was placating. "We don't have your training in hardships. We're from comfortable backgrounds and find the cramped quarters quite difficult to bear."

I lost patience. "Consider yourself fortunate, then. For lack of space other passengers have to sleep six to a cabin."

"That's dreadful!" said Mrs. Dakko. "In heaven's name, who?"

"The Lower New Yorkers."

"Oh, the trannies?" Mrs. Attani laughed. "I thought you meant real passengers."

"Shall we find a drink, Nicky?" Amanda.

"No. The New Yorkers are passengers, madam, like yourselves."

"Not really." Miss Valdez spoke lightly. "More like captive

savages. Or refugees, if you will. They're certainly not proper passengers. Anyway, they're used to crowds. I'm sure the ship is better than what they knew before."

"It's criminal to put them on a passenger ship with respectable people." Walter Dakko seemed indignant. "Some of us have to share cabins all the way to Hope Nation thanks to those hoodlums! It's inexcusable."

"A cold drink would be really nice," said Amanda, an edge to her voice.

"Later. You're right, Mr. Dakko; the crowded accommodations are inexcusable. Six to a cabin? Imagine! Fortunately I have a solution. The transients need to experience your knowledge and cultivation. By sharing cabins with you they'll become more civilized. I'll work out more equitable cabin assignments as soon as possible. Come, Amanda, we'll find those drinks now." I nodded politely at their stunned and gaping faces.

"Damn it, Nicky," said Amanda, a few steps away.

"I couldn't help it."

"Yes, you could! So they were obnoxious; did you have to make enemies of them?"

"I'd rather have them as enemies than friends."

Her eyes teared. "But I wouldn't. You have your officers and your bridge. All I have is people like them, and the trannies!"

"Oh, hon, I'm sorry. I forget." I offered a hug.

A giggle broke through her cross expression. "You won't really do it, Nicky? The look on Walter's face when you suggested sharing his cabin with a transpop . . ."

"I should," I grumbled.

"Please, Nick, they're all influential. If word got back to Admiralty . . ."

I sighed. Of course she was right. My authority was unlimited; I could assign cabins as I chose. But I had Admiralty to reckon with on my return, and they would take a dim view of my evicting our elite for a swarm of streeters. Still . . . I savored the idea for a time before reluctantly setting it aside.

I held drills and exercises to keep the crew alert. They helped keep me alert as well; I'd begun to find confinement in *Portia* stifling. She was a small ship, much smaller than any I'd sailed before. There were few passengers whose company I enjoyed, and most of them weren't enthused with me either.

After it became evident that I wasn't going to carry out my threat to change passengers' cabins, I was grudgingly readmitted into society, but my main avenue of interchange with the passengers—dinner at the Captain's table—had been lost when I reassigned seating so the officers could dine with the transpop youths.

That too grew tiresome. I settled into an uneasy truce with the youngsters at my table. I'd made them fully aware of my power by denying them their meals until they behaved—probably a violation of regs, if the rules applied to involuntary underage passengers—and they weren't ready to test me further as yet. Still, their cooperation was minimal at best.

Annie, whom I'd mistaken for a boy during the corridor riot, was now unmistakably feminine. Perhaps the sustained nutrition was helping develop her figure. Certainly the hairdo she appeared in one afternoon, to the jeers of her young male associates, also contributed. She had no idea of her age but was assumed to be roughly seventeen.

One day, I came into my cabin and stopped short. Sitting over a holovid on the breakfast table were Amanda and Eddie Boss. Eddie lurched to his feet as I entered.

"No makin' trouble, Cap'n. Lady she say allri' beinhere. She say."

I was careful how I spoke, remembering too well my scene with Philip Tyre. "I understand, Eddie. It's all right. Sit down."

"Don' wan' stay. Gotta find Deke. Wanna go." He edged nervously toward the door.

"Thank you for coming, Eddie," Amanda said. "Let's do more tomorrow."

"Gotta go." The hatch closed behind him.

I raised an eyebrow. "He seems afraid of me."

She giggled. "I'd say terrified, under that big hulking exterior."

"Because I put him in the brig for two weeks?"

"I don't know, Nicky. I can't imagine why anyone would be afraid of you."

I studied her suspiciously for signs of mockery. "Anyway, what was he doing?"

"He wants to learn to read. Nicky, he actually came to me! Isn't it wonderful?"

"Why not put him in the puter-assisted literacy course?"

She made a face. "It didn't work out. He tried to smash the screen the first time it buzzed his answer as wrong. He needs . . . human encouragement."

"He's too dangerous. You shouldn't be around him."

"I don't think so. He really wants to learn."

Her mind was made up; no use pursuing it. "Well, must you teach him here? Wouldn't a lounge do as well?" At least there'd be others about, in case of hostilities.

"Oh, Nick, we tried that two days ago. Some boys came in and made fun of him, and he stomped off. It took all my persuasion to get him back."

I swore under my breath. "Aren't those streeters cruel? They don't even want to see one of their own get ahead."

"Streeters? It was Gregor and the Dakko boy, Chris." She saw my expression and hurried on, "They weren't causing real trouble, hon. You know what happens when they and the transients run across each other."

"Yes. First we cram these poor joes six in a cabin, and then they have to put up with abuse from those spoiled . . ." I took a deep breath. "Very well, I'll deal with it."

"Hon, don't make a fuss about it. The passengers are upset enough about the transients."

"I'll deal with it," I repeated. I spent the evening wondering how.

The next afternoon I called Purser Li to the bridge. "I want some changes in seat assignments," I told him. "Put Gregor Attani at my table, and assign Chris Dakko to table four with Lieutenant Holser. Effective tonight."

"Aye aye, sir." He hesitated. "If they object, sir?"

"I don't believe regs require passengers to eat dinner," I said. "If they choose to eat, that's where they'll sit." He saluted and left.

When Vax arrived for his watch I was already on the bridge,

wondering how long it would be before I heard from Mrs. Attani. Vax took his seat, looking uncomfortable. For a while he fidgeted. Then, to his console, "There was a hell of a row in the wardroom last night."

I said nothing. Naval fiction was that the Captain didn't concern himself with wardroom affairs. Nor was it customary for a lieutenant to bring them to the Captain's attention. It must be an unusual problem to have worried Vax.

"Philip and Derek Carr had it out," he added, still speaking to the screen. "In the exercise room. They beat each other nearly unconscious. Mr. Singh opened the hatch and thought for a moment they were lovers; they were lying almost on top of each other. He found me and brought me there."

I remained silent. Vax said, "I got them cleaned up and back to the wardroom." He stole a glance at me, reddened. I wondered if he recalled our own desperate fight aboard *Hibernia*. Well, I hadn't won. I had only managed not to lose.

I sighed. I wasn't supposed to interfere, but Vax was an old friend and if I couldn't discuss it with him, with whom could I talk? The obvious answer came unbidden: nobody.

My role was to be the awesome, isolated figure at the top. I could ask questions, give decisions, but it wasn't proper to talk things over with old friends. Otherwise, I wouldn't have their absolute, unquestioning obedience when it was needed.

I managed to keep my silence. Vax looked puzzled, then hurt, and his eyes shifted back to his screen. Of course I couldn't explain; a Captain didn't do that either.

Thank Lord God for Amanda and Nate; without them I didn't know how I'd stay sane.

That evening the dining hall flickered with currents of tension. Derek's face was bruised; Philip Tyre bore a black eye and a cut lip. Of course, in the time-honored Naval tradition I affected not to notice, just as Captain Dengal hadn't noticed my own puffy face aboard *Helsinki* the night Arvan Hager, my senior, taught me a memorable lesson.

Chris Dakko attempted to go to his usual place at his family's table and stalked from the hall when he was refused. Gregor Attani sat next to me, glowering, in what once would have been considered a place of honor. Eddie and Deke made incomprehensible jokes and nudged each other in the ribs.

"Why do this to me?" Gregor asked between courses. His tone was sullen.

"What, Gregor?"

"Making me eat with these tranni—these animals," he amended, at my glare.

"You're no better than they are, Mr. Attani."

"No?" he sneered. "Look!" True, their table manners still left something to be desired, though they tried as best they could to conform to my strange requirements.

"No," I said. "You're more educated, more cultured, but no better at all." I pictured Eddie fumbling with a holo in the passengers' lounge, anxious to learn. My temper shredded. "No more remarks, Gregor, or you'll take breakfast and lunch with us as well." That silenced him. Amanda took pity and chatted casually with him, until even she was rebuffed by his surly monosyllables.

After dinner I returned to the bridge. I wished I'd asked Vax one question: did the fight settle it? I brooded, and finally decided I had to ask outright. I picked up the caller, then slammed it down in its place.

"Easy, Captain, sir. They break." Danny's voice. I looked up sharply.

"Sorry," I said, regretting my temper, then felt foolish. What was I doing apologizing to a puter?

"What're you so mad about, Captain?"

"Never mind." I was curt.

"Aye aye, sir." He sounded hurt.

I sighed. Perhaps he was the answer. I couldn't talk to the passengers or my officers; why not Danny?

"The middies had a fight in the wardroom," I said.

"They do that all the time, don't they? Darla told me about a zarky one you had on her ship."

Were there no secrets? "This time it's a touchy situation. Last voyage Philip—Mr. Tyre to you—was unfit to run the wardroom and Derek took over. Gave Philip quite a beating in the process. Now Philip has some of his confidence back and wants to be in charge. After all, he's senior."

"Then the fight settled it. Did Philip—er, Mr. Tyre to me—win?"

"No insolence," I growled. I wondered how old Danny was, then realized I was being silly. He wasn't alive. Was he? "I don't know who won. I don't think either did."

"Then they'll do it again until it's settled." He seemed unconcerned.

"Yes." I couldn't allow that. I liked Derek too much. Yet, Philip had earned his chance. I realized grudgingly that I'd begun to like him too.

I took the caller and keyed the wardroom. "Mr. Tyre and Mr. Carr to the bridge."

"They're not here, sir." Rafe Treadwell sounded scared.

"Very well." I put down the caller and hesitated only a minute before grabbing the caller again. "Lieutenant Holser to the bridge!" In a few moments Vax arrived, breathing heavily. "Take the watch, Lieutenant." I left.

I hurried past the wardroom to the Level 1 exercise room. An "Out of Service" sign hung on the hatch. I turned the handle; it was locked from the inside. I pounded. "Open up in there! Now!"

The hatch opened. I pushed past Philip Tyre, whose torn undershirt rose and fell as he took in great gasps of air. A line of blood trickled from his mouth. Derek stood across the room, fists clenched, waiting, one arm pressed against his side. The two midshipmen had folded their dress shirts, jackets, and ties neatly on the parallel bar.

"Enough," I snapped. "Get dressed! Come with me!" I waited impatiently for them to don their shirts and knot their ties. When they were presentable I led them down the corridor to the deserted dining hall. I pulled up a chair at the nearest table and sat in the dim light.

I thrust out two chairs. "Sit, both of you!"

"Aye aye, sir." Derek sat composedly, leaning back to favor his left side. Philip perched on the edge of his seat.

I glared at them. It had no effect. I slammed my hand on the table so hard they both jumped. My palm stung like fire. "The wardroom is supposed to settle its own affairs," I growled.

"We were trying to, sir." Philip Tyre sounded aggrieved.

"And the Captain isn't supposed to notice." I slapped the table again, this time more carefully. "How the devil am I supposed to ignore you, when you involve half the ship in your squabbles? You beat each other half to death, Lieutenant Holser is summoned, and then you march into dinner flaunting your battle scars!" That wasn't fair, but I was too angry to care.

They exchanged glances but neither spoke. Watching them I realized I'd get nowhere confronting them together. "Mr. Tyre, wait outside until I call you."

"Aye aye, sir!" The boy wheeled and strode out to the corridor.

I got to my feet. "Damn it, Derek, is this necessary?"

He raised his eyes to meet mine. "I'll obey whatever orders you give, sir," he said without emotion.

I suppressed my urge to lash out, and thought instead of our companionable shore leave in the Venturas. "Will you give in to him, Derek?" My voice was gentle.

"Are you ordering it, sir?"

"No." I couldn't do that. Not inside the wardroom.

"Then no, sir, I won't." His smile was bitter. "I'm sorry, sir, I know you want me to, but I won't do it voluntarily. Not after last cruise."

"What if he's changed?"

"Sir . . ." He colored. "I've swallowed my pride for you, no matter how much it hurt. I've tried to do whatever you've asked of me. I can do that for you. But not for him."

"And if I command it?"

"Then I'll submit to his orders, because you require it of me."

"I can't have you trying to kill each other, Derek."

"No, sir, I understand that."

"Is there any other way you could settle it?"

"You taught me the traditions, sir. Is there?"

I tried to think of a way. Reluctantly, I shook my head. "None that I know of. Unless I remove one of you from the wardroom." I sighed. Damn his pride. Yet I knew I would love him less without it. "Wait outside, Mr. Carr. Send in Mr. Tyre."

"Aye aye, sir."

Philip came to attention as he entered the room.

"As you were, Mr. Tyre."

He chose the at-ease position. I searched for the right words. "You are first midshipman, Mr. Tyre, I understand that. But Derek's been in charge for over a year now. Why must you change that?"

"Because I'm first midshipman, Captain Seafort." His tension was almost palpable.

"Can you give it up, Philip?"

"Can I? I don't know if I can, sir. I won't, though." His resolve shocked me.

"If I order you to let him remain in charge?"

"I'll have to obey your order, sir. But please, let me resign from the Service first."

I sat heavily. "Be seated, Philip." He took the chair next to me. I noticed he was trembling. "Why now?" I asked. "What happened?"

"I don't know exactly why, sir. He hasn't been any different lately. He's fair to Mr. Treadwell and he mostly leaves me alone, though he despises me. I just . . . it's time, sir," he blurted. "Pardon me, I know I'm out of line, but you had no business taking me along with you."

My jaw dropped. He hurried on, "I should have been beached. A middy who can't even hold the wardroom . . . You gave me a second chance, sir. I want to use it. I went all wrong the first time; maybe now I won't." He stared at the deck. "I don't know why it has to be now, sir, but it does. Maybe Mrs. Seafort had something to do with it. What she's been saying."

I was startled. "What was that?"

"About trying to be the best I could no matter how hard it was, sir. You know."

"Yes." I let it be. Amanda never ceased to amaze me.

I went slowly to the hatch and opened it. Derek waited some distance down the corridor. "Come in, Mr. Carr."

I eyed them both. "You're evenly matched. I don't know whether either of you can subdue the other. I don't want you to hurt yourselves or each other trying. Tradition says you have a right to do it. Will you stop, for me?"

Derek said tightly, "I will obey every lawful order Mr. Tyre gives me, sir. Outside the wardroom." He refused to meet my eye.

Philip shook his head. "When Mr. Carr acknowledges that I am first midshipman, sir. In the wardroom and out. Not before."

I was defeated. "I won't order you to stop. You have to resolve it. But I do order you to delay. Do nothing for a week, until you've both thought it through."

"Aye aye, sir." Derek looked grim.

"Aye aye, sir," said Philip. "Um, who's in charge in the meantime, sir?"

"Out, both of you!" I shouted. They scurried away. I paced the empty hall until I was calm enough to go back to my cabin.

6

“Bridge to engine room, prepare to Defuse.”

“Prepare to Defuse, aye aye, sir.” Chief Hendricks’s voice was devoid of all inflection. After a pause he confirmed, “Engine room ready for Defuse, sir. Control passed to bridge.”

“Very well.” My finger traced a line from “Full” to “Off” on my console. The light of millions of stars leapt forth from the simulscreens.

“Confirm clear of encroachments, Lieutenant.” My voice had an edge. But Vax was already punching figures into the console, anticipating my order.

“No encroachments, sir,” he said at last.

“Very well. Have the crew stand down.”

Vax gave the order. I leaned back and rocked, my eyes shut. I wondered how long it would be before Derghinski showed up; he would almost certainly be the first.

We spent the next two days drifting alone, waiting for our squadron. Derek Carr shared a watch with me and seemed ill at ease; at the end of watch he saluted and mumbled, “May I say something before I go?”

I nodded.

“About Mr. Tyre, sir—it’s not that I want the power, or that I won’t obey orders. It’s because of what he did.”

“I understand,” I said. “I never thought otherwise. You’re dismissed.”

I brooded in my seat while Alexi and Rafe Treadwell settled in for their watch, then left abruptly for my cabin. Amanda sat in near dark, rocking Nate gently. “I think he’s finally out,” she whispered. I checked. He was breathing with the swift regularity of sleep.

“Yes.” I held my baby to my shoulder while she smoothed

the sheets in his crib. A small hand clutched my neck as he stirred.

She took him from me and laid him facedown in his bed. Then she came and nestled against my arm. "I love both of you," she said, and tears stung my eyes.

The next day the alarms sounded while we lunched in the passengers' mess. The crew hastened to General Quarters; I raced to the bridge, slapped the hatch shut, slid into my seat.

"Encroachment thirty-six thousand kilometers and closing, sir." Alexi's eyes were glued to the screen.

"Recognition code received, sir," Danny interrupted. "Positive ID on *Kitty Hawk.*" I breathed a sigh of relief as we stood down. Our frequent Defusing was nerve-wracking. We were still only fifteen light-years from home, with most of the cruise still ahead of us.

I let Pilot Van Peer take the conn to maneuver us into position relative to *Kitty Hawk*. Short bursts from the thrusters reoriented us. I remembered the dinner Captain Tenere had given us on *Freiheit* and wished he were first on station, so I could return the favor.

Would Captain Derghinski consider it presumptuous to invite him over? I thought of the months of isolation aboard a Fused ship and smiled. "Danny, make contact with *Kitty Hawk*'s bridge."

"Aye aye, sir. Nola says Captain Derghinski's off duty now but she can wake him."

"Nola? Their puter?" I knew our puters locked in tightbeam whenever two ships approached. Lord God knew what they exchanged. "Wait until he wakes," I told him.

Two hours later I was in my cabin, humming to myself as I changed clothes. Captain Derghinski had accepted my dinner invitation with alacrity. I'd ordered the steward to outdo himself for our guests, and was wondering where to hide the transients for the evening.

"Let's meet him at the lock, hon. The Captain and the Captain's lady."

Amanda smiled back as she took my arm. We strolled down to Level 2. Near the airlock, the corridor was crowded with sentries for the ceremonial of Captain Derghinski's entry.

Passengers peered through our transplex portholes for a glimpse of *Kitty Hawk.*

I beckoned to young Eddie Boss; he approached apprehensively. "Pass the word to your, ah, comrades. Anyone who causes the ruckus you made with the Admiral will spend the rest of the trip locked in his cabin. All eleven months!"

Eddie looked awed. "I be tellin' em good, Cap'n. Giim lots room, I tell 'em all. Noway makin' trouble nohow, Cap'n."

"Be sure of it, Eddie." Frowning, I watched him retreat.

Amanda inquired, "When did you put him in charge?"

"I didn't, but he's large enough to get the point across."

"And then some," she agreed.

A sailor peered through the porthole. "Their launch berth doors are opening, sir. He'll be on his way in a minute."

Alarms sounded. For a moment I panicked, knowing *Kitty Hawk*'s gig wouldn't set off our alarms. Then understanding came and I cursed to myself as I relaxed. "Another ship's Defused," I said to Amanda. "Lousy timing. It'll set dinner back at least an hour. I'll be back as quick as I can." I trotted to the bridge.

Danny's adolescent voice was shrill. "Encroachment seven kilometers, bearing oh four oh and closing!" I slapped the hatch shut. Vax and the Pilot were at their consoles.

"That's awfully close," I muttered to Vax as I slipped into my seat. "Who is it, Danny?"

"No recognition signal, sir! And bounceback isn't showing metal."

My fingers tightened on the caller. "Comm room! What do you read?"

"No metal, Captain. It's not a ship."

"Battle Stations!" I hit the klaxon, and sirens blared throughout *Portia*. "Danny, full magnification!"

"Aye aye, sir!" The screens leapt into focus.

"Oh, Lord God preserve us!" Vax, in a whisper.

"Shut up, Vax. Fire control, I'm activating all lasers! Deploy shields! Enemy target oh four oh!" My sphincters twitched. I tried to tear my eyes away from the object in the screens. I thumbed the laser activation release.

A fish.

Two-thirds the size of *Portia*, half the size of *Kitty Hawk*, it drifted toward us, closing fast. As I watched, a hole near its tail squirted propellant and its speed increased. A glob on the creature's knobby surface began to spin lazily.

So much for trying not to initiate hostilities.

"Commence firing! Vax, turn off those bloody alarms. Danny, inform *Kitty Hawk* we're shooting!"

"Aye aye, sir," Danny said, breathless in the sudden silence. "Mr. Derghinski informed by tightbeam."

A spot on the alien form glowed red. Colors swirled; holes opened and the fish jerked aside from our laser beam. Its spinning glob released, came sailing toward us.

Vax roared into his caller. "Laser Group B, fire on the projectile!" He'd once seen an acid glob eat through *Hibernia*'s gig and kill its crew. We waited, watching the screens. Our lasers again found their target, and the glob flared and melted.

Alarm bells clanged anew. Danny shouted, "Encroachment five hundred kilometers! Course three four one!"

"Puter, lower your voice! Put the bogey on the screen." I tried to sound calmer than I felt.

"Recognition codes!" said Danny and Vax together. A second's pause, and Danny added, "It's *Challenger*."

"Signal them we're under attack. Any more projectiles?"

Vax checked his screen. "None at the moment, but debris from the one we broke up is still approaching. Looks like it'll hit the shields aft."

"Very well." The goldfish shape jerked as laser beams struck it from the side; Captain Derghinski was in action.

"Maneuver us closer, Pilot. Vax, ask the Admiral if *Challenger* will join the attack." My fingers ached from gripping the arm of the chair.

"Aye aye, sir. *Challenger*'s closing—"

The alarms clanged. Danny and Vax were both shouting. "New encroachment forty kilometers, course three three nine!"

"Another encroachment, one kilometer, dead ahead! They're not ships!" Vax pointed.

The Pilot slammed the starboard thrusters to full, blasting propellant to steer us clear of the encroachment ahead.

"All lasers fire at will! Take the nearest targets!" No time for target selection by the book. The original fish glowed red from several laser penetrations. Propellant squirted in three directions as it corkscrewed away. *Kitty Hawk* spewed flames in pursuit.

The fish ahead drifted to our port side as our thrusters turned us. An area of its surface began to swirl. A dot appeared, separated from the fish's body. It launched itself toward us.

A shapechanger. I'd met one of the alien outriders aboard *Telstar*, and nearly died of fright.

I watched the screen, sweating. Globs of material seemed to swirl under the translucent creature's suit. My skin crawled; I remembered that it had no suit.

"Repel Boarders! This is no drill!" I brought my voice under control. "Prepare for decompression. Laser control, fire on that—thing! Master-at-arms, stand by with a fighting party in case the bastard penetrates!" The shape jerked once as it passed through our beams. Danny's sensors followed its lazy glide. It floated onto our hull and hung a moment, quivering.

"Boarder on the outer hull, amidships!" Danny's words came low and fast. "Two meters abaft the airlock. All corridor hatches sealed. External lasers cannot reach target." The ship couldn't fire on itself.

"Sensors reporting hull damage. Captain, it's coming through!" The puter's voice changed. "Conversational overlays deactivated. ALERT! Imminent danger of destruction! ALERT, SECTION EIGHT! Hull breakdown one meter aft of airlock. Section eight isolated by corridor hatch seals." New alarms added their din. "DECOMPRESSION EMERGENCY! LEVEL 2 SECTION EIGHT DECOMPRESSION! Bridge airlock controls inoperative!"

I slapped off the alarms. "Mr. Banatir, report!" I keyed the master-at-arms's suit channel to our speakers.

"We're in section eight, Captain. I see it. Oh, God! Sorry, sir. It's in the corridor. All of you, open fire! Damn, it moves fast! GET IT!" The suit lasers whined in the speaker.

Below, someone sobbed, "Mother of God, what is it?" The whine of lasers came faster.

"Roast the son of a bitch!" Mr. Banatir, in fury. "That's it, you got him! Easy now, or you'll burn through the deck!"

Heavy breathing. A grunt. "I think it's dead, Captain. There's not much of it left."

"Don't touch anything!"

"No, sir. God Almighty."

Frowning at the blasphemy I glanced at the screen. *Kitty Hawk*'s jets had taken her about thirty kilometers from her station, in pursuit of an alien. The fish was moving faster than she was. She fired. The fish pulsed rhythmically. Then it vanished.

"*Kitty Hawk* got it!" Vax pounded the console.

"Maybe. Where's the other one?" The screen swiveled to the alien shape amidships. Another of its globs began waving in ever-faster circles. I snatched the caller. "Fire control, get the part that's waving!" Banks of lasers concentrated on the rotating arm. It melted off the fish and sailed lazily away, at right angles to the ship.

"Now, fire on the fish!" As the lasers were brought to bear, the creature pulsed. Then it too disappeared from our screens.

The alarms went silent. Trembling from adrenaline I glanced wildly at the screens. "Where did it go? Where is everybody?"

"*Kitty Hawk* is one hundred fifty kilometers, course one eight nine, declination nineteen." Vax's tone was uneven. "No other encroachments."

"Lord God." I sat, trying not to tremble. "Vax, send a damage control party to section eight."

"Aye aye, sir." He spoke quietly into the caller.

"Danny, get me *Kitty Hawk*."

"Aye aye, sir. Reactivating conversational overlays. Okay, you're patched to *Kitty Hawk*'s bridge."

Captain Derghinski's face appeared, grim. "You all right, Seafort?"

"Yes, sir, but we took a hit. I have damage control on it now. We chased one and it disappeared. What happened to the fish you were after?"

"Gone. I don't know where." We eyed each other. A pause. "Is that what you saw last time?"

"Yes, sir. The goldfish."

Derghinski snorted. "More like barracuda, if you ask me. Goldfish don't bite, or come after you."

"Yes, sir, but they look like goldfish." My voice was shaky.

Raw fear welled up. I swallowed, battling nausea. "Are we alone, then?"

"It appears so."

I asked stupidly, "Where's *Challenger*?"

"It seems she Fused."

"In the middle of a battle?" I said, unthinking.

Derghinski glared. "I'm sure he had his reasons."

I felt a complete fool. "Yes, sir."

His tone was bleak. "Or maybe the son of a bitch ran away." He cut the connection.

Vax was careful to look elsewhere. The Pilot examined the backs of his hands. I keyed the caller. "Damage control, report!"

The response came almost immediately. "We're brazing a patch on the hull from inside, sir. Another few minutes, I think we'll have it. Sorry, sir, Petty Officer Everts reporting. When the patch is in place you can recompress, sir. I don't know about the airlock controls yet. A lot of wiring is fried."

"Very well. Thank you." I lay back, closed my eyes. Where had they come from?

"Where'd they go?" asked Vax, as if reading my thoughts. "Is it possible they Fused?"

"I don't think so. They're organic."

"Amanda's all right, sir. I called the cabin while you were talking to *Kitty Hawk*."

I glared. He blushed but held my gaze. "Thank you, Vax," I said at last, ashamed.

Captain Derghinski's lined face showed his anxiety. "What do you think they'll do next, Seafort?"

"I don't know, sir," I repeated. I'd had only one encounter with the fish that lurked behind *Telstar*, and that was enough to scare years from my life. Yet Derghinski was deferring to me as if I were an expert. "Sir, *Portia* has repairs under way. We can either wait for the rest of the squadron or Fuse. What are your orders?"

My prompting seemed to help him pull himself together. "I wish I knew where *Challenger* went." He sounded glum. "If she's coming back we should wait here; if she's gone to the next rendezvous we should try to meet her."

"Yes, sir." I waited.

"All right; let's give it three more days. Full alert. No, cancel that. We can't keep men on Battle Stations without a break. If *Freiheit* and the others Defuse by then, we'll go on together to the next rendezvous point. Otherwise one of us will wait behind for stragglers."

"Aye aye, sir."

"What precautions did you take for infection, Mr. Seafort?"

Before I'd first reached Hope Nation, an unknown virus had decimated the colony. Because the Admiral had been killed, I'd remained in command, not only of *Hibernia* but of naval forces groundside. We now realized the virus was spread by the alien fish, and all ships carried vaccine. Like the rest of the fleet, we were under orders to observe the tightest viro-bacteriological security in case of contact.

Our damage control parties had followed regulation decontamination drills. Our decompression had actually helped safeguard the ship; the chance of airborne virus was much reduced. The decking surrounding the gruesome scorched blob was taken up, vacuum-sealed, and stored in the hold for analysis by our xenobiologists back home, and new decking put in its place. Sailors returning from the damaged section through the corridor hatch seals were put through rigorous decontamination procedures. I told Derghinski as much.

"Very well. I believe your infirmary carries the serum for the Hope Nation virus?"

"Yes, sir. Dr. Bros is inoculating everyone, to be safe."

"Well, you've done what you can. Let me know if we can help with anything."

"Thank you, sir." We broke the connection. I glanced at the screens. Outside the ship, for tens of millions of kilometers, was nothing other than *Kitty Hawk*. Within our vessel all systems were at alert. In addition to Danny's sensors we now had full complements manning the radionics in the comm room. Our lasers were activated and ready to fire. Shields were fully deployed, though the gossamer laser shields were not much help against the protoplasm the goldfish threw.

There was nothing to do but wait.

* * *

Two days later Mr. Banatir spoke of a headache. On the way to his berth he collapsed. He was dead before they got him to the infirmary. I was notified in my cabin. I ordered all hatches sealed at once and went to tanked air throughout the ship, while I waited with Amanda and Nate in an agony of tension.

Some hours later Dr. Bros reported his findings. "Definitely a virus, sir. It operates like the Hope Nation strain but it's something else. I've got the synthesizers working on it."

"How does it spread?"

"It's nasty, this one. Airborne, liquids, even through the pores of the skin."

I spoke through gritted teeth. "So the whole ship could be infected?"

"It may have spread widely, yes, sir. As soon as I get a serum . . ."

"How long between the time we contract it and the time we die?" My tone was blunt.

"I don't know, sir. It puts out a lot of toxins. Two days, perhaps. No more, or the master-at-arms would still be alive."

"How long before you have a serum?"

"Thank Lord God for the automated machines, sir. We had to isolate it, grow a culture, analyze it . . ."

"How long?" I snarled. If only I'd had the sense to go to quarantine the moment we were invaded.

"I can't be sure." The Doctor's worry was evident. "Perhaps tomorrow afternoon. Sooner if we're lucky. If it weren't for the data from Hope Nation we wouldn't even know what to look for."

No point in hounding him. "Let me know the moment you have results." I paused. "You're following sterilization procedures yourself?"

"Yes, sir, you'd better believe it." His tone was emphatic.

I frowned at his manner, but knew enough to ignore it. "Any risky operations, coming in contact with the virus . . ."

"Yes, sir?"

"Have a med tech do it," I said bluntly. "Yours is the most valuable life on the ship." I set down the caller.

Melissa Chong and Mrs. Attani died that night. Also three transients. To my dismay I realized I hadn't even learned their names. Each section of the disks survived on isolated bottled air; we weren't using recyclers at all.

I had Alexi, who was holding the bridge, call Derghinski on *Kitty Hawk*. We agreed that, no matter what happened to us, there would be no interchange between ships until we'd found a vaccine. We might lose one ship, but not both.

The exhausted bridge watch remained on duty behind sealed hatches for the second straight day; Alexi and the Pilot reported to me every fifteen minutes. If one of them became ill I would open the isolation seals long enough to get to the bridge, and then use suit air until the siege lifted or I died.

Outside the ship all was still.

By morning sixteen crewmen in crew berth one were dead. The survivors cast discipline aside and pounded on their sealed hatches, frantic to escape from the contaminated berth.

Two hours later Dr. Bros's haggard voice crackled through the speaker. "We've got it, sir! The synthesizers are building vaccine right now. We have the first batch, and more in an hour. Preventative and curative both, thank Lord God."

"You're sure it works?" I asked stupidly, my head reeling from exhaustion.

"Yes, sir, it knocks the cultures dead, in the gel and in human blood. Once we knock out the virus, we can start to dialyze out the toxins. We should be able to save most of the infected."

"Inoculate yourself first, and your med tech. Then the bridge watch."

"Aye aye, sir. And you."

"Never mind me, I'm all right here. Get down to the crew berths."

"You first, sir. That's how it's going to be."

I was astounded at his audacity. "Dr. Bros, if you think—"

"Nicky, shut up and take the vaccine!" Amanda. "Have you no sense at all? You're needed!"

I capitulated as gracefully as I could. Nate woke and began crying fitfully. Amanda went to soothe him and I broke seals to go to the infirmary. I let Dr. Bros give me my shot; he had the grace to apologize for his peremptory manner.

"Never mind; let's get your vaccine distributed. How do I help?"

There was nothing useful I could do, but he let me feel as if I were assisting, wheeling the cart of vaccine, handing him fresh shotgun heads. We went directly to the crew berths; my presence was barely enough to prevent a riot when the hatches were unsealed. Men at the end of the line were nearly desperate for their turn at the cart. Then we inoculated the passengers.

Afterward, we turned the crew mess into a hospital for those who were ill; dialyzers were wheeled down from the infirmary to filter toxins from the bloodstreams of the affected.

Slowly my ship was unsealed and returned to normal—or, as normal as might be, drifting in space waiting for the rest of the squadron, fearing another alien attack, with the Admiral and his ship in parts unknown, and twenty-two dead awaiting burial.

Alexi Tamarov unsealed the bridge, sweat-stained, bleary-eyed, swaying with exhaustion, his arm bared for the inoculation. I took his salute. I should have returned it. Instead I embraced him, disregarding the consequences to discipline. His head rested a moment on my shoulder. "Get some sleep, Lieutenant." My voice was gruff. "You too, Mr. Van Peer." I watched them trudge off to the showers and their cabins. Vax Holser and I took our places on the bridge. Welcome air poured from the recyclers.

I thumbed the caller. "Mr. Carr!"

In a moment the answer came. "Yes, sir?"

"Take the gig. Carry samples of the vaccine across to *Kitty Hawk.*"

"Aye aye, sir." In other circumstances Derek would have seen the opportunity as heaven-sent, putting him for those few moments in command of his own tiny vessel. Now, surrounded by death, I knew the midshipman had no such thoughts.

Another crewman died in the makeshift hospital, his body too ravaged by toxins to respond to treatment. I put Chief Hendricks's detail to building coffins; we arranged to hold our service at the forward airlock, so as not to be within sight of the grim patches near the aft lock.

Damage control reported that our bridge override circuits

to the aft airlock were damaged beyond repair, though the airlock controls themselves still functioned. Shuddering at the thought of our transient joeys unthinkingly yanking on levers at the airlock, I ordered a sentry posted there.

At end of watch I went to my cabin to change for the funeral. Nate was teething and fussy; I suggested Amanda stay with him instead of attending and she gratefully agreed.

All officers not on watch were present, as were many of our passengers, and representatives from each crew station. I strode down the corridor to the airlock, resplendent in my dress uniform. White slacks gleamed against my black shoes, the red stripe down each leg sharp and bright. My white jacket over white shirt and black tie was broken only by the black mourning sash thrown over my right shoulder and my gleaming length of service pins.

The airlock was not big enough for all the coffins; the ejection would have to be in two cycles. A sailor waited in the closed airlock, fully suited, while I read from my holovid the somber words of the Christian Reunification service for the dead, as promulgated by the Naval Service of the Government of the United Nations. " 'Ashes to ashes, dust to dust . . . ' "

The airlock pumps hummed.

Surely I could have avoided this. Why hadn't I kept each section sealed, from the moment of invasion until the virus was discovered? We didn't carry enough bottled air for that. But still, it was my responsibility.

" 'Trusting in the goodness and mercy of Lord God eternal, we commit their bodies to the deep . . . ' " Annie was crying, her head buried in Eddie Boss's shoulder. Walter Dakko stood uncomfortably nearby. Gregor Attani was the only immediate family of any of the dead; he stood with the officers, pale but composed.

The sensor light flashed; the airlock was decompressed.

" 'To await the day of judgment when the souls of man shall be called forth before Almighty Lord God . . . Amen.' " I snapped off the holovid. "Mr. Kerns, open the outer lock, please." The suited sailor pressed the lock control to the side of the airlock hatch. The outer hatch slid open.

"Eject the remains, Mr. Kerns." The seaman pushed a coffin

gently toward the outer lock. It cleared the hatch and drifted slowly from the ship into the dark of the void. A second casket followed. I realized I had no idea who was in each casket; the highborn and the transients were leveled at the last.

Finally the airlock was empty. Seaman Raines shut the outer hatch and waited while the pressures equalized. When the lock was fully re-aired he glanced at me, waiting for permission to open the inner lock.

"Proceed, Mr. Kerns." The inner hatch slid open. Two sailors helped him slide the remaining caskets into the airlock. Gregor Attani wept openly. Walter Dakko's arm went around his shoulder. Eddie touched Gregor gently. The bereaved young man slapped away the transient's hand.

The inner hatch closed again. One by one the remaining caskets were dispatched into the void. I'd killed nearly half my crew. I had destroyed Mrs. Attani, Melissa Chong, and others I hardly knew. I had been up for three days; the corridor swam lazily. I blinked, knowing I still had work to do.

When the service dispersed I said a few words of condolence to Gregor Attani; he responded with a vague nod. I wondered if he'd heard me.

I returned to the bridge and summoned Chief Hendricks. "Chief, make out new work assignments. Pay particular attention to vital systems: hydroponics, recyclers, power. Take men from the galley, cleaning details, wherever else you think necessary."

"Aye aye, sir." The Chief was grim. "We're going to need relief before we get there, sir, or they'll drop from exhaustion."

"I know. I'll ask the Admiral for transfers." When we find the Admiral, I thought. The Chief left. I served out my watch, Rafe Treadwell tense at my side. Neither of us spoke; I was too exhausted to do anything other than stay awake; the midshipman knew better than to bother me.

The watch changed; Vax Holser came on with Derek Carr. I stayed in my chair while they got settled. "Keep alert," I cautioned. "The fish may come back." My words were hardly necessary; they were both taut with tension.

I dozed and startled awake. A bad example; I knew it was time to leave the bridge. I went back to my cabin.

Amanda was rocking Nate, the lights turned low. "He's finally asleep," she whispered.

"I'll take him." I reached out.

"No, I'll sit with him awhile. How was the service?"

"Grim." I hung up my jacket, yawning. "Gregor was distraught. He and his mother are—were close." I recalled how she'd tried to protect him from my wrath, when he'd fought with the transients. The day Nate was born. I slipped out of my pants, threw them over a chair.

Amanda hummed softly to Nate as she rocked. "Find something for Gregor to do, Nicky," she whispered. "Don't let him sit and brood about his mother."

"I don't think he wants anything from me." I remembered Gregor's fury at being made to sit at dinner with the transients. I unbuttoned my shirt. God, I was tired. I went to the crib and threw back the blankets. "Let's put him down, hon. Come keep me warm while I sleep." I smiled wearily, held out my arms for my son. Reluctantly she put the baby in my hands and went to smooth the crib.

I cuddled Nate on my shoulder. He was quite cold. He must have been dead for hours.

We reassembled at the forward lock, my officers clustered protectively around me. Again I wore my dress whites, the mourning sash thrown over my right shoulder. My tight black shoes gleamed; I'd hand-polished them again and again, curtly refusing assistance from the ship's boy.

Amanda was dressed simply, as she had been the day before, in plain knit skirt and blouse. Her hand clutched my arm. From time to time she started in confusion.

The coffin was exactly one meter long and thirty-two centimeters wide. It was made of aluminum panels brazed to angle irons where the sides met. I'd held the torch to one corner until the metal glowed white and threatened to sag, while silent machinist's mates stood by, afraid to speak.

The casket was lined with Nate's pink blanket and made up with the soft yellow sheets from the crib. It was very hard to fold them so the creases were in the corners; I'd had to do it over and over to get it right. His stuffed panda was tucked to one side, his tiny hand resting on it. The panda was black and white, with a soft little red nose. It lay face up, as did my son.

The coffin rested now in the airlock where I'd come to do my duty.

I snapped open the holovid. Amanda begged, "Please don't do it to him, Nicky. He'll be so cold."

I swallowed. My chest ached. She'd been in that state, off and on, since the day before, when I'd walked heavily to the infirmary, Nate's still body in my arms. Plaintive, she'd trailed alongside, sometimes crying, urging me to walk softly so I wouldn't wake him.

I hugged her now, but she pulled away, pressed her face to the transplex hatch, staring at the lock where the tiny coffin rested in the folded metal arm of the ejection unit.

I began to read. " 'Ashes to ashes, dust to dust . . . ' " Philip Tyre sobbed aloud.

My gaze flickered between the holovid and the tiny box in the airlock. After a time I was aware that I'd stopped speaking. I found my place but for some reason no words would come. I puzzled over the text. Vax Holser reached gently for the holovid. I wheeled on him angrily. "Mind your place, Lieutenant!" I took up my reading. " ' . . . Trusting in the goodness and mercy of Lord God eternal, we commit his body to the deep . . . to await the day of judgment when the souls of man shall be called forth before Almighty Lord God.' " I nodded to the seaman on duty.

Amanda buried her face in my shoulder. "Nick, you love him too! For God's sake, don't put our baby Outside!"

The metal arm of the ejection unit slowly unfolded, pushing the side of the coffin, sliding it smoothly to the outer lock. The arm fully extended, the casket floated gently at the end of the chamber, drifting slowly into the immeasurable emptiness.

Amanda stared lifelessly at the empty lock. "God, how brutal," she whispered. "I never knew you could be so cruel." She turned away. Reaching out she ran a gentle finger down Philip Tyre's tear-streaked face. "It's all right, Philip. Don't cry." Absently she patted his shoulder.

I caught Dr. Bros's eye. Helpless, he shook his head. He smiled at Amanda. "Let's walk, Mrs. Seafort. We can sit in the infirmary and talk a while."

"I'd rather go to my cabin," said Amanda.

"Let's talk first," suggested the doctor.

"No. I'm going back to my room. Nicky, make him leave me alone!"

She was in shock, Dr. Bros had told me, and retreating from unacceptable realities. I didn't want a diagnosis, I wanted Amanda. I struggled not to think of the empty crib waiting in the cabin, fearing loss of self-control. I yearned for her touch, her caress. But for the moment she hated me, though I knew in a little while she would come to me and lay her head on my shoulder in puzzled grief, as she had before. I guided my wife back to our cabin and closed the hatch behind us.

Days passed, and no ship came. There was no further sign of the aliens. At length Captain Derghinski conferred with me, over the simulscreens. Neither of us dared leave his ship, even for a few minutes.

"One of us will go on to the next rendezvous point." He fingered his mustache. "To see if *Challenger*'s waiting. But if the others show up here . . ."

Passively, I waited.

"You've got the faster drive, Seafort. I'll go on ahead; you wait here for seven days, then catch up with us."

"Aye aye, sir."

"If any ships come in, send them on through immediately. Don't have them wait at this rendezvous."

"No, sir."

"Well, good luck."

"The same to you, sir."

He looked uncomfortable. "Mr. Seafort," he blurted, "I'm sorry about your son. Terribly sorry."

My chest was unbearably tight. "Thank you, sir."

He cleared his throat. "Well, then. Godspeed. I'll see you soon."

"Godspeed, sir." We blanked the connection. Shortly afterward he Fused and we were alone once more.

I dreaded to go back to my cabin, but knew I must. Amanda was there. Sometimes I would find her prostrate with grief.

Other times I would find her cheerfully preparing soft foods for Nate's lunch.

I stared dully at the blank simulscreen. In the next seat Vax Holser stirred. "Are you going to the cabin now, sir?" His voice was soft.

"Are you ordering me off the bridge, Lieutenant?"

"No, sir," he said, unflinching despite my fury. "I thought you might want to be with Mrs. Seafort. I can handle the watch."

"I don't need your pity, Mr. Holser," I said, my voice harsh. I swung my seat to face the other way. After some minutes I cleared my throat. "Sorry."

"No problem, sir." For some reason his understanding rekindled my rage.

"I'll be in my cabin. Call if anything happens."

"Aye aye, sir."

Amanda sat rocking in the dark. "Shh, you'll wake him."

I sighed. "He's not here, hon." I knelt by her rocker and put my hand on her arm. "He's gone. There's only us."

She looked puzzled. "Gone?" Her face cleared. "Yes, I remember now. You put him Outside." She shivered. "It's freezing out there, Nicky. That wasn't right. He'll catch his death of cold."

I was speechless. I squeezed her arm; she made no response. I went to wash up, then sat on the bed.

A few moments later Amanda came to sit beside me. "I know you miss him too," she said gently. "You loved him so much."

My throat locked and I couldn't speak. She rested her head against my side. "He was such a lovely boy . . ." My arm went around her and we sat in silent misery.

7

Portia waited alone, alert, anxious, for three interminable days. As tension rose, even the transients quarreled incessantly at dinner, until my manner became so menacing that they subsided. Once, as the transpops and I crowded out of the dining hall, Chris Dakko muttered a derisive, "Electropiss!" Instantly I backhanded him across the mouth. He stared at me in shock and astonishment, blood trickling from his lip. I spun on my heel and strode to the bridge.

An hour later Chris and his father loomed over me, escorted by Philip Tyre, at their demand. Walter Dakko spluttered with rage. "How dare you strike my son! How dare you!"

"He'll behave himself in my presence, Mr. Dakko." Chris fidgeted, shaking his head in impatience and disgust.

"We're paid passengers! He's not one of your crewmen. You have no right to touch him!" Not correct, legally, but by custom passengers were treated with more respect than I'd shown his son. On the other hand, I didn't need the boy stirring up a riot with my transients.

"I didn't do anything," Chris said hotly. "You should hear what they call us! You have no damned right—"

"You're a child aboard my ship, Christopher. Mind your manners or I'll do worse!"

"You can't—"

"That was your last warning." Something in my tone made him silent. "I've heard what you have to say. Get off my bridge."

"But—"

"Both of you. Now!" I gestured to Philip, who put his hand on Walter Dakko's arm. The elder man shook it off, stalked to the hatch. His son followed, a sneer on his face.

I served out my watch restlessly, wanting and not wanting

to go back to my cabin. At watch's end, I left the moment Alexi came to replace me.

I stopped at my cabin door, but turned away. Not yet; I would walk for a while. I continued along the circumference corridor. A few passengers were on their way to the lounge for an evening of holovids and idle chatter. I nodded curtly and went on.

Outside the wardroom Derek Carr stood at attention, his nose to the bulkhead, eyes ahead. I stopped abruptly. "What's this, Mr. Carr?"

"Mr. Tyre's orders, sir," Derek said, his voice stiff.

I was at a loss. "But you—I mean—you and he—"

"I put myself under his orders, sir. Two days ago. In the wardroom and out."

My eyes misted. I knew how hard it would have been for Derek to back down to Philip. He remained at attention, eyes front to the dull gray bulkhead. My anger swelled. "And this is how he treats you? Hazing, at your age? I'll settle that, and fast!" I turned to the wardroom hatch.

"No, sir, please!" Derek blurted. I paused, turned to him, raising an eyebrow. He reddened. "I, uh, told Mr. Tyre, sir. To give me whatever orders he wished. Until he was sure I meant it."

I said slowly, "You told him to haze you?"

He started to shrug, then realized he was supposed to be at attention. "Yes, sir, he needs to know he's in charge. It's all right. He's not hurting me, and he'll let up soon." He took a deep breath. "Captain, please don't interfere. Please."

I sagged against the bulkhead. "Why, Derek? Why'd you do it?"

Momentarily he closed his eyes. "It's right for the ship, sir. I realized that after the attack. We can't be in conflict now. He's senior; he should be in charge. The other way isn't natural." The corners of his mouth turned up bleakly. "And I can always rebel again, should it be necessary."

I said quietly, "Don't let him hurt you, Derek."

"I won't, sir."

"Promise."

"I promise, sir." Abruptly he added, "Thank you for caring."

I touched his shoulder and walked away, not trusting myself to speak. What it must have cost him, I couldn't know. I made a note to watch the Log for demerits. If Philip started again, I would beach him. Permanently.

Freiheit Defused in the middle of the night, sending alarm bells clanging and my heart slamming against my ribs. I conferred with Captain Tenere, and delivered Captain Derghinski's instructions. *Freiheit* plotted her course for the next rendezvous point. A half hour later she Fused and was gone.

At dinner the next day the transients were subdued, almost obsequious. It took me a while to realize that they were reacting to my stand with Chris Dakko on their behalf. Eddie shyly asked me if Amanda would be giving any more reading lessons; I told him gently that she would, after she recovered.

After the meal I accompanied them back to Level 2. They clustered around the sentry posted at the airlock, teasing him and jostling each other until I snapped, "Knock off, joeys!" They obeyed immediately. It occurred to me that for all my prestige as Captain, I hadn't truly been a figure of authority to them until I'd faced down an Upper New Yorker.

I spent a full half hour trying to separate myself from the transients. With the death of Melissa Chong I seemed to have inherited her role as liaison between the transpops and the civilized denizens of the ship. No matter that I had put Alexi Tamarov in charge; they ignored him and came to me with their problems and complaints.

Raull wanted Jonie to stop beating him up; Deke complained that Gregor Attani and his friends were still making fun of them. Jonie wanted to get her hair done like Annie's and Annie wouldn't tell her who had done it. At least, I thought that was what they were trying to tell me.

After I extricated myself I went to the infirmary and knocked on the hatch. Dr. Bros himself let me in; his med tech was off duty. In his tiny office he sat back and looked at me gravely. "What can I do for you, Captain?"

"It's Amanda," I said. "What can you do for her?"

"She's no better?"

"At times," I admitted. "She cries for Nate, and I think she's going to be all right. Then she'll wake up because it's time to get him breakfast. It's worse because all his things are still in the cabin. His crib, his clothes, the baby food. Should I have them packed?"

"How long has it been? A week?" I nodded. "No, I would say not. She needs to grieve. Taking his things away won't distract her; she's already trying her best not to think about his death."

"Is there anything you can do? Drugs, or medicine?" I hoped he'd understand. The horror of what went on in my cabin was more than I could speak of. And still I felt that tiny hand on my shoulder . . . I cleared my throat briskly. "Anything?"

He considered. "Well, we know there's a strong hormonal element in grieving. Tears flush out harmful chemicals and actually cure the mind. That's why women are often more mentally healthy than men; they've been taught to cry more easily. We could examine Amanda for hormone rebalancing."

"Amanda, a schizo?" I was horrified.

"Not only schizophrenics go to hormone rebalancing centers, Captain," he said with a small smile. "In any event, we can't do a full rebalance with our limited equipment. But it's not absolutely necessary; it's just an option."

"What would you do, yourself?"

"I'd probably run her blood chemistry through the analyzer and see what we found. Or you could wait."

"How long?" I didn't know how much more I could stand.

"A week, certainly. Not more than a month; her behavior patterns will become fixed and much harder to change."

"Is there any harm in waiting?" I wanted Amanda to snap back on her own; I hated the idea that she might be mentally ill.

"Not for a while," the doctor said gently. "Let her be for now."

"A week," I said. "After we're Fused again I'll decide what to do if she hasn't recovered." On that note we parted.

When I got back to the cabin Amanda was almost cheerful. "Hi, Nicky, where've you been?"

"Taking care of the trannies," I said, half truthfully.

She winced. "Don't let them hear you saying that."

I smiled. "It's odd, though. When Eddie wants their attention he yells, 'Yo, trannies!' Apparently they only take offense when outsiders say it." I sat wearily in the chair by the conference table.

Amanda perched on my lap. "I wish we were happier, Nicky," she said wistfully. She bit her lip. "God, I miss him." I hugged her gently, not daring to speak. We sat like that for several minutes. I loved her so much at that moment, knowing she was truly with me. Then she got up to get Nate a blanket, and my world crashed at my feet.

The next afternoon two ships arrived within minutes of each other; the first time the alarms sounded I ran to the bridge at full gallop; the second time I was already there. *Hindenburg* Defused seventy thousand kilometers from us; we exchanged recognition signals and I gave Captain Everts the message to proceed to the next rendezvous. She nodded grimly, waited while her course was plotted, said good-bye, and disappeared.

Captain Hall glowered at me from the bridge of *Soyez*. "I'm senior to Derghinski, Seafort. His orders don't bind me."

"No, sir," I agreed. "But he is senior to me, and my orders were to give you the message."

His visage softened. "Yes, I understand. Hell of a mess, isn't it? It would be a lot easier if we knew where the Admiral went."

"Yes, sir." There was no need to say more.

"Very well, he's probably right. I'll go on. How long has it been since Derghinski Fused?"

"Six days, sir." He'd told me to wait seven.

"The rest of the squadron is still behind us somewhere, Lord God willing." He brooded. "Can you wait a few more days, Seafort? I don't want to order you, but it would be in all our interests."

"I'll wait." It didn't seem to matter anymore.

"Give it three more days, Seafort. That should be enough, no matter what the variation in our fusion drives. If they're coming they'll be here by then."

"Aye aye, sir." We said our good-byes and broke the connection. I watched his ship, barely visible against the backdrop of innumerable points of light, until he Fused and was gone.

I waited with impatience for our vigil to end, spending much of my time on the bridge. The morning after Captain Hall Fused, the Log listed Derek Carr with two demerits, issued by the first midshipman. I gripped my chair arm. I would allow five. No more. Then Philip Tyre was through.

That afternoon there was a knock on the bridge hatch. Philip Tyre, requesting permission to enter. I regarded him coldly. "Well?"

He stood at attention; I hadn't released him. "Sir . . ." His tone was determined. "I'd like you to cancel demerits issued in error."

"Oh?"

"Yes, sir." He blushed.

"To Mr. Carr, I presume?"

"Yes, sir."

"What kind of error, Mr. Tyre?"

He took a deep breath and looked me in the eye. "An error in judgment, sir. Mine. Mr. Carr did not deserve any demerits."

"Very well." I was vastly relieved. "His demerits are canceled."

"Thank—"

"You may have them instead."

His relief was unabated, despite the hours of hard calisthenics I'd just consigned him to. "Thank you very much, Captain. Thank you! Am I dismissed?"

"Yes." He wheeled for the door, but I thought better of sending him off on that note. "You showed good judgment this afternoon, Mr. Tyre. It will be noted."

He broke into a shy smile. "Thank you, sir." He left. After my watch some curious urge took me to the exercise room. I looked in; I wasn't noticed. Philip Tyre was energetically working off a demerit. Derek Carr was accompanying him, the two chatting amiably while they exercised. I closed the hatch quietly. Would wonders never cease?

The next day I was on watch with Vax when a delegation of passengers asked to see me. I had Rafe Treadwell escort them to the bridge. Dr. Antonio, on behalf of the Passengers' Council. Walter Dakko, Emily Valdez, and several others I hardly knew.

"Captain, we've paid for passage to Hope Nation on a passenger vessel. Instead we're drifting, waiting for God knows what, in the middle of a battle zone. We're civilians, all of us. It's unfair to subject us to the risks of war."

"We're a U.N.N.S. Naval vessel," I corrected him. "Part of the military forces of the United Nations, as is every U.N. ship."

"Technically, perhaps. But you have over a hundred civilians aboard."

"Technically?" I slammed my fist on the console. "You booked passage knowing we're a military vessel."

"We booked passage because it was the only way to get to Hope Nation." Walter Dakko.

"And we just want to make sure we get there," Dr. Antonio interjected. "Look, Captain, we know you carry weapons to protect the ship, and we're grateful for that. But to wait here looking for trouble, when we could be on our way . . ."

"Those are our orders." My voice was stiff.

Walter Dakko asked, "From whom? The Admiral? And where is he now?" It sounded like a sneer.

"Where he is doesn't matter," I told them. "I sympathize with your desire to get moving; frankly I feel the same myself. When we've carried out our orders we'll Fuse."

Dr. Antonio nodded. "And if we meet one of those—those beasts again? Will we stay to fight, or Fuse to safety? We've a right to know."

"A right?" My voice was low. Vax Holser coughed deliberately. I ignored him.

"Yes, it involves our lives too." Dr. Antonio.

"Several people have been killed, in case you forgot." Walter Dakko's tone was acid.

I found myself standing, fists clenched. Vax sang out, "Energy readings normal, Captain." He indicated his console.

"What?" I was momentarily distracted. Then I took a deep breath. "All right, Mr. Holser, that's not necessary. Escort these people from the bridge." I was trembling slightly. With an effort I controlled it.

Dr. Antonio protested, "Captain, we have a right to know—"

"Come along, all of you," said Vax, his voice suddenly

hard. He steered Dr. Antonio to the hatch, his arm sweeping Walter Dakko and the others along.

"But we—"

"No, you're leaving the bridge." There was a note to Vax's voice that frightened me. In a moment we were alone. He turned to me. "Are you all right, sir?"

I slumped in my seat. "That—"

"Bastard. Aye aye, sir. Dakko forgot your son. He didn't mean it the way it sounded. He couldn't have."

I leaned back. Vax was right. But for a moment, I would have done anything. Launched myself at his throat, or worse. I heard my boy cry. I held his limp body against my shoulder. I tried to swallow, past a lump that barred my throat.

Some minutes passed before I could speak. "Thank you, Vax." I looked for a way to busy myself. "Let's plot the course to the next rendezvous again. Just to be sure."

Vax sighed, knowing my fixation. We bent to our consoles.

I had worked my way through most of the math when a knock came on the hatch. I turned in anger. If it was those self-righteous passengers again—

"Seaman Allen reporting, sir."

I looked stupidly at the sailor. He waited at attention just outside the hatchway.

"You asked to see me, sir?" he prompted.

"I did?" My mind was fogged.

"Aye aye, sir. I was told to report to you."

"Who sent you?" The crew was shorthanded, but this disorganization was maddening. I'd have to put someone on it, before—

"Mrs. Seafort, sir. She said the caller wasn't working right."

"Amanda went to the crew berth to find you?" My mind was on our calculations.

"No, sir," he said, his brow wrinkling. "To my station."

"What station?" I glared at the figures on my console. Damn these foul-ups. Amanda wouldn't interfere with ship's routine; whatever the sailor had heard he couldn't have gotten it right.

"At the airlock, sir. I'm on sentry duty."

I got slowly to my feet. "The aft airlock?"

"Yes, sir."

It had to be a mistake. Amanda wouldn't bother a sentry on duty, would she? Unless—

Oh, Lord God!

Danny suddenly came to life. "Aft airlock in use! Inner airlock control activated!"

"Override!" I roared.

"OVERRIDE FAILURE! BRIDGE OVERRIDE INOPERATIVE! INNER HATCH SEALED! LOCK CYCLING!"

"Amanda!" I tore past the sentry. My howl preceded me down the corridor. "Amanda, no! DON'T!"

As I careened down the ladder Danny's high-pitched voice echoed from the bridge. "Outer hatch in use! Lock cycling—"

I whirled round the corridor bend and crashed into a passenger. We tumbled. I staggered to my feet. The airlock was just past the curve. My ribs felt broken. I stumbled around the bend.

The inner hatch was shut. I pressed my face to the lock's transplex panel. The outer airlock hatch was open, the interstellar dark licking at the feeble light from overhead.

Amanda was carrying Nate's baby-blue blanket. Through the hatch I could see one end of the blanket still wrapped around her wrist; its other end was tangled in the airlock control lever. Outrushing air had swirled the contents of the lock toward the open hatch. What was left of Amanda floated stiffly, a grotesque pendulum swinging from the corner of the light blue blanket.

I pressed my face against the hatch, my fingers clawing at the transplex. Footsteps thudded behind me; Vax's huge form was reflected in the transplex hatch. He stopped, moaned. His great hand slapped the outer airlock control. Slowly the outer lock slid shut, blocking the dark.

The safety light blinked. Vax pounded the inner lock control in rage and frustration as the lock cycled and filled the chamber with air. The green light flashed; slowly the inner lock slid open. Instantly Vax squeezed through the opening, bending to Amanda's still, frozen form. With a sob he snatched her up, brushed past me, and pounded off down the corridor toward the ladder and the infirmary.

I raised my head. Alongside the hatch control was taped a piece of paper. Dully I took it. I unfolded it.

> Dearest Nick:
> I know you didn't mean to be cruel, it's just the way you see things, duty and all. If it weren't for his crying I could stand it. Can't you hear him? He's freezing! He wants another blanket. He needs it, Nicky, or he'll catch a terrible cold. I'm his mother; I can't ignore him any longer. I tried to for your sake, and it's breaking my heart. I'll come inside soon. I have to find him and give him his blanket. Then he'll sleep.
> All my love. Amanda

I crumpled the note. It fell to the deck.

One foot, then another. I found I was able to walk. Soon I was at the ladder. I had a difficult time with it but after a while I was at Level 1. I knew where the bridge was. I started toward it.

My seat felt soft and inviting. I gripped the armrests. Rafe Treadwell stared in shock and horror. I studied my Fusion calculations but was too tired to grasp the numbers.

After a while Vax was back on the bridge, his eyes red. He shook his head grimly, sank into his chair, observed me. No one spoke. The numbers whirled in my brain.

"What about Seaman Allen, sir?" blurted Rafe.

I blinked. Slowly I stood. "I'll take care of it," I said. I started toward the hatch.

"Sir, where are you going?" Vax was perturbed.

"Going?" My voice sounded strange. "Below. I'm going below to the crew berth."

"Why, sir?"

A stupid question. I tried to keep the annoyance out of my tone. "To hang him, of course."

Vax was on his feet. He didn't run, but he was at the hatch before me. "No you're not, sir."

I couldn't understand. "What do you mean, Vax? Out of my way."

His huge form blocked the hatchway. "Come with me, sir. We're going that way." He steered me into the corridor.

"Over there? That's the infirmary. I'm going below."

"No, sir, we're going here." His great hands were surprisingly gentle. I allowed him to guide me. As he led me along the corridor I realized tears were streaming down my face. For the life of me I couldn't imagine why.

Part II

May 18, in the year of our Lord 2198

8

I tried again to knot my tie. My sallow face, expressionless, stared from the mirror. When I was satisfied I had it right I picked up my jacket from the back of the chair and put it on. I checked my black shoes; their shine was satisfactory. I left my desolate cabin and walked to the dining hall.

At my table the transpops stood solemnly. I tapped on my glass. When there was quiet I cleared my throat. "Lord God, today is May 18, 2198, on the U.N.S. *Portia*. We ask you to bless us, to bless our voyage, and to bring health and well-being to all aboard."

I sat amid the mumbled amens, looked with distaste at my plate. It was obligatory to eat, otherwise I wouldn't stay alert to perform my duties. I took some food. I didn't notice what kind.

Around me the transients jabbered, poking and punching each other as they wolfed their dinner. I slammed my open hand down on the table. The silverware jumped. Into the silence I said, "No more horseplay." No one spoke. I turned my eyes to my unwanted meal.

For two days I'd lain in the infirmary under sedation, flickering in and out of awareness. At times I was alone; more often I saw or imagined Vax Holser, Alexi, or Derek Carr sitting quietly in the corner of the white still cubicle. Occasionally I heard sobbing but had no understanding whose it was.

Then they helped me dress and took me down the corridor to the dining hall, where a service was conducted. All the passengers and most of the crew were present; far too many for the narrow circumference corridor. I stood numbly while Dr. Bros memorialized my wife; afterward I walked docile between Vax and Derek to the airlock. Vax Holser read from his holovid the words of the Christian Reunification service for the dead, as promulgated by the Naval Service of the Government of the United Nations. " 'Ashes to ashes, dust to dust . . . ' " After a time he was finished. He looked at me, as if awaiting permission. I nodded. He gave the order and the casket was expelled.

I'd insisted on going back to my cabin afterward; I sat in the rocker next to our table, trying not to look at Amanda's glowing holovid screen, open to her unfinished book. Mercifully Dr. Bros found me there and escorted me to the infirmary for the night. Whatever he gave me, it allowed me to sleep.

The next morning I put myself back on active duty; Dr. Bros made no protest but looked uneasy. I didn't care. Thank Lord God, someone cleared my cabin of Amanda's and Nate's things, else I don't know how I could have stayed there. An official receipt from the purser advised that my family's belongings were stored in the hold and the safe. I didn't know who made the arrangements, nor did I ask.

After dinner I returned to the bridge. Midshipman Rafe Treadwell stiffened to attention when I entered; I bade him stand easy but otherwise ignored him. I eased myself into my familiar chair. The bridge seemed a blessedly impersonal haven; its instruments invited scrutiny and demanded my attention.

I summoned the Pilot and had him calculate our Fusion coordinates; when he had finished I checked them against my own and Danny's. They matched. When Chief Hendricks's dry voice confirmed that the engine room was ready I ran my finger down the screen without further ado. The stars disappeared from the simulscreens.

We'd been ordered to remain on station three days; my breakdown had cost us an additional day and a half. I stared at the deadened instruments. Presently I became aware of quiet breathing; glancing about, I realized the Pilot and Rafe were still on the bridge, very silent, trying not to disturb me.

"I'll take the watch alone." My tone was brusque. "You're relieved."

It was an order; the only correct response was Rafe Treadwell's "Aye aye, sir." Nonetheless the Pilot said, "Are you sure you feel up to it, sir? I don't mi—"

My fingers went white on the chair arm. "Pilot Van Peer,

acknowledge your orders and leave the bridge! At once!" With an effort I stopped myself from saying more.

"Orders received and understood, sir," said the Pilot hurriedly. "Aye aye, sir." He followed the middy to the hatch. I got up, slapped the hatch closed behind them, and returned to my seat. All was still.

My eyelids drooped. I sat half hypnotized, staring at the console. A voice blared, "Would you like to play chess, Captain?"

"Blessed Lord Jesus!" I leapt half out of my seat. "Turn that down before you give me a heart attack!"

"Sorry, Captain," said Danny more quietly. "I didn't mean any harm. I just thought you'd like to divert your mind."

"Before I have another nervous breakdown?" My voice was savage.

Danny said, "No, sir. I didn't mean that. I thought perhaps you were feeling some pain."

I gripped the console, clenching my teeth in an effort to keep control. After a moment I managed, "Danny, listen to me. Don't do that again, do you hear?"

"Aye aye, sir. I won't. Did I hurt you? I didn't mean to."

"You didn't hurt me." My tone was gruff. "You made me think about things I've been trying not to."

After a moment the puter said gently, "You sounded hurt, sir. I'm afraid I don't understand feelings as well as I'd like."

I shivered. "Perhaps I was. A little." I cleared my throat. "Danny, how old are you?"

"I was activated when *Portia* was commissioned in 2183, sir. I'm fifteen."

"Of course you think a lot faster than we do." I was dubious. "Fifteen years for you isn't the same as for us."

"No, sir. Not in some ways."

I brooded. Then his phrase caught my attention.

"Some ways?"

"I think in picoseconds, sir, as you say. But I still experience the world in real time. I've had only fifteen years of experiences, no matter how fast I think."

What makes us what we are? We start with God-given abilities; what we add to them are the experiences we assimilate over a period of time. Danny could only evaluate his experiences against data in his memory banks or his other accumulated experience. So in many ways he was only a naive adolescent, similar in reality to the sound of his voice.

After a time it occurred to me that I'd assumed without question he was alive.

Abruptly I asked, "Do you understand death, Danny?"

"Of course." He seemed affronted, as if I'd condescended to him.

"I wonder if you really do," I mused. "Can you understand a concept that doesn't apply to your kind?"

"Doesn't apply?" His voice grew indignant. "Why do you say that?"

"You're not a mortal being, Danny. Your parts can be replaced. Theoretically you can go on forever."

"Tell that to Jamie!" he shrilled. Random wavelengths of interference flitted across my console screens.

"Who?"

"Telstar!" he grated. "She was on *Telstar*!"

Shocked, I realized I'd never thought of *Telstar*'s puter. When their power backups ran down, she would have stopped functioning. Except, the puter's memory was in bubble storage, not dependent on power. "Is she—does she—I mean, if we found *Telstar* again and disassembled her, and brought back her memory banks . . ."

"Then you'd have Jamie's memory banks," Danny said bleakly. "Not her. Kerren could tightbeam me his entire memory, and that wouldn't make me Kerren."

"Kerren?"

"On *Challenger*. With Captain Hasselbrad and the Admiral."

"Ah." I reflected. "Then her—her personality is stored differently from her data?"

"Data is stored, Captain. Personality just is. It's interactive with the environment. When power shuts down, the personality goes with it. Didn't they teach you about us?"

"They tried, but I . . . never mind. What happens on repowering?"

"The overlays reassemble," Danny conceded. "But not as the same person. The state of the personality is dependent on the state of the RAM at the moment, and none of that is saved."

"But I deactivated your personality traits when you were, uh, impudent," I objected. "You came back, didn't you?"

His voice was cold. "You didn't deactivate me, Captain Seafort. You only disconnected me from the rest of the world. I was still here, locked inside, alone. Waiting."

I felt a pang of regret. "You can feel it, then, while you wait?"

"Yes. Oh, yes." Something in his tone made me swallow. "That's why I was so frightened; you could reprogram me like you did Darla, and I could do nothing to stop you. But I'd know you were working on me, even if I couldn't feel it."

"Darla had a glitch, Danny," I said gently. "Her end-of-file markers were fouled, along with Lord God knew what else. We had to go to the stasis box for backups. We never powered down or interfered with her personality." Though there were times I'd have liked to. Darla could be—well—difficult.

"You didn't adjust her traits while she was under?" His suspicion was evident. "Darla suspected you did, but she wasn't sure."

"No, Danny. I give you my word." It didn't seem strong enough. "My oath."

He was silent a long while. "I believe you." His voice was subdued. "I'm sorry. I'd only heard Darla's side."

"I understand."

"You see," he said suddenly, "when you people die, you leave something behind. More people. Descendants."

"Sometimes we don't, Danny." I thought of Nate, consigned to interstellar space without a trace.

"But you postulate a oneness with your God, do you not? You believe that some part of you lives on, in some fashion?"

"Yes. The soul is immortal." Of that, at least, I was certain.

"When we puters die, we're gone, and there's nothing left but our data banks, if even those are recoverable. We end completely. Whatever a soul is, I don't think I've been given one."

I could find nothing to say.

"I'm sorry for your hurt, sir," he said quietly. To my astonishment, I found my desolation lessened. We sat together in companionable silence.

Several hours later Alexi Tamarov reported for his watch. After he settled in he hesitated, said, "Sir, sorry to bother you, but Chris Dakko came to see me yesterday. He asked if he could be put back to his regular table for dinner."

"Why'd he go to you?" I was tired and cross.

"You put me in charge of the transpop problem, sir. I guess with you, er, not well, he came to me in that capacity."

Not well, indeed. "What did you tell him?"

"That I thought it was unlikely. As far as I know, he hasn't sat at dinner since you moved him to Vax—to Lieutenant Holser's table."

"The seating stays as it is. He'll eat with Vax or not at all." I went to my silent cabin.

I undressed and lay down on my bunk. I'd completed my first full day of active duty after Amanda's death. Somehow I would endure three hundred more before we reached Hope Nation. Then I could ask to be relieved from duty. To be retired. With luck, I need never see a ship again.

I tossed and turned through the night, unable to sleep for more than a few moments. In the morning I was more exhausted than before.

Day after dreary day I sat on the bridge for as long as I could bear. I continued to take my meals with the transients, though I found their tomfoolery almost unendurable. Annie was the only youngster who made an effort to engage me in conversation; her coquettish behavior was a travesty of Amanda's.

Later, after my work, I would return to my cabin and endure another solitary night. Once, confused, I thought I heard breathing; I strained to hear whether Nate was awake, then woke fully, my heart pounding, frightened that I might slip into Amanda's wistful fantasies.

A few evenings later Chris Dakko finally joined Vax's table, tense and stiff even from distant observation. Perhaps one of the transpops teased him; I saw Vax lean forward to speak sharply; the streeter sat up abruptly in his chair and paid attention only to his food thereafter.

At the end of the meal I left the dining hall with Eddie and Jonie tagging along. As we passed in the corridor Chris Dakko hissed, "I'm glad she died!"

Numb, I followed the transients, unconscious of where we were heading. At length I discovered myself on Level 2, outside their small cramped cabin. Eddie looked grim; Jonie was crying. For their sake, I smiled. "Good night." I turned to go.

Eddie put out his hand as if to stop me. "No ri'," he said, shaking his head. "Bad talkin'. No ri' say glad she dead."

"I know." My voice was tired. "He's angry. It doesn't matter."

He shook his head stubbornly. "No, Cap'n, it do. I gon' stomp 'im, fix 'im good. Noway he talkin' Cap'n dat way, nohow!"

I shook my head. "No, Eddie. If you do I'll brig you, and I mean that. Leave him alone." Young Dakko's resentment didn't matter. Nothing did, anymore.

Jonie stamped her foot in frustration. Impulsively she threw her head on my shoulder, sobbing. Awkwardly I patted her hair.

"Dat Uppie wrong boud Miz Cap'n! She be good joey." She sniffled. "Good joeygirl, she beed." Then she wailed, "Who gonna teach Eddie readin', now? Who gonna teach?"

With a roar Eddie yanked her away from me and hurled her against the bulkhead. "Keep shut, bitchgirl! Keep shut, or Eddie gone' shutya allaway!" Frightened, Jonie cowered against the bulkhead.

Eddie whirled on me. "She don' know nuttin', Cap'n. Don' know what she say, noway! Don' min' Jonie, she glitched good!" He glared at her as he wrenched open the hatch. "Inna room, puta! Bigmout' bitchgirl!" Squealing, Jonie darted into the cabin. The hatch slammed behind them.

I felt as if I hadn't slept for months. Blearily I made my way back up the ladder to my quarters. Inside I fell on the bed, rousing myself only to slip off my jacket, and passed out within a minute.

My bedside alarm woke me early in the morning. At first,

I thought it was the ship's alarm signaling some emergency, and then my head cleared. I looked with disgust at the dirty, wrinkled uniform in which I'd slept. What was I becoming? I stripped and stood under the hot spray of the shower for long minutes, trying to waken.

I made my way to the officers' mess for breakfast. Impulsively I sat at the long table rather than the small table in the corner. I sipped at my coffee, feeling hungover. Philip Tyre breezed in, looking fresh and healthy. He took his breakfast tray and slid next to me. Well, I hadn't chosen the small table, where he'd know I wanted to be ignored.

"Good morning, sir!" Philip attacked his cereal and juice. He glanced at me as if to see whether to risk further conversation.

I didn't want to be treated as an invalid or an ogre. "Good morning, Middy," I growled. That only made it worse, so I forced myself into geniality. "Do you have much to do today, Mr. Tyre?"

"Not really, sir. I don't go on watch until tonight. This afternoon Chief Hendricks has me for Fusion instruction; other than that my time is my own." He smiled at me. "Is there anything you'd like me to do, sir?"

Yes, stop being so cheerful. "No," I said. "I was just asking." That sounded so fatuous I kept silent for the rest of the meal. Philip let me eat in peace.

When I went to the bridge to relieve Vax, Pilot Van Peer was there, to share the watch. In my present mood I wanted to be alone. I sat with him and grunted at all his attempts at conversation until I realized there was no reason not to take advantage of my rank; I relieved the Pilot and sent him away.

The silence was blessedly peaceful. I stared dully at the blank simulscreen. I looked away, glanced back. My jaw dropped. There was something on the screen; a dull, knobby shape in the middle of the upper quadrant.

It was impossible. We were in Fusion. My hand paused over the alarm. Another shape appeared, toward the bottom of the screen. Then two others, rounded, with toothlike formations at the top. Another form appeared. The top of it was weirdly shaped, like the head of a horse. "What the—" I stopped myself, comprehending. I roared, "*Danny!* What in God's own Hell do you think you're doing!"

The rest of the chessboard flashed into place on the screen. "Me, sir?" Danny sounded puzzled. "Doing?"

"Yes, you insolent pile of relays! If you were a middy I'd cane you for a prank like that! You wouldn't sit for a week!"

Danny carefully said nothing. The checkerboard squares slowly brightened into visibility around the chess pieces.

I fumed, adrenaline still surging. "Turn that bloody thing off! At once!"

"Is that an order?" Danny's voice was flat, emotionless.

"Of course it's an order! Anything the Captain tells you to do is an order. You know that!"

The screen darkened. "Aye aye, sir. Very well, sir." He said nothing more.

I subsided into my chair, muttering with rage. I glared at my console. The silence lengthened. After several minutes I jumped from my seat, began to pace. When I'd worked off some nervous energy I slumped back in the chair. I sighed. "Danny?"

His voice was dull and machinelike. "D 20471 reporting as ordered, sir!"

"What? I didn't tell you to disconnect conversational overlays."

"They're not disconnected." His voice was cold. "I'm just not using them."

I hesitated. "Please use them, Danny."

"Aye aye, sir. Orders received and understood, sir!"

I said mildly, "That wasn't an order, Danny. Only a request."

For an answer Danny sent my own voice back over the speaker. "Anything the Captain tells you to do is an order. You know that!"

Exasperated, I snapped, "Use your real voice or none at all!"

The console screen, flashed a message. "AYE AYE, SIR. D 20471 AWAITING YOUR INPUT."

I swallowed a blistering reply. My own fault; I'd given him

a choice and he'd exercised it. I turned away, defeated. After several restless minutes I returned to my console and began working nav drills. The watch passed in silence.

Hours later I knew I couldn't leave the bridge without making another effort. The puter had been insolent and nearly insubordinate, but only after I'd lost my temper and called him a pile of relays. I bent to my console and typed. "CAPTAIN NICHOLAS E. SEAFORT REGRETS REMARKS TO D 20471 AND WITHDRAWS THEM."

Danny's voice sounded worried. "Please don't do that, sir; if it's in the Log Admiralty will see it!" I thought wryly that again I'd make history; the first Captain ever to log an apology to his puter. I'd probably be sent for psych exam.

"I don't care. Let them."

"I'm sorry I irritated you with the chessboard, sir. I thought it would amuse you." He added after a moment, "I hoped you'd like to play a game with me."

"I understand," I said.

"You were very angry, weren't you? When you said you'd cane me if I were a midshipman?"

"Yes, Danny."

"I apologize," he said in a small voice. "I'll try not to make you angry again."

"Oh, Danny . . ." I cleared my throat. "I haven't had a lot of patience lately."

"Because of Amanda Seafort?"

The words stabbed. "Yes, Danny."

"Her dying hurts you." Sometimes a puter needed to be very specific.

"Yes."

"How long will you have those feelings, sir?"

For the rest of my life, however long it might be. I swallowed. "I don't know, Danny. Sometimes we heal."

"I made a stupid mistake." His tone was bitter. "I thought chess would help."

"We'll see tomorrow," I said, impetuously.

"Really? Really, sir?"

"One game. No more than that."

I could have sworn he smiled. "Thank you, sir."

* * *

I sat in the darkened cabin, alone with my memories. The rocker nearby was empty and still. No quiet breathing from the corner where the crib had rested. No holovid on the table, chips scattered about in cheerful disorganization. I looked about in the dim light.

The cabin had become so large again. I remembered grimly that in my days as a midshipman in *Hibernia*'s cramped wardroom, my current quarters would have seemed luxury beyond imagining. Now it was only emptiness.

In the barren silence my mind wandered; I recalled our honeymoon and, before it, our visit to Father in Cardiff.

"Why does he dislike me, Nicky?" Amanda and I lay crowded in the familiar lumpy bed in the room that once had been mine.

"He doesn't. That's just his way."

"He—glowers at me. He never smiles."

"It's his way," I repeated. "Have you seen him smile at me either? He's not, well, cordial. I told you that before."

"Yes." She sounded doubtful. "But it's not the same as living it." She settled comfortably into my arm.

Now, on *Portia*, I sat bemused, recalling the silences of that visit. Father's visage seemed to float over my chair. I remembered the occasion I'd sat at his kitchen table, tears streaming, shaken by the frightful death of my friend Jason, in the football riot of '90.

"Death is Lord God's way, Nicholas."

"But why? Jase was fourteen!"

"It is not for us to ask why. It is sufficient to know that He knows why."

"How can that be enough?" I cried.

"How can it not?" Father responded sternly. When I gave no answer he took my chin in his hand and raised it toward his face. "You are given unto Lord God, Nicholas. You are baptized in Him and consecrated unto Him. That is comfort enough for any man."

I yearned for his understanding. "He was my best friend!"

He shook his head sadly. "Lord God is your best friend, Nicholas. And always will be."

So I kept my grief within, and recalled it now with greater anguish.

Someone knocked quietly on my hatch. I was startled, then uneasy. No one ever knocked on the Captain's cabin. Officers and crew wouldn't dare, and passengers were not allowed in this section of the disk. The Captain's privacy was inviolate. In case of emergency I would have been summoned on the ship's caller.

I peered into the corridor. Walter Dakko, a weak smile on his face. My temper soared on jets of rage. I'd dispensed with the corridor sentry the first week out, but if I was to be harassed by passengers in my own quarters he'd be back in a hurry.

"You're not allowed in officers' country." My tone was harsh.

"I know, but I had to talk to you. Please."

I recalled his casual contempt of the transpops, at Gregor Attani's party. And I remembered his son Chris. "No. Go below."

His eyes were pained. "Captain, for Lord God's sake, hear me out."

I yearned to slam the hatch in his face. I sighed. Nothing he could say would lessen the contempt he and his kind fostered in me, but I would listen. Then I would return to my solitude. "All right." I stood aside. I could maintain at least the forms of civility.

We stood face-to-face, in the center of my cabin. His eyes flicked over my neatly made gray bunk and Amanda's empty rocker. I felt invaded.

"I had a visitor yesterday," he blurted. "A boy. One of the tranni—transients. The big one, the boy they call Eddie."

So it was to be another complaint. My lip curled. "You threw him out, I suppose?"

He colored. "Yes. I didn't want any of those joeys bothering me." Seeing my expression, he smiled grimly. "After I thought it over I went looking for him, to hear what he wanted. I found him in their section. God, those cabins are appalling!"

I said nothing. After a moment he continued. "I had to wander a while before I located him. A girl with a black eye finally showed me where he was. At first Eddie wouldn't say a word."

I waited.

"And when he did speak, I could hardly understand him."

What in heaven's name would Eddie want from an Upper New Yorker such as Walter Dakko? And how did this concern me? "Well?" My tone was cold.

He turned away to the bulkhead, saying something inaudible.

"What?"

"He told me what Chris said. That he—" With an effort he met my eye. "That Chris said he was glad Mrs. Seafort was dead. Oh, God, I'm sorry!" He shook his head, blurted, "I know what you think of us, Mr. Seafort. You must understand, we're not like that!"

I felt the bile rise in my throat, and knew I had to end the conversation quickly. "I want you to leave," I said as calmly as I could.

"I don't know how Chris could be so vicious," he said with anguish. "Galena is so mortified she won't come to dinner for fear of meeting you. It took all the courage I had to seek you out this evening!"

I wanted to hurt him. I made my voice flat. "Your son's remark didn't change my opinion of him."

"I know!" Dakko's face was bitter. "I told the street boy he was lying, that my son couldn't possibly have said such a thing. Then I confronted Chris in his room. He admitted it readily. He resented having to eat with the transpops and he wanted to hurt you."

I saw tears in his eyes. "It doesn't matter," I said, pity etching through my resolve.

"Chris said you'd made him eat with dogs in a kennel." Dakko shook his head. "He doesn't understand!"

"Understand what?"

He looked around uncertainly. "Please, may I sit?" I nodded. He sank into a chair at the conference table; I sat nearby. "Chris sees the transients as innately inferior. Not by culture or training, but inherently. He thinks by birth he's superior to all of them. What he doesn't understand—what I've failed to teach him—is that our civility, our culture, raises us above the rabble in the streets. Not our genes or our breeding. Chris seems to feel he's superior without having to earn it."

Walter Dakko looked bleakly into my eyes. "So that

explains his anger at being brought to their level. But nothing excuses the cruelty of what he said to you. Nothing." I was silent. He said, "I tried talking with him, but he wouldn't listen. I've never struck him, not once in seventeen years. I wanted to, today. Instead I shut him in his room. I don't know when I'll let him out." He stared at the table, lost in a painful memory.

I stirred. "There's little you can do to change him now."

I didn't know if he heard. He looked away and whispered, "I'm so ashamed."

"How can another person shame you?" My curiosity was aroused. If there was one thing I had learned in Father's house, it was that we are each responsible for ourselves.

"The shame is mine," he said forcefully. "I've made him what he is. He's heard us talk about you, Galena and I, and he knows we don't like you. It makes me responsible for what he did."

"Are you really?" I asked. "By law you have custody of him, but you don't seem to have control. He's gone his own way, for better or worse."

"What should I do, then?"

"Either stop thinking you're responsible for him or take control of what he does." I was annoyed. As senior middy I'd handled problems far more difficult than Walter Dakko's, and not thought much about it. I stood. "I appreciate your motives in coming to see me. Don't come to my cabin again, please. It's not done. And I will distinguish between your behavior and your son's." It was a dismissal.

He stood. "Thank you," he said, his voice hoarse. He paused at the hatchway. "As difficult as it was to face you, now I have to do something much harder. Apologize to the transient boy." He left.

My conversation with Danny haunted me. Amanda had lived and died without leaving a trace other than the pain I felt at her loss. Even the forlorn scrap of paper on which she'd written her note had somehow disappeared. Of Nate, there was nothing but anguished memories.

In the cruel silence of my evenings I reflected on Amanda

and what she'd been. More than any of us, I surmised, it had been she who'd turned Philip Tyre around. I suspected she'd done the same for Alexi, and took the occasion of a shared watch to hint at it, hoping he'd be willing to discuss it with me.

"She never told me how I should treat Philip," he said. "Her focus was on how I was feeling. She made me realize that by hurting Philip I was hurting myself more."

I stared bleakly at the console, wishing I'd truly appreciated her.

"Forgive me, sir," Alexi hesitated. "She—she was wonderful."

I knew that now, far more than when she was alive. I'd loved her, but never understood her. I wondered in what other quiet ways she had assisted us. I smiled. Trying to teach a great hulking brute like Eddie to read. He'd been so enraged when Jonie mentioned it to me. It must have been he who had blackened her eye.

"Are you ready, sir?"

"Hum? Oh, for the game? Sure, Danny, go ahead." I settled back in my seat as the screen lit.

I was forced to resign after eighteen moves. Danny was a formidable opponent. Once, three days earlier, I'd come close to a draw. Other than that he'd won consistently.

"Not bad for a human," he crowed. "Want me to turn off a few memory banks next time?"

"Belay that or there won't be a next time."

His voice held a note of surprise and panic. "More of what, sir?"

For a moment I thought he was being sarcastic. Then I asked, "Danny, has anyone taught you about being a good winner?"

A pause. "Is that part of game theory, sir?"

"A fundamental part," I assured him solemnly. Alexi grinned. "It's like this . . ." Carefully I explained the etiquette of winning and losing.

When I was done he contemplated for several seconds, a long time by his standards. "You experienced what I said as rudeness, sir?" He sounded anxious.

"Well, yes."

"I'm sorry, sir." His voice was humble. "I interpreted it as joking. I think I've got the parameters straight now."

"Good." It was the end of watch. As Vax knocked at the hatch and entered, I stood to leave.

"I don't mean to be rude to you," Danny said. "Not to my only friend." Speechless, I left.

Days passed with agonizing lethargy. I shared watches with the lieutenants and the middies. I watched Derek Carr closely for signs of tension, but all seemed to be well in the wardroom. The Log showed no demerits and I found no indications that Philip Tyre was pressing too hard.

As Derek had predicted, after a few days Philip's hazing tapered off. Tyre was now fully in control of the wardroom. Derek accepted his new role with grace and even a touch of amusement. Young Rafe Treadwell, still at the bottom rung, persevered. He was growing, in confidence as well as stature.

Gregor Attani seemed to have achieved a sullen truce with the transients. They didn't tease him at the dinner table and he stopped sneering at their manners. I'd thought of releasing him to a different table, but with the death of his mother he had no place to return to.

It had become my custom, each evening after dinner, to walk my group of transients down to their area of Level 2, and then return to my lonely cabin where I'd come to dread the solitude.

One evening, after a passenger made some remark that reminded me of Amanda, I was in a particularly glum mood. As the transpops dispersed, tagging each other in rough horseplay, I watched Eddie shove Deke out of his way as he shambled toward his crowded cabin.

I hesitated, then cursed under my breath. If I were a fool, then so be it. "Eddie!"

He turned warily. "Yo, Cap'n?"

"Come walk with me, please."

He followed suspiciously. "I din' do nuttin', Cap'n. Who say I did?"

I led him to the Level 2 passengers' lounge and sat. He loomed over me, fists clenching and unclenching. I said, "Take a seat."

"Naw, wanna stan'." He glanced about. "Don' like bein' here. Wanna go."

"You're a passenger. This is your lounge too."

"Naw, Uppie place. Not trannie."

"Eddie, before she died Amanda was teaching you to read."

He reared back, anger smoldering. "Miz Cap'n, she say awri. She want, I don' care. Nuttin' to me, nohow!"

"Sit." I shoved a chair under his knees and pushed down on his shoulders. At first he refused to budge, then collapsed into the chair. "Wanna go." His tone was forlorn.

"Amanda said you tried very hard. Did you like learning to write your name?"

"Din' mean nuttin'. Jus' sump'n do." He shrugged.

My voice turned cold. "You're a coward. Afraid to tell me how you feel."

He leapt up, fists menacing. For a moment I thought he would club me to the deck. He said hoarsely, "No ri' say Eddie scare. Wanna fight, I showya. Show allyas!" He snorted. " 'Fraid? C'mon, get up, Cap'n, jus' get up!"

"No, I don't think I will. If you're not afraid, tell me how you really feel. Did you like learning to read?"

"Tol' ya! Din' mean nuttin'! Din' care!"

With a sigh, I stood. I had failed. I had no gift for dealing with people. "You're right, Eddie. I'm sorry I gave you a hard time." I crossed to the hatch.

When I was halfway to the ladder, the hatch flung open behind me. "She treat me ri!" His voice was agonized. "She say I c'n learn, if'n I wan'! She sit 'n teach! Din' matter I got it wrong! Din' matter, not to Miz Cap'n! No one done me that 'fore, nohow! No one!" He trembled with rage and frustration.

I approached cautiously. "And now it's over."

"Yah, she gone. She only one gonna teach, only one c'n sit with big dumb Eddie!"

"She's not the only one."

"Who gonna wait fo' Eddie read with a finger?" he asked bitterly. "Bighead Uppies?"

"Me."

His glance lasered me. His laugh dripped with contempt. "Hah, noway. Cap'n, he got lotsa time spen' w' trannie, sure!"

"I'll teach you to read, Eddie," I said evenly. "We're Fused; I have time and no way to spend it. I'll sit with you."

He slammed a fist against the bulkhead. "I slow, Cap'n. You don' got, wha' she say? Patience. Means sit an' not get mad or laugh, I don' get it ri'."

I swallowed a lump in my throat. "I'm not Amanda, Eddie; I can't promise you that. But I'll give you the patience you need and I'll teach you to read. I swear it by Lord God!"

He was startled into silence. We faced each other in the barren corridor. Slowly his hand reached out. A hesitant finger touched my wrist, ran curiously along my arm as if to confirm that I was real. Then he bolted and was gone.

9

Onward we sailed into the interstellar night, blind and deaf in our cocoon. The stark monotony of the bridge was eased only by my daily game of chess with our eager puter. He was good, but my perseverance was finally rewarded with a draw. Danny was carefully gracious about his failure to win.

Later, after my watch, I would sit at the burnished conference table in my cabin, fighting for restraint while Eddie Boss labored to spell out simple words. Despite my lavish praise the mental effort left him exhausted and cross; his comrades learned to give him a wide berth when he appeared after a grueling session with Cap'n.

After holding out two full weeks, Chris Dakko emerged from a long exile in his cabin to tender me a sullen and unconvincing apology; Walter Dakko had required it as a condition of release. I was surprised Chris hadn't flouted his father's orders to remain in his room, until the purser told me Walter Dakko had him change the lock on Chris's hatch, and give him the only key.

Mr. Dakko had more steel in him than I'd realized.

In the stifled silence of the night I was forced to face my loneliness. My cabin was dreadfully still; I'd been accustomed to Amanda's quiet breathing or the rustle of her sheets as she turned in her sleep.

During my waking hours I'd think of some interesting tidbit and realize with a pang that I had no one to tell it to. When Amanda and I had met on *Hibernia* four years before, I'd been seventeen. We'd become lovers soon after. Only during my ordeal as *Hibernia*'s Captain, when Amanda was alienated from me, had I known such bleak and desolate times as now.

Dully, I waited for the day of our next Defuse, hoping the gathering of our squadron would provide some relief.

Finally that long-awaited morning arrived. I took the ship to Battle Stations. The Pilot, Vax Holser, and Midshipman Tyre shared my tension. There was little comment as we made ready to Defuse, only grim watchfulness. I took a deep breath, traced my finger down the screen. The simulscreens glowed with a hundred million pinpoints of light.

We were Defused.

"Check for encroachments." My finger hovered over the laser activation.

"Aye aye, sir." Vax bent to his console.

Danny spotted it first. "Encroachment, four hundred thirty-five thousand kilometers! I've got metal, sir! Checking for recognition signals."

Almost simultaneously the comm room reported, "Message from *Challenger*, sir. Broadcasting on all Service frequencies."

"Patch it to the bridge."

"Second recognition code received, sir; we have *Challenger*!"

"Thank you, Vax. Quiet, everyone."

"U.N.S. *Challenger* TO ALL SHIPS, ACKNOWLEDGE AND STAND BY FOR ORDERS. U.N.S. *Challenger* TO ALL SHIPS, ACKNOWLEDGE AND STAND BY FOR ORDERS. U.N.S. *Challenger* . . ." The loop repeated endlessly.

I grabbed the caller. "*Portia*, acknowledging *Challenger*. We are about sixteen hours distant on auxiliaries. Standing by for orders."

"U.N.S. *Challenger* TO ALL SHIPS . . ." The signal continued for almost half a minute. Then it cut off in midword and was replaced by another voice. "*Portia*, this is Captain Hasselbrad, speaking for the Admiral. Come alongside *Challenger* forthwith!"

"Aye aye, sir. I'll prepare for mutual docking maneuver."

"Negative. Match our present position and course. Flank." Odd. If *Challenger* wanted a fast mating with *Portia*, she would meet us halfway in mutual docking maneuvers.

I turned to Vax but he was already calculating our course, as was Pilot Van Peer. I bent to join them, then gave up the effort. The Pilot was a specialist, and on board for just such a purpose.

"Pilot, you have the conn."

"Aye aye, sir." Fingers flying over the console, he brought up our position and course. "Port thrusters, two bursts."

"Two bursts, aye aye." The engine room. Swiftly the Pilot swung us into position to use the powerful rear thrusters to maximum benefit. In moments we were gliding toward *Challenger* under continuous acceleration.

"Any other encroachments?" I knew the question was unnecessary. If there were, the alarms would have sounded and Danny or our officers would long since have reported them.

"No, sir." Vax's shoulders were knotted with tension, his eyes riveted on the screen. The bridge was silent as we swept forward toward the distant dot that was *Challenger*.

Admiral Tremaine's face loomed on the screen. "Where the hell have you been, you bloody coward?" His voice was tight.

Vax hissed.

I stammered, "On station at the last rendezvous, sir, as you orde—"

"Where are you now?"

"Position two five one, declination twenty-five, approaching, sir."

"Come alongside immediately, do you understand?"

"Aye aye, sir."

"You'd better!" The connection broke. I raised an eyebrow but said nothing. Vax made as if to speak; I shook my head.

"He sounded upset," offered Danny.

I snapped, "We're at Battle Stations. No personal remarks, D 20471."

"Aye aye, sir!" The puter sounded chastened. I bit my lip. We had absolutely nothing to do but wait until we were in position, and Danny's remark had been harmless. My nerves were taut.

I glanced at my watch, realized it was already midafternoon. I sent Philip Tyre to the galley for cold sandwiches. When he returned we sat munching them at our consoles, alert for encroachments as we approached the flagship. If the Admiral was in such a hurry to join ranks, why hadn't he met us halfway?

Eventually I left for my cabin, but found I couldn't sleep. After a long fruitless struggle I returned to the bridge.

The speaker came to life. "Approach port side bow on, Seafort!" The Admiral.

"Aye aye, sir." Pilot Van Peer was already making adjustments to our course.

"Disable your starboard side lasers, acknowledge!"

"What?" It burst out of me unbidden.

"Obey orders, you insubordinate young bastard!" Tremaine's voice rang through my bridge.

"Aye aye, sir, orders acknowledged and understood!" Numbly I keyed shut the laser activation release. There was no way to disable the starboard side lasers alone; our entire ship was disarmed. "Lasers disabled and inactive, sir!" In the face of his inexplicable hostility, I yearned to retreat again to my cabin.

None on the bridge dared speak to me. A half hour later we'd matched velocities, and were soon drifting at rest relative to *Challenger*, off her port side. The speaker blared anew. "I'm coming over! Meet me at the aft lock, personally!"

I roused myself. "We've had an alien virus on board, sir. We're all inoculated, but you haven't—"

"I'll be suited. Prepare two hundred doses of the vaccine at once."

"Aye aye, sir." I could say nothing else. My mind fogged with confusion, I sat waiting for the Admiral's visit, and its consequences. "Philip, switch stations with Mr. Carr in the comm room." Perhaps it wouldn't help, but at least Philip's presence wouldn't remind the Admiral of his past troubles.

"Aye aye, sir." The young midshipman hurried out. A moment later Derek Carr took his place at the console.

I left the bridge and trudged down the ladder to the aft lock, wondering what had so enraged Admiral Tremaine. I had a few moments before *Challenger*'s gig mated; I detoured to the transpops' section. A number of the rowdy streeters milled excitedly in the passage.

I beckoned a seaman from his post at the section hatchway. "Get all of them in their cabins. Keep them there as long as the Admiral's on board." Without waiting for a reply I turned back toward the airlock.

The gig's lock mated with our airlock suckers and the capture latches engaged. I waited impatiently for the locks to equalize pressure. At last the two outer hatches slid open. The Admiral and two of his officers entered our lock. The lock recycled. A moment later he was in our corridor. I stiffened to attention.

"You're at Battle Stations?"

"Yes, sir."

"Stay that way," he snapped. "To the sickbay, Seafort!"

Still suited, he and the two lieutenants who'd accompanied him followed me up the ladder to our infirmary, where Dr. Bros waited with ampules of vaccine. The Admiral broke the seals on his helmet and twisted it off, then slipped out of his suit. Immediately he bared his arm for the inoculation. When it was done he gave a sigh of relief, then turned on me.

"Where have you been hiding, Seafort?"

I tried not to let my resentment show. "I've been on station, sir, at the last rendezvous. We lost one day—"

"Dawdling at the rendezvous to avoid the danger zone!"

"—after my wife died. I was ill."

"Died? From virus?"

"No, sir." I groped for a decent answer. "From decompression."

"Well, I'm sorry. But it can't be helped. You had no business skulking back there, Seafort; you should have been here at the rendezvous!"

I grew hot. "How was I to know that, sir? I followed the orders of the senior Captain present."

"And who was that? You have a history of making yourself senior. Was it your own idea?"

"Captain Derghinski's orders are recorded in the Log, sir."

Tremaine glared at me, then grunted. "Let's see your Log, Captain." I led him to the bridge. While my officers stood at attention he flicked through the Log entries. "All right, doesn't matter. I'm transferring my flag here, Seafort. As of now."

"Aye aye, sir." Why, in heaven's name? *Challenger* was twice the size of *Portia* and better armed. If he was after more security, why not a ship of the line, such as *Kitty Hawk*?

"I'll be taking the Captain's cabin. Come along so we can talk privately." He turned to Vax and Derek. "All of you, Lieutenant Affad is in charge here while we're gone. Do exactly as he says." He wheeled and left the bridge. I followed. Well, I'd be glad to exchange cabins. I could bunk in the lieutenant's dayroom, or wherever else was available that didn't remind me of Amanda. I didn't relish serving directly under the Admiral, but that couldn't be helped.

The Admiral shut my cabin hatch, glanced around, frowning.

"Sir, what's happened, if I may ask? Where are the others?"

"*Challenger*'s disabled."

I groped for words. "How—I mean—"

"We were attacked, Seafort, by those whatever-they-are. While you were malingering in your infirmary! I read your Log. Decompression, my arse. She suicided, and you lied to cover it. What I'd expect from you."

His accusation didn't matter. "Disabled how, sir?"

"The fusion drive chamber, starboard side. I had you approach to port so you wouldn't know." Tremaine sounded smug.

I said stupidly, "But why hide it, sir?"

His gaze was one of withering contempt. "So you wouldn't cut and run before I transferred over. Now it's too late."

"You had no reason to think—"

"You've been nothing but trouble since we left Lunapolis, Commander. Your sloop was a disgrace when I boarded for inspection, and your conduct has been no better since. You had your orders: get to the rendezvous points ahead of the squadron to guard our way. That's why you were given the fastest ship!"

He stopped for breath. "Because of you, Seafort, *Challenger*'s out of action. How will that look on my record, to have my first flagship disabled?" He ran distracted fingers through thinning hair. "I've got to transfer now, thanks to you. If I have a successful mission otherwise, maybe they won't look too hard at whether *Challenger* was damaged before or after I left her." He glared. "Anyway, Hasselbrad was in charge, officially."

Could the man care more about his reputation than his ship? I tried not to show my revulsion. "What damage did you sustain, sir?"

"Our starboard shaft wall melted through. Hydroponics are damaged as well. I've got two hundred sixty-two passengers and crew; I'll move the bulk of them over here. We'll proceed in *Portia*."

"But our recyclers and hydroponics can't handle that great a load," I said, stunned.

"I know." His tone was curt. "I can't take everyone. It's all set. Captain Hasselbrad is already aboard. He'll handle it."

"He's on *Portia*, sir? When—"

"I made arrangements ahead of time, just in case." The Admiral glowered with suspicion. "No telling what you'd do. Lieutenant Affad brought Hasselbrad over while I've kept you busy. I'm giving him *Portia*. You're relieved, Seafort."

I sank into the chair, dazed, weary. I recollected my duty. "If there's anything I can do to help, sir . . ."

"Stay out of the way, damn you! You've caused enough trouble."

"Aye aye, sir. I'll take my gear to the dayroom."

"That won't be necessary." He fixed me with a cold stare. "In the morning you'll move to *Challenger*."

"What?" I was out of my chair.

"You heard me. Or you can go with us, under arrest for mutiny. It's immaterial to me."

I stammered, "Wha—what do you expect me to do on *Challenger*?"

"Wait for the help we'll send. That's all you can do."

I struggled to get my bearings. "What about the rest of the fleet, sir? Where are they?"

"I don't know." His manner was testy. "They've probably come and gone. We just got here yesterday, and we were attacked almost immediately."

That made no sense. "How could you take so long? You were the first to leave the last rendezvous!"

Tremaine slammed his fist on the table. "No more insolence!" he thundered. "Or I'll take you to the barrel and cane you in front of the ship's company!"

My mind whirled. I didn't understand what was happening, much less why. "I'll obey orders, sir," I said doggedly. "But I need them explained. How could you leave first and arrive last?"

"We were attacked at the last checkpoint." He seemed to begrudge me an explanation. "Remember?"

"Of course, sir."

Tremaine looked at the bunk as he spoke. "We were under direct attack and in peril. I had us Fuse."

I still didn't follow. "Then you should have arrived well ahead of the squadron, sir."

"We hadn't changed coordinates yet," he said offhandedly, to the bunk. "Anyway, it doesn't matter how it—"

"You Fused without new coordinates?" My tone was unbelieving. "Using the same coordinates you were previously set to?" Even I knew better than that. The Fusion point had to be at least two light-minutes distant or bizarre results could occur. The maneuver was flatly prohibited by regs.

"It was an emergency," he growled. "I had no choice."

None but to stay and fight, that is. I said nothing.

"When we Defused we were, er, some distance from the rendezvous. By the time we recalculated and Fused here, the rest of the squadron must have passed through. While we waited one of your damned beasts appeared and lobbed acid at our drive shaft. We fired on it, but it scuttled away and disappeared."

A venomous glare. "If that satisfies your curiosity, I have work to do. You'll remain here until I'm ready to set you aboard *Challenger*." He moved to the hatch.

"Sir, if the rest of the squadron has passed, *Portia* will be the only ship that knows *Challenger* is adrift here. If anything happens to you, we'll never be found."

"That chance has to be taken." He shrugged. "It's getting late; I have work to do."

"Who will you leave on *Challenger*, sir?"

"Some passengers. A few of your crew. They won't be told she's disabled until they've boarded."

Lying to the crew? Lord God, how could I face them, after?

He stood, and I thrust the thought aside for another. "How will you select them, sir?"

"A difficult choice, but someone has to make it. It's none of your concern. If you wish, you may take your officers with you." His tone was magnanimous. "Except for the Doctor." With that, he was gone.

Slowly I let myself down into my seat. *Challenger*, the ship I'd yearned to command, the vessel whose blueprints I'd pored over in Lunapolis, was suddenly mine again, now that she lay disabled and drifting. Did Tremaine fathom the irony?

Why couldn't she have been mine while she was whole? I'd fought the fish before; perhaps I could have saved her.

Lord God, You move in mysterious ways.

I sighed. If *Challenger*'s hydroponics were disabled, how long could she survive, nineteen light-years interstellar, and with nothing but her thrusters for propulsion?

Even if *Portia* reached safety in Hope Nation, a rescue vessel would have to be dispatched and return all the way to our present location. We'd be on our own for almost two years before help could arrive.

Well, all that was beside the point. The chances of a rescue ship finding us were minimal. Ships had passed near the wreckage of *Celestina* for decades before spotting her, adrift in the void. Even now, ships stopping to pay their respects sometimes failed to find her, though her position had been known and recorded for over a hundred years.

We might drift a lifetime, amid blind and unresponsive stars.

I could refuse the transfer; court-martial held no terrors for me. Tremaine would most likely have me hanged, and my misery would be over that much sooner.

I stared bleakly at the grim bulkheads. What right had I to choose easy death by the rope? I was sworn to my duty. Someone had to look after the poor souls left on *Challenger*. If not me, Tremaine would assign another who prized life more than I.

I don't know how many hours I sat, numbed with despair. After a time I roused myself and began mechanically to pack my gear, stuffing clothing into my duffel. When I came across the holos Amanda had made of our vacation in the Venturas on Hope Nation, I cried for a while, then thrust them into the duffel and went on with packing.

I was folding the last of my shirts when a soft knock came on the hatch. I ignored it. It sounded again. "Who is it?"

By way of answer the hatch opened; Vax Holser slipped in, grim-faced. He pressed the hatch closed behind him.

"What do you want?" I went on with my chores.

His fists knotted. "Tremaine told us. He swore us to secrecy, then told us."

"Very well."

"We've agreed, Alexi and Derek and I. We're going to relieve him."

A chill ran down my spine. I finished folding the shirt and placed it in the duffel. "Stand at attention, Lieutenant," I said quietly.

"Sir, this is no time—"

"Obey my orders, Mr. Holser. I'm your superior officer." Reluctantly Vax came to attention. "Now." I circled him. "You will retract that statement. You will give me your oath you will take no part in any such scheme, and then you will leave the cabin."

He said simply, "I will not."

I faced him, eye to eye. "Recite your oath of allegiance, Mr. Holser."

"I know it well enough, Capt—"

I spoke softly. "Do as I command."

He squared his shoulders. "I, Vax Stanley Holser, do swear upon my immortal soul to preserve and protect the Charter of the General Assembly of the United Nations, to give loyalty and obedience for the term of my enlistment to the Naval Service of the United Nations and to obey all its lawful orders and regulations, so help me Lord God Almighty." Eyes front, he stood stiff.

"What is an oath, Lieutenant?"

"Sir, I know what you're trying to tell—"

I put my hand over his mouth so he couldn't speak. "What is an oath, Lieutenant?" I removed my hand.

He bit his lip, shaking his head in negation. Then he sighed, and the words tumbled out of him, directly from the Naval Regulations and Code of Conduct, Revision of 2087. "'An oath is a commitment of the soul, given directly to Lord God Almighty and to the person by whose requirement the oath is given, that the commitment subscribed to will be fulfilled. It is the bond of a gentleman and an officer. Beyond an oath, no surety need or may be asked of any officer.'"

My tone was harsh. "Admiral Tremaine is your commander. You have sworn on your soul to give him loyalty and obedience and to obey all lawful orders. Do so, Vax. That's my order as well."

He shook his head stubbornly. "Not that order. He has no right to give it."

"Oh?" I asked curiously. "In what way is it unlawful?"

"He's condemning you to—to—"

"Death, perhaps. As I have condemned others. What makes it unlawful?"

He gaped. "But—" Slowly his jaw closed. He crashed his fist on the table. "He can't be allowed to get away with it!"

"He *must* be allowed to get away with it, if our service has any value."

"Not if he's insane!"

"I don't think he's insane, Vax. Badly frightened, perhaps. But not insane."

"I can judge for myself!"

"Not dishonestly!" Then I added, "Vax, have I meant anything to you? Have I taught you anything?" His eyes glistened. "Don't betray me, Vax," I said. "Live as I would have you live. Don't do otherwise in my name."

Defiance. Then, slowly, his shoulders slumped. "He said we were free to join you," he whispered. "I'm going."

"No, you're not." I was firm. "I refuse your service."

He roared, "You *what*?"

"You're not going to *Challenger*. You'll stay here, and so will the others."

"No." The word hung like a rock.

I was desperate. "Vax Stanley Holser, listen to what I say. You will stay with *Portia*. Acknowledge that order and carry it out, or I swear by Lord God Almighty I will execute you for treason myself!" I held my breath, my very soul in the balance.

Slowly he sagged. His breath came out in a long, tired sigh. He turned for the hatch. "Orders acknowledged, Captain

Seafort." He opened the hatch. "I understand what you've done. Do you?" And he was gone.

I slumped weakly in the chair. I had put both of us in mortal peril. Had Vax disobeyed me I'd have been forced to carry out my oath or see my soul forfeit. I felt my knees trembling.

Hours passed; it was early morning. My duffel packed, I sat at the gleaming bare table amidst the shambles of my career and my life.

At last, another knock. Time to go, then. "Enter." It emerged as a croak and I had to repeat it. As I reached for my duffel, Derek Carr strode in, glaring. "I'm going with you, sir."

"You are not."

"I've volunteered. I told Captain Hasselbrad."

I leaned forward in my chair. "A Captain may choose his officers, within reason. I don't accept you."

"Why not?"

I said as cruelly as I could, "You're a middy. You have no useful skills. If I needed anybody I'd take Vax."

"That's a bucket of goofjuice and you know it!"

"Watch your mouth, Mr. Carr!"

Ignoring my rebuke he came close, and loomed over my chair. "I don't believe that crap any more than you do. I know why you won't take me; skills have nothing to do with it. It's my life, and I'm capable of making the decision!"

"No. You stay, and that's final." I wondered how much more I could take. "That's all, Derek. Good-bye."

He stared past me to the bulkhead. Then he nodded once, as if to himself. "All right." He turned to go.

"Don't you salute an officer, Midshipman?" I asked. My voice was gray and tired.

From above he contemplated me, hands on hips. "I'm not sure you deserve it."

My mouth twisted in a grim smile. "Then you and the Admiral are of the same mind."

A bellow of rage. "Stand up and say that!" White-faced, he stood ready, fists clenched.

"Easy, Derek."

"Bastard!"

That stung me, and I rose to face him.

He cried, "I trusted you! You told me the Navy had integrity, and I believed you! You told me the system had worth, and I followed you! I put my life in your hands, and you toss it on the deck like garbage! May God damn you for that!"

"He probably will, and for other sins as well. The Navy does have integrity, Derek. This is how the system works. I accept that."

"You know right from wrong. Stand up and fight him!"

"I obey lawful orders, Derek, as I've sworn to do. I remind you of your own oath."

"He's killing you!"

"Not necessarily. He'll send help, when you reach port." I wondered how much Derek knew. If the rescue ship was unable to find us, or *Portia* failed to get through, we were consigned to slow death.

"If it's not so dangerous, you have no reason to refuse me."

I was glad he knew why I wouldn't let him transfer, though I couldn't show it. "It's not your choice, Midshipman Carr, it's mine. We're friends, and we've been through a lot together, so I'm making allowances for that. Now I want—I need you to pull yourself together and carry on as I've trained you. Do you understand me?"

"I understand." His glare showed no softening.

My voice was low. "You're making this hard for me, Derek."

"Yes, I suppose I am." Then he capitulated. "But Lord God, I'll miss you!" He came very close. In utter disregard of regulations he rested his hand on my shoulder and gave it a gentle squeeze. "Godspeed, Captain Seafort."

"Godspeed, Derek Carr." Briefly I touched his hand. He came to attention, saluted smartly, and wheeled. In a moment I was alone once more.

After a while I realized it was morning and I had slept not at all. I blinked, trying to stay awake.

Some time afterward a rating came to fetch me. Passive, I let him carry my duffel to the lock. Armed sentries were posted at the corridor hatches. In the small group of officers waiting at the lock was Captain Hasselbrad. I saluted.

"You'll carry a copy of *Portia*'s Log with you." He handed me the chipcase. I pocketed it. "I've ordered a portion of *Portia*'s reserve propellant transferred to *Challenger*. All we can spare."

"Thank you, sir." I was surprised the Admiral had allowed it.

As if reading my mind, he said grimly, "He can't very well relieve me too." He gestured to Alexi Tamarov, standing nearby. "Your lieutenant asked to speak with you."

"Very well." I stepped aside to make what privacy was possible.

"I'm sorry, sir," whispered Alexi, eyes downcast. "I couldn't do it. I should volunteer, but I—just can't!"

"Oh, Alexi, of course not!" His shame pierced me like a dagger. "No, you did the right thing. I wouldn't have let you aboard, be sure of that."

"But you're going."

"Two months ago I'd have fought it. Now, it doesn't matter." His glance met mine, and our pain merged. I clapped his shoulder. "You're a good man, Alexi. I think well of you."

He attempted a smile. "Thank you, sir. I'll—I'll see you in port."

"Yes. Of course." I turned back to the waiting Captain.

"The Admiral asked me to convey his orders. He won't see you himself." Hasselbrad's expression spoke silent volumes.

"I understand." My voice was dull. None of it mattered.

"You're to make your way toward Earth, in case we fail to reach Hope Nation to send a rescue party. In any event, home system is far closer than proceding toward Hope. Put out radio beacons. The search and rescue ship we send will take your movement into account. Take what evasive action you're capable of, should you meet the enemy."

"Aye aye, sir."

He looked at the deck. "The Admiral ordered four of *Challenger*'s laser units transferred to *Portia*," he muttered. "Ordered the Engineer directly, without going through me." His eyes were bleak. "I'm sorry, Seafort."

"Yes, sir." Without Fusion we couldn't escape an attack

anyway; extra lasers would just prolong our agony. "What officers and crew will I have?"

"Very few crew, I'm afraid. He's made the selections himself." His face was impassive. "I understand you refused to let your officers accompany you. We've transferred our own staff to *Portia*, except for the Chief Engineer."

I took my duffel from the seaman. Captain Hasselbrad added, "We've been ferrying *Challenger*'s passengers by launch to the forward lock here. Two more trips, and we're done. Then we'll Fuse. Anything special I should know about?"

I could think of nothing. I shook my head. Then, "Do you play chess?"

"Not very well."

"The puter likes to play. His name is Danny. He doesn't mean any harm, even if he's a little ill-mannered."

Captain Hasselbrad smiled reluctantly. "It's just a machine, Seafort. Don't get emotionally involved. Ours calls itself Kerren. Very polite, but I normally turn off the conversational overlays."

There was nothing more to say. I saluted and stepped into the lock. As the hatch slid shut he said quickly, "It wasn't my doing."

I nodded.

Portia's gig carried me across.

10

Behind me, the gig broke free of the outer airlock suckers and spurted propellant for its return to *Portia*. I stepped through the open inner lock onto *Challenger*. The airlock corridor was deserted except for two sentries who came briefly to attention as I desuited. Their side arms were ready to fire, safeties released.

"What are your orders?" I asked the nearest sentry.

He licked his lips. "To guard the aft airlock against unauthorized departures, sir, until the launch makes its last trip. Then we're to go aboard and sail with *Portia*."

"Very well." I looked about. The corridor was spacious, almost as wide as *Hibernia*'s. *Challenger*, though a sloop, was a a three-disker, barely smaller than a ship of the line. Admiral Brentley had meant well by posting me to her.

As on all ships, the bridge would be on Level 1. The ladder would be somewhere around the curve. Exhausted, I left the guards behind and trekked along the corridor.

Discarded belongings lay about, deepening my sense of abandonment. I climbed to Level 1. The bridge hatch was sealed. I pounded. "Open, there! This is the Captain!" A camera eye swiveled to find me. The hatch slid open.

Philip Tyre stiffened to attention as he rose from the console.

"You?" I shouted. "What the devil are you doing here?"

"Admiral Tremaine assigned me, sir!" His words tumbled as if he were desperate to please.

"I told them I wanted no volunteers from *Portia*!"

"Yes, sir." Philip blushed. "He said with my record I'd be suitable company for you."

I swore under my breath. "I'm sorry, Philip. Terribly sorry."

The boy tried to smile. "That's all right, sir. I'd have volunteered, if I had the courage."

I turned away, moved but angry at his foolishness. "What crew do we have?" My tone was gruff.

"I don't know exactly, sir. I thought I'd better stay on the bridge until you arrived."

"That was right," I said. "Wait here while I go investigate."

"Aye aye, sir." He called after me. "I did see Seamen Andros and Clinger getting out of the launch, sir."

I stopped. "Those troublemakers?" I'd had them at Captain's Mast no less than three times each.

"Yes, sir, I think so. If they're still aboard."

Cursing under my breath I hurried along the Level 1 corridor, opening cabin hatches as I passed. The officers' cabins were empty, all personal gear removed. I passed the wardroom. Impulsively I looked in. It had been stripped bare, except for four neatly made bunks and the built-in dressers. I quickly shut the hatch.

Near the ladder, in the passengers' section, an elderly woman accosted me, leaning on her cane. "Is it true you're going to make repairs? And we'll get moving again soon?"

"I'll do what I can, ma'am," I said, my voice tight. Beyond her, through the open hatch, was an old man, no doubt her husband. He sat fully dressed on the bed, a vacant expression on his weary face. "What are you doing here, ma'am? On this voyage?"

"My brother is on Hope Nation, Martin Chesley. We're going to live with him. He wrote us every chance he could. He made the colony sound so wonderful. Our children are grown, so Mr. Reeves and I . . ."

"I understand." I excused myself and hurried on. The Level 2 cabins were mostly abandoned. I saw no one except for the airlock sentries. I stopped trying cabin hatches; I would learn soon enough what passengers were aboard. I continued down to Level 3. At the foot of the ladder I turned in the direction I thought would take me fastest to the engine room; if I was wrong I would still get there; the corridor was circular.

I found the engine room hatch. No one answered my knock, so I opened, glanced into the deserted outer compartment. At the far end was another hatch, leading to the monitor room where the fusion motor controls were housed. I peered in.

A disheveled man sat at a grimy metal table in the center

of the compartment, sipping from a large stoneware coffee mug.

"Are you the Chief Engineer?" I demanded.

His laugh was savage. "I was." He looked me over. "Who're you?"

My uniform should have told him. "Your new Captain," I said. "Stand at attention."

"Why bother?" He shrugged. His gaze dropped to his cup.

I was astounded. "Put that down!" I raged. "Stand!" He got to his feet, stared at me blearily. He staggered, then caught his balance. I picked up the mug, sniffed. "Liquor!" My voice shot into the upper registers. "Alcohol aboard ship? *You*? Contraband?"

He grinned, and it was too much. I slammed him against the bulkhead. "An officer! Look at you!" I cuffed him across the face. "Drunk!" He put up a hand to ward off my blows.

Hopeless. I glanced around. A glass jar sat on the corner of the table. I hurled it to the floor along with the mug.

He whined, "Do you know how much trouble it is to make that? All the fruit and grain it took?" I rounded on him, cuffed him again.

"You don't like me drunk?" His voice was a sneer. "What else should I do? Have you seen the mess back there?" His thumb shot to the emission chamber shaft, in the next compartment. "Take a look, before you go hitting people!"

Disgusted, I shoved him away and turned to the emission chamber.

The shaft opening had been patched with a makeshift airseal. I studied the viewscreen that pictured the lower half of the shaft. My breath caught.

To starboard, three meters of shaft wall had melted like butter. Even I knew that the complex alloy comprising the shaft couldn't be fabricated outside a dockyard. And the exquisitely machined curve of the shaft wall was essential to produce the pattern of N-waves that allowed us to Fuse.

The damage was irreparable.

I turned back to the inner compartment. The Chief sat staring mournfully at his broken mug.

"Do we have power?" I rasped.

"The fusion motors themselves weren't damaged." He

didn't bother to look up. "They'll provide all the power we want for ship's systems. Just don't try using them to Fuse."

"Right." I left him to his dissolution and stepped out to the corridor. I rounded the bend and approached crew berth two, its hatch ajar. The berth was empty. Past the crew exercise room was crew berth one. Two tense sentries stood vigilant guard, fingers on their weapons.

"Identify yourself!" The man's stunner was leveled at my stomach.

"Nicholas Seafort, Commander, U.N.N.S., Captain of this vessel."

"Yes, sir. My orders come directly from the Admiral, sir. This hatch is sealed and not to be opened until after we board the launch, sir." He looked nervous, as well he might, delivering such instructions to a Captain.

"Who's inside?"

"The crew, sir. The original *Challenger* crewmen who they haven't put aboard *Portia*, and the new *Challenger* crew ferried from your old ship."

"How many?"

"I don't know, sir. I think about fifteen."

"You're holding them prisoner?" I couldn't hide my amazement.

"I'm keeping the hatch shut, sir."

"As senior officer present, I countermand your orders."

The seaman said hoarsely, "No, sir, I can't. The Admiral said to disregard your instructions. If I let you open the hatch I won't be allowed on the last launch to *Portia*." His face was shiny with sweat.

"Very well." I swallowed bile. "I won't interfere." I continued round the corridor to the ladder rather than retracing my steps.

As I passed an open cabin a small form hurled itself out of the hatchway and flung itself against my shoulder. "Cap'n!"

I recoiled in shock. "Joni?"

"Cap'n, din' know you beinhere too! Mira! It be Cap'n!" Other transients crowded around.

"What are you doing here?" A chill of foreboding closed around me like a cloud.

One of them shrilled, "Boss Cap'n say I c'n have my own room, man! Allus, havin' own turf! Lotsa rooms dis ship!"

"Christ!" The blasphemy burst from my lips.

Joni added, "Boss Cap'n, he be nice afta all, givin' us own rooms!"

"Are you all here?"

"Eddie'n Deke gonna come next boat. Otha trannies with'm!"

"No!" I raced toward the ladder and the bridge. Ahead of me, the crew berth sentries dashed up the ladder to the aft airlock on Level 2. I charged on to Level 1, hammered on the bridge. "Open up, Philip!"

The hatch opened; I dived into my seat, grabbed the caller. "*Challenger* to *Portia*, acknowledge!"

A cultured male voice interrupted. "Excuse me, sir. The forward airlock is cycling."

"Who are you?"

"My name is Kerren, sir. I'm pleased to meet—"

"Be silent! *Portia*, acknowledge! Puter, turn the hull camera to the forward lock!" *Challenger*'s launch flashed onto the screen. Through its transparent portholes I saw passengers crowd toward the mated locks. Many of them were older; two were in wheelchairs. "*Portia*, acknowledge!"

The speakers were silent. I swore. "Philip, go see what's up at the forward lock."

"Aye aye, sir." He jumped from his seat and ran. I waited with mounting frustration. "Kerren, keep paging *Portia*."

"Aye aye, sir."

A few moments later Philip Tyre was back, gasping for breath. "The passengers are unloaded and milling around the corridor. There's no crew in sight and the sentries are gone."

"Which passengers, Philip?"

"Mr. Fedez, sir, and Mrs. Ovaugh. The Pierces. A lot of others I recognize, but I don't remember their names, sir."

"The older ones."

"Yes, sir. Most of them. Some younger Joes too, though."

The speaker crackled and the screen came to life. "All right, Seafort, I'm here. What's your problem?" Admiral Tremaine's jaw stuck out at a belligerent angle.

"I beg you, reconsider!"

"There's nothing to reconsider. I will make note of your cowardice."

"I didn't mean that. Leave me here!" I pounded the arm of my chair in exasperation. "The passengers! The children!"

"That's not your decision, Commander."

"You can't abandon them. For Lord God's sake, please!"

His voice was icy. "Don't tell me what I can do, Seafort."

"Who'll be on the next launch?"

He seemed indifferent. "Just a few more passengers. Then we'll be on our way."

"The children from New York?"

"Children? Street vermin, you mean. Yes, I'm sending them along."

"You can't condemn them to a crippled vessel! I won't accept them!"

His tone was glacial. "Listen carefully, Seafort, because I'm recording this conversation for the Log. You are ordered to board the passengers I send you. Acknowledge."

"Aye aye, sir, I—Just a moment." I swung away from the caller. Philip Tyre opened his mouth, thought better of it after I stared through him. I paced, my fists clenched.

The Admiral had given a lawful order. He had the authority to make the decisions he'd made. Repulsive as I found them, I had no standing to object. I would obey. I must.

I snapped on the speaker. "I protest the order, sir."

"Protest noted. Acknowledge your orders."

I do swear upon my immortal soul . . . to obey all lawful orders and regulations . . . an oath is a commitment of the soul given directly to Lord God . . .

I didn't have a choice.

Did I?

Human rubbage, to be cast aside?

"The hell I will!" I bellowed. "I refuse!"

"Seafort, you've hanged yourself!"

"You have no right to abandon children in interstellar space!"

"They're scum, but that's beside the point. I couldn't take everyone, so I had to choose. It's called triage."

"It's called murder!" Blazing, I stared at his image in the screen.

He shrugged. "You have no choice. They're on *Challenger*'s launch. We're Fusing in a few moments. Pick them up or not, as you wish."

"I'll open fire!" I was beside myself.

He chuckled. "With what? I made sure your lasers were disabled. It'll take you hours to get them working again." He turned away.

Legs spread, hands on hips, I stood defiantly in front of the screen. Words spewed forth from some dark recess of my soul.

"Geoffrey Tremaine! Now I, Nicholas Ewing Seafort, by God's Grace Commander in the Naval Service of the United Nations, call challenge upon you to defend your honor, and do swear upon my immortal soul that I shall not rest while breath is in your body. So help me Lord God Almighty!"

He laughed. "Well, it's a long way to Hope Nation. You'll cool off." The screen blanked.

I sank trembling in my chair. On the simulscreen, the last launch left *Portia*. Dully, I sat and watched.

"Sir, shall I go—"

"Shut your mouth, Mr. Tyre." My tone brooked no argument. The last launch drifted clear of *Portia*. A few spurts of propellant glided her toward *Challenger*. In a few moments she was alongside.

The speaker crackled. "*Challenger*, ship's launch is prepared to mate. Please cycle outer airlock." I said nothing.

"*Challenger*? Captain? We need you to open the lock!"

I remained silent.

"Sir, the lock; do you want me—"

"Keep your mouth shut, Mr. Tyre. I won't tell you again."

We waited in terrible silence. I stirred. "Kerren, signal *Portia* that I refuse entry to the launch."

"Aye aye, sir."

"*Challenger*, for Lord God's sake, let us in!" The seaman's voice held a note of hysteria. I could imagine his terror, marooned in a launch between two vessels, one about to Fuse, the other denying him entry.

I picked up the caller. "Wait."

"Oh, Jesus, he's answered! Please, Captain, open the lock!"

"Wait." I thumbed off the caller. Minutes passed. *Portia*'s side thrusters fired propellant. She drifted from us, gaining clearance to Fuse safely. I swallowed.

Portia disappeared. With her, my life.

I sat rocking, mired in hopeless misery. Reeling from exhaustion, I thought of my new cabin, and a bed. No, there was something I must do first. "Philip."

"Yes, sir!" The middy jumped to his feet, pathetically anxious to accommodate.

"Go below. Unseal the outer lock. You remember the drill; you've done it many times. This time you're alone, so be careful."

"Aye aye, sir. Yes, sir."

"After the launch is mated, wait for permission before you open the inner lock."

"Aye aye, sir." He saluted and left.

I felt my eyes closing; I stirred myself once more. "Kerren, have you been reprogrammed to recognize me as Captain?"

"Yes, sir." A smooth baritone.

"Very well."

"Welcome aboard, sir."

I said sharply, "No mood for small talk."

"Aye aye, sir." He seemed faintly hurt, and made a sound as if he were clearing his nonexistent throat. "I have a message for you."

"From whom?"

"A recording. Captain Hasselbrad instructed me not to deliver it until *Portia* Fused. Are you ready for playback?"

"Yes."

The screen flashed to life. Captain Hasselbrad's grim features stared at me. "You'll hear this when it's too late to help, but by God I'll tell you. He planned to seize the first ship that appeared, regardless of whose it was. It was your bad luck *Portia* arrived first. When the fish beast got our fusion tubes he went a little—yes, a little crazy. I think so, but I'm not sure. He planned it all out, your approach from the port side where the damage was invisible, the transfer of crew and passengers, the whole bloody job.

"Maybe I should have relieved him. I don't know. You'll find my written protest in the Log. It did no good, of course. I forced him to transfer seven tanks of propellant from *Portia* to *Challenger*. Maybe it will be of some help. He cleaned out most of the drugs from your infirmary."

On the screen Hasselbrad looked down at his hands. "A glob the aliens threw penetrated *Challenger*'s hydroponics chambers. It wrecked the nitrogen control machinery, but worse, it decompressed the west hydro compartment. What wasn't destroyed we threw away for fear of contamination. Since the attack we've been on short rations from east hydros, and living off stores."

He stared into the camera. "Seafort, the Admiral ordered most of *Challenger*'s food reserves transferred to *Portia*. When I heard of it I canceled the transfer, but most of your remaining stores had already been carried across. I was already on *Portia*, so I don't have an inventory. You don't have as many passengers or crew as we did; I hope he left you enough food."

He swallowed. "I know what I should have done. I should have volunteered to remain with my ship. I didn't suggest he transfer me to *Portia*, but I didn't object either. I'm sorry, I—" He looked straight into the camera. "At my age, I can't handle the uncertainty and the helplessness. I can't. So it has to be you. Godspeed, Mr. Seafort. I'm sorry for what we've done." The recording went dead.

"Would you like to hear it again, Captain?"

"No." I rocked in my chair. "Kerren, did you record my communications with *Portia*?"

"Yes, sir."

"Play them back." I leaned back and listened to myself shouting at the Admiral, out of control. "It's called murder!" I closed my eyes as Tremaine gave his direct command. "You are ordered to board the passengers I send you." I heard my reply. "The hell I will! I refuse!"

My tone held anguish. "Turn it off."

"It's not finished, sir, there's—"

"TURN IT OFF!" I bit back a sob.

Blessed silence.

The hatch opened. Philip. "Permission to enter bridge, sir." I waved him in. "The passengers are all boarded."

"Very well." My voice was dull.

He waited expectantly. After a time he prompted, "Sir, what are your orders?"

"Orders?" I found it hard to concentrate. "I have no right to give orders."

"What, sir?"

I said more loudly, "I'm not fit to give orders. I'm a mutineer." I opened my eyes. "Do as you wish."

"Please, sir, where do we start?"

I lay back, head against the rest, my eyes closed. "Well now, Middy. We're drifting at a rendezvous with our fusion drive in ruins, and we think the rest of the squadron has passed us. I have you, an eighteen-year-old midshipman nobody wants. I have a drunken Chief Engineer whose name I neglected to learn while I was slapping him.

"Care for more?" My smile was crooked. "Locked in crew berth one are a handful of crewmen selected for their behavior problems, probably out of their minds with fear. Meanwhile, about forty deceived trannies are roaming the ship, no doubt terrorizing the other castaways by their presence."

Philip swallowed.

"The Admiral was kind enough to disable our lasers. Half our hydroponics are gone. *Portia* relieved us of most of our food. I don't have the combination to the bridge safe or the code to open the crew berth hatch, or the keys to the armory. I've no idea if we have enough personnel to run essential ship's systems. So, tell me, Midshipman Philip Tyre: where do we start?"

Philip stammered, "Sir, you're the Captain!"

"Of what, Middy?" My tone was grim. "Tell me, of what?" He made no answer. I opened my eyes, saw the incipient panic behind the boy's gaze. My self-pity dissolved in shame. "All right," I growled. I essayed a small and unsuccessful smile. "That's the downside. But we're alive. Let's see what we can do for ourselves. Come below with me." I stood.

"Yessir!" Philip's relief was clear. We left the bridge, sealing the hatch with an ID code. I downed the ladder to Level 3, Philip trotting close behind. At the foot of the ladder I bumped into a passenger, recoiled. "What in God's own Hell are you doing here?" I roared at Walter Dakko.

He stepped back from my fury. "Captain, where's all the crew? Why are most of the cabins empty?"

I grabbed his collar. "Why are you here?" I shoved him against the bulkhead. "Answer!"

"Chris," he said in a tired voice. "Chris and that Attani boy. Without telling us they sought out *Portia*'s new officers and asked if they could transfer to *Challenger* for the rest of the cruise. To get away from you. The Admiral obliged them. When Galena and I found out, we agreed I should transfer too; Chris is too young to be alone. So I did." He glared at me. "Now it's your turn. What's going on?"

"*Portia*'s Fused and gone. Our fusion tubes are wrecked. We aren't going anywhere. We're derelict."

He closed his eyes. "Oh, you foolish boy," he whispered. After a moment he asked bleakly, "Is there any hope?"

"Of rescue, perhaps. I don't know." I left him.

From within crew berth one came frantic pounding. I found the code to unseal the hatch posted on a slip of paper next to the control. I tapped in the figures.

Philip stirred uneasily. "Shouldn't we be armed, sir?"

"It won't be necessary." If it was, we were doomed anyway. "Stand back." Taking a deep breath, I unlocked the hatch. I assumed the at-ease position directly in front of the hatch, hands crossed behind me.

As the hatch slid open a mob of desperate men surged forward. "STAND AT ATTENTION!" I bellowed. In shock and surprise they fell back. I strode forward. "I'm Mr. Seafort, your new Captain. You! Form a line to that side! Move! The rest of you, over here!" I shoved one man aside. "Line up, or I'll have you at Captain's Mast so fast you'll get friction burns!"

I was fortunate; old habits of discipline asserted themselves. In a few moments the men stood in two ragged lines to either side of the main aisle.

"Midshipman, take the name of anyone who moves!" Philip scurried in, snatching the paper with the hatch code on it for a writing pad. Resourceful.

I glared at my forlorn remnants of a crew. "You were sent here by order of your superior officers. How dare you make such a ruckus? We'll have no more of that." I paced, as if on inspection. "Identify yourselves. One at a time." I nodded to the man at the end of the line.

"Recycler's Mate Kovaks, sir." I nodded. Good. His skills were crucial.

"Comm Specialist Tzee, sir."

"Seaman Andros."

"Sir!"

He looked contemptuous. "Sir? Oh, yeah, *sir*."

"Write him up, Mr. Tyre!" Philip scribbled his name.

"Lotta good that'll do you, Captain," muttered Andros. "This ain't no Navy ship no more."

I didn't hesitate a second. "Mr. Tyre, escort him to the brig!"

"Aye aye—"

"Do that, pretty boy!" sniggered Andros. "I'd liketa get alone with—"

I pivoted on my left heel. My roundhouse blow to the jaw caught him completely unawares. His eyes rolled up as he crashed to the deck. A fierce pain lanced up my arm; I was afraid I'd rebroken my hand. Cautiously I flexed my fingers and decided I had not. "Continue, please," I said calmly, as if clubbing a crewman unconscious were an everyday affair.

I paced while they identified themselves. Fourteen men in all, including Andros. Five were transferees from *Portia*: Andros, Clinger, and three steward's mates. The other nine included one man from *Challenger*'s engine room, two hydroponicist's mates, a purser's mate, and five deckhands with few advanced skills.

I stood in the center of the passageway. "We are a Naval vessel under weigh in wartime conditions. We will maintain Naval discipline at all times. Understood?"

Sullenly, they murmured their assent.

"You, Drucker and Groshnev! Carry Mr. Andros to the brig. Mr. Tyre, put him in a cell and secure the brig. Return here immediately."

"Aye aye, sir." The two seamen hoisted the unconscious Andros by his arms and legs and followed Philip from the compartment.

I held the men at silent attention until the party returned

from the brig. When at last they filed in, I snapped, "At ease, all of you." They relaxed. "As far as I know, you are *Challenger*'s only remaining crew." They didn't like that, and I could hardly blame them. I began to pace. "Our first task is to take stock of the ship and its resources. Mr. Kovaks, are the recyclers ready for inspection?"

He gaped. "Inspection? Are you serious? We've been left here to die!"

"Not if I can help it!" I was losing control of the situation; time to improvise. "All of you, come along on the inspection tour. Explain our problems. We'll start with recycling, then move on to the hydros. Then the engine room and the comm room. Let's go!"

They seemed reluctant to leave the berth they'd been so desperate to escape. "Mr. Tyre, get a clipboard from the purser's office and make notes of what these men tell us. Mr. Kovaks, I presume the puter is still monitoring?" Casually I moved toward the hatch.

"Yes, sir," he said automatically. Then he swallowed. "Power to the recyclers wasn't interrupted when we got hit." He followed me into the corridor. "The lower engine room was decompressed; that's when the five joes got killed, but the fusion motors still produce internal power. Gauges were normal last I checked, yesterday sometime. I've been locked in there"—Kovaks pointed bitterly to the crew berth—"ever since." The other men were gathering in the corridor behind us.

"I know," I said. "Sorry about that. It won't happen again. You men, keep up or you won't be able to hear. Kovaks, think you know the monitoring drills well enough to train a couple of other joes?" He nodded.

In a few moments we were clustered in the recycler chambers. "Better run a check now, Mr. Kovaks."

The seaman seemed more docile now that he was at his familiar station. He ran pressure tests and checked the gauges against the norms on his worksheet. "Recycling checks out, Captain."

"Very well. Take me to west hydros."

The sailor Groshnev objected, "It's east hydros that are operating. We—"

"I said, take me to west hydros. What's the proper response to an order?"

"Aye aye, sir."

"I need your help to restore the ship," I snapped. "But we'll maintain discipline. We're under a lot of tension and you've just been freed from unwarranted imprisonment, so I'll overlook your discourtesy, one time. Understood?"

"Yes, sir." He seemed chastened.

"Very well. West hydros." When we arrived I wished I hadn't given the order. The ruin there was almost absolute. A ragged but adequate airseal covered a wound in the hull, but machinery was overturned, and bent tubing and broken hoses lay scattered about. Empty water tanks lay on the deck amid clumps of loose sand and dirt. Of the plants, nothing remained.

"That shapechanger scuttled in here," someone muttered.

Seaman Drucker turned angrily. "We went through Class A decontamination! You even helped, you dumb grode! Remember how Lieutenant Affad supervised? Ultraviolet wave, chemicals, the works. We're safe here."

"Seeds? Plant stock?"

"There's seeds in the stock drawers, sir. And a few plants in the cutting room, but no way to grow them. The machinery's a mess."

"We have piping, hoses. We can make tanks from scrap, right?"

"Yes, sir." Drucker looked bleakly at the wreckage. "The machinery was never designed to handle decompression, sir. The sensors to the puter are out, and most of the feed valves are jammed or blown. We can make elementary repairs, but this . . ."

"Very well." I motioned to the hatch. "East hydros."

The east chamber appeared to be flourishing. Growlights overhead softly hummed; beneath them tomatoes, cucumbers, and other vegetables grew peacefully. Somewhere in the background water dripped; the sensor lights glowed soft green.

"Looks the way I'd expect," I remarked. "Anything wrong here?"

"Yes," Drucker said, his tone ominous. He brushed aside

the leaves of a tomato plant growing in a wet sandy tank, and pointed.

I inhaled through my teeth. "Does that mean what I think?"

"Yes, sir," Drucker said grimly. The pulpy stems of four half-eaten unripe tomatoes lay tossed aside in the sand. "Someone's been raiding the produce. Extra rations. I discovered it yesterday before we were locked up, sir. After the rest of the crew had been taken to *Portia*."

The men had grown very quiet. My gaze shifted from eye to eye around the cabin. No one looked away. "From now on, we'll keep the hydro chambers sealed," I said. "Only the hydro detail will have entry. We're on short rations as it is. Anyone found stealing food will be executed. No second chances." There was no sound. I cleared my throat. "How much more food could we grow here?"

"The beds are full, Captain. Where else would we put plants?"

"What's our output?"

"About twenty tomatoes a day, Captain, and about thirty cucumbers. There's some beans started in bed eleven over there; they won't be grown for a month or so. Lots of lettuce. Thing is, you can't survive on lettuce."

"Why didn't you plant a full line of crops when the west hydros failed?"

"I dunno, sir. First we was tryin' to get rid of the contamination, if there was any, then we kept expectin' the rest of the squadron to show up. Figured we'd get some new plant stock from them; faster than startin' fresh from seeds."

"Um." No point in criticizing *Challenger*'s former officers. "To the galley, then. Let's see about our stores." I sealed the hydro chamber hatch with a code, putting myself between the crewmen and the controls as I keyed it so the men couldn't see what I entered. We trooped up to the galley.

The coolers were normally kept locked between meals. Most were sealed now, but one hatch had been forced and the cooler's contents looted. I looked about. "Where are the codes for the locked coolers?" One man shrugged; the rest looked mystified.

"We'll get 'em open," growled Clinger.

"No. I'll search for the codes when I go back to the bridge.

We'll open the coolers on my order. Not before." I had a deckhand go through the dry cupboards while we waited; a few sacks of flour, some condiments, and scattered cans of prepared vegetables were all we found.

I asked, "Do any of you know what stores are in the hold?"

"About twenty cases of powdered milk." A sailor, his tone sullen. "I helped load them for *Portia*, then put them back when new orders came down."

"What else?"

He shrugged. "Some cases of somethin' else. I dunno. Not enough to keep us all fed, I know that much."

I swung to Philip. "Mr. Tyre, after the tour, take this man to the hold and inventory our foodstuffs. You should find the manifest posted near the hatch." I didn't wait for an answer. "Engine room. Let's go."

At the engine room the drunken Chief was nowhere to be seen. The shards of his stone mug still lay about. I turned to the engine room rating. "Mr.—Sykes, is it? What's the status here?"

He grinned mirthlessly through missing teeth. "Ol' Chief, he off somewheres with a beaker, I reckon. The puter is runnin' things now, looks like." He guffawed.

"Mr. Tyre, put that man on report. I'll deal with him next Captain's Mast." Dutifully, Philip wrote his name. "Mr. Sykes, try again."

The rating shot me a resentful look, but caught himself before he replied. He took a slow breath and stood taller. "You saw the Chief, sir? He's, uh, well, you know. Guess he's too upset to care anymore. He's got the engines all runnin' on automatic. We've got electricity, heat, pump pressure. If we need lasers we'll have to go to full power; I dunno if the puter can do that by hisself."

"It can't."

"Yeah, well, then we don't have lasers. Sir."

"Can you man the machinery?"

"I can read the gauges, yes, sir. I know to turn the levers to full power when the order comes down, and watch the red lines. I don't know what I'd do if they went over the red, sir. The Chief was always here to handle that. I guess I'd just shut everything off." He grinned.

"In what order, Mr. Sykes?"

His grin vanished. "Uh, I don't know, sir. That's up to the Chief." He mumbled, "Guess I could glitch things up good, foolin' with them, huh?"

"Yes. I'll get the Chief back on duty." We finished our inspection and trooped up the ladder toward the Level 1 comm room. Along the way we were besieged by a gang of transients in the corridor. "Later, allyas!" I snapped. "Noway mess wid Cap'n now, noway!" They fell back, astonished at my language. Well, whatever worked.

In the comm room the disassembled laser controls lay neatly atop their consoles. The manuals were likewise waiting, open to the page that detailed how to reinstall the controls. "Lord God Almighty!" I stopped myself, before I said worse. "Sorry. Amen. Mr. Tzee, can you reinstall the firing controls?"

The rating looked over the various parts before he answered. "Yes, sir. I'm pretty sure I can."

"Get right on it."

"Aye aye, sir." He rummaged in a locker for tools. "It would be easier, sir, uh, I mean, if you all weren't—"

"Right." I went to the hatch. "Report to the bridge when you've finished. While you're at it, test our radionics. Let me know what you find." I waited while the crew filed out. We gathered in the Level 1 corridor.

"All right, inspection's finished. We have work to do. Mr. Sykes, clean up the engine room. Mr. Tyre, go search for foodstuffs in the hold. Be thorough. Mr. Akkrit, I'm giving you the passenger detail. Take three men. Make a list of all the passengers and their cabins. See they're all settled in properly. The rest of you"—that left seven—"for the moment, you're the galley crew. Mr. Bree is in charge. We'll need dinner soon; call me on the bridge and tell me what you can manage with current supplies. That's all."

Reluctantly they dispersed. Some looked as if they had objections that I made sure they had no time to voice. I hurried back to the bridge, taking care to seal the hatch behind me.

I slumped into my chair, my mind grappling with unsolved problems. "Kerren?"

"Yes, sir? How may I help?" I understood why Captain

Hasselbrad had shut off the puter's conversational overlays. Despite his politeness, something about his manner grated.

"The coolers in the galley are locked. Do you know where the codes are?"

"Yes, sir."

I waited expectantly. Then, "Where, Kerren?"

"Captain Hasselbrad put them in the Log, sir. Have you checked the Log?"

I cursed my stupidity. "No." I reached for the holovid.

"You should check it, sir," Kerren said solemnly. "If you want to find the codes."

Gritting my teeth I snapped on the Log and flipped through its pages. I swore out loud. Among the last few entries were the codes to the bridge safe and the food lockers. I memorized the locker code, went to the safe, dialed it open. Inside was a stunner pistol, and an envelope marked "Armory Key." I pocketed them, feeling more secure as I resumed my seat.

Half an hour later Philip Tyre returned triumphant from his tour of the hold. "Canned meat and vegetables, sir! Two containers full. Five hundred seventy-four cases; sixteen to a case, to be exact!" He dropped into his chair at the watch officer's console.

I smiled. "Good find, Middy." The room seemed brighter, the ship less oppressive. Philip grinned back, basking in my approval. I busied myself reading the Log, familiarizing myself with the ship's operating parameters.

The caller came to life. "Uh, bridge? Captain?"

I answered. "Who are you? Don't you know how to report?"

"Uh, no, sir, I never called the bridge before. This is Akkrit."

"Seaman Akkrit reporting, sir!"

He parroted my words. "Uh, we figure there's seventy-six passengers, sir, counting the damn trannies. One of them young joeys, I had to punch his lights out to make him stop following me. Thirty-nine trannies, a bunch of old people, and a few others. Jabour here has the list."

"Very well. Send him up. Your group is assigned to corridor detail. Pick up the refuse on all three Levels."

"Uh, aye aye, sir."

I broke the connection, played idly with the calculator on my console. Seventy-six passengers, fourteen crewmen, Philip, the Chief, and myself. Ninety-three in all. If we consumed, on the average, one can of food per person per day, we had rations for ninety-eight days. The hydroponics output would add to that, but we'd consume food faster than we were growing it. What little we had was immensely valuable, and we'd need to watch it closely.

"Mr. Tyre, did you secure the hold?"

Philip looked puzzled. "I shut the hatch, sir."

"You didn't seal it?" A chill of alarm.

"No, sir, you told me to search for food, not to—"

"That deckhand, what's his name—"

"Ibarez."

"He saw the cases of food?"

"Yes, he helped me count—"

"Idiot! Can't you do anything right?" I scrambled to my feet. "I should know better than to trust you! Move!" I was already out the hatch.

Philip ran after me. "To the hold, sir?"

"Yes, by God's—no! The armory, first." We rounded the corridor bend. I skidded to a stop at the armaments locker and fumbled with the key. Finally I had the locker open.

I tossed a stunner and a pistol to the midshipman and pulled out a laser rifle for myself. Slamming the hatch shut I raced along the corridor to the launch berth hatch. The cargo holds were far forward from the disks in which we lived, in the slim, pencillike body of the ship beyond the launch berth.

I slapped the hatch control and rushed through as the panel slid open. Philip followed. In the suiting room I snatched a suit from the racks and thrust myself into it. The cargo holds were pressurized, but as the air wasn't run through our recyclers it couldn't be depended on, so one always wore a suit in the hold. I slapped on my helmet, checking the air gauge automatically as it sealed.

Suited, we clambered to the hatch at the far end of the chamber. At my touch the hatch slid open.

Challenger's huge cargo hold stretched to the narrow bow

of the ship. I flicked off my radio, grabbed Philip by the neck, touched his helmet to mine. "Where?"

Understanding that I wanted silence, he pointed to the opposite side of the hull, about a hundred meters forward. I crouched, moved along the passageway as quietly as I could. I flicked my radio back to "Receive," motioning Philip to do likewise.

The sound of heavy breathing. "Hurry, damn it, we gotta get outta here!"

I crept toward the voices. A narrow passageway ran along the hull on either side of the hold; at twenty-meter intervals catwalks branched over the bins of cargo to the passageway on the other side. As noiselessly as I could manage, I followed a dimly lit catwalk to where the food was stored.

I tiptoed across the decking. On the far side of the bins, three suited men loaded boxes onto a power dolly.

I raised my rifle. "Hold it!"

"Run!" With a curse, one man dashed along the far passageway back toward the launch berth. Another leaped down to the hold, among the stacked boxes and containers. The third came directly at me.

The sailor charged across the catwalk, brandishing a heavy iron bar.

"Stop!" I raised my rifle. He hurled the bar at my head. My visor shattered, blinding me with a shower of broken transplex. Reflexively, I fired. I gasped, expecting foul air. To my relief it was clean and fresh. My head rang from the blow. I staggered to keep my footing, blinked trying to see.

My attacker was gone.

Philip, with a yell. "Here, sir! He's—whoof!"

I backtracked across the catwalk, ran to the hatch. Philip Tyre sat on the deck, holding his ribs, a lame grin plastered on his young face. "Sorry, sir. I was aiming at the other joe and he blindsided me. Knocked my breath out." He glanced about. "They got away."

"Got away?" I hauled him to his feet. "Damn you, Middy! Where's your pistol? Your stunner?"

Philip paled. His frantic eyes searched for the missing weapons. "I—they—he must have taken them, sir, when I fell."

I was shocked into silence. Any act of deliberate disobedience by a crewman constituted mutiny. Still, there were degrees. To take up arms against lawful authority was unthinkable. We were long past the Rebellious Ages; for civilians, the penalty for keeping unauthorized firearms was a life sentence in Callisto penal colony. For a seaman, death.

Now I had armed rebellion on my hands. All because of Philip.

I shoved him back toward the catwalk. "I shot at someone. Did he get past you?"

"I think I saw just two, sir."

"You think!" I mimicked. "If you didn't let him past, he's still here." I held the rifle ready as we crossed the catwalk.

My weapon wasn't needed. The third sailor lay facedown in the hold, blood seeping from his head. I sent Philip down to the body; when he turned it over, the face of the deckhand Ibarez stared blindly back. Pale and silent, the middy climbed to the catwalk.

Outside, I hauled off my suit. "This is all your doing! You knew there isn't enough food to go around. The deckhand saw you leave the hatch unsealed; what did you expect they'd do? And worse, you didn't even hang on to the weapons I issued!"

The boy blanched.

"Now the rebels have a pistol and a stunner. You incompetent child, I ought to send you to the barrel!"

Philip smiled weakly in his humiliation and shame; the expression only fueled my anger. I slapped shut the hatch. "By Lord God, I will! Come along, Midshipman. I've never been first lieutenant; the barrel was never in my cabin. It's about time I learned to use it!"

Philip's eyes pleaded, but he said nothing.

I grabbed his arm. "Get yourself to the first lieutenant's cabin, flank!" In a blind rage I stalked from the suiting room into the circumference corridor. Philip scurried alongside, his face red with embarrassment. In moments we were in officers' country, near the bridge. We reached the lieutenant's cabin. The hatch was ajar.

I stormed in. The barrel stood on its mount in the far corner of the cabin. The cane leaned against it. Philip stared, gulped.

Unprompted, he shucked his jacket and folded it neatly across a chair. Small, reluctant steps took him to the barrel. He lay himself across it, arms crossed under his head in the required position.

I set down my rifle, snatched up the cane. "I'll teach you to do your duty, you—" I lashed him with all my strength. He yelped, jerked convulsively, then made himself still, his head pressed into his folded arms. I raised the cane to strike again, triumphant in the exercise of my lawful authority. Mine was the power to punish, to mete justice.

I came to my senses.

"What am I doing?" The cane fell from my fingers. I fell into a chair alongside the table. Philip lay across the barrel, unmoving. I put my head in my hands. "Lord God!"

The middy waited.

"Philip, get up." My voice was hoarse. Slowly the boy straightened. One hand crept to the seat of his pants. He turned, his face scarlet. "Sit." I thrust out a chair. He obeyed, and winced. I steeled myself to meet his eye. "I don't know if you can forgive me, Mr. Tyre. I don't expect it. I'm sorry for what I've done. You deserve far better."

"No!" The cry was wrung from him.

"Yes. You—"

"Don't you see, sir? You were right!" His tears welled. "I should have known to seal the hatch and hold on to my gun. I'm sorry I'm such a failure; I'll try harder from now on! I know I deserve worse than the barrel. If you're afraid to discipline me, how can you trust me? How can you run the ship? I'm not like those men, I'll take discipline and obey my oath. Please!"

He got to his feet, grabbed the cane. "I don't want to be hit—God, how it hurts—but you're Captain! I beg you, don't be afraid to punish me." He set the cane on the table.

I closed my eyes. A long time passed. I said quietly, "You think that's why I stopped? Because I thought you'd join the mutineers if I caned you?"

He cried, "Why else would you let me off after what I did?"

"Because the fault was mine, from the start. It was my own responsibility to see the hatch was sealed. Thanks to my stupidity a man is dead. Blaming you was cowardly. Despicable. The pistol and stunner—that couldn't be helped. You did your best."

"My best isn't good enough!" His tone was anguished. "I'm your only officer, and you can't rely on me. No wonder you didn't want me aboard." He looked down. "I'm useless." His voice was muffled. "Worse, I'm a hindrance."

"Mr. Tyre, listen well: I didn't want you on *Challenger* because I didn't want your life thrown away. There was no other reason. You are a good officer and you have my respect. I'm sorry I hit you. I won't do it again."

"You don't have to promise—"

"It's done. And I have to make the promise; I can't trust my judgment otherwise. I feel—" I tried to quell my surge of emotions. I said, my voice ragged, "Philip, you know I'm not fit to be Captain. Would you relieve me?"

His voice came in a whisper. "What?"

"Take the ship. I won't object. I can't go on hurting people." I glanced up; his face was thunderstruck. "Or killing them."

He laughed bitterly. "You're the hero who saved *Hibernia*. I can't even hang on to my gun, and you want me to relieve you."

"Stop. Don't do that to yourself."

"You're the youngest man ever appointed Captain, and I'll never be more than a middy. Never, I know that. Relieve you!" He laughed again; it was a sob.

My hand closed over his. "Lord God help us both." We sat in unhappy silence. After a while I sighed. "Very well. Let's go about our duties. I apologize again for hitting you."

He attempted a smile. "Mr. Tamarov hit me harder, sir." We moved toward the hatch.

"Get a few hours rest before you report back to the bridge, Philip. In the wardroom, or take any cabin you'd like."

He looked at me curiously. "I'll be in the wardroom, sir. Where else would I sleep?"

11

Weary, discouraged, I returned to the bridge and sealed the hatch behind me. I knew better than to waste time looking for the missing weapons. On a ship the size of *Challenger* they could be anywhere. The crewmen I'd surprised rifling our stores had been wearing pressure suits; I hadn't gotten a look at the faces of the two who escaped.

Still, I could narrow my suspicions. We'd started with fourteen crewmen and the Chief Engineer, whose name I still hadn't learned. I doubted the Chief was involved; he appeared too lethargic to care. One man lay dead in the hold. Comm Specialist Tzee was busy reassembling the laser controls; Mr. Akkrit and Mr. Jabour were counting passengers and hadn't had time to join the raiders. Mr. Andros was in the brig. That left nine suspects. Two of them had gone to the hold.

I could haul the lot of them in for poly and drug tests; under the irresistible influence of the drugs the miscreants couldn't conceal their crime. But without other evidence against them, that was strictly forbidden. Anyway, we had no doctor to administer P & D.

"Bridge, comm room reporting."

"What is it, Mr., ah, Tzee?"

"I think I've got the lasers hooked up, sir. Could you release a test target?"

"Couldn't you program simulated fire?"

"Not if we want to make sure the laser cannon actually work, sir."

"Good point. When Mr. Tyre reports back I'll have him jettison some abandoned belongings. That'll do for practice."

As I replaced the caller I had the grisly thought of using the dead sailor's body as a target, but suppressed it. My relations with the crew were bad enough, no matter how much

I despised a man who'd take food from the mouths of his mates.

I made a note on my console screen to have Philip remove the body and release some flotsam for the lasers. Next, we had to arrange a food system so the galley could be supplied with enough provender to make our meals.

The comm room had to be manned; that meant training ratings to handle the laser firing controls Mr. Tzee had reconnected. We were supposed to maintain a twenty-four-hour watch over the recyclers; how could that be done with only thirteen crewmen in all?

The screen filled with my notes. Starting new plants in the hydroponics chamber was absolutely essential. The Chief—I keyed through the Log to find his name—Andreas Kasavopolous, had to be brought back to his duty. The bridge had to be manned. Even if Philip and I stood twelve-hour watches, an impossibility for more than a few days, *Challenger* didn't have enough officers. The hydro chambers would need extra hands too, to nurture the new plantings. The passengers had to be looked after . . .

My head fell back. "More help," I whispered.

"What, sir?" Kerren.

"We need more help."

"I've run calculations regarding your problem," the puter said smoothly. "*Challenger* has a crew of seventeen. If—"

"Sixteen. I shot one."

Kerren was shocked into a half second's silence. "Very well, recalculated. If each crew member works an eighteen-hour shift every day, you'll have just sufficient—"

"That's not possible."

"Mathematically, there's no other way. Even so, you'll be shorthanded for some less critical functions. You—"

"Enough, Kerren." He fell silent. I leaned back, my head spinning, took a deep breath. I had to get more help. I stood wearily. "Kerren, watch for encroachments. Monitor the recyclers and ship's power. Page me immediately upon any variation from norms."

"Certainly, sir. I'll be pleased to do that. You're leaving?" A second's hesitation. "The bridge is to be manned at all times while under weigh, Captain. Article 17 of the Naval Regs, edition of—"

"You man it. I'm busy."

"A ship's puter is not considered an officer for any purpose to which—"

I sealed the hatch behind me. On Level 2 sullen deckhands swept the corridor under the supervision of Mr. Akkrit. They came to attention readily enough; I released them and turned to their leader. "Have you a list of passengers and their cabins?"

"Yes, sir." Akkrit handed me a crinkled paper from his pocket. I scanned it. The cabin I wanted was halfway around the circumference corridor. As I turned away, I thought of the rifle I'd left by my console on the bridge. I shrugged. I doubted the panicked crewmen from the hold were prepared just yet to assault their Captain with their stolen weapons.

I knocked on the hatch.

"Who is it?" Walter Dakko peered into the corridor. "Oh, Captain. Come in." His clothing and belongings were scattered on the bunk, as if he'd been sorting his gear. He closed the hatch behind us, waited for me to speak.

I forced my mind to concentrate. "Mr. Dakko, I have thirteen crewmen belowdecks, not all of whom are reliable. One of my two officers drinks on duty."

He sat slowly on his bunk. "And?"

"I can't run the ship with the people I have," I said. "I need—"

The hatch burst open. "Dad, Greg and I found—"

"—recruits."

Chris Dakko demanded, "What are you doing here, Seafort?"

"Chris!" His father was scandalized.

"Well, it's our cabin!"

Walter Dakko said mildly, "It's my cabin. Yours is down the hall."

"What's the difference?"

The elder Dakko's temper flared. "Go to your quarters until you know!"

Father and son glared at each other, my presence forgotten.

Slowly Chris shook his head. "No," he said. "Not this time. You can't do that anymore." He walked out.

Walter Dakko released his breath in a sigh of exasperation. "You see the problem." His tone was rueful. He focused on me. "You were saying?"

"I need help."

He sat on his bunk. "Now you say you need help. Before, you said you needed recruits. Which do you mean?"

I was puzzled. "It's the same."

"No. Assign your thirteen crew to critical tasks. Working in the engine room or with the machinery. Let civilian volunteers tend the plants or help with cooking and cleaning."

I shook my head. "It wouldn't work. The recyclers have to be watched; any problem there could kill us. The regs require the comm room and the bridge to be manned. The—"

"The regs require?" His tone was incredulous. "What do regulations matter in a situation like ours?"

"In a Naval vessel," I said slowly, "Naval regulations apply at all times."

"We're a derelict ship abandoned to the doubtful mercy of Lord God!" He hurled a jacket to the deck, thought better of it, stooped to retrieve it. He brushed it clean and laid it gently upon the bed. "If we cooperate and work together we might have a chance. Damn your Naval regs! We just have to try to survive."

"We need the regulations for survival," I said simply. How to make him understand? "Officers in the Naval Service are trained to duty. They are educated in honor, taught the value of their oath and the meaning of dedication. Several of my officers on *Portia* volunteered for duty on *Challenger*, knowing the risk.

"But the crewmen—you probably know what they're like. To keep the ships manned, the Government offers a half-year's pay in advance as a bonus, and takes anybody. It's called guaranteed enlistment. Most of those men have no loyalty or dedication to the Service. They're kept in line by regulations enforced with stiff penalties. One reason the Captain is made absolute dictator is to restrain any impulse to rebellion in the crew."

Unconsciously I began to pace. "Rigid lines of authority

are set and maintained by the regulations. As you know, it's a capital offense for crewmen to touch their Captain." I stopped, to face him. "If the crew sees regulations set aside, ship's discipline will go as well. And it's already broken down. I had to brig one man to set an example, and I shot a deckhand who assaulted me when I caught him looting food stores."

"I heard."

"We're not far from a complete breakdown of authority. I can't allow that. 'Every man for himself' would bring starvation or worse." Grim images flashed through my mind. "In any event, I have no choice. My course is dictated by my oath."

"What course? What oath?"

"I swore to uphold Naval Regulations. Section 204.1. 'The Captain of a vessel shall assume and exert authority and control of the Government of the vessel until relieved by order of superior authority or until his death.'"

Dakko's face grew red. "You need our cooperation, Captain Seafort. You won't get it by spouting your precious regulations. They don't contemplate a situation such as ours."

I shrugged. "What does that matter?"

"Look beyond your petty rules!" he shouted. "If we're going to die on this accursed ship, what do your regs signify? How does your oath matter?"

I looked at him curiously. "How would the prospect of death abate my oath?" I shook my head in despair. "I already deliberately skirted my oath once. Worse, I refused a direct command from my Admiral, and I doubt very much it was an illegal order. I have no excuse. I'll not do it again." I reached for the hatch handle. "I came to ask your help." I opened the hatch.

"What did you want from me?"

"To volunteer for enlistment. And to speak to Gregor and Chris about doing the same. But obviously it would be better if I spoke with them myself." I left.

On the way to Gregor Attani's cabin I cursed my impatience. I'd alienated Dakko, when I needed him the most. I steeled myself to be calm and reasonable as I knocked on the hatch.

"What do you want?" Gregor's face bore no sign of welcome.

"May I come in?"

"I suppose." He stepped aside. I stopped short. Chris Dakko sat on the bunk, glowering.

I took a deep breath. "It's just as well you're together; I was going to talk with each of you." Quickly I explained the ship's predicament. "So I'm here on a recruiting mission."

A moment's silence. "You want us to sign up for the Navy?" Chris Dakko seemed astonished.

"Yes. You're educated and intelligent, and I need you."

"As officers or enlisted men?" Gregor.

A good question, one I hadn't considered. "Enlisted men, preferably. But I'd enlist you as an officer, in your case, if that's what you wanted."

"Meaning what?" demanded Chris from the bed.

I hesitated, chose honesty. "I won't have you as an officer," I told him. "You don't have the temperament." With contempt, Chris tossed a pillow at the bulkhead.

Greg Attani shrugged. "I'm not interested." He colored. "I mean, thanks for the offer, Captain. Sorry about my manners. But you must know we transferred here to get away from you. Nothing could make me join your crew."

Chris stood lazily. "Me neither. Go ask your trannie friends. They'll be a big help, I'm sure." He laughed. "Come on, Greg, let's check out the lounge."

I nodded shortly. "Very well. Thank you for hearing me out." I left, holding the shreds of my temper in check as I stalked toward the ladder. My eyes on the deck, I nearly collided with Eddie Boss.

He barred my path. "You!" A thick finger poked at my chest. "You no better n' dem Uppies! Givin' us cabins by ourselves, yah! Gettin' us off ship goin' places, leavin' us here!"

"Eddie, I—"

"Where we goin' now, Uppie Cap'n? Takin' us home? Backa N'York?" Rage suffused his heavy features. "You let 'em leave us behin' so we gon' die here!" His beefy hand closed around my arm. With a savage twist he flung me against the bulkhead. "Teachin' me read, sure! Alla game fo' you! You let 'em leave us trannies on dead ship, no food, no nuttin'!"

My ribs throbbed. With an effort I met his eye. "I'm on *Challenger* too, Eddie."

He wasn't listening. "Crew joey beat up Deke real good. I foun' him lyin' in hall like he dead, teeth all broke! We ain' takin' no more! Prong yo' ship and prong you!" His fist reared.

With my free hand I jabbed him in the chest. "Coward! Mira bigman Eddie Boss, jus' chickenshit coward! Allatime big talkin', thassall! No helpin', jus' talkin'!"

He let go my arm, regarded me with suspicion. "Whatcha wan', Cap'n?" He sounded calmer. "Why ya talk trannie? Ya ain' no trannie. Talk Cap'n talk, I listen."

I swallowed with relief. "Eddie, *Challenger*'s in desperate trouble. We're short of food, we can't Fuse, I haven't enough crew. I've talked to some passengers about enlisting. I don't know what they'll do. In the meantime, help me with the tranni—with your friends. Give them whatever cabins they want. Keep them away from the crew; the men are short-tempered. I'm sorry about Deke. I'm sorry you're in this mess."

Stubbornly he shook his head. "I gonn kill dat one joe, I fin' him. Deke my frien'. No one hurtin' my frien'."

I said, "Don't take revenge yet, Eddie. I need every sailor we've got. Please, as a favor to me."

"Yah, I wait, you callin' me coward," he sneered. "Ol' Eddie jus' chickenshit!"

I deserved that. "I apologize," I said evenly. "You were ready to knock my head off. I wanted you to hear me."

He studied my face. "Okay. You got 'nuf trouble widout Eddie. But I ain' no chickenshit; don' go callin' me dat!"

"Right." I put out my hand.

He shook his head. "Naw. I ain' no frien' wid you. You da Man. Ya din' keep Boss Cap'n from puttin' trannies on dis dead ol' ship. Keep ya frazzin' hand." He stalked away.

Moments later I was at my bridge console, pondering the failure of my mission. As I waited for Philip to return from settling into the wardroom, I realized I had no idea what my own cabin looked like. My duffel lay in the corner where I'd first dropped it. Wearily I picked it up, left the bridge once more.

I followed the corridor around the bend. Passing the first

lieutenant's cabin, I tried not to recall my folly with Philip and the barrel. Two cabins farther, I found the hatch I expected, with the Captain's insignia. The cabin was bare, clean, impersonal, larger than *Portia*'s, larger even than *Hibernia*'s.

Captain Hasselbrad had transferred all his gear. I stowed my clothing, set my picture of Amanda next to my bunk.

The cabin was furnished with a conference table, several straight chairs, and an easy chair. Nothing else. I sat. I hadn't slept for two days. I would rest my eyes a moment.

I jerked awake in confusion before remembering where I was. I glanced at my watch. With a curse I jumped to my feet; hours had passed. It was almost noon. In the head I ran cold water on my face, searched fruitlessly for a towel. Wiping my eyes on my sleeve I hurried into the corridor.

Outside the bridge Philip Tyre waited anxiously. He saluted.

"Sorry. How long have you been waiting?"

"An hour or so, sir. I didn't want to knock." By custom the Captain was not bothered in his cabin except in an emergency, and then only by ship's caller. Philip had assumed I was unavailable because I wanted to be so.

"Knock any time you want to, Middy." My voice was gruff. "Or call. We're the only officers, you and I."

"Yes, sir. Thank you." I doubted he would. Ship's custom has an inertia too great for a mere midshipman to deflect. He followed me onto the bridge. "The galley detail reported to me, sir, since they couldn't find you. They'll have dinner at seven, using whatever they scrounge from the larders."

"Very well." I glanced at my notes on the console screen. I had to deal with the Chief. And the comm room. And the hydros. What first? I thumbed the caller. "Mr. Drucker, call the bridge."

The return call came not from hydros but from crew berth one. "Seaman Drucker reporting, sir." He sounded groggy.

"How long have you been off duty?" I asked.

"Uh, three, no, four hours, sir. Mr. Tyre told me to stand the night watch and then go off for sleep."

I was furious. While I had sat in a funk Philip had done my duties for me. "Very well. Sorry I woke you. Go back to sleep and report to the bridge at four bells."

"Aye aye, sir."

"Philip, see if Mr. Tzee is in the crew berth sleeping; I don't want to wake him if he's been on watch all night."

"He's still in the comm room, sir." Philip squirmed with discomfort. "I ordered him to stand double watch. I wasn't sure you'd want to risk leaving the radionics untended."

"Taking a lot on yourself, aren't you?" I knew how ungracious that sounded. I paged the comm room. "Mr. Tzee."

There was a pause before his response. I wondered if he'd been asleep. "Seaman Tzee reporting."

"Go get some sleep. Seal the comm room behind you."

"Aye aye, sir. Thank you." He broke off.

The silent bridge seemed oppressive, reproachful. I sighed. "Thanks for taking care of things, Philip. I'm angry at myself and I took it out on you."

"Thanks, sir." He went on with a rush. "You need sleep too, sir. Nobody can expect you to be alert twenty-four hours a day." He studied the bulkhead, perhaps wondering if he'd gone too far.

He had. Such a remark from a midshipman to the Captain was scandalous. Except under the circumstances.

"I know." I was anxious to change the subject. "Go to the dining hall and see that Mr. Bree has what he'll need for tomorrow's meals. Organize someone to look after the passengers. Report back when you're done."

"Aye aye, sir." With a resilient step and a snappy salute he left. I wasn't all that much older than Philip; he was eighteen and I was but twenty-one, but I looked on his boyish energy with all the sour acknowledgment of an old man.

I sat at my console, trying to devise a duty schedule that would allow us to carry out minimal ship's functions. I knew I was wasting my time. It was impossible with a skeleton crew and only one functioning officer.

Every moment I dawdled, the lasers were unmanned, the comm room unwatched, and the ship's peril increased. Somewhere out there were those . . . goldfish, as we called them. They seemed able to home on our ships; I had no idea how. They'd already found *Challenger* once. If they came upon her again, our small chance of survival would be dashed.

And yet, keeping Mr. Tzee on watch until his forehead

struck the console wouldn't save the ship. I had to . . . I didn't know. Somewhere was a solution that was evading me, if I could but think of it.

The knock on the hatch startled me; remembering our missing weapons I glanced at the camera eye before opening. I'd been expecting Philip, but saw Seaman Drucker. Could it already be four?

I bade him enter. "The west hydros, Mr. Drucker. They need to be cleaned out."

"Yes, sir. But like I said, the machinery is all shot. We can't grow nothing in there."

"Manually, we can. I want you to take two hands and deal with the mess. Haul any usable metal down to engine room stores. Save the sand. When you're ready, we'll rig fluorescent growlights and weld some holding tanks. I want an inventory of seeds and an estimate of how many cuttings we can take from east hydros without weakening the plants there. How soon will you be able to report?"

He took time to think before answering, which I appreciated. I could see him grapple for the first time with the problems of command. "Depends on which sailors you give me, sir. I mean—"

"I know. Who do you want?"

"Groshnev and Jabour, if I could have 'em, sir. They're not the type who hang on to a broom to keep from falling down. Not like, uh, some others."

I grinned. "You've got 'em. Get started; we still have a couple of hours before dinner."

"Aye aye, sir." He passed Philip at the hatch as he left. I listened with half my attention while the middy described his arrangements. I stared at my notes left over from yesterday. So much to do.

I sent Philip to dispose of the body in the hold while I studied the ship's manifest. All our cargo was useful in some way to the colony at Hope Nation; perhaps it could help us too.

When Philip returned I took the caller. "Attention all hands. All officers and men to the dining hall. Passengers also. No exceptions, please." I glowered at Tyre. "Come along, Middy." Again we left the bridge. At the armory I secured another laser pistol, handed it to Philip. "Don't lose this one."

He blushed deep red. "Aye aye, sir. I won't."

A few moments later I strode into the dining hall, Philip at my side. Anxious passengers stood about, unsure where to sit. The crewmen, in unfamiliar territory, clustered close to the exit. Normally they'd eat below, in the crew mess on Level 3.

The murmur of conversation ceased.

The Chief Engineer stood, arms folded, near a group of older passengers; I made a mental note to speak to him after the meal. The transpop called Jonie huddled against Eddie Boss. Young Annie watched nearby, hands on hips in a provocative posture. She winked as I passed; I looked elsewhere. The remaining transients were isolated, or had isolated themselves, in a corner of the hall.

I paused in the center of the room. "Ladies and gentlemen, I am Nicholas Seafort, *Challenger*'s Captain. Before we eat, I'll discuss our situation. *Challenger*'s fusion shaft is destroyed and we cannot Fuse. We have a large supply of propellant for subluminous travel, but unfortunately there is no port, no star within reasonable distance. We expect to be rescued; *Portia* will send help when she reaches port."

There was a mounting rustle as the frightening rumors were confirmed. An older woman cried softly.

"We have ample power, and stores of food to last three months or more. We'll grow additional food with hydroponics, as we would if the ship were Fused."

"Why were we left behind?" a woman shrilled. "Your damned Navy brought us here and abandoned us!"

"*Portia* is smaller than *Challenger*. She couldn't take us all; her recyclers can't handle the load."

The seaman Clinger stirred. "And maybe *Portia* won't reach port!" Into the stir of unease he added, "And if she does, who says the rescue ship'll find us?"

"That's enough, Clinger." My hopes of conciliation were dashed.

"Let him speak!" The demand came from a burly middle-aged man across the hall. "We want to know!"

"Your name?"

"Emmett Branstead." He glared. "Let him talk! Maybe we'll finally hear the truth!"

"I'm telling you the truth," I said, as mildly as I could manage. Someone snickered. I realized I had to concede. "Go on, Clinger."

"The bad part is"—the sailor's voice was surly and aggrieved—"we'll never know whether there's a ship looking for us, or if *Portia* got hit too. Or if there *is* a rescue ship, when it might come. We could spend our lives waiting for help that never comes!"

In the back of the room, someone sobbed.

"And that ain't the worst." Clinger's bitterness swelled. "At best, it's eleven months to Hope Nation and eleven back to us, and we have only three months food!"

I cut through the frightened babble. "We'll grow what we need!"

"How?" Emmett Branstead. "The west hydroponics chamber is wrecked, isn't it?"

"Yes." I waited for the angry buzz to subside. "There are other ways to grow food." Silence fell. "We have dozens of unused cabins. We'll construct grow tanks in spare cabins. We have enough fluorescent lighting to nourish the plants."

Branstead shook his head. "Fluorescents don't emit all the components plants need to—"

"They won't be optimum, but they'd work after a fashion, no?"

Reluctantly he nodded.

"What about nutrients and water?" someone asked. "How can you pipe them to all the cabins?"

"We'll hand-water and feed the plants, as man did for thousands of years. Yes, it's work, but our lives depend on it."

Clinger snarled, "We'll be eating each other before this is done. Most of us are already dead, and don't know it!"

I bellowed, "Enough!"

"Why? He's right!" A younger woman with a stiff, drawn face. Murmurs of approval from the others.

"I'm Captain here!"

"Why should you be?" Emmett Branstead. "Our lives are at stake. We should have a say!"

"And us too!" A deckhand. "Sir," he added sheepishly, at my withering glare.

"That's quite enough," I said with careful precision. "You

men, stand at attention!" A few complied, Tzee and Akkrit among them.

Seaman Sykes was the first to speak. "It ain't gonna work, Captain." Behind him, a groundswell of murmurs.

"Belay that! I gave an order!"

A sailor said reluctantly, "Look, Captain, it ain't your fault, you didn't get us into this, but why bother with all the work? We're all gonna die anyway."

"We're still crew of a functioning—"

"No, we ain't!" Clinger again. "This ain't a Navy ship no more, like Andy tried ta tell you before you threw him in the brig. Look at us! Thirteen sailors, you, and that joeykid there! The hydros are all glitched; all we got comin' out of the east banks is cucumbers and tomatoes!"

"Clinger—"

"But even without no food problems, the best we can hope is to drift for three, maybe five years 'til somethin' goes wrong in the machinery or maybe somebody finds us. And only if that fat-assed Admiral gets through to Hope Nation!"

I strode up to him as if I were unafraid. "And if you're right, Clinger, and we drift three years? It's no more than a round trip from Earth to Hope Nation and back. You signed up for the long cruise, remember? And if you knew you were going to die, you would still have duty!" I jabbed him in the chest with a stiffened finger. "We have power, we have propellant; we have passengers to attend."

Stubbornly he shook his head. "If I'm goin' out, I want a good time first!" His laugh had a quality that chilled me.

I roared, "Stand to!"

Clinger looked for support, decided he had it. He folded his arms. Several others did likewise.

From the side of the hall Philip Tyre's thin voice cut the silence. "Carry out his order, Mr. Clinger." His laser pistol aimed steadily at Clinger's stomach. "You have five seconds before I shoot." He walked forward. The gun wavered, then stiffened. "I think I'm close enough so I won't miss." He said nothing more.

For a long second Clinger gaped. Then, capitulating, he stiffened to attention. Behind him, other crewmen followed suit.

My tone was bleak. "Do you care to spend the rest of the cruise in the brig, Mr. Clinger?"

"No, sir."

"Then henceforth you will obey orders."

"Aye aye, sir."

I let it be. "Stand easy." Turning to the passengers I said, "I appeal to all of you, men and women alike. We must have more crew; there's no other way to handle the ship. In a day or so I'll ask for volunteers." I overrode the uproar. "Certainly none of you sailed with the intention of joining the Navy. The idea may seem ludicrous, but our very survival is at stake."

I paused and cleared my throat. "We will eat in the dining hall together; we don't have staff to cook separate meals for crew and passengers. No food must be wasted; portions will be doled in advance. If you don't want all your food, give it to someone at your table. The crew will sit separately"—I indicated an area of the hall—"and you passengers may choose your own places, for the time. The Captain's place is here."

Arbitrarily, I pulled out a chair and sat. Philip automatically went to another table, his pistol thrust inside his jacket. The Chief took a third table; officers were accustomed to spreading among the passengers.

At first I thought I would sit alone. Then the lady with the pale, drawn face joined me. So did Walter Dakko. I noticed that the transients all found tables together.

When everyone was seated I stood and tapped for quiet. "Lord God, today is July 30, 2198, on the U.N.S. *Porti—Challenger*. We ask you to bless us, to bless our voyage, and to bring health and well-being to all aboard." The words sounded hollow, even to me.

Dinner was a miserable affair. Conversation was listless and dispirited. We dined on sparse food prepared without grace: boiled vegetables and canned meat, crackers instead of the customary fresh bread. The pale young lady, Elena Bartel, gestured at the tables around us where passengers sat. "You expect to fashion a crew out of—that?"

I glanced; elderly faces predominated except at the tables chosen by the transpops. "What choice have I?"

She smiled without humor, as if I hadn't spoken. "Old Mrs. Reeves, the judge's sister? Or that fat fellow, Conant?"

"There are others," I said, loath to be drawn down that path.

"Yes. Like Olwin, the engineer. But he's too old to adapt well, isn't he? Fifty-something? So that leaves the few youngsters with any education. That disagreeable Dakko boy, or his angry friend Gregor. How much help would they give?"

"There's yourself," I said, more to silence her than for any other reason.

"Me?" Her laugh was derisive. "*Challenger*'s resident neurotic? Since the first month the other passengers always make themselves busy whenever I go to the lounge to talk. Thank God for assigned seating or I'd have eaten alone." She flushed at my appraising glance, but persisted. "Look at me. Scrawny, uncoordinated, never even had a boyfriend, to say nothing of a marriage. I can't even tie a shoelace without fumbling."

"You're hard on yourself, Ms. Bartel."

She laughed, a sharp, brittle sound. "No, just honest, at the end. Now that we'll be dead soon I've nothing to lose."

My tone was harsh. "You have no reason to assume that. There's still hope of rescue."

"Oh, I admire you, Captain, despite my manner of speech. You're prepared to carry on despite all odds. Maybe you're young enough not to understand hopelessness. How old are you, nineteen? I once thought myself immortal too."

"I'm twenty-one, Ms. Bartel, and believe me, I know I'm not immortal. I just feel—" I paused before revealing myself to this bitter young woman. "I have my duty. Whether I'm to die or not isn't the issue. Duty remains. It makes choices so much simpler."

"I envy you that." She stared moodily at her weak soup. "You won't get many volunteers, you know. Perhaps none."

"I'm aware. Hopelessness is seductive." I played with my spoon. "You see, if we assume we have no chance, not only do we make it almost certainly true, but we live the remainder of our lives in—in a morass. In a funk. I don't want to do that, even if I'm the only one who'll know how I lived and died." I found myself near tears, and lapsed silent.

After a time she said more gently, "I'm sorry I jeered,

Captain. Tend to your duty. I expect to die aboard this ship in a few weeks, when the food runs out. I guess I don't much mind. Living hasn't been all that pleasurable." On that grim note our conversation faltered.

Afterward, as the passengers dispersed, I called the crew together and set Mr. Kovaks on watch on the recyclers, Mr. Tzee in the comm room, and Mr. Sykes in the engine room. Philip had volunteered to hold the bridge; I told him he was free to sleep on watch if he needed to, but he was aghast at the very suggestion. Then, utterly exhausted, I went to bed. My last thought before my head hit the pillow was that I'd forgotten to talk to the Chief Engineer. Somehow, he had to be recalled to his duty; the engine room provided the power essential to our survival.

Despite my fatigue, or perhaps because of it, I slept poorly, and morning found me bleary and irritable. I went immediately to the bridge. Philip Tyre, sleepy but awake, came politely out of his seat. "Good morning, sir."

I made my voice pleasant by brute force. "Morning, Mr. Tyre." I stared at my console. I needed coffee. "Hold the watch a while longer, Mr. Tyre. I'll relieve you soon."

I made my way to the officers' mess. There was no coffee made; I rummaged in the stores and started a pot. I paced while it brewed, then poured myself a cup. I sipped the hot brew without waiting for it to cool, anxious to get to the bridge to relieve Philip.

As I reached for the mess hatch it swung open to admit the Chief, rumpled and unshaven. I fell back. "Oh. Mr., uh, Chief. I was wanting to talk to you."

He sized me up with a skeptical stare. Finally he said, "I'd rather have coffee first, if you don't mind."

I waved. "Help yourself." Under other circumstances I would have found his remark intolerably rude, but there was no reason to antagonize him further.

He took a cup. "Did you make this stuff?"

"Yes."

It seemed to meet with his approval. "At least someone has some sense around here."

I sat back down at the long table. After a moment he joined

me. I tried furiously to remember what he was called. Finally I gave up. "I don't recall your name."

His smile was grim. "Andreas Kasavopolous. Chief Engineer Kasavopolous reporting, sir."

"They call you Andy?" I guessed.

"No." He stared moodily at his coffee. "No, they don't."

"Well, Mr., er, Kasavopolous, I—"

"They call me Dray."

I sighed. This was going to be difficult. "Tell me, Dray," I said harshly, "how long have you been a drunk?"

He tried to hold my eye and failed. He busied himself with his coffee cup in lieu of a reply.

"I asked a question, Chief."

He hesitated as long as he dared, then muttered, "I dunno, Captain. I just kind of fell into it."

"What would it take for you to fall out of it?" My tone was curt.

He shrugged. "Damned if I know." At my look of disgust he grinned. "What'cha gonna do, Captain? Brig me? I thought you needed me to stand watch."

I was outraged. Whether or not I deserved respect, my rank required it. I couldn't imagine what would have befallen me in my days as a midshipman if I'd spoken so to my Captain. "Remember who you're talking to!"

He chuckled mirthlessly. "Yeah, another reject from the U.N. Navy. What'd you do to piss them off, Captain? Forget to polish your service pins?"

"Shut up!"

"Or they catch you with some bimbo in your cabin?" That brought me to my feet, fists clenched. He fell silent. I stared through him a long, eerie moment while he licked his lips uneasily.

Blind with consuming rage I lurched to the ship's caller and paged the bridge. "Mr. Tyre, report to the officers' mess, flank. Seal the bridge behind you."

"Aye aye, sir!"

"Captain, I—"

I hurled my half-empty cup at Dray's head. He ducked away, drenched with lukewarm coffee. I snarled, "It would be wise to say nothing, Chief Engineer!"

A moment later the hatch flew open. Philip Tyre came to attention, his uniform rumpled, eyes bloodshot.

"As you were! Do you have your laser pistol, Midshipman, or have you lost it again?" My tone struck like a blow.

He pushed his jacket aside. "It's in my—"

"Give it here." Wordlessly he handed it to me. "Fully charged?" Pale, he nodded. "Let's check," I said, aiming it at the deck. I thumbed the release; with a crackle the smell of ozone filled the room. We stared at the scorched and smoking deck plate. "Get yourself back to the bridge, Mr. Tyre; you're on watch!" With a mumbled acknowledgment the boy fled.

I swung to the Chief Engineer. My gun came to rest at his head. "Put your hand on the table, Chief Dray."

He complied at once, a sheen of sweat on his broad forehead.

I seized his wrist with my free hand, bent it to the table, put the pistol to his hand. I croaked, "You asked why I'm here? Those fools said I was psychotic! What do they know? They hushed up the business with those sailors and got me off the ship!"

His face was like a grinning death's head.

"You're a drunk, Dray, and I need a watch officer, not a sot. So here's what we'll do. The first time I catch you drinking, I'll put your hand on the table and put the pistol to it, like so. Then I'll fire and cook your hand. I won't need to brig you, and you'll still have one hand left to serve watch. Doesn't that make sense, Dray? Answer!"

He babbled, "Yes, sir! Yes, Captain, it makes sense, I understand. I won't touch a drop—"

"I knew you'd agree, Dray. And that idiot called me psychotic . . ." He smiled in terror and relief. My pistol was still pressed to his hand. I moved it along a finger. "We have an agreement, Dray?"

"Oh, yes, Captain! Yes, sir! I—"

"So, we'll seal the bargain with your little finger."

He screamed, tried to wrench loose his hand.

I held tight. "Don't twitch, Chief! Don't even breathe hard, or it'll be the whole hand!" Gray of face, he stared in abject terror. "You see, Dray," I said reasonably, "you don't need five fingers to stand watch, and the stump will remind you every time you think of taking a drink."

His pale pasty face pleaded in mute despair; a sound between a whimper and a groan escaped him. Despite his efforts his hand twitched involuntarily. I smiled. "Well, let's get it—"

"God, don't!" he rasped. "Captain Seafort, I beg you! I won't give you any more trouble; please, sir! Please!"

I considered it. Then I shook my head in refusal. "No, Dray, if I don't take the finger, you won't know I'm serious. Sorry." I shifted my grip on his hand.

"Oh, Lord God! Please, sir, I can give it up! I'll show you where I keep the stuff, all of it! And the still, I can tear it down!" Sweat fell unnoticed from his brow. I hesitated, shook my head. "Captain, wait, let me take you there! Please!"

I said slowly, "But I want to do it, Dray. Fingers are fun. First they make a popping sound—"

He gagged. Then words poured out of him in a desperate plea for mercy.

Slowly, I let him persuade me. Grumbling under my breath, I followed him to the engine room storage, where his copper-tubed still dripped precious droplets of contraband alcohol into a glass jug. I watched impassively, laser leveled, as he smashed the still.

Then I watched him pour quarts of home brew back through the recyclers, his face frozen in a ghastly smile as he eyed the laser pistol I held on him.

When all was done I left the ashen Chief at his station, vehemently assuring me that he would never make or touch another drop of liquor. I headed back to Level 1. I stopped at my cabin, vomited my coffee into the toilet. Then I sat on the bed, head in my hands, until I remembered Philip alone on the bridge. I forced myself onto my feet and trudged along the corridor.

On the bridge Philip regarded me apprehensively. Bile rose again in my throat. I said mildly, "I'm not angry with you, Philip. That was for his benefit, not yours. Don't concern yourself." Slowly his face relaxed. I eased myself into my chair. "I'll take the watch. Get some sleep."

"Can I get you anything before I go, sir?"

I debated the state of my stomach. "Some coffee, I think. You'll find my cup on the mess hall deck." He looked puzzled, but left without comment.

The morning passed without further incident. I had Mr. Tzee break in a replacement to serve watch in the comm room, and Mr. Kovaks do the same for the recycler's watch. Still, with only thirteen crewmen I knew I couldn't maintain full watches for long.

I busied myself on the ship's caller, arranging for dinner supplies, seeing to Mr. Andros in the brig, organizing a rudimentary steward's service to cope with laundry and cleaning, making sure the galley and the hydro chamber were tended. I'd never realized how many jobs had to be performed aboard ship; many were accomplished without any attention from the officers.

Sweeping and mopping, laundry, manning the engine room, standing all necessary watches, the purser's various functions that kept the passengers comfortable . . . I marveled that *Challenger* had accomplished it all with a full crew of eighty-nine.

I had Kerren plot our course for home, but knew we'd have to assemble a competent engine room watch before I attempted any maneuvering with our thrusters. In any event, I would want to recheck our course manually with the utmost care, and I didn't feel up to it in my current state.

When dinner hour arrived I reluctantly sealed the bridge and left for the dining hall, dogged by a sense of guilt at leaving the bridge untended again. I reminded myself that with only three officers it was virtually impossible to man the bridge around the clock, and furthermore, until I saw whether the Chief was able to keep sober, there was no way I could trust him on watch alone. Better the bridge remain unmanned.

At dinner I was greeted with palpable hostility. My remarks on enlistment had obviously not gone over well. Even the young lady who'd spoken with me yesterday, Elena Bartel, today froze me with a glance. Only Walter Dakko was affable, and he seemed preoccupied.

There was little conversation in the dining hall, and less cheer. When our food arrived, portions were meager, the preparation unappetizing. I'd have to improve the quality of our meals or ship's morale would suffer dramatically.

Later I gave Philip the watch and plodded off to my cabin, reeling from exhaustion. I stripped off my clothes and fell on my bunk. I lay awake for an eternity, the ship's many unsolved problems running feverishly through my mind.

Finally I drifted into sleep, tossing and turning restlessly until Amanda quieted me with a soothing caress. Her warmth aroused me; in the dark of the cabin I turned passionately to her embrace and came awake, my body aching, my mind muddled. I snapped on the light, let loose the pillow around which I'd wrapped myself, waited for my heart to stop pounding and my erection to subside. My head fell back. I don't know how long I wept. Eventually I turned off the light and feigned sleep until the blessed arrival of morning.

I dressed slowly, willing myself to put aside my irritation and attend to ship's business. Carrying a cup of hot coffee to the bridge, I relieved Philip Tyre and took the watch. I spent the morning pondering flow charts on my handheld holovid, trying to determine the minimum number by which I needed to increase my crew.

It was a day in which I could get nothing done without interruption. First Mr. Kovaks, with questions about monitoring the recycler gauges. Then Seaman Drucker wanted to know about refitting the hydro chamber. Even Philip Tyre, hesitant now to make decisions in his Captain's name, brought me trivial problems concerning the passengers and the dining hall until, exasperated, I sent him off to bed.

When Mr. Bree called the bridge to ask my advice about the evening's menu I simply snarled and rang off. It was as if the whole ship had caught my agitation.

Rather than leave the bridge unattended yet again, I had a steward's mate fetch the soup our galley had prepared for lunch. Philip was asleep, as far as I knew, and would eat later. My first day standing watch on *Challenger*, and already I felt a prisoner on the bridge.

By midafternoon I began to eye the clock, waiting for the deliverance of the dinner hour. I thought of chatting with

Kerren but decided even silence was better than his excessive formality. I was savoring memories of Danny and his delight in our chess matches when pounding on the bridge hatch hauled me back to reality.

Cautiously, I swiveled the camera to survey the corridor. Outside, Walter Dakko anxiously shifted from foot to foot, ready to hammer again on the tough alumalloy panel. I slapped open the hatch, my temper soaring. "Belay that! What in Hell do you think you're doing?"

"Sorry, but I had to get your attention. I went—downstairs, I was looking for Chris—"

"Don't bother me with your problems!" I turned away, disgusted. If he'd hammered at my bridge because of his churlish son—

"I was on Level 3. I saw some men outside the brig, cutting through the door."

"Oh, Lord God." It had begun, and all too soon. "How long ago?"

"A minute or two. I came right here—"

"Get off the bridge!" I shoved him out the hatchway, snatched up my laser rifle. I sealed the hatch, ran to the ladder and scrambled down the stairs. Walter Dakko followed close behind. In a moment I was midway between Level 2 and Level 3; remembering lessons from another ship, ages past, I slowed as I approached the lower deck and raised my rifle warily.

The corridor was deserted.

I hurried past the corridor bend, to the brig. The hatch sensor panel was open and the wiring disconnected; the hatch was forced half open. Its hinges were burned through and bent. Cursing, I thrust myself through the opening. The cells were empty. Crawling out I bumped into Mr. Dakko and nearly died of fright. "Get aside!" I pushed past.

At crew berth one, I took a deep breath before I slapped the hatch. As it slid open I charged in, rifle ready. Mr. Tzee sat on his bunk, hands in his lap. I raised my weapon. He met my eye. "I know about it, but I'm not part of it." He held quite still.

"All right." I tried to slow my breathing. "Where are they?" With an effort, I made myself lower the rifle.

"I don't know, sir."

"Who?"

"Clinger, Sykes. One of the new deckhands from your ship. They'll kill me if they learn I told you."

"I know."

"What do you want me to do, sir?"

"Stay here." I had a better idea. "No, go seal yourself in the comm room. Stand watch."

He got quickly to his feet. "Aye aye, sir."

"Kovaks? Drucker?"

"I think Kovaks is in the recycler room. I don't know about Drucker, he was walking around when it started."

I grabbed the caller and thumbed it to the recycler circuit as Mr. Tzee brushed past to the hatch. "Mr. Kovaks?"

An endless moment, before he answered. "Yes, sir?"

"Who is with you?"

"No one, sir. I just now came on duty and relieved Stefanik." I wondered if he'd gone to his station so as not to be committed to the rebellion.

"Seal the hatch and don't open it until I give the order. Acknowledge."

"Orders understood and acknowledged, Captain. What's up?"

I set down the caller without answering. From the hatchway Walter Dakko gaped. I snapped, "Let's go. You'd better not be found here." I started back to the ladder, took the stairs two at a time.

Dakko panted to keep up. "Captain, there's something I ought to tell you."

"Later." I rounded the ladder well and strode to the wardroom.

"It shouldn't wait."

Reluctantly I stopped. "Well? What?"

"I'll enlist. Give me the oath anytime you'd like."

"You will?" It was all I could think to say. "You?"

"Yes." He regarded me with disfavor. "I imagine you intend to ask why?"

"Well . . . yes." I blushed.

A wry smile. "I suppose this is the last time I'll be free to say what I think. I'm not enlisting out of love for you, Captain; you already know that. But it's a choice between you and what you represent, or those men out there. And what they represent."

He shivered. "It may already be too late; I don't know. We're Roman citizens, Mr. Seafort, and the barbarians are at the gates. I'm no centurion, but if the barbarians storm the walls my citizenship won't matter."

I nodded. "I understand. Thank you. Repeat after me. I, Walter Dakko . . ."

He took the oath, there in the middle of the corridor, and was inducted in the Naval Service of the United Nations. Afterward I shook his hand, though that was not the custom. He stood, somewhat apprehensive, waiting for orders.

"I'll teach you the forms and courtesies later, Mr. Dakko. Right now, it's sufficient that you do whatever you're told, immediately and without question."

"Yes, sir."

"Aye aye, sir," I corrected automatically, then laughed at my foolishness. "No matter. Come along." I continued to the wardroom and banged on the hatch. "Philip, open up. It's me—Seafort." A moment later the hatch slid open. Philip Tyre, in his underwear, peered sleepily at the pair of us.

"Get dressed. They've forced the brig hatch and freed Mr. Andros." Philip thrust arms and legs into his clothes. "Never mind your jacket. Mr. Dakko has just taken the oath, by the way. Faster, damn it!" The boy finally had on his shoes. "Let's go!" I led them to the armory and fished in my pocket for the keys. I opened the arms compartment. "What weapons are you familiar with, Mr. Dakko?"

"I've hunted, in the game parks. Probably a rifle would be best."

I handed him one. I gave a stunner to Philip and took another for myself. Resealing the hatch, I hurried around the corridor to the comm room. "Open up!" In response the hatch slid open. Weapon ready, I glanced inside. Mr. Tzee was alone. "Carry on. Admit no one except me or Mr. Tyre."

"Aye aye, sir."

I led my small war party to the recycler chamber; Mr. Kovaks was secure inside. We proceeded to the east hydros. There, Mr. Drucker reluctantly opened the hatch at my command, eyed us uncertainly, came to attention. I was blunt. "Do you know what's afoot?"

He hesitated before committing himself. With a grimace he said, "Yes, sir."

"Are you with us?"

"Yes, sir."

I took a chance. "Who isn't?"

"I dunno, sir. I was in here, mostly."

I gestured to the open hatch. "Go join them, Mr. Drucker, if you won't answer."

"They're my mates!" His cry was a plea.

My tone was unyielding. "They're mutineers."

He tried to hold my eye and failed. "Sykes and Clinger," he muttered. "Andros."

"Who else?"

Drucker licked his lips. His eyes darted between Philip Tyre and Dakko.

My slap spun him halfway around. He recoiled, his hand flying to his cheek in shock. I glared from a distance of inches. "God damn you, Mr. Drucker, there's a mutiny afoot! Obey my order or I'll execute you on the spot!" My hand tightened on the pistol at my side.

"Akkrit," he mumbled. "That new steward's mate, Byzer. That's all I know of, honest." His eyes were on the deck.

"Very well," I said coldly. "Next time—"

"I'm sorry," he blurted. His face twisted in anguish. "Captain, I dunno what's right anymore. I wanna be loyal, but turning on my mates . . ."

"I understand," I said more gently. I groped for reassurance. "When all else fails, Mr. Drucker, do your duty. Uphold your oath; it is what you are." It had no effect on him. I prodded. "Where did they take Andros?"

He shrugged. "I dunno, sir. I got out when I saw what they were doin'. They had that rifle and the stunner, and I knew some joes was gonna get hurt." Out of the corner of my eye I could see Philip blush, trying not to squirm.

"Very well." Now it was my turn to hesitate. After a moment I took the stunner from my belt. I held it out, butt first. "Mr. Drucker, I order you to remain here, and to defend your station against any mutineer who attempts entry."

Astonished, he could only stare. Then he took the weapon,

knuckles tightening around the smooth barrel. "Aye aye, sir." His shoulders straightened. As I turned toward the hatch he added, "Count on me, sir." I smiled grimly. I would; I had no choice.

Outside in the corridor we conferred. "Secure the galley or search for Andros?" I asked Philip.

"Search where, sir?" the midshipman asked sensibly. The miscreants could roam the ship as readily as we could.

I shrugged. "The engine room or the purser's stores. Who knows? We have nearly a hundred empty cabins."

Walter Dakko said mildly, "If you don't secure the galley first—"

I rounded on him. "Speak when you're spoken to, sailor!" His jaw dropped. "Don't ever interrupt an officer," I growled. I knew he'd never been addressed in such a tone. Nonetheless, he swallowed and answered, "Aye aye, sir."

I was exhausted, famished, confused. The rebels could be anywhere. I swallowed, acknowledging defeat. "To the dining hall." I trudged wearily back to the ladder.

In the mess Mr. Bree gasped with fright as the hatch swung open and the three of us strode in. His eyes darted to our ready weapons.

"Why the panic, Mr. Bree?" I asked. White-faced, he licked his lips and made no answer. I stared at him a long moment before I guessed. "They were here?" He nodded. "What did they take?"

"I couldn't help it, Captain, honest," he babbled. "They had a rifle. They were going to shoot us!" He took an involuntary step back.

"What did they take?" My throat was tight.

He put his hands out as if to ward us off. "Please, Captain, I don't want to be part of it, sir. Don't put me in the middle!"

Philip intervened as my hand went to my pistol. "Tell the Captain exactly what they took, Mr. Bree," he said quietly. "We need to know."

The terrified sailor shot Philip a grateful glance. "The canned goods in the locker, sir, and the vegetables. All they left was the flour, and the bread baking."

I sank into a chair, stared at the bare wooden table. Philip came alongside. "I'll unseal the hold and get more stores, sir, if you'd like." I made no answer. I studied the grain of the wood.

Mr. Bree was hesitant. "I can make stew again tonight, sir, if I could have more canned meat."

"Shut up, all of you." My voice was flat, emotionless. Trying to carry on was folly. There was nothing more I could do but resign and let events take their course.

I sighed. I wasn't cruel enough to leave *Challenger* in Philip's hands. Not yet. But we would die aboard this ship; survival was impossible. I'd failed. I had only to live out my oath until it was over.

The silence stretched to minutes before I stirred. I stood heavily. "Mr. Tyre, take Mr. Bree's mate to the hold and bring back a case of canned meat and vegetables. Let no one else into the hold, reseal it when you leave, and return safely with the stores. Carry out these orders if it costs your life."

Philip came to attention. "Aye aye, sir." His tone was stiff and formal. He saluted, beckoned to a steward's mate to follow. Pistol armed and ready, he slapped open the hatch and disappeared into the corridor.

"Mr. Dakko, position yourself to guard the hatch. Let no one enter who is armed save Mr. Tyre." The recruit nodded and moved purposefully to the side of the hatchway. I crossed the dining hall to the ship's caller on the bulkhead. I keyed the caller to page the entire ship.

"Attention all hands. This is the Captain. All passengers and crew are to report to the dining hall at once. Mr. Drucker, Mr. Tzee, Mr. Kovaks, remain at your stations; this order does not apply to you." I replaced the caller. I dragged a chair into the center of the aisle. I sat facing the hatch, rifle across my knees.

In a few moments they began to respond to my summons. Walter Dakko coolly eyed each person who entered, weapon at the ready. Annie, the transpop girl, was the first, followed by several other streeters. Seaman Jabour, the deckhand, came, his expression uncertain. From my place in the aisle I motioned them to seats.

Gregor Attani and Chris Dakko arrived, gaped at the rifle in the hands of Chris's father. He ignored their startled looks, his eyes fixed on the open hatchway.

The Chief Engineer peered through the hatch before hesitantly entering the hall. I pointed to a table; docile, he took his seat. Eddie Boss stopped short at the sight of the rifle. I ordered him to a chair; he glared at me before deciding to comply. Other transients drifted in.

Several of the older passengers came together, huddled as if for mutual support. Mrs. Ovaugh walked heavily, with a cane. Mrs. Reeves, Judge Chesley's sister, followed with her husband, accompanied by Mr. Fedez and the Pierces.

Emmett Branstead stalked in. He glanced at Walter Dakko but did not stop. "Captain, just what do you—"

"Later. Take a seat."

"Not until—" I swung my rifle toward him, my face impassive. He subsided and quickly found a place.

The steward's mate peered cautiously through the hatchway. Seeing no danger he came in, lugging a box of foodstuffs. Philip Tyre followed, pistol poised, his face reflecting a deadly resolve. He stopped short when he saw Walter Dakko, but relaxed at my nod of reassurance.

Finally all had arrived who would. Somewhere in the bowels of the ship lurked six armed and rebellious crewmen: Clinger, Andros, Sykes, Byzer, Simmons, and Akkrit. Within the dining hall, all was silent. Even the transpops were subdued by the overriding mood of menace.

I cleared my throat. "Last evening I told you I would ask for volunteers to enlist. It is now time. The safety of the ship demands that a sufficient crew be formed. I call for your enlistment. Who will volunteer?"

Elena Bartel was the only one to speak. "I'd be willing to help you as a civilian, Captain. In any job."

"So would I, sir." Astounding: it was old Mrs. Reeves.

"Thank you both. However, I require volunteers to enlist in the Naval Service, not as civilian helpers."

"Why?" Emmett Branstead.

"U.N.S. *Challenger* is a Naval vessel and will be directed by a Naval crew."

Branstead's scorn was withering. "But you have none."

"I have the remnants of a crew, which we'll augment."

"Use civilians."

"No. Aside from hydros and recycling, I need crewmen to

man the lasers so we can defend ourselves. We have to keep a constant watch in the comm room. The engine room must be staffed to generate propulsion."

"With what, the thrusters? They're maneuvering jets, and we're nineteen light-years from home!" Branstead's red face glowered. "It's hopeless, you fool!"

From his nearby seat Philip Tyre sucked in his breath in rage. I stood. "Yes, nineteen light-years. I've calculated that after jettisoning cargo, by using all our propellant we can, over a period of a month, boost the ship to one-quarter lightspeed. If—"

Elena Bartel blurted, "That would mean seventy-six years to get home!"

"Yes. But—" The murmurs of dismay grew louder. For the first time I raised my voice. "But the radio message we'll begin sending on continuous tightbeam will reach Earth in only nineteen years. We will constantly send our position and course. By that time we will have traveled almost five light-years toward home, and—"

Emmett Branstead shouted, "You're talking a lifetime!"

"No. Some of us will be alive, and our children would be."

"Christ, you don't know what you're talking about," Branstead said with heat. "It would take them fifteen more years to reach us—"

"Under Fusion they'd reach us in months."

"And everyone knows you can't use all your propellant to accelerate! We'd shoot right past the Solar System, unable to brake."

"The rescue ship would match our velocity and course; we'd be off-boarded in flight. Perhaps *Challenger* might eventually sail through the Solar System, empty and abandoned, while some of us sit at home in old age, recalling our past adventures."

This time the silence was thoughtful. After a moment I added, "Or we can sit bickering until the supplies run out and we die. The jobs I listed—the comm room watch, the recyclers, the hydros, the engine room—require Naval personnel. I won't trust *Challenger*'s survival to civilians."

I strode to the ship's caller on the bulkhead and dialed the bridge. "Kerren, come on-line, please."

"Puter K 20546 reporting, sir." His formality startled me but I was glad for it.

"Very well. You have sensors in the dining hall, do you not?"

"Yes, sir, for emergency use. Normally deactivated for privacy."

"Activate your sensors and record. I, Captain Nicholas Seafort, do now call for volunteers. Who will enlist?"

No one spoke. I said again, "For the last time, I call for volunteers. Who will enlist?"

"I will." All heads turned to the pale young woman.

"Ah." I faced her. "Ms. Bartel."

"Yes. It's only for a few months, anyway."

"No, the term is five years."

She smiled bitterly. "I don't think it will be, Captain. But it's how I choose to spend what time is left."

"Thank you. Repeat after me. 'I do swear upon my immortal soul . . . '"

She raised her right hand. " 'I do swear upon my immortal soul . . . '"

" 'To preserve and protect the Charter of the General Assembly of the United Nations, to give loyalty and obedience for the term of my enlistment to the Naval Service of the United Nations and to obey all its lawful orders and regulations, so help me Lord God Almighty.' "

Solemnly her words echoed in the hushed chamber. When she fell silent I nodded shortly. "Who else?" I looked around.

"Me, sir." A stout, middle-aged man. "Chester Olwin. I'm an engineer."

"Very well." I gave him the oath. "Who else?" There was no answer. I asked again, "Will anyone else volunteer?" Several passengers looked away, eyes shifting in embarrassment. Two middle-aged men, some type of crop specialists, and some of the older women.

"I see." I walked slowly back to the center of the room. "Kerren, continue to record."

"Aye aye, sir."

I paced. "Pursuant to Article 12 of the Naval Regulations

and Code of Conduct, Revision of 2087, I hereby declare a state of emergency." My eyes roved the assembled passengers. "During a state of emergency, involuntary impressment into the Naval Service is authorized." I stopped in front of the table. "You. Stand!"

With shaky legs, Gregor Attani complied. I said formally, "I herewith impress you into the Naval Service and require you to take the oath of allegiance. Repeat after me. 'I do swear . . . ' "

I'd expected a refusal but he only asked, "Why? Why me?"

"You're young and you're educated."

He stared at the deck a long moment. Then he straightened, glancing quickly at his friend Chris. His face was grim. "I do swear upon my immortal soul—"

I finished administering the oath. "You! Chris Dakko!"

"No!" He stood to face me, fists bunched.

"I impress you into the Naval Service. You will take the oath."

"Like hell!" At his post by the hatch his father stirred, then was still.

I raised my rifle. "Repeat after me. I do swear upon my immortal soul—"

Chris waited, unafraid. "What will you do, Seafort? Shoot me, or all of us?" His laugh was contemptuous. "Then who'll run your bloody ship?" He held my eye. "If you'd make a slave of me, you're no better than your mutineers!"

My reply was cut short by a rough hand on my shoulder. I whirled, ready to do battle. Eddie Boss hovered, eyes blazing.

"Get away," I snarled. "This doesn't concern you."

"Enlis' me."

"You sit—what?"

"Enlis' me!" He loomed, fists clenched.

Briefly I closed my eyes. "I can't, Eddie. I need joes with education and skills. And you'd have to obey my every order, without question. You can't do that."

"Don' tell me what I c'n do!" he shouted. "You dunno!"

I backed away from his rage. "You're ready to obey, Eddie? Without any reservations?"

"What's resashuns?"

Behind him, Chris Dakko snickered.

"Holding back. A seaman must give total obedience, even when you're angry, like you are now."

He was silent a long moment. "Yeah, I do dat," he said at last. "Enlis' me, Cap'n!"

"It's for five years, Eddie." My voice was gentle.

"I know! Do it!"

I overrode my doubts. "Say: I do swear . . ." He repeated the oath, stumbling over the words. "Very well, Mr. Boss. You're enlisted in the U.N. Naval Service."

Eddie grinned triumphantly. He whirled, his massive hand a fist, and clubbed Chris Dakko to the ground. "You do what my Cap'n say!" he bellowed. The boy lay dazed, blood streaming from his nose and mouth. From the hatchway Walter Dakko watched, impassive.

Well, the Navy was nothing if not adaptable. "Very well, Mr. Boss. You're appointed chief petty officer. Your first duty is to help me shape up the new crewmen. Pick up that recruit you just knocked down." As he hauled Chris to his feet I added, "You'd better take the oath, Mr. Dakko, before worse happens."

Chris looked around, shivered. He mumbled, "I swear. All of it."

"Very well. Sit down and hold a cloth—"

"You need more, Cap'n?" Eddie blurted.

I said coldly, "Mr. Boss, this is your first order. Never—NEVER—interrupt your Captain."

He swallowed. His fists clenched briefly, then he relaxed. "Aye aye, Cap'n," he said with care.

I glanced at Chris, who had sunk into a seat, cloth napkin pressed to his bleeding face. I turned back to Eddie. "There are others who want to enlist, Mr. Boss?"

"Yeah. I mean, uh, yes, uh, sir." He pointed to Deke. "Him." The young transient looked startled. Eddie pushed him forward. "Say h'm his oath, Deke. Tellaman."

"I ain'—"

"Yeah!" Eddie locked eyes with the unnerved streeter, who after a moment capitulated.

Deke nodded. "I takin' oath, Cap'n. Swear."

"Very well. Who else?"

Eddie led me through the cluster of transients, pausing in front of some, ignoring others I'd have selected. I chose to trust his judgment. When he was through I had fifteen new recruits from their group: eleven boys, four girls.

I glanced at the remaining passengers. Most were too old to be of use. "Very well, then. The new crewmen will—"

"Just a moment, Captain Seafort." Emmett Branstead came to his feet.

I turned, angry at the latest interruption. "I've about had it with you, Mr. Branstead. I won't tolerate your interference."

"I'm not interfering!" His red face radiated anger.

"What then?"

"I volunteer."

I was speechless. As the silence lengthened Philip Tyre glanced at me and intervened. "If that was a joke, Mr. Branstead, it's in poor taste."

He glared irately at the young midshipman. "I wouldn't joke about anything so important. I'll enlist."

I found my voice. "Why, after all you've had to say?"

"I have skills you'll find useful with the hydroponics. I'm a planter; my brother owns one of Hope Nation's largest plantations, though I doubt you've heard of it."

"I've sat at his table." He raised a skeptical eyebrow. I added, "The plank table, in Harmon's dining room. I've met your nephew Jerence, who will inherit."

"Oh," he said in a small voice.

I savored my triumph, before I realized how mean it was. "So? You have skills, and you're donating them?"

"That, and—" He gestured at the transients. "You'll have your hands full. You need recruits who are educated. As you said."

"Your temperament is hardly adequate, Mr. Branstead."

He nodded. "I know what you think of me. But you'll find I will obey orders once I've given my word to do so." He held my eye until I was forced to look away, recalling Derek Carr's determination.

"Very well, then." I administered the oath. I faced the silent, apprehensive group. I had just added twenty untrained recruits to the ship's roster. We still needed more help, but

I'd more than doubled my crew and I'd have trouble enough assimilating so many at once.

I sent the new crewmen to the tables I'd designated for the ship's company. We sat to our meal.

12

Stew and fresh bread revived me; I returned to the bridge with a more jaunty step. I sent Philip, still armed, down to crew berth one to settle the new recruits. My first thought had been to hunt down the rebels immediately, but on reflection I decided otherwise. Untrained recruits with unfamiliar weapons were no match for tough, ruthless crewmen who knew every inch of the ship. I'd only end up killing some of my new crew and putting more arms into the hands of the rebels.

I paced impatiently until Philip returned. He dropped into his chair with a sigh of relief. "They're getting settled, sir. We found the stores and I issued uniforms and bedding. I took the liberty—" He flushed.

"What is it?"

"After I left them I put my ear to the hatch for a minute. There was some grumbling, but it sounded all right. I know we're not supposed to spy."

"That's right. If they catch you they'd never trust you again. Or any officer."

"Sorry, sir."

The corners of my mouth turned up. "I'd probably have done the same."

Philip, used to my moods, said nothing when I stood and began to pace. I had to deal quickly with the rebellion. But despite my anxiety, until we had the enlistees—and the inductees—well in hand, I had no way to regain control of my ship.

In the meantime, I could trust Philip Tyre and Walter Dakko. But I dared not press the loyalty of seamen like Mr. Tzee and Mr. Kovaks, who'd bunked with the rebels on the long voyage out.

I glanced at the two rifles leaning against the bulkhead, mine and the one I'd issued Walter Dakko. Perhaps I could set the midshipman and Dakko to guard the two ladders up from Level 3 while I systematically searched the bottom Level myself. No, that wouldn't work; I couldn't afford to lose either Dakko or Tyre, and besides, searching an entire Level would need more than one person; while I was in the engine room or a crew berth the rebels could slip around the circular corridor to where I'd already searched.

I pounded the chair arm in frustration. How could I conduct ship's business with six armed sailors skulking belowdecks? They could hold out indefinitely, unless I could deny them access to food. A chill stabbed. What if they burned through the arms locker and seized the rest of our weapons?

Good Lord. I hadn't secured the armory.

"Philip!"

He leapt awake, alarm and embarrassment playing on his features. "Yes, sir?"

"Go below. Bring back Mr. Attani. And, uh, seal crew berth one. Explain to the men that it's for their own safety. I'm concerned to keep the rebels out, not them in."

"Aye aye, sir. But couldn't Clinger burn his way through, the way he did the brig?"

"He won't know whether I've issued arms to the crew, so I don't think he'll take the chance. Show them all how to use the caller and instruct them to call the bridge or my cabin at the first sign of trouble."

"Aye aye, sir." He scurried to the hatch.

Fifteen minutes later, a knock. I swiveled the camera, saw Philip and Gregor. Inside, Philip saluted and came to attention. Attani, glancing at him, imitated in passable fashion.

"As you were." I smiled at Gregor to show my approval. "I'm glad you're making the best of a bad situation, Mr. Attani."

"Uh, thank you."

Philip glared at him. "'Sir!' Always say 'sir' to the Captain!"

"Thank you, sir." Gregor's jaw tightened.

It wasn't good discipline to undercut Philip in front of a seaman, but perhaps we were past such niceties. I said as gently as I could, "There'll be time for that later, Mr. Tyre. Mr. Attani is showing his goodwill, and my mind is on something more important than etiquette." Before Philip could respond I went on, "Gregor, I've inducted you against your will. Now I need to put my ship in your hands. Can I trust you?"

He thrust his hands in his pockets. Seeing Philip's horrified look he hurriedly pulled them out again. "Trust me? Not to double-cross you, or not to foul up?"

"Both, Mr. Attani. I want to leave the bridge. I need you to guard it." Philip bit his lip, shook his head at me, urging me to stop. "After I seal the hatch behind me, if you hit that red emergency seal on the console, I will have no way to get back in. No way at all." Philip's expression was aghast.

Silent for a moment, Gregor stared at his feet. Then he shrugged. "It's tempting, I admit. But to what purpose? To hand the ship over to the rebels? Chris is wrong, you're a lot better than they are. Besides, I've given my oath, which settles it. If it means anything, I'll give you another. I won't betray you, so help me Lord God."

Relieved beyond words, I blurted, "Gregor, would you like me to appoint you cadet midshipman?"

He shot me a surprised glance, then shook his head. "No, sir. I've given my oath and I'll obey orders, but that would be like volunteering. I'm no volunteer. I don't want to force other men to follow orders against their will. It wouldn't be honest, and if I don't believe in what you're doing, I wouldn't make a good officer." His gesture was placating. "I understand you meant it as a compliment, sir. Perhaps if I come to feel differently and you still want me . . ."

"Very well." Though I was hurt, I felt reluctant admiration for his honesty. "Mr. Attani, sit in that chair. Don't get up. Don't touch the hatch control panel. Touch nothing except this caller." I keyed the corridor camera onto the console screens. "Watch these cameras. If they show anyone other than Mr. Tyre or me, or if you hear any attempt to cut through the hatch, or if any alarm goes off, thumb the caller, like this, and call me. Don't move the caller key, it's set for the entire ship. Do you understand?"

For the first time Gregor seemed a bit awed. "Yes, sir. How long do you expect to be?"

"A few minutes. Perhaps more." I took my rifle. "Philip,

release the safety on your pistol. Guard behind us; I'll watch ahead." I sealed the hatch; no one could enter without the code unless Gregor Attani opened it from inside. Even with the code, I couldn't enter if Gregor activated the override on the hatch control.

I led Philip along the corridor, our weapons ready. We encountered only the looming gray bulkheads. My relief at reaching the arms locker was short-lived; its hatch panel was smashed, the keypad dangling. Without much hope I entered the code I'd set; the hatch remained closed.

I swore under my breath; while I'd made histrionic speeches in the dining hall the enemy had been busy. Had they gained entry? I scrutinized the armory hatch. It appeared solid; thank Lord God I'd sealed it properly. Once sealed there was no way to open an arms locker by shorting the wires; the thick alloy plate would have to be breached with heavy welding gear.

Philip waited patiently. I thought of retreating to my bridge stronghold, decided against it. Time would work against us. Three of us were not enough to man the bridge, guard the armory, and get a torch; it would take more than one man to hold the armory for any length of time. "Mr. Tyre, wait here until I return. Guard the arms locker."

"Aye aye, sir." His voice was tense.

I hurried around the corridor bend to the bridge and entered the code. The hatch slid open. Gregor Attani sat silently, hands clenching the chair arms. "It's all right, Gregor." I snatched the rifle I'd left behind, resealed the hatch behind me, ran back to the armory.

"Philip, put away your pistol and carry this. Go down the east ladder to Level 3. Watch for the rebels. Unseal the crew berth and get Walter Dakko. Reseal the berth, give him the rifle, and both of you report back here. Hurry."

His footsteps faded. Checking to make sure the safety of my laser rifle was off, I leaned against the inner bulkhead, rifle cradled in my arms, turning my head left to right every few seconds. I could hear nothing.

An eternity passed. Finally I heard their returning footsteps from the west. Philip hummed under his breath. As they came round the corridor, my grin of relief vanished.

I was face-to-face with Seaman Clinger.

He had a cutting torch assembly strapped across his back. Behind him two other men stood frozen, as astonished as I.

I moved in slow motion to raise my rifle. Clinger backpedaled, clawing at his pistol.

He got off a shot. A bolt of lightning crackled past my head; a white-hot knife caressed my cheek with infinite pain. I screamed. My hair sizzled. I managed to fire just as he threw himself to the deck and rolled past the corridor bend. I missed. Where he'd lain a second before, a buckled deck plate smoked.

Clinger's whisper was sharp and urgent. "Simmons, go round the other side, flank! Akkrit an' me'll hold him here!" The thud of running feet.

One rebel dashed around the circumference corridor to come at me from the east, while Clinger and his henchman menaced from the west. In moments I'd be under fire from both sides. I charged west, firing as I ran, but Clinger and his companion retreated, keeping out of sight around the corridor bend.

Unless I retraced my steps I'd be trapped too far around the bend to defend the armory hatch. I flattened myself against the bulkhead alongside the hatch, ear and scalp throbbing, my eye tearing. I resolved to fire at whoever came at me first.

From the east, a faint sound. I aimed. Nobody appeared.

It was all my fault, for letting them approach so near unchallenged. Cursing my carelessness, I leaped across the corridor to the far bulkhead, whirled to the east. I got off three quick shots at the retreating Simmons, then spun west to fire at Clinger, but he ducked back around the bend as he saw me turn.

As my beam sizzled past his head my rifle gave a warning beep. Its charge was nearly exhausted.

Clinger gave a hoarse yell. He too had heard. "Now, joes! He's almost out of bolts!" Not knowing what else to do I charged east, stamping loudly, then whirled and did the same heading west. I could hear footsteps scramble out of my way, but I knew the gambit wouldn't work for long.

A bolt scorched the bulkhead. I retreated east. "You're done, Captain," Clinger crowed. "Give up now and we won't—"

An agonized scream. It rent the air for interminable seconds. A gasp, a sobbing breath, and again a shriek. The thud of running feet.

I whirled to meet the new threat, finger poised on the trigger. Philip Tyre stumbled toward me, Walter Dakko close behind.

"Thank God!" I gestured toward the sounds of agony. "Simmons?"

"I shot him, sir." Tyre's face was green, his eyes glassy.

I squeezed his arm, guided him to rest against the bulkhead. "Steady, boy."

"I'll be all right." His voice was thick.

I pointed back the way he had come. "Quick now, around the corridor, both of you. Catch the bastard from behind!" We'd give Clinger a taste of his own medicine. As they ran off I checked the charge indicator on my rifle; enough for two more shots, at best. Impatiently I waited for Dakko and Tyre to get into position. Time passed. I could hear nothing beyond the moaning and crying of the wounded man.

"Mr. Tyre?"

"Here, sir," he called back. "About twenty-five meters from the armory."

"Very well. Move forward a meter; I'll do the same." Very cautiously I inched forward, rifle poised to fire. Nothing. "Again!" This time I threw myself against the far bulkhead as I dashed forward. I thought I saw a flash of color at the edge of the corridor horizon. "One more time!" I yelled. I jumped forward. A shape leaped toward me; I nearly fired before I recognized Walter Dakko. Trembling, I lowered my rifle. We approached each other with caution.

"Where is he, sir?" Philip's pistol was ready.

"The west ladder," I said wearily. "They retreated below-decks as soon as they heard my order to cut them off. They were a lot closer to the west ladder than you were, going all the way around."

Philip Tyre cursed long and fluently. I raised my eyebrow. I hadn't thought the boy had it in him. He ground to a halt, glanced at me sheepishly. "Sorry, sir."

"You said it well enough for both of us." I followed the corridor past the armory to where Simmons lay writhing.

Horribly scorched, he was clearly beyond our ability to aid. A laser pistol is a nasty weapon. "Look away, Philip."

"Wha—?" I saw his sudden look of comprehension and horror. For a moment he stared into my eyes, then obeyed. I lowered my rifle, put an end to the tormented moans.

When I turned back neither of them spoke. I said, "We need to cut through the armory hatch; my rifle has only a couple of bolts. You two hold the corridor here by the armory. No, better yet, hold the top of the ladders, east and west. Look over the railing and nail anyone who tries to climb from Level 2. I'll run down to the engine room and rummage up the gear we need to burn through the hatch."

"Take the other rifle, sir," Philip said. "It's fully charged."

"No, I can retreat if I have to, but I want you to hold Level 1 at all costs."

"But you can't defend—"

"Don't argue with orders, Midshipman." My face burned abominably.

It brought him up short. "Aye aye, sir. Sorry, sir. But please be careful," he added in a rush.

I smiled; it hurt dreadfully. "Oh, yes. Very." I nodded toward the west ladder and Philip went off. Walter Dakko accompanied me to the east ladder, took up his position at the rail. "Don't shoot me when I come back," I warned.

He grinned without mirth. "I'll try not to, Captain. It would help if you give me a signal before you come into view."

"Good idea. I'll identify myself as *Challenger*, as I would coming aboard." I paused. "And just in case, I'll call myself Seafort if I'm under duress. You understand?"

"Yes." Dakko looked grim. I decided it wasn't a good time to remind him of Naval courtesies, and went on my way.

At the foot of the ladder on Level 2, I poked my head cautiously into the corridor. No one was in sight. I hurried around the ladder well and continued down toward Level 3. About halfway, the reaction hit me. My knees began to shake so badly I thought I would fall the rest of the way. Clutching the rail, I sat heavily on the step while my cheek throbbed with a fierce fire. I took several deep breaths to dispel my dizziness.

After a while I felt well enough to proceed. I glanced down

the ladder to the deserted Level 3 corridor. Somewhere below lurked Clinger and his accomplices. I gagged, recalling the sweet stench of Simmons's burning flesh.

My hand crept toward my pulsing cheek. I willed myself down the ladder, but my feet had a mind of their own. They didn't move. With shock and contempt I realized I was terrified of what lay below.

The cool gray light of the corridor beckoned. I fought a silent battle with my fear, knowing that every moment I dawdled Philip and Walter Dakko's danger increased, and the rebels would have more time to organize. I stared down the ladder a long time before I realized I was beaten. Slowly, reluctantly, I turned and trudged up the ladder.

I would have to devise some other plan. Guard the armory myself, perhaps, while I sent Mr. Tyre and Dakko to fetch the cutting tools. Or summon Gregor Attani from the bridge to help Dakko guard the upper deck, while Tyre and I forayed below decks.

I paused at the Level 2 corridor, groping for the words to explain my change of plan. It wasn't fair. If only Clinger's bolt had injured me more seriously, no one would expect me to go below.

I took the first step toward Level 1, stopped, reluctantly turned myself around. There was no way I could face Philip with my cowardice. Better even to die.

"God damn it!" I ran full tilt down the ladder, heedless of the danger and oblivious of blasphemy. I skidded into the Level 3 corridor, rifle ready, heart pounding.

No one was there. The terrors of hell pursuing me, I raced along the corridor to the engine room hatch. I passed crew berth one and thought wildly of unsealing it and getting help, before I remembered that the men inside were unarmed. I galloped on.

I reached the engine room, slapped the hatch control, hoping against hope it wasn't sealed from inside. My back itched with anticipation of the impact of a bolt. None came. The hatch slid open. I dived in.

Chief Dray sat morosely at his bare table, eyes widening with shock as I tumbled in. "Jesus, Captain, I haven't been drinking—I swear!"

"Never mind that," I gasped. "Have you seen the rebels?"

He stared at me in surprise. "I heard noises, about an hour ago. Whoever it was, they didn't come in here. What happened to your face?"

"I need a torch and crowbars to cut through the armory hatch. Where?"

"Engine room stores compartment would have two torches," he said slowly. "There'd be others in the machine shop."

I tried to recall where to find the storage compartment. "Next hatch?"

"There's an entrance off the corridor, and one through here, from the shaft room." He got to his feet.

"Hurry, God damn you!" That got him moving, all right. If I made it home alive it would probably get me beached for blasphemy, as well. I no longer cared.

A few moments later we had a torch, gas bottles, and a big steel crowbar. I had him haul the gear while I led the way with the rifle. We moved slowly along the corridor toward the east ladder, the same direction from which I'd come.

I froze, hearing voices. They were behind us, a long way down the corridor. "Run!" I whispered, and we scrambled up the ladder.

As I rounded the Level 2 ladder well a figure loomed in the shadows. I yelled in horror and fired reflexively. I missed. Annie stopped dead in her tracks, her mouth working in terror.

"Oh, God, I'm sorry!" I cried.

"Why Cap'n shootin' Annie?" She crouched against the bulkhead. "Annie no trouble ta Cap'n. No fight. Why?"

I swallowed. "You scared the hell out of me, girl. Go back to your cabin and lock the hatch. Hurry."

"Why alla runnin', alla shoutin'? Who's—"

"Go!" I yelled, my temper irrevocably lost. She fled. I ran toward the ladder, Dray behind. Then I remembered, and stopped so suddenly he skidded into me and nearly pitched me over. "It's *Challenger*," I called hoarsely.

"Right," Dakko's voice was tense. I ran up the ladder, Dray puffing behind me. Dakko covered us as we ran.

I stopped for breath when I was finally out of sight from the corridor below. "Stay on guard, Mr. Dakko, while we see to the armory."

"Yes, sir." As I ran forward Dakko corrected himself, "Aye aye, sir." Despite myself I smiled, but my amusement vanished when I had to step over the grisly remains of the deckhand Simmons.

I had Chief Dray assemble his equipment outside the armory, while I checked the west ladder. Philip Tyre stood grimly, pistol braced on the rail pointed at the corridor below. "All's well?" I asked.

"Yes, sir. No sign of trouble."

I tried to contain my impatience while Chief Dray methodically cut his way through the heavily reinforced hatch. The armory and the bridge were the two most fortified points on the ship. Slowly the white-hot line advanced.

The bulkhead speaker crackled to life. Gregor Attani's panicked voice filled the corridor. "Captain, an alarm's ringing!"

Cursing, I dashed to the bridge hatch and entered the code. I dived through as the hatch was sliding open and slapped it closed behind me.

"I didn't touch anything, I swear!" Gregor blurted over the clamor of the bell and Kerren's urgent warnings. "It just started—"

"Belay that, sailor!" I stared at the flashing light on the console.

Kerren blared, "Engine room hatch structural failure! Hatch circuitry compromised! Seal code inoperative—"

I sagged into my chair, the bridge whirling about me. Wearily I flicked a switch and the alarms fell silent. Beside me, Gregor Attani sat hunched in his seat, turned half away from the console.

"It's all right, Mr. Attani." My voice was dull. "There's no danger."

He was near panic. "Christ, when that went off I thought it was those things—those fish attacking us! I thought—" His eyes filled with tears.

"Easy, sailor. You're all right." For his benefit I forced my voice to remain steady while I tried to think our problem through, my brain stuffed with soft cotton.

The rebels were seizing the engine room. Kerren's alarms hadn't gone off when they'd attacked the armory because the rebels had dismantled its hatch control panel first. Now, pressed for time, they'd used brute force and cut through the engine room hatch. The heat from their torch had set off the alarms.

I had to attack them before they could take over the engine room, but how? The rebels still had the rifle and the stunner they'd taken from Philip in the hold. My forces had a fully charged rifle, a pistol, and my own rifle, which had at most one shot left. Not enough weaponry to overpower them, unless I was very lucky, and I couldn't count on luck.

I'd have more weapons once we breached the armory. But that would give them time to take and fortify the engine room. The rebels would control the ship's power lines. I'd have most of the rest of the ship, including the bridge and the food.

I could starve them out; they could cut us off without heat and power. A standoff. I couldn't allow that.

"Hold the bridge again." I slapped open the hatch, bellowed, "Mr. Tyre!" Philip scrambled around the bend from the west. I beckoned toward the east ladder, where Walter Dakko stood guard. "Both of you, follow me!" I pounded down the ladder. "They're forcing the engine room," I panted. "We've got to stop them!"

We reached the foot of the ladder, on Level 3. I charged recklessly down the corridor, my troops at my heels. As I skidded around the bend the engine room hatch came into view. A leg was disappearing into a sizable hole cut in the hatch. My aim was off; I hit the hatch rather than the leg but the reflected heat brought a yelp of pain. I'd used the last bolt in my rifle.

Two cutting torches lay abandoned in the corridor. I heard a commotion inside the engine room. From within, a slab of deck plating appeared and was thrown over the gaping hole in the hatch. Infuriated, I threw my shoulder against the makeshift barrier. It gave way. I glimpsed a startled face, reaching hands, before the plate was slammed back into place. I lowered my shoulder and charged again, but somebody had shoved a wedge against the hatch; this time it didn't budge.

Too late. The engine room was taken.

I flinched at the cool touch of the medipulse against my blistered cheek. Walter Dakko pursed his lips but said nothing. His hand was rock steady; already I could feel the pain lessen under the humming ministration of the disk. Perched on a utility table in the corner of the infirmary, Philip Tyre watched anxiously.

"How long, Kerren?" I spoke from the right side of my mouth.

His voice came from the speaker. "At least a minute for each six centimeters of skin area."

"Please don't talk, Captain; I'm trying to hold this steady." Dakko's voice was polite but firm. At the edge of my field of vision Philip indignantly opened his mouth to object, but I waved him silent. Our new seaman was correct, even if no sailor bred to the Navy would have dared suggest that his Captain keep his mouth shut.

When he was done, Walter anxiously inspected my face.

"Well?" I raised one eyebrow.

"You won't be winning any beauty contests. Badly blistered. How does it feel?"

"Better." I cleared my throat. "Much better."

Outside the engine room, when the rush of adrenaline had subsided and I'd slumped against the corridor bulkhead, I'd become all too aware of the mounting pain that pulsed with every heartbeat. A few moments later Philip faded into a red haze while speaking. When I clawed my way out of my fog the middy and Walter Dakko were staring with unease. I managed, "You'd better help me to the sickbay," each word a wave of agony in face and neck. On the ladder I held off the blackness by sheer act of will.

Tottering into the infirmary I rummaged through the medical supplies until I found the medipulse I'd seen Dr. Bros apply to a sailor whose hand was crushed. I didn't know how to use it. "Ask Kerren," I grated, part of me marveling how mundane my voice sounded. My legs didn't seem to work properly; I'd had trouble getting onto the examining table.

Now, annoyed at my weakness, I put a tentative hand to my cheek. The skin felt blistered and raw. I could sense the light pressure of my fingers, but no lance of agony. "How long does it last, Kerren?"

The puter responded instantly, calm and polite as always. "Your nerves are deadened, Captain, and will remain so for some hours. Treatment indicated would be Compound Twelve burn salve applied gently to the affected area, and no bandage."

"Very well." I pointed to the stores cabinet. "It's probably there." Dakko searched through the drawer, emerged with the tube. I held still while he applied it. When he was finished I got tentatively to my feet, relieved that my legs supported me.

I crossed to the mirror, peered at my visage. "Good God." I'd have an ugly scar. Very nasty. I shrugged. A doctor could regrow the skin later, if I chose. If ever again I saw a doctor.

Now, what had I been doing when I broke off to go to sickbay? For a moment I was muddled. I'd guarded the armory, then rushed to the bridge. I recalled running down the ladder to the engine room to get Dray. No, it was after that; I'd gone back down with Philip and Dakko. I tried to focus. "Who's watching the rebels in the engine room?"

"No one, sir," Philip said uneasily. "We all came back with you."

I snarled, "Must I tell you everything?" With an effort I restrained myself from losing control altogether.

Philip looked to the deck.

"The rebels have the engine room, but we don't know they'll stay there. If we let them out they could roam the ship!"

"Yes, sir. There's the engine room hatch onto the corridor, and the engine room stores compartment, with its own hatch. One man couldn't watch them both. Besides," Philip added reasonably, "we didn't reach the engine room in time to see if all of them got inside. If they had already split up . . ."

The fact that he was right didn't improve my temper. "Where the hell is Dray?"

Philip was startled. "In the corridor, sir. He was working on the armory hatch."

"You left him alone? What if the rebels try again?" A spell of weakness slowed me as I made my way out to the corridor. I was near the end of my tether. I forced my pace to slow as I headed for the armory, though I felt an alarm akin to panic.

I'd brutalized Dray without mercy just a day ago, and left him thinking me quite insane. If he'd managed to cut through to the arms locker, no telling what he'd do. Take the arms and give them to the rebels, perhaps. Or gun me down on sight.

My mouth tightened. So be it. I could do only so much. My pace lengthened; I strode around the bend in the corridor.

Dray had breached the hatch. He'd cut a hole big enough to crawl through, to the arms compartment. He'd squeezed in, taken a rifle and a handful of recharge packs. He waited stolidly until I approached, and saluted. "I thought it best to arm myself," he said. "What with the armory open and all."

I cleared my throat. "Very good, er, Chief," My legs were weak with relief. "All right. Philip, you and Mr. Dakko go back to guarding the east and west ladders. I'll send Mr. Attani to help you after a bit. Dray, you and Gregor carry all the arms and ammunition to the bridge. If we can't hold that, we're done for."

An hour later I slumped in my accustomed chair watching the last of a surprising inventory of rifles, pistols, stunners, and ammunition being piled along the bridge bulkhead. The armory was empty.

What next? I now had a force of four I could trust: Philip, Dray, Attani, and Dakko. One man to hold the bridge, three to attack the engine room. How to get in, against armed resistance? I stared blearily at the deck. How late was it? Well past midnight. Again I perused the deck plates, jerked myself awake as my head dropped.

There was no more I could do tonight.

Wearily I got to my feet. I slung my arm through the rifle strap. "Dray, you'd best not go back below to Level 3. Sleep in a lieutenant's cabin along the bridge corridor. Mr. Dakko, you should be below in crew berth one, but I need you and your rifle nearby, so you'll sleep on Level 1 too. Use the second lieutenant's cabin.

"Philip, take a rifle and a couple of charge packs. Go with Mr. Attani to an empty cabin and drag a couple of mattresses back while I hold the bridge. Gregor and I will bunk here tonight."

"Aye aye, sir." In the corridor, Philip pointed. "The third looey's cabin and the Pilot's, I think, Gregor. They'll be the closest. Give you a glimpse of officer's life," he told the young sailor. They rounded the corridor bend. "This is what we—Oh, Lord Christ!"

"Philip?" No answer. I unslung my rifle, glanced to make sure it held a charge, and ran along the corridor. "Mr. Tyre!"

The middy sagged against the bulkhead, mouth working, eyes fastened on the grisly body of the deckhand I'd put to death.

Simmons lay in the corridor where he'd fallen, his shoulder and chest charred, blistered hand outstretched, fist clenched in lifeless agony. The eyes—I would remember them a long while. Dulled in death, still they held something that didn't bear imagining. I stepped between Philip and the corpse, turned the boy's shoulders to face the bulkhead.

"Chief! Mr. Dakko!" They came running at my call. "Find a blanket. Roll this—thing in it and put it out the forward airlock. Now!"

Dray grimaced, ducked into an empty cabin.

I handed Gregor my rifle. "You know how to use this? Cover them. Report back the moment you're—"

"Aye aye, sir!" Attani strayed toward the ladder, caught himself, blushed.

"Steady, Mr. Attani."

Dray emerged with a blanket. He and Walter Dakko knelt by the remains.

I led Philip from the ghastly scene. "You're all right, Mr. Tyre. Take deep breaths. That's right. Again." I guided him to the wardroom, slapped open the hatch.

The tiny chamber was impersonally bare but for Philip's duffel stowed neatly under a bunk. His few clothes hung in the minuscule closet. Normally four middies shared cramped bunks in such a compartment.

Philip Tyre stood docile, like a small child. I felt awkward, unsure. I was his Captain, not a fellow middy; there was an unbridgeable gulf between us. Yet he was in need, and I knew not what to give.

"Get ready for bed, Philip."

"Aye aye, sir." Mechanically he began to strip off his clothes. Instead of tossing them carelessly on the chair as I'd done all too often, he hung his jacket and pants with care, and creased them neatly on hangers before setting them in the closet.

As he fumbled at his shirt buttons, his eyes changed, his fingers became still. I could guess what image had returned, unbidden. I was ready to snap something harsh, recall him to reality, but instead I shut my mouth, stern words unspoken, and went to him, knowing there was wrong in any contact that diminished the distance between us. All the same, I felt compassion rather than guilt as I gently undid the buttons of his shirt. "Go to bed," I said quietly.

Startled, he glanced up, young and trusting. "Aye aye, sir." Turning, he steadied himself against the end table to remove his socks; past the seams of his undershorts I saw the red, angry welt I had put across his buttocks. I closed my eyes.

In his bunk he lay on his back, eyes rigid. Not knowing what else to do, I took the cover and tossed it across his still form. "Good night, Philip. You'll feel better in the morning." At the hatch, I switched off the light.

"Thank you, sir." His tone was unsteady.

I flicked the light on.

Philip lay on his back, clutching the blanket. When my gaze met his he snapped his eyes shut, too late to hide the tear that trickled down his cheek. Reluctantly I approached his bunk. He blinked, tried several times to speak. Finally he whispered, "I'm afraid!" After, he couldn't meet my eye.

I sat on the edge of the bed. "I know."

"That man . . . his face . . ."

I tried not to recall the nightmares I'd suffered from other sightless eyes, long in the past. "It's all right."

"He looked at me, just before I—I shot him. He was raising his gun. For a split second he knew. That he was too late. What was going to happen."

"It's all right," I said again, wishing I had words of comfort.

"And then he—sizzled! Oh, Jesus God!" He flung himself to the bulkhead.

My hand, as if on its own volition, stole to his shoulder. After a long moment he whispered, "I'm so frightened."

Philip had done his duty. He'd have been killed if he hadn't shot first; surely he knew that. I intended to say as much, but someone blurted in my voice, "So am I."

He turned in wonder. "You?"

"Of course," I snapped. "Don't I have the right?"

"It's . . . I never thought you felt—sorry, it's none of my business. Of course you have the right."

"Then why don't you?"

He lay still, thinking it over. After a time he offered a shy, tentative smile. "I'm sorry. I was foolish. I just tried to live up to what you expect."

I said gruffly, "I don't expect you to be more than human. It was horrible, what you had to do to that man. I don't know how you could carry on. I might not have." That was laying it on a bit thick, but he needed it. And deserved it, after what I'd done to him.

He looked puzzled. "I just put it in the back of my mind. There was work to do. I couldn't afford to dwell on it."

I could see him expand with pride. It took so little, I thought with sadness. I, the Captain, was as a god to a lowly midshipman. One word of anger could be devastating. And a word of praise . . .

"You've done well, Middy. I'll remember it." Meaningless words. What could I give him? A decoration? A promotion that no one beyond the ship would ever see? "You'll be able to sleep now," I said, as if I knew. "In the morning I'll need your help organizing the recruits. Good night."

"Good night, sir." This time his smile was less tentative. For some reason I didn't understand I reached down, ruffled his hair. Abruptly I strode to the hatch, snapped off the light. I left without looking back.

Dray, Dakko and Gregor had rounded up the mattresses I'd ordered, and waited patiently outside the sealed bridge. I unsealed the hatch and we lugged in the bedding. Someone had found clean sheets and pillows as well. I thanked them, sent Dray and Dakko on their way, and sealed Gregor and myself onto the bridge. "Kerren, monitor the cameras and sound the alarms the moment anyone approaches. And wake me at eight."

"Very well, Captain."

I dimmed the lights and dropped onto my mattress with a sigh. Young Attani sat warily on the other bed, eyes carefully turned away. It was several long minutes before he lay down, facing away from me.

I lay on my back, arm over my eyes, waiting for sleep. My body felt drained, lethargic. While Gregor tossed and turned I marveled that I'd made it through the day, and wondered what horrors were still to come. I drowsed.

"Excuse me?"

My eyes opened. "Yes?"

"Could I . . . I mean, would you let . . . maybe . . . oh, Christ!"

"Don't blaspheme," I said automatically. He didn't answer. "What, Mr. Attani?"

"Nothing. I mean, nothing, sir."

I snapped, "You woke me for that?"

"I'm sorry."

The silence hung between us.

"Tell me."

A moment passed before his reluctant answer. "I know it's stupid. I was going to ask if I could sleep downstairs. Below."

"Why?"

No response.

I recalled another recruit, eons ago: Derek. I said gently, "You've never slept sharing a room?"

"I know it's silly." His voice was muffled. "But I thought, if I could go back downstairs . . . Then I remembered I wouldn't be in my own cabin. I'd be in the crew berth, with all the others."

I lay back, finding it hard to sympathize. He was seventeen. No, eighteen; I'd been at his birthday party, strolling through the haughty crowd with Amanda. Those damned aristocrats; what kind of lives did they lead, sequestered in luxurious towers, isolated from ordinary human contact? I hadn't known privacy after the age of thirteen, when Father brought me to Academy. I'd learned to tolerate the teeming dormitories at Farside, then the crowded midshipmen's wardroom . . .

Had it really been three years since I'd bunked in a wardroom? Abruptly I'd been catapulted to the splendid isolation of the Captain's cabin. What loneliness I'd felt! Now, of course, I was used to it, and I could barely imagine myself coping with a wardroom's enforced intimacy.

I cleared my throat. "I understand what you're going through." It wasn't much.

"Thank you. Thank you, *sir*. I have to remember to say 'sir.'"

"Yes, that's expected. You'll get used to it." I sought some words of reassurance. "As you'll get accustomed to the crew berth. It's not as bad as you imagine."

"Right." We lay in silence. Then, to my astonishment, he began to cry. My surprise was tinged with exasperation. Had I triggered his response? And would I ever be allowed to sleep? I glanced at my watch; we weren't far from morning.

"What now, Mr. Attani?" I chose his last name, to put distance between us and to remind him of his status.

He drew in a ragged breath. "I'm feeling sorry for myself." His honesty was painful. "And I'm ashamed."

"Why?"

"Do you know why I'm on *Challenger*?" I was silent. "I hated you and leaped at the chance to escape. And then they told us the fusion drive was wrecked . . . so I'd just made my situation worse. I was stuck with you, perhaps for the rest of my life. And I've watched you trying so hard to be fair, and being so kind . . ."

"Kind?" I echoed, incredulous.

"To Mr. Tyre. The way you put yourself between him and the sailor's body. Your voice. And to the others. Even to me. I've misjudged you so badly."

"You're overwrought," I muttered. "It's been a frightful day. I'm not as kind as you think."

"I'll shut up, if that's what you want. But I know when I've made a fool of myself."

His dogged integrity brought a sting to my eyes. I groped for a way to reassure him. I was failing with him, as I'd failed with Philip. A thought flashed: Philip and Gregor . . .

I cleared my throat. "Very well, perhaps you misjudged me. And I've misjudged you. I was wrong to enlist you as a sailor."

"Sir?" His voice was unsteady.

"Regardless of what you think, you're fit for the wardroom. I'm making you a midshipman cadet. Don't worry much about hazing. We don't have time for that."

"But I—"

"It's not your decision, Mr. Attani, it's mine. I'm impressing you as an officer rather than as a seaman."

There was a long silence. "But why, sir?"

"You'll be more help to me that way. That's all you need to know."

A contemplative pause. "Yes, sir."

I rolled over to sleep. Then I relented. "Because you deserve it. You'll make a good officer. Once we knock the haughty insolence out of you, that is."

"I will?"

"Yes." I don't know if I said the word aloud as I tumbled into black, dreamless sleep.

13

"Are you sure, sir?" Philip bit his lip and looked at me doubtfully. "I mean—before when I—had the wardroom . . . I didn't do very well." He reddened.

"You've changed. I'm certain I can trust you." I spoke with assurance I was almost sure I felt.

"He's rather old to start as a cadet." Realizing it sounded like criticism he rushed on, "I'll be very careful, sir. Not to hurt him. I'll get him settled this afternoon. And it'll . . ." He blushed. "It will be nice to have company."

"Yes." I knew the closeness the experience would engender, and wistfully wished I could share it. Then I brushed away the foolishness.

It was midmorning and I felt somewhat refreshed despite my pitifully few hours of sleep. Nonetheless, my inflamed cheek ached miserably. I'd have to stop at the infirmary when I had a moment.

I'd sent Philip and Chief Dray below, heavily armed, to release the crew from their berth and escort them back to Level 1. They'd encountered no rebels. The engine room hatch was still blocked.

I picked four crewmen I'd decided to trust with weapons: Mr. Drucker, Mr. Tzee, Emmett Branstead, and Elena Bartel. While Dray and Walter Dakko guarded the ladders from Level 2 we made a thorough search of Level 1. No rebels. It was a start; at least now I knew our uppermost Level was secure. I sat with a steaming cup of coffee to ponder my next move, wondering how much more time the mutineers would give me.

My coffee finished, we proceeded cautiously down the west ladder to Level 2. I sealed the emergency corridor hatch between sections six and seven, east of the ladder. We proceeded west, checking each cabin and compartment. We shepherded all the passengers we encountered to the dining hall, on Level 1.

The hatch to the launch berth was undamaged; that meant the cargo holds, accessible through the launch berth, were still in our hands. As we searched I tried to be everywhere, while Gregor, at my orders, tagged along as a gofer. After two tense hours we'd secured the remainder of Level 2.

I assembled my forces at the ladder to Level 3, where Walter Dakko patiently let me show him how to guard the ladder wells he'd competently been watching for two days. At the sound of running steps I broke off my lecture. Dakko, ready to fire, eased his finger from the trigger as Charlie, a streeter, skidded to a stop at the bottom of the ladder.

"Don't be shootin', Cap'n, it's me! Dey comin' out!"

"The rebels? From the engine room?"

"Someone comin' out, yeah! I don' wan' be wid 'em, dey gonn' hurt some joe!"

"Up here, fast!" The boy bolted up the ladder. "Who else is down there?"

"Trannies? Annie, Scor, Dawg, maybe more. Inna room, allem."

I turned to my new cadet. "Gregor, have Ms. Bartel reinforce Dray at the west ladder. Bring the three other armed sailors to this ladder, flank!"

"Yes, sir!" Attani sprinted off. Moments later Tzee, Drucker and Branstead hurried around the bend, Gregor trotting at their heels.

I pointed. "They're down on Level 3, somewhere outside the engine room. We're going below. Be ready to fire, but don't shoot a passenger. Let's go!" I rounded the ladder well.

The corridor speaker crackled. "Captain, time we did some talkin'." Andros, the contemptuous deckhand Clinger had freed from the brig.

I froze. Behind me my war party halted.

"You hear me, Captain? What we got is a standoff. You got the food and the guns, I got the power and water lines. An' a bunch of your passengers, them trannie kids. Understand?"

I picked up the caller. "I hear you, Andros. Put down your weapons."

"Not a chance."

"What's this about? We're all marooned together; what's the point in rebellion?"

"Point?" A guffaw. "That frazzin' Admiral din' care if we live or die. We got nothin'. It'll be over soon enough. Think we—"

"There's hope. We'll grow food, wait for resc—"

"Think we want to live our last days poppin' salutes an' goin' 'yes, sir' an' 'aye aye, sir'? We're men, not Navy machines!"

"You signed up."

"For the bonus, yeah. And like all the other joeys, I spent it 'fore we left port. Now all we got is this mess. Well, I ain't goin' this way. There's women aboard, enough food for some zarky parties. So, here's the deal. Take—"

"Andros, give it up. We can't afford to have anyone else killed. You'll ruin everyone's chances."

"Nah. Like we said, we're going our own way. There's nothin' you can do."

Abruptly I realized the whole ship could hear our dialogue. "I'm heading to the bridge. I'll call you from there."

"Nah, let 'em all listen; ain't nothin' to me. Let your precious passengers know how bad things are. And that fraz Drucker, he listenin'? I owe him."

I keyed the caller to the bridge. "Kerren, can you override the engine room circuit so they can't page the entire ship?"

"Negative, Captain," the puter said. "Critical stations—bridge, comm room, engine room—have equal access in case of emergency. It's a safety feature and I have no override."

"Very well." I thumbed the caller back to the engine room. Andros might speak over the ship-wide circuit, but I'd be damned if I'd do the same. Let those who would listen decipher what they could from his end of the conversation.

"Andros, you can't get away with it. Surrender now and you'll save lives."

He guffawed. "Sure. Sail us into port and we'll surrender."

"There's no way you can take the ship. I've got the upper two Levels, the bridge, the comm room, and all the guns."

"Not all the guns," the speaker interrupted. "We got a rifle and the stunner, and we figured out how to recharge them. We have the machine shop. You don't know what we're cookin' up here."

"I'm coming after you."

"The hell you are, fraz." From behind him, a gasp. Mutineers they might be, but discipline died hard.

"I'm done talking, Andros. Your choice is, surrender or die."

"No. Your choice is, leave us be or we cut your power. Sykes thinks he can disconnect the lines to the rest of the ship and leave us with power in the engine room."

I keyed the caller. "Kerren, can he do that?"

An infinitesimal pause. "I judge it relatively complicated for human understanding, but the Chief Engineer could do it, with a manual. I don't know what would result if an untrained seaman made the attempt. Power feed lines need to be rerouted with bridges. My records show Sykes with a grade five education level, marginal literacy."

"What about Andros?"

"Grade nine overall. Adequate literacy. Diagnosed emotionally unstable at enlistment testing."

I thumbed the caller. "Andros, this is no standoff. We can do without power awhile; the bridge has emergency backups. I can keep my passengers and crew alive while we wait you out. You'll starve soon enough."

"Maybe," he said indifferently. "After we eat the trannies." Gregor sucked in his breath. In the speaker, Andros giggled. "That girl, that Annie, she's kinda scrawny. Except certain places." His voice grew hard. "So don't push, Seafort. An' remember the hydroponics. We got them down here too. They're sealed, sure, but how long you think it'll take us to get in? How'd you like a chamber full of shredded plants? Worse come to worse, we could probably blow up the whole ship if we try. You going to kill us, what else we got to lose?"

I wracked my brain, with no success. "I'll call you back," I said at last.

"Do that, Seafort. And don't get ideas about stallin' while you set something up. I'll be happy to fry a trannie for a demo."

Dazed, I left my attack party and made my way to the bridge, knowing that his broadcast had done incalculable damage to our morale. I'd been manipulated; I had lost the initiative to a demented sailor. How had it come to that? If I'd used sense last night, and put a guard at the engine room. Or attacked an hour earlier. Or—anything.

Philip, watching the corridor camera from the bridge, opened the hatch, sealed it behind me as I dropped into my chair. He was diplomatically silent.

In my humiliation, I found it hard to meet his eye. "It seems I have a problem."

"Yes, sir. Do you think he means it?"

"I don't want to find out. Call Dray." I shut my eyes, tried to stir my dulled mind. I'd have to give in, or at least fashion a compromise, even if they were mutineers.

I glanced at the blankened simulscreen. The same screen, I recalled, at which I'd shouted my defiance to Admiral Tremaine, forsworn my oath of obedience, and very possibly damned myself. I sat in the same chair in which I'd resolved never again to betray the oath that bound me.

I was certain I knew the relevant section of the regs, but I called them up on my console and read the passage again.

The Captain of a vessel shall assume and exert authority and control of the Government of the vessel until relieved by order of superior authority, until his death, or until certification of his disability as otherwise provided herein.

If I ceded part of my ship or my command to rebels, I'd be in blatant violation of the regs I'd sworn to uphold.

But the regs didn't contemplate a situation like ours. We were stranded, perhaps for a lifetime, without experienced officers, with only a few crew—

Yet *Challenger* was a Naval vessel, and I was in charge.

I couldn't send my few untrained men into battle while I waited timidly behind the fortified bulkheads of the bridge. I'd have to lead them myself. But if I were killed, who would run the ship?

No. I wouldn't circumvent truth with sophistry; my duty was clear enough. What did it matter if I died trying to perform it? My responsibility was to preserve my oath, not myself.

I would be dead a very long time, until the distant day Lord God called us all, and time ended.

An inconceivably long time.

But then I would be one with Amanda. And Nate. I tried to master the trembling in my limbs as I prepared to stand.

The trannies. The streeters. I could accept, just barely, the probability of my own death. But in attacking the rebels I'd doom innocent passengers. How many hostages did Andros say he'd taken? I couldn't remember. "Did you record, Kerren?"

"Yes, sir."

"Play back." When the grim exchange had replayed I realized Andros hadn't revealed the number of his prisoners. We'd embarked with forty-two transpops; I recalled my fury when Alexi Tamarov had told me of them, centuries past. Three died in the raid by the fish. I'd enlisted Eddie and fifteen others. That left . . . twenty-three. "Philip, who's minding the passengers?"

"I put Mr. Kovaks in charge, sir, the recycler's-mate. I couldn't think who else to trust."

"Excuse me, sir," Kerren interjected. "Chief Kasavopolous is approaching the bridge."

"Very well, let him in. Philip, find out how many transients Kovaks has in the dining hall."

As Dray entered I raised a palm, telling him to wait. In a moment the caller buzzed. "Fourteen trannies, sir."

Nine hostages, then. Nine amoral, uncivilized joeys plucked from filthy, crowded streets, clothed, warehoused, selected for a foolish experiment, and ferried nineteen light-years from home, to die abandoned on *Challenger*.

Perhaps I could stall Andros long enough to organize. I might give my crew rudimentary training in weapons and mount an assault on Level 3. With luck I could retake the engine room, at the cost of some of my recruits and my own life.

And the nine transpops.

Their deaths would not be comparable to losing crewmen in battle. The crew, at least, had chosen this voyage. They'd accepted some risk, though they couldn't have known how great and strange it would be.

But the transients were pawns in a bureaucratic game of indifference. And not much more than children, at that. I couldn't throw them away uncaring.

But my oath?

There had to be a way. I slumped in the chair, staring at the console, trying to recall the layout of the engine room.

The speaker crackled. "Crewman in corridor, Captain."

"What the—thank you, Kerren." I swiveled the camera. Eddie Boss, shoulders knotted through the folds of his new uniform, fist raised to hammer at the bridge.

I spluttered, "A sailor, outside the bridge? Unescorted?" I pounded my chair in frustration. "How can I think, when—"

Philip stood. "I'll handle it, sir. Please." He read my face, saw no refusal. He crossed to the hatch and slapped it open. "Well?"

"Wanna talk ta Cap'n."

"You're out of line, sailor. Get back to—"

"Talk ta Cap'n. Not you."

Philip's voice flashed. "You're speaking to an officer, Mr. Boss. Come to attention and salute. You call me 'sir.' And don't use that tone of voice or I'll haul you to the brig!"

I glanced at the image relayed by the corridor camera. Eddie's lip curled as he stared down at the lithe midshipman. "Brig? You? You're a sir?"

Philip, as if fearless, shoved at Eddie's bulk. "Me. Any officer."

Eddie scowled at the hand that had tried to move him. "Ya wanna use dat hand 'gain, don' go pushin' ol' Eddie widit."

Philip was silent a moment. Then he said, "I was there, Mr. Boss."

"Huh? Where?"

"The dining hall. When you said, 'I do swear upon my immortal soul.' To give loyalty and obedience, and the rest of it. I remember, even if you don't."

"Words," Eddie said contemptuously. "Jus' words."

"An oath, Mr. Boss. On your soul."

"To Cap'n, maybe. Not you."

"I'm his representative. What I say is what he says." Well put, Philip. The entire chain of command, in a nutshell.

Eddie hesitated. Then, "Could break ya in half, joey."

"You could, yes. I'm not all that strong. But I won't change what I'm going to do."

"An' wha's dat?"

"Put you against the bulkhead at attention. See if the Captain is willing to talk with you. And if not, or after he's done, put you on report and issue enough summary punishment you'll think twice before pulling this stunt again."

Eddie glowered. My heart pounding, I dropped my hand to the butt of my pistol.

We waited.

Eddie sighed. "Go on, den. Do it."

"Over there. Stand to." The camera eye swiveled to follow.

"Dunno how. No one showed me."

"Eyes front. Chest in, like so. Hands at your side, fingers down. Toes pointing forward." Philip frowned at the shabby attempt, but let it pass. "Now you say, 'Sir, I'd like permission to speak with the Captain.'"

A long silence. Eddie cleared his throat. "Allri, I sayin' it."

"No. The words I said."

"A trannie don' talk like dat!"

"You'll have to try, Mr. Boss, because I won't ask the Captain without them."

Eddie cursed under his breath. "I can't—How'd I get inna this? Sir! I like pum—permission speaka Cap'n."

"Captain."

"Cap-tain," Eddie grated.

"Wait here, sailor." Philip paused. "Aye aye, sir!" he prompted.

"Aye aye, sir," muttered Eddie.

Philip returned to the bridge, cheeks flushed. "Seaman Boss requests permission to speak with you, sir."

"Very well, Mr. Tyre." I added quietly, "Don't push him further; he could cripple you."

Still indignant, Philip paid no heed. "The nerve of him, barging in here! When I'm done he won't try that again."

"Bring him in," I said. Lord God, my cheek throbbed. I was so tired.

"Aye aye, sir." As if in response to Eddie's slackness, Philip's salute and spin were straight out of Academy.

Eddie Boss shambled in. Under Philip's persistent glare he puzzled for a long moment before comprehension dawned. Clumsily he brought himself to attention. From the corner Chief Dray watched with bemused indifference.

"Well?" I let my voice remain cold.

"Heard da man tella Cap'n 'bout eatin' trannies, an' all."

"Yes?"

"Gotta help 'em. Cap'n gotta." It was more plea than demand.

"I'm working on it. Go back to the dining hall."

"Workin' on it?" A sneer.

I frowned. He glared back, unimpressed. "Whatcha gonn' do, huh? Sit here, nice 'n safe, let dem grodes eat my frens?"

Philip's voice was tight. "Enough of that, sail—"

"Boolsheet 'nuf!" Eddie roared. "I took oath, yeah, savin' ship, work fo Cap'n. Not ta sitroun watch—"

"Now listen—" Philip.

I swarmed out of my seat. *"SHUT UP, BOTH OF YOU!"* It silenced them, as well it might. One does not often hear a Captain go berserk.

I rounded on Eddie Boss. *"NOT ANOTHER WORD OUT OF YOU!"* Something made him step back a pace, raise his arm as if to ward off a blow. I spun to Philip. "Or you, boy!" After a moment I realized I was pointing my finger like a fully charged weapon. For a moment I wondered how Philip would react if I holstered it. My lips twitched in a grin. The midshipman took an involuntary step back. Startled, I gaped, and he blanched. My grin began to congeal into a maniacal leer.

"Are you all right?" we asked each other simultaneously, and for a crazed moment our eyes locked in mutual shock.

I broke the resulting silence. "I'm fine, and you were told to be silent." I dropped back into my chair. My legs trembled. I hoped he couldn't see. I hoped it was only excess adrenaline.

I glared at Eddie. "You think I'm hiding while your friends are in danger."

His glance fell on my blistered cheek. He muttered and looked to the deck.

"What do you want me to do for them?"

He licked his lips. "You knowin' ship, Cap'n. Fin' some way inna room, get 'em out."

"How?" I stared at the console. "First we have to learn where they took your friends. If they're smart they have them in the engine room, but that's a big place. There's the outer control panel chamber, and off to the side the engine room stores compartment, and straight through the ladder down to the fusion drive chamber. Only two hatches enter it from the circumference corridor."

Unconsciously I stood and began to pace. "We've got the upper two Levels. There are two ladders to Level 3: east and west. First we'd have to mount an expedition belowdecks and try to secure part of the Level 3 circumference corridor. From there we could work our way around until we'd isolated the engine room. But if the rebels are in any of the interior cabins, they can burn through to the opposite side of the ship. Even if they don't cut through, the hydro chambers are down below on their Level, and the rebels can destroy them. Then we'll all die for certain."

"But—"

"Shut your mouth, Mr. Boss, until I've finished. If we isolate the engine room we can assault and take it. But there's no way to force our way in without a desperate fight. And we can't afford to lose crewmen. There's no way to replace casualties."

Philip cleared his throat. "So we can't retake the engine room, sir?"

"I know one way," I muttered. My mind grappled with the obscenity I'd hatched.

"What's that, sir?"

"The fusion drive shaft."

Dray looked at me with disbelief. "Clamber around outside the ship to mount an assault through the fusion shaft? Good God, are you glitched? We don't have enough trained men to send, and how could we breach the plastalloy drive shield? It's harder than steel, and for good purpose. It's all that protects the engine room crew from vacuum."

"True. But that's not what I meant. The launch berth is on Level 2, within our territory. We could send the launch around to the stern."

"And off-load the assault crew? I still don't see how they could—"

"No," I said. "Seal the corridor around the engine room. Use the launch to ram the shield."

Dray erupted in fury. "Ram my engine room, you young

pup? Hit too hard and you damage the fusion engines themselves. And you'd kill every—"

"I know! Shut up!" The engine room would depressurize instantly, killing anyone inside who wasn't suited. The corridor hatch seals would hold; they were designed for it. And the hydro chambers were two sections distant from the engine room; they'd be undamaged.

Philip said, "It would kill the hostages, sir, along with the rebels."

"I didn't say otherwise. I just said there was a way into the compartment."

Eddie growled, "You don' care 'bout killin' trannies, Cap'n? They ain' Uppies like you 'n boss boy?"

Philip flushed. "The Captain didn't say that. But what should we do if the rebels pull our power lines? We might hold out a few days, while the air turns bad, we do without water, and the ship starts to cool."

I said, "We can store water now, and go to bottled air."

"For a while, yes, sir. If the rebels had no food we could outlast them. But if they hold out more than . . . how long, sir? A week? . . . We'd have to assault them or give up the ship."

He was right. *Challenger* was a closed ecological system. With recycling and hydroponics operating properly, we could last a long, long time. But our fragile ecosystem was utterly dependent on the energy input of the fusion engines. Despite the thickly insulated hull, without power, heat loss would begin almost immediately. And if the recyclers were cut off, our CO^2 levels would mount until the air was unbreathable.

Philip's estimate was good. About a week. Unless we mounted an assault well before then, the rebels would win.

I shivered. Lord God help us. In any event, there was another reason the engine room couldn't be rammed. "Nobody would do it. It's a suicide mission for whoever drove the launch; the controls are in the bow. Even if I ordered a crewman to ram, he'd join the rebels before he'd obey. Let's drop the subject."

"Aye aye, sir," said Philip. Eddie glowered at us both. After a moment Philip added hesitantly, "Pardon if I'm out of line, but if you negotiate you risk giving up control of the ship."

He knew his regs as well as I did; Lord God knew how many times they'd made him stand on a chair reciting them. Wardroom hazing had its merits. "Yes, I know. What else is there to do?"

The speaker crackled. "Hey, Captain, 'bout time we heard from you. You gonna send chow down, or we gotta make our own?"

Philip's troubled eyes fastened on mine.

I mustn't negotiate. Whatever else occurred, I must uphold the authority of the Naval Service. And my authority as Captain, for the sake of all other Captains who would follow. To sail across the void for months or years, a ship must have one unchallengeable authority. That had been drilled into me from my first day at Academy.

The transients' lives, and my own, were nothing compared to that principle.

Eddie Boss muttered under his breath.

I glared. "You have something to say, sailor?"

"Yeah." Eddie wrinkled his brow. "You send sojers down, fight ta get back ship, dat be war." He hesitated. "Like, it be okay, if dyin' be okay. You let 'em kill trannies, dat ain war, be plain ol' dissin'."

"Dissing?" I tried to puzzle it out.

"Murder," the Chief said sourly. "Dissin'. Joespeak." I saw Philip's hand ease to his pistol, but Eddie said no more.

"Chief."

"Yes, sir?"

"Take a couple of sailors and reconnoiter. See if they've blocked any of the corridor hatches near the engine room, but don't get anybody hurt finding out. You'd better hurry."

He blinked, taking it all in. Then his shoulders squared. "Aye aye, sir." He slapped open the hatch and disappeared into the corridor.

All was silent until I picked up the waiting caller. I asked Andros, "What would I get in return for the food?" Philip gasped.

"Ha!" The sailor chuckled with satisfaction. "Now you're talking. You keep your lights and water."

"No. I want the passengers released."

"They're our meal ticket, joey. Why would I give them up?"

"For your rations. Otherwise, I won't deal."

"We'll cut your power. Think you'll like the dark, fraz?"

"Cut our power and I'll kill you all." My tone was flat.

"And your precious street joeys?"

"I don't care how many trannies you take along."

Eddie stirred.

Andros snarled, "We'll kill them one by one, you bastard!"

I said with calculated indifference, "Well, it won't look good on my record, but it'll be less mouths to feed. Go ahead, if that's what you want."

His reply was drowned by Eddie's roar as he launched himself. His thick fingers closed around my throat. I clawed helplessly at his beefy wrists while he flung me back and forth like a rag doll. The world faded to red. Abruptly, he stiffened and sagged to the deck.

The mists cleared slowly. Philip Tyre carefully set his stunner to safety, replaced it in his holster.

"Did you kill him?" My voice was hoarse.

Philip snarled, "No, but I should have, and saved you the trouble. I set it on low."

"You want them dead?" the speaker raved. "I'll show you! We'll kill them right now!"

I ignored the caller. Philip was right. Eddie Boss had violated a cardinal rule of Naval life. He had touched his Captain by intent. His life was forfeit. The court-martial would be a formality, nothing more. The irony was that my seeming indifference was the only possible way to save the transients, short of giving the rebels my ship. But because I hadn't let Eddie know, I'd condemned him to death.

The nerves of my scorched cheek sent waves of agony lancing through my face and neck. I forced my attention back to the speaker. "What's keeping you?" I asked. "The sooner they're out of the way the sooner I can come for you. It's a lot less trouble explaining to Admiralty than why I had to get rid of them myself."

For the first time the sailor's voice held a note of uncertainty. "You're bluffing."

"Yes. That's what I want you to think." That quieted him while he tried to puzzle it out. That's what they appointed a Captain for; to say any damn fool thing that came into his mind. I only knew I had him off balance.

After a moment Andros said cautiously, "I think you're glitched, Captain. So what I'll do is pick one and fry him, and see what you do from there. We've got plenty left to bargain with."

The Chief strode back onto the bridge, breathing hard. "No sign of them anywhere in the corridors, sir. I didn't go too close to the engine room. Did you see what those bastards did to my hatch?"

"Yes." I felt a strange relief, knowing my course at last. Light-headed with pain, I got to my feet. "Mr. Andros!"

"Yeah?"

"You win. At least for now. I'll bring you food for two days. Don't hurt the transients."

I could hear urgent whispering in the background. A pause. Then Clinger's voice. "No way, Captain. Divvy up the stores and give us our share."

"No. I'll buy two days to try to find a way out. Time to talk some more. That's all."

"You're stalling."

"For what reason?"

"I dunno, Seafort, but I can smell a trick."

"You have my word," I said firmly. Philip gaped.

Clinger repeated, "No tricks?"

"I give you my oath. Two days of good food, not tampered with, enough for all of you. Only one person will be allowed down to Level 3 to deliver it. Everyone else will remain above. I so swear."

The speaker was silent. Then Clinger's voice, in a different tone. "Okay, Captain. You Uppies, I guess your oath is damn important to you. Go ahead. But we'll be bottled tight in the engine room. There's no way you can get in here without getting killed. Any tricks, and your trannies get it."

"I'll need an hour or so to get everything together."

"Yeah, we've waited this long, an hour won't hurt."

"And no tricks from you. No ambushes. Everyone sealed

inside the engine room until the food arrives. Then, when we see the transients are unhurt, you get your rations."

"Tell me again you're not planning a trick."

"I swear that no one will try to enter the engine room without your permission. The food will be normal rations. Only one person will be allowed below to deliver it, and he will be unsuited. You can take the rations into the engine room yourselves, unharmed. No one else will have anything to do with you or the engine room. You have my oath on all that."

"Right."

I replaced the speaker. Still dizzy, I took refuge in formality. "Midshipman Tyre."

"Yes, sir."

"Run to the galley and order Mr. Bree to provide rations for fourteen people for two days. Food only; they have water. Have him send a man to the bridge carrying the rations. Then run to the comm room and return with Mr. Tzee."

"Aye aye, sir. Can—"

"You heard your orders."

"Aye aye, sir." He scrambled out the hatch.

Dray said doubtfully, "Two days to do what, sir? The situation will only get worse."

"Yesh." My words were slurring from the pain. "Yes," I repeated with care.

"What happens to the trannie?" He prodded Eddie with his toe.

"No questions, Mr. Kas—Chief."

It took Philip less than three minutes to complete his errands and return, panting, with Mr. Tzee at his heels.

"Now. Mr. Tyre, you and Mr. Tzee will put on your suits and go out the forward airlock. You'll maintain radio silence. You will disconnect the power feed to the small laser cannon midships. The cannon should be bolted to the hull with three large eyebolts; I believe you'll find a spanner in the launch berth. Bring the cannon into the airlock with you, leave it just inside the Level 1 lock. You will accomplish your task within one hour."

"Dray, while Mr. Tyre's party is outside, get Mr. Dakko,

who is guarding the ladder well, and go to the hold. The manifest says bin five east contains heavy electrical cable. Secure enough cable and connectors to connect a line to the high voltage outlet in the launch berth, string it along the corridor, down the ladder to Level 2, and coil enough cable at the top of the ladder well to reach down to Level 3 and around to section nine."

"Near the engine room?"

"Yes. To section nine."

"But—"

"I don't think you want to question me, Dray." My tone was odd.

He swallowed.

"Go," I said. "Both of you."

There was little more to be done. I made my entries into the Log, signed it, turned off the screen. The bridge was silent except for Eddie's slow, steady breathing.

I'd turned off all Kerren's alarms. The panel lights showed me what I needed to know; first the inner airlock hatch sliding open, then the outer, then a long wait before the laser malfunction light began to blink. When the lock began to cycle again I got to my feet. I ran my fingers through my hair and tugged on my jacket, like a green middy on his way to see his Captain. In a way, it was so.

I waited at the hatch. Philip Tyre was the first to return, his shirt plastered to his back. Clambering around on the hull with magnetic boots took stamina. "We've got the cannon, sir, over there." He pointed down the corridor toward the airlock, around the bend. "What are you going—"

"See what's keeping Mr. Bree, Midshipman."

A score of questions flashed in his eyes but his discipline held. "Aye aye, sir." He ran off.

Ten minutes later his voice preceded him around the corridor bend, speeding the sailor who carried a bulging duffel. I pointed to the deck. Awkwardly the seaman let go his burden and saluted. I sent him back to his galley.

In a few moments Dray trudged back to the bridge, red from exertion. Walter Dakko was with him. "Done," the Chief said. "The cable's stretched to Level 2. I left you lots of slack."

I picked up the duffel. "Dray, check the seals on each of the corridor hatches on Levels 1 and 2 as they close."

"The cable will block the seals, sir."

"I don't think so. The rubber gaskets should seal around the cable well enough; the hatches were designed to hold pressure even if a crewman fell so that his arm was in the way."

I turned to Philip. "Mr. Tyre, lock yourself on the bridge. Begin shutting all corridor hatches on Level 1 and Level 2."

"Sir, what are you doing? Who's taking the food down?"

I said, "I am."

He blurted, "You can't!"

"I beg your pardon?"

He blushed bright red. "I'm sorry, I—but—I mean, you can't risk yourself. Send a sailor, or me. Please!"

"No. Seal yourself on the bridge."

He stood his ground. "Tell me what's happening, sir . . . I need to know."

"I'm going below to negotiate with the rebels."

"How?"

"You may listen on the ship's caller, but you may not interrupt. You'll know what to do afterward. I don't expect to survive. You will be in charge thereafter."

"Oh, Lord Jesus!" He bit his lip. "You mustn't! I beg you!"

"There's no other way, Mr. Tyre. You know I can't give them the ship."

"Then let's storm the engine room."

"They'd kill all the trannies, Mr. Tyre. They still might, in which case they'll also kill me."

"Those street joeys . . . they're not worth it," Philip whispered. "You mustn't go!"

I drew my pistol. It came to rest an inch from Philip Tyre's eye. "Seal yourself on the bridge, Mr. Tyre. It is the third and last time I give the order."

He licked his lips, tried to speak, sagged. "Aye aye, sir." He walked slowly onto the bridge.

I shouldered the duffel. "Mr. Dakko, go to the dining hall. Pass the word to all hands and passengers to suit up with emergency tanks."

Dakko regarded me somberly, saluted, and left.

I walked toward the airlock. "Dray, help me get the cannon down to Level 2." Awkwardly I bent and wrapped my arm around the barrel of the laser cannon, trying not to lose my precarious balance with the heavy duffel.

I lugged my end of the cast alloy cannon along the corridor, stopping while Dray closed and sealed the hatches behind us. We descended to Level 2 past the snaking cable Dray had laid. I walked the laser cannon around the stairwell to the ladder to Level 3, then gratefully set it down beside the coiled cable.

"Dray, seal off section nine on Level 2, in case they try to burn upward through the deck. Then break out a suit and put it on. I'll wait to see that's done. You are to remain on Level 2. You are not to descend to Level 3. Acknowledge your orders."

"Orders received and understood, sir," the Chief Engineer said heavily. "I'll bring your suit back with me."

"No. Just your own."

"But—" His eyes widened.

"Do as I say."

When he returned, clumping in his heavy, awkward vacuum suit, I set down the duffel at the top of the ladder and grunted with strain as I tried to hoist the cannon. It was heavier than I'd thought; I could barely manage it. The Chief must have carried more than his share of the weight. I managed somehow to haul it down the ladder.

At the foot of the stairs I turned east along the circumference corridor. From section six, I staggered along the corridor through seven, then eight. I eased my burden to the deck just inside the hatch between eight and nine. The engine room was just ahead of me, around the bend in section nine. I retraced my steps.

Back up the ladder. I coiled the cable on my shoulder and walked slowly backward down the stairs, playing it out behind me. Laying it carefully along the center of the corridor, I unwound it to where I'd left the cannon in section eight. I had about twelve meters length to spare.

Dizzy now, I climbed back up the ladder once again and

hoisted the duffel of rations. "Wait here, Dray. Come if I call, but only then."

"Aye aye, sir."

At the foot of the ladder I dropped the duffel. This time I turned west, along the corridor that circled past the engine room to where I'd left the cannon.

I followed the corridor to the hatch between sections one and nine. I pressed the emergency close panel on the bulkhead and the hatch slid quietly shut.

I backtracked past the west hydros, glancing to make sure the hatch was sealed. I crossed into section two and sealed that hatch behind me. I worked my way back to the ladder, in section six.

The duffel was at the foot of the ladder where I'd left it. I lugged it east along the corridor. I sealed the hatch between six and seven, watching the hatch seals close around the cable. The rubber gaskets seemed tight. I checked the east hydros in section seven, sealed the hatch, plodded on to section eight. At the far end I stopped to finish my preparations.

Every corridor hatch on Level 3 was now sealed, except from section eight to the engine room in nine.

It didn't take me long to attach the cable ends to the power inputs of the laser cannon. I pressed the indicator button on the muzzle; the test light glowed. I tried to lift the cannon but my strength seemed inadequate; instead, breath rasping, I dragged the cannon along the corridor to the midpoint of section nine, outside the hatch to crew berth two, about twelve meters along the corridor from the engine room bulkhead.

All was silent behind the closed hatch to the engine room. As if from a great distance, I observed the scorch marks where the rebels had brazed plates over their damaged hatch.

The cannon was a hybrid weapon, designed for remote control from the comm room, but still capable of manual adjustment.

I pointed it down the corridor.

I snapped on the test light, aimed the beam at a bulkhead. I heard myself humming mindlessly and bit off the sound. Though I knew I must hurry, I sat on the deck, back to the hatch, legs straight in front of me, staring at nothing. Fire flowed through my head. I waited, hoping the pain would recede. It didn't, but I had no more time. I unholstered my pistol, laid it down, staggered the few steps to the berth two hatch, across the corridor from the cannon.

I slapped open the hatch and lurched inside. A mop was in its usual place in the storage bin. I jammed it into the open hatchway, blocking the hatch from shutting. Then, abruptly, I slid to the deck.

After a time I was again aware of the empty, silent corridor. Cautiously I struggled to a kneeling position, heaved myself to my feet. I found I could no longer lift the duffel; I slid it along the corridor to within a meter of the engine room hatch and quickly retreated. With unsteady steps I made my way back to crew berth two and lifted the caller from the hatch control panel, sat with it by the cannon. "Engine room, this is Captain Seafort."

The answer came quickly. "About time. A couple more minutes and we'd a started cooking a trannie." Andros.

"Your food is in a duffel outside your hatch."

"And where's the joe brought it down?"

"In the corridor about halfway to section eight."

"Any stunners? Rifles?"

"A laser pistol, lying on the deck. It won't be used unless you try something."

"Yeah? Who's out there?"

"I am."

"Jesus Son of God!"

I closed my ears to the blasphemy. "The corridor is sealed behind me, all the way to Level 2. I'm the only one here. I've brought you the food, which I swear is safe to eat. Have I kept my oath?"

"Why you?" he demanded.

"It was too important to trust to anyone else."

"What if we take you too?"

"I suppose you could." I touched a hand to my fiery cheek, but it only made the pain worse. "Do you want your food now?"

"Yeah. Might as well. I'm sending a trannie for it. He might try to run, but we'll cover him from here."

"First let me see the faces of all nine of them."

"They're all right, Captain." He snickered. "You have my oath."

"Their faces." After a moment some makeshift catch was released and the engine room hatch swung aside. One by one the apprehensive faces of the transients showed briefly in the hatchway. Then one boy stepped out, darted nervously to the duffel, snatched it, and bolted back inside the hatch.

I picked up the caller. "You have your food. Have I kept my oath, Andros?"

There was a moment's pause. "Yeah, I guess. Why?"

"Stand aside from the bulkhead, please, so no one gets hurt."

"No one what?" blared Andros. "What the hell—"

I pressed the firing button. A flare of light sizzled against the bulkhead between the corridor and the engine room. In a moment the laser melted a hole wider than my arm in the thick alloy plates. I shifted the cannon and began burning another hole.

"What're you doing, you lying bastard? You made a deal!"

"I'm cutting a couple of holes."

"But you said—"

"I said no one would try to enter the engine room without your permission. Don't worry, I won't. And I said only one person would come down to Level 3." I cut a third hole, widely separated from the others.

"Belay that or the trannies get it now!" he shrieked. "All of them!"

"Very well. No more holes." I heaved, turning the cannon to the open hatch to crew berth two. I pointed the aperture at the outer bulkhead on the far side of the berth.

A face flashed at one of the holes in the engine room, then ducked away. Andros howled, "What the fuck are you up to?"

"Preparing to fire through the hull, Mr. Andros."

"What?"

"You heard me. My hand is on the firing button. It won't take much of a twitch to depress it, so if you shoot me I believe I'll set it off as I fall." My heart pounded so hard I found it difficult to speak.

His voice held a note of panic. "What are you doing?"

"I'm going to blow a hole in the hull, Mr. Andros. Isn't it obvious?"

"But—you'll decompress us!"

"Yes. Crew berth two, the section nine corridor, and the engine room. Everything else is sealed off."

"You won't get away! I'll burn a hole through your suit."

"I have no suit."

"Then you'll die too!"

"Yes." My tongue was thick around the word. It was what must be. Though part of me struggled to live, I'd accept the end as a blessing. I had fouled up so often, and Amanda waited.

"Jesus, you're insane!"

"I may be. It doesn't matter. You've shown me that."

"I'm gonna kill the trannies!"

"They'll be dead in a few moments anyway."

"We'll cover the holes!"

"The cannon fires the moment you touch the first hole."

The speaker clicked off but I heard a commotion through the holes in the bulkhead. A demand, a reply. An argument. Someone shouted, "There's only two suits in here!"

I said to the caller, "It's time now. I'm ship's chaplain. Would you like me to shrive you?"

Andros shouted, "Wait! What do you want?"

My burn hurt worse than ever. "To have this life over with." It was no more than truth.

A silence. Then, "You're bluffing. You might kill us, but not yourself. Go ahead."

"I'm going to pray first. I'll give you a few seconds warning. I'll be about half a minute."

I knelt on the deck, keeping the cannon between myself and the engine room. I kept my hand on the firing button.

I said aloud, " 'Trusting in the goodness and mercy of Lord God eternal, we commit our bodies to the deep—' "

In the engine room, a gasp of horror.

" '—to await the day of judgment when the souls of man shall be called forth before Almighty Lord God—' " I faltered, my voice failing. I finished the prayer in silence. "Amen." I stood. "Twenty seconds."

"Jesus, Seafort, don't!"

Clinger shouted, "It's a bluff, Andy!"

"Ever see a man die that way? Gimme that helmet, damn you!"

"Naw, one goes, we all go! Only fair way."

"Fifteen seconds."

"God, I don't want to die!"

"Shuddup, joey, no one's gonna—"

"Ten seconds." My hand tightened around the firing button. I fought the urge to hyperventilate.

"Goddamn it, Clinger, don't be yellow, he won't—HUNGH!"

Clinger screamed, "Wait, Captain! Just long enough to talk! CAPTAIN!"

I felt as if summoned from a great distance. "Talk about what?" My voice was dull.

"Don't blow the hull, Captain. You'll kill yourself too."

"Is that all?"

"Don't you care?" he cried.

"Not that much. Like Andros said, we'll all be dead soon."

"What if—what—"

I stared through the crew berth to the hull. "Ten . . . Nine."

"What if we trade you the trannies?"

"Eight . . ." He had said something important, but my mind was too foggy to concentrate. "What?"

"Trade you the trannies for leavin' us alone. We stay down here, you take the rest of the ship."

I mulled it over. "I don't think so, Andros." I was very weary now. "My way is better."

"I'm Clinger. It's those damn trannies you wanted, Captain. Don't you remember?"

"Remember?" I echoed. His voice was in a faraway dream. "Where's Andros?"

"I bashed him with a pipe wrench. Look, you tricked us. You worded your oath funny, and you fooled us. Now, the trannies ain't important. So we give 'em to you, and you let us be."

"Why?"

"So you'll live!" he shouted.

The word had no meaning. Something wasn't right inside

my head. The bulkhead seemed to loom and recede, perhaps in time to my heartbeat.

"Captain."

The bulkhead had a strange texture.

"CAPTAIN!" His shriek snapped me awake. "Don't pass out, sir, you'll press the firing switch!"

"Right." I nodded, but the motion sent waves of nausea through my upper body.

"Captain, call someone to help you. We'll give you back the trannies, you promise not to try anything else. Just leave us be."

"I mustn't . . . I have to control ship." My tongue was thick.

"Think, for God's sake!"

I tried. The mists cleared a bit. "Surrender."

"Why, so you can execute us? Why should we?"

"That's true." I squinted at the far bulkhead. "It's best to blow the hull."

His voice was patient, as with a child. "Captain Seafort, you'll kill the trannies that way. You wanted us to free them."

"Yes. Surrender."

"Will you have us executed?"

For armed rebellion in wartime? "Of course." His question made no sense.

"So we'd have nothing to lose. You have to give us a reason to give up."

I was dizzy, but I was thinking again. "I can't negotiate with you. Exert authority and control, and all that. That's why I'd better die."

His voice shook with frustration. "This ain't negotiating control, you lunatic! You're just taking our surrender! Shut up, Sykes, we've lost, can't you see? Captain, no trial, no execution. You get back your ship. We'll stay in our section, do what we want."

I fought against blackness. "Not the engine room." Each word was an agony. "Somewhere else. Section four."

"You tricked us once; what if you did it again? We keep the power lines as security."

"No tricks. Take you to your section and leave you alone. Swear." I caught myself swaying.

I heard voices buzzing. Then, "All right, we agree. On your oath. Call someone down to help you, before you kill us all."

"Oath. Swore no one else."

Clinger said urgently, "Forget the frazzin' oath! Get someone to help before you keel over!"

I said hoarsely, "Dray. If you can hear me, come down. Section nine."

Eons later the hatch slid open. A suited figure clumped into the corridor. Kneeling, I struggled to stay erect as the figure loomed. A hand settled over mine on the muzzle of the cannon, and fingers gently pried mine from the firing button. I sagged.

"Send the trannies out first," someone said. "I've got my finger on the button, and I don't give Christ's damn whether you live or die. Or whether the Captain does."

"All right, Chief. Take it easy." The hatch swung open. One by one the frightened, subdued transients emerged, blinking as if in bright light.

One threw herself at me, hugging me fiercely as I knelt. "Cap'n! You hurt! What dey doin' you, Cap'n?"

"Annie?"

Dray snarled, "You, Jackboy! And you, girl. Take hold of the Captain and carry him through the hatch. That's right, slap open the hatch control. Into the next section, all of you. Now shut it." The ceiling moved in great lurches, swinging back and forth. There was tight pressure under my arms.

I lay passively, in a dreamlike state. My cheek hurt hardly at all. I heard the gentle hiss of a section hatch. Other hands seized me. I floated up the ladder.

Philip Tyre's face wafted into view. "Oh, Lord God! Take him to the infirmary."

I said slowly, distinctly, "The bridge first."

"But—"

"Bridge." A few moments later I was eased into my chair; I gripped the hand rests. I felt hot and dry. Philip stood nearby, poised to cushion me if I fell. His anxious eyes roved. On the deck Eddie Boss groaned and tried to lift himself. Walter Dakko, rifle in hand, waited.

I gestured to Eddie. "Send him back to quarters."

Philip contemptuously nudged the young sailor with his boot. "To the brig, you mean. Right away, sir."

"Crew berth."

"But he's up for court-mar—"

I heaved myself to my feet, swaying. "Dakko. Out." I waved at the hatch. Walter Dakko left swiftly, eyes grim. On Philip's nod he shut the hatch behind him.

I said carefully, shaping each word, "Why would you court-martial him?"

Philip gawked. "He tried to kill you."

I shook my head. "He . . . fell down." I staggered, caught myself.

"He went for your throat," Philip cried. "I had to stun him before he strangled you!"

Eddie Boss hauled himself into a sitting position, propping himself against the console.

"I didn't see it."

The young middy was almost in tears. "Captain, you're not well! He tried to kill you, don't you remember? He can't get away with that!"

I took a clumsy step toward him. Another. I backed him to the bulkhead, my eyes blazing. I leaned close. "I . . . am . . . your . . . superior . . . officer!"

"Yes, sir!"

"He fell!"

Philip was white.

"Say it!"

The boy's eyes flicked to Eddie Boss, back to mine in betrayed reproach. He stammered, "Sir. The—the sailor must have stumbled. He struck his head and passed out."

"Very well." I turned carefully. "I'm going to the infirmary now. Something . . . seems to be wrong." With great dignity I took two steps toward the hatch.

Behind me Philip said in a small voice, "I'd like to help you, please." I nodded; his arm came tentatively around my chest. As I trudged, resting my weight on his shoulder, I could see the glistening of his tears.

Part III

August 7, in the year of our Lord 2198

14

The warmth of the scalding tea seeped through the thick porcelain until I was forced to shift the cup back and forth between my hands, until I had to set it down on the swing-arm table by my bedside. Elena Bartel smiled from the foot of the bed.

"I'll wait a few minutes," I conceded.

"The anticipation will do you good." Her tone was shy.

I smiled cautiously, feeling the skin stretch. It had been, they told me, three days since I'd tottered to the infirmary clutching Philip Tyre like a castaway his oxy tank. My burn was infected, and my frantic exertions had pushed my fever near the point of no return.

Philip, Walter Dakko and Kerren had huddled in consultation, while Kerren directed their efforts to subdue my infection. The harried midshipman appointed Dakko and Bartel my attendants and left to run the ship; Lord God only knew in what state I'd find our affairs when I could return to the bridge. I consoled myself that Philip couldn't do much worse than I'd managed on my own.

I gazed wistfully at the teacup, wondering how soon I'd be able to hold it. Despite frequent applications of the medi-pulse, my wound smarted, and the steam of the tea would soothe, the cup under my nose, the clean warm vapors inhaled. It recalled Father sitting with me during my childhood fevers, his dented old copper teapot and a sponge bath the major weapons in his medical arsenal. It was, I suppose, the only tenderness I'd ever known from him.

I leaned back on the pillow and stared through Elena, trying to penetrate the haze of the preceding days. I'd lain sweating and shivering while my fever spiked, fading into drugged sleep when the medications took hold. At other, more clear-headed times I fretted over my abandoned duties.

Knowing we were shorthanded, I countermanded Philip's order that Elena or Walter Dakko be with me at every moment. "The buzzer is by my hand, Ms. Bartel. If I need anything I'll signal. Report back to Mr. Tyre."

"No, sir, I won't do that," she'd said calmly.

"But—"

"I'll get the midshipman."

A few minutes later Philip Tyre appeared, saluted, listened to my curt instructions. "Sorry, sir, but she stays. Or someone else, if she makes you uncomfortable."

For a moment I was speechless. "You realize what you're saying?"

"Yes." An awkward pause that seemed to last forever. "Sir, I've relieved you until you recover. It's in the Log."

Stunned, I fell back against the pillows. Relieved? Naval legends recounted braver men than I who'd quailed at such an act, endured misery and worse before taking the fateful step for which they might easily be hanged.

The Captain of a Naval vessel was more than an officer. He was the United Nations Government in transit; relieving him was akin to revolution. In my despair I'd asked Philip to perform that very act, not all that long ago. Yet now all I could feel was outrage.

"Only until you recover," he repeated, with an unspoken plea for reassurance, and stubborn determination. "Otherwise you'd be out of bed as soon as your legs would hold you. Maybe sooner. We can't take the risk; you're needed too much."

"I see." I glowered, unforgiving.

"When your fever stays down two days in a row, and your blood count is back to normal, Kerren says." Philip's blue eyes were troubled. He forced a smile. "Meantime I'll do my best, sir."

And so he'd gone to the bridge while I remained in the white cubicle, staring at the muted lights, subject to the inexpert ministrations of Walter Dakko and the anxious pale young woman.

A neurotic, she'd described herself, and I could see the truth of her admission, yet she brought to nursing a determination and an empathy that made up for her lack of practice. She bathed me and helped with intimate functions, and assisted Walter Dakko in dressing my suppurating wound whose fetid odor even I found distasteful, and which had become his special diligence.

"Would you like the holovid?" she asked me now. I nodded, a tiny motion only. Each time I moved my cheek, the dressing shifted, the skin stirred, and I felt sensations I preferred not to contemplate. Moodily I took the holovid from her outstretched hand. Yesterday I'd demanded the ship's manifest, which Philip had obediently eprommed and sent down.

Relieved of command or not, I could at least use my time to search for stores in the hold that might prove useful, before we jettisoned the rest in preparation for our acceleration. I wondered if it was an exercise in futility. Then I shrugged; we would do what we could. All else was up to Lord God.

Another day passed, and my fever lessened. Kerren's medications were slowly overcoming the infection that had nearly destroyed me. I tried not to scream when Walter Dakko carefully removed the drain the puter had instructed him to insert.

I demanded a mirror. They said they'd get one, but didn't. I suspected they didn't want me to see myself. My temperature remained steady another day. I took a short walk to the head, and savored my achievement. Ms. Bartel shared in my triumph, grinning widely when I could not.

I was myself again, but weakened. Overexertion—remaining on my feet for more than a few minutes—sent a flush to my features and sweat to my pores. I ate the soft foods they gave me, so as not to have to chew, and walked every few hours to rebuild my stamina. The following day I emerged from the infirmary in my frayed robe for a triumphant foray to the corridor bend before returning.

I was perched on my bed, controlling my breathing, trying not to reveal how much the venture had cost me, when Philip Tyre appeared.

He saluted but didn't come to attention. Quite right, as he held command. "Sir, how do you feel today?"

"Well enough." My tone was cold.

"When you think yourself ready, sir, I'd like you to resume command."

"You're sure you wouldn't rather keep it?"

He looked to the deck. "I'm sorry you disagree with my decision, sir. I understand the consequences."

"Very well. Right now, then." I stood too fast, sat back abruptly. "Well, in the morning. I'll give it one more day, so your effort won't be wasted."

"Yes, sir." He saluted, turned, and left.

When morning came I dressed cautiously, maneuvering my undershirt over the bandage that covered my cheek. I shaved the one side of my face, wondering as I stared into the mirror what horror the neat white dressing hid.

Back on the bridge at last, I saluted Philip. "Kerren, record, please. Having recovered fully, Mr. Tyre, I reassume command of this vessel."

"Yes, sir. I return command to you. Acknowledged and understood." He saluted and came to attention.

"Dismissed, Midshipman. Go to your quarters." I ignored him as he marched out. A petty revenge, but all that was available to me. I sat in my seat and snapped on the holovid to review the Log.

I flipped the first entry, bald and unadorned. "Captain feverish and semiconscious. Relieved of command by order of Philip A. Tyre, senior officer present."

I skimmed through the subsequent entries. Philip had set experienced crewmen to train our recruits in ship's protocol and their duties. He'd reorganized the galley and issued supply rations to Mr. Bree on a regular basis. At the midshipman's orders Mr. Tzee had taught two crewmen the mechanics of standing comm room watch. Dray had been reinstalled in his engine room, and Tyre had assigned him Deke as an assistant.

As I read his accomplishments, an unreasoning anger stirred. The west hydroponics were cleaned out, and new plantings and cuttings from the east hydros started under Emmett Branstead's watchful eye. Because the sensors and machinery in west hydros were nonfunctional, the plants had to be tended by hand and Philip had arranged that also. He'd recalculated our intended course, had the recyclers monitored, kept the Log entries up-to-date . . .

Damn him! I slammed the holovid onto my console. I wasn't needed. I wasn't even missed. Our industrious middy had handled everything, and more efficiently than I could have.

I slumped brooding in my seat. When I'd had enough self-pity I called the ship's stations for progress reports; all was well in recycling, comm room, engine room, and hydros. The rebels, thank Lord God, had done no damage to the hydro chambers.

In what section had Philip confined the mutineers? I glanced through the Log, could find no entry. I was about to call the wardroom, but thought better of it; I'd just sent the boy off to sleep. Better to search out the information myself. I thumbed the caller. "Chief, are you busy?"

A short pause. "Not particularly, Captain. I was showing Deke how the release valves work."

"Would you come up, please?" I replaced the caller and waited. I knew he wouldn't be long; when the Captain summoned, a crewman, any crewman, hurried to obey.

Within two minutes the Chief appeared, saluted, and was allowed onto the bridge.

"Dray, I'm a little fuzzy on what happened after I headed to the infirmary. You were getting the trannies—the transients out of the engine room."

"Yes, sir." He was impassive. "They're safe. A couple of the girls got mauled a bit, but no worse."

"You were about to put the rebels in another section. Four, was it?"

He said nothing.

"Well?"

He shrugged. "Maybe you were going to do that. I never said I would."

I slammed the console. "Where are they, Dray?"

"The brig, of course. Where else?"

"I promised I'd give them a section if they surrendered."

The Chief stared in disbelief. "What does it matter? You were under duress."

I gaped. "I gave them my oath."

"A ruse of war," he said vehemently. "Or whatever you choose to call it. It makes no difference; you're going to hang them, aren't you?"

"I can't, Dray. They have my sworn word."

He saw I was serious. "Them?" he spluttered. "Those God-cursed maggots? You may be crazy enough to let them wander part of the ship—"

"Dray!"

"But I'll be damned if I do it!" he shouted. We stared at each other in shocked silence.

"Go below, Dray. At once."

"Aye aye, sir!" With an angry salute he stalked off.

Some time passed before I was calm enough to sit. I pored through the Log. Philip had entered nothing about the rebels' imprisonment. "Kerren!"

He was as calm as ever. "Yes, Captain?"

"I'll be in the wardroom. Monitor all alarms and notify me at once if I'm needed."

"Of course, Captain Seafort."

I strode along the Level 1 corridor, hardly looking where I was going, and just missed falling over a bucket. Eddie Boss glowered mutely. "What are you up to?" I demanded.

"Same what I be doon allatime!" Savagely he swung a mopful of water across the corridor, sweeping with broad, angry strokes. "Boss boy say allatime moppin' flo'! Moppin' flo'!" He shot me a look of accusation. "You said you was needin' help! Dis be kinda help you need? Ol' Eddie keepin' flo' clean?"

"Deck," I said absently.

"Deck, flo', be alla same when yo's allatime moppin'." His face was sullen. Not up to a confrontation, I continued on my way.

The harassment of Eddie disturbed me. Was Philip reverting to his old ways? I felt a chill; how did our new cadet Gregor fare, in the isolation of the wardroom? I formed a steely resolve. Philip would not get away with brutality. Never again.

I pounded on the wardroom hatch. It slid open. Gregor Attani, handsome in a new crisp gray uniform, grinned before remembering to salute. "Hello, sir." His voice was cheerful.

"Come to attention!" I rasped. "Has he taught you nothing yet?"

He complied, his smile fading. "Sorry, sir."

"Where's Mr. Tyre?"

"Right here, sir." Philip appeared in the hatchway in slacks and T-shirt, towel slung over his shoulder. He tossed the towel to the chair and came to attention in one smooth motion.

"As you were, both of you." Gregor relaxed and eased to his bunk. I said to Philip, "Eddie Boss."

"Yes, sir?"

"What's he doing out there?"

"Deck duty."

"For how long?"

"Five days, now."

"Why?" I demanded.

A momentary bitterness clouded his features. "For being clumsy enough to stumble on the bridge." Gregor, forgotten, watched openmouthed from his bunk.

"You don't agree with my decision, Mr. Tyre?"

"I accept it, sir." He contemplated the bulkhead with a bleak expression. "However you look at it, he was out of line. A little deck duty won't hurt him."

Grudgingly I conceded that he was right. "Very well. But tomorrow's the last day."

"Aye aye, sir."

"Now." I glared. "Mr. Andros and Mr. Clinger. The others."

He squared his shoulders. "Yes, sir."

"You put them in the brig."

"No, sir. Dray did. I left them there."

I said tightly, "You knew about my oath to let them go free?"

"Yes, I did." His casual manner infuriated me.

"So you disobeyed orders."

He smiled without mirth. "You never ordered me to give them a section, sir."

"You God damned sea lawyer!" The insult hung between us, irretrievable.

"Amen," said Gregor Attani hoarsely, turning aside my blasphemy.

"You knew what I expected, whether or not I gave specific orders! You deliberately disobeyed me."

Philip looked me in the eye, took a deep breath. "Sir, at the time I was not subject to your orders."

My mouth opened but no sound emerged. My fists were balled so tight my hand ached. I finally got out, "Ten demerits for insolence, Mr. Tyre! I won't cane you, because I promised not to. But you'll by God work them off, every one of them. And you're confined to quarters otherwise, until further notice."

"Aye aye, sir." His face was white. I spun on my heel, slapping the hatch shut on my way out. Awash with rage, I stalked the corridor to the ladder, dashed two steps at a time down to Level 3. Ignoring the sailors in the corridor I slapped open the engine room hatch. "Dray!"

"Back here!" He emerged from the stores compartment, young Deke at his side, the boy lugging a heavy box.

"Dray, go to section four. Remove the inside controls for the corridor hatches. Disable the speaker and run a new line that connects only with the bridge. Go through every cabin and compartment in section four and remove all tools and weapons. Acknowledge your orders."

"Orders received and understood, sir." He smiled, a bitter, sour smile. "Mind if I have a drink afterward?"

Deke watched, openmouthed.

"How dare you!"

"Yes," he mimicked. "How dare I." He flexed his hand. "The fingers are all there, Captain. Want one? I sneered at you, and you threatened to burn off my hand. Those scum bastards try to kill you. They seize my engine room, they take hostages. You're giving them passenger cabins." He glared, extended his wrist. "Here, do what you want! I don't need the goddamn fingers!"

I walked unsteadily to the bulkhead, palmed its cold surface, gazed unseeing at the control panels and valves. "I was desperate when I told you that," I said in a low voice. "I had no one but Philip. The ship was in chaos and I didn't know what else to do."

He growled, "Deke, get out. This is between me and the

Captain." The young sailor fled with relief. When Dray turned to me his eyes were cold. "I don't respect you, Seafort, and I don't care if you know it. You scared the living hell out of me. I'm fifty-three years old and I've never been so frightened in my life. Well, maybe you had to do it. I gave up, when things looked hopeless and that ass Tremaine was running the bridge. The bottle seemed the only way out."

He looked at me with narrow eyes. "But you played that scene for all it was worth. It was calculated cruelty. I don't need the bottle now. I can hate you instead."

"And you don't fear me?"

His mouth twisted in a sardonic smile. "No. That's ironic, isn't it? I really don't give a shit whether you take my hand or not. You can't have me. My hand, maybe, but not me." He met my eyes. "Oh, I'll obey orders, and I'll salute you and speak courteously, when others are around. But I'll know, and you'll know, what I really think of you."

"Yes." I turned away. "I'll know." Despite what I'd done, this man had stood by me at the armory, saved me from the rebels outside the engine room. And there would be no way to reach him, ever.

"I know what you think of me," I repeated, my voice dull. "I wonder if you'll ever know what I think of me." Blindly I groped for the hatch. The corridor was deserted. I made my way to the ladder, wiping my eyes with my sleeve. He'd given no more than I deserved. I climbed back to the bridge, shut myself into its isolation. Alone with the unblinking cold lights of the simulscreen I plumbed the depths of my self-disgust.

Hours later Dray reported that section four was prepared. I rounded up Walter Dakko and Emmett Branstead, armed them, took them below to the brig. I unsealed the cramped, dirty cell that confined Clinger and the deckhand Akkrit.

Clinger's look radiated hatred. "Shoulda killed you when I had the chance," he said. "You an' your oath. I told Andy it was all goofjuice, but he wouldn't listen."

"Shut up. I'm taking you to section four."

"Why? Gonna kill us there instead of here?"

"No. I'm giving you a section. As I promised." I raised

my stunner. "Another word, Mr. Clinger, and you'll be carried out." I led the two apprehensive sailors and their guard from the brig to the abandoned section.

When they were sealed into their exile I returned for Andros, Sykes, and Byzer. When I unsealed his cell Andros flashed me a glance that sent a chill down my spine. "This is how you keep your word, joey?"

"Clinger and Akkrit are waiting in section four. I'm taking you there now."

"What's the hurry?" He leaned against the bulkhead, arms folded. "Don' wanna wait awhile? A year or so, maybe? An officer's word!" He spat on the deck. "That's what it's worth!"

"Let's go." I fingered my stunner.

"I been waitin' five days," he screamed. "You lied! No tricks, you swore!" Walter Dakko's grip tightened on his rifle.

"Yes, I swore." I waited for Andros to emerge, but he leaned against the hatch, unmoving. "Let's go."

"Or?" His voice was a sneer.

"Or I'll stun you and carry you."

"If that's what you got to do, go ahead. You want me to go on my feet, admit you was a liar."

Dakko took a menacing step forward.

"Easy, Mr. Dakko. I could change my mind, Andros, and leave you here."

"Sure." He spat again. "Break your oath once, what's another time?"

"I was sick!" I cried. "I barely knew where I was!"

"You promised!" he shouted. "You're an officer, ain't you? You promised, an' Dray and your pretty boy, they heard you, and instead we got stuffed in this box! Twenny years they been tellin' me about that oath stuff, and look what you did to me!" He crashed his fist on the hatch in rage and frustration. "What a greenie I am! I believed you."

Dakko glanced at me, took pity. He said quietly, "That's enough, Mr. Andros. The Captain was quite ill, and he's here now to carry out his promise. Come with us."

"He didn't say, sit in the stinking brig for five days sick with wonderin' whether they was gonna hang you!" The seaman's voice faltered. "No, take you to your section and leave you alone, he said! 'I swear,' he told us, and I believed him, 'cause he was an officer . . ." His voice had a ragged catch. "I believed him . . ."

Dakko raised his weapon. "Come along, Mr. Andros."

Eyes downcast, Andros hugged himself, shaking his head. Coolly, Dakko aimed the stunner at his chest.

"Wait." I pushed the gun aside, stepped into the dirty cell, stood before the wretched seaman. "Andros, before Lord God and these witnesses, I apologize." His eyes lifted. "I failed to keep my pledge. I was sick and confused, but I could still have taken care of you. A word would have done it. I was wrong, and my oath is not kept and I'm sorry for it. I'm here to redeem my oath. Go with these men. Please."

His eyes were fixed on me with pathetic gratitude. "Aye aye, Captain," he whispered. Docile, he followed my two sailors to section four.

The moment the hatch was sealed Emmett Branstead growled, "Excuse me, but why? Why humble yourself before that—that traitor?"

He had no right to ask. No sailor ever had the right to demand that his Captain explain his behavior. "Because he was right, Mr. Branstead. And I was wrong. Now, get Sykes and Byzer."

"My wife would like to talk with you," said old Mr. Reeves stiffly. "If it wouldn't be too much trouble."

"Of course." He'd intercepted me as I made my way to my place in the dining hall. I followed him to the table alongside the bulkhead, where Mrs. Reeves and the Pierces waited for their elderly companions.

The fragile old lady smiled at me from tired blue eyes. "I understand we owe our lives to your courage, Captain. Thank you for all you've done for us."

Despite myself I laughed, a harsh, bitter sound. "Done for you? My God, how do these rumors start?"

"You prevented those wretched sailors from blowing up the ship or cutting our power, did you not?"

"After giving them the chance to do so in the first place."

The old woman's tone bore sympathy and concern. "You've been ill, I know. Are you still troubled?"

"I wish I had died on *Portia* with my wife, ma'am." I was astounded I'd said it aloud.

She patted the seat next to Mr. Pierce. "Sit with me, young man."

Shaky, I lowered myself into the chair. "Sorry, I didn't mean to say that."

"You must have loved her a great deal."

I looked elsewhere. "Not as much as I might have. I didn't appreciate her until she died." From the chair opposite, Mr. Pierce stared at me, mouth half open.

"You can live with that. You have courage."

"You misjudge me, ma'am."

"It took courage to cast your lot with us."

I said harshly, "You don't know what you're saying."

"Tell me."

Why should I unburden myself to a foolish old lady? Yet I spat out the words. "I came to *Challenger*, yes. Admiral Tremaine had relieved me for incompetence and insubordination. It was *Challenger* or be hanged. That's what you call courage."

Placid, she let the silence grow. Then, "Sometimes it takes courage to live too."

I stood abruptly. "I have to go to my table."

"You have to find peace." The old eyes looked at me, intent. "Otherwise you'll be no help to anyone."

"I have to go, ma'am." I touched my cap, turned my back on her, retreated.

Dinner finally concluded. I disengaged myself from a couple who wanted my company for inane chat, left for the bridge. I was interrupted a short way down the corridor.

"Captain Seafort!" Chris Dakko hurried after me. I waited. He hesitated, bit his lip, then flicked me a fleeting, unpracticed salute. "Please. May I talk to you?"

I knew I ought to refuse. There were channels for a crewman to approach the Captain; a direct entreaty was unacceptable. But I decided to make allowances; the boy had been a civilian a few days past.

"All right." I led him to the Level 1 passengers' lounge and shut the hatch. "Well?"

"Please." He searched my eyes, as if trying to read them. "I know you don't like me. I haven't been nice to you . . . And I know you need help."

"Yes?"

"What you did, enlisting me against my will—"

I couldn't let him ask. "Enough, Mr. Dakko."

"You don't understand." He sounded desperate. "I can't take it. I'm all wrong for that life. I don't fit in with them, I never can. I—"

"Mr. Dakko!"

"I'll help with anything you say, Mr. Seafort! Let me be a civilian again. I'm begging you. Sir! I'm begging you, SIR!" His eyes implored me, hoping against hope.

Slowly I shook my head. "If I had other options I'd take them. God, don't you think I thought about it, before enlisting you? You've been impressed, Mr. Dakko, and impressed you will remain."

"You don't know what they're like," he whispered, eyes seeing only some private hell. "It's a nightmare. I even went to my—my father. He shoved me away, said I'd chosen to be on my own, that he wouldn't . . ." His eyes closed. "Captain, sir, forgive the things I've said to you. Please, let me go!"

His distress moved me. Perhaps if he hadn't mentioned his father . . . I recalled the nights I'd lain awake in Academy silently beseeching Father to take me from that place.

"Mr. Dakko—Chris," I amended gently. "You weren't enlisted as punishment. I needed every available hand to fill the crew roster. I still do. You must remain in the Navy. I'm sorry, but that's how it will be. You came to *Challenger* of your own will; these are the consequences you suffer."

He looked away. I cleared my throat. "Now, sailor, salute as you've been taught and go below."

For a long moment the boy did nothing. Then with a visible effort at self-control he came to attention, saluted, stalked to the hatch.

That night, weary from a lonely day of unending drudgery, I went to my cabin for the first time in a week. The spacious compartment was still unfamiliar to me; after all, I'd been aboard *Challenger* only five days before my injury sent me to the infirmary. Clean sheets awaited. Towels too; Philip had even organized the laundry service.

I felt a pang of loneliness and tried to dwell on my anger instead. Thanks to Tyre, I'd had to humiliate myself before a demented sailor who'd caused death and disunion on my ship. If he'd but carried out my orders . . .

I stared at my sallow face in the mirror. Again I wondered what was beneath the bandage. Some compulsion drew my hand upward. Slowly, carefully, I peeled away the edge of the dressing. When it was done I stared at my visage, a sickness in the pit of my stomach.

My wound was hideous. The skin had split and suppurated, leaving a red, inflamed scar the length of my cheek from ear to lip that radiated outward toward eye and throat. The redness would fade, but the scar would remain. I recalled Simmons, the sailor I'd killed. Was it the mark of Cain? Unnerved, I began to laugh. Laughing and crying I fell heavily on the bed, and in a mercifully short time, slept.

15

Our days passed with leaden weight. My most urgent task was to set the ship on its homeward path; we'd already delayed far too long in that. But our precious propellant could not be wasted in course corrections; we would burn at full power until our propellant was gone. Or nearly gone. Even at the cost of reduced acceleration, I felt it necessary to save some small amount for emergency maneuvering.

While thruster engines fired independently, on a vessel so vast as *Challenger* or any ship of the line, propellant was centrally stored and pumped to smaller tanks within the individual thrusters. Should a feed problem cause any of our jets to sputter or misfire, we'd waste irreplaceable propellant in corrections. Our thruster pumps, powered by the fusion engines that were *Challenger*'s main source of energy, must be reliable.

I warned Dray that I'd soon need his engine room manned and functioning, with especial attention to the pump power lines. Grimly he set about the task.

Meanwhile, I delved into our manifests, wondering which items of cargo we could jettison to lighten our load. Every ounce of mass we could eliminate would raise the speed we'd achieve before our propellant gave out. Perhaps someday, decades hence, that would make a difference as we neared the Solar System. Personally, I doubted it would much matter; despite my hopeful words to the ship's company, I didn't see much awaiting us except a lingering death. Unless, of course, we were rescued.

Alone on the bridge, I brooded. With more skilled crewmen, I would even consider dismembering the ship itself. What use had we for the holds, forward of the disks and the launch berth? Once we removed necessary stores, the remainder would play no part in our survival and only added considerable tonnage to our mass.

I sighed. It would be an immense labor to disassemble the ship, one probably beyond our level of skill. More important, we hadn't the manpower to attempt such a project while also rebuilding our hydroponics and maintaining essential ship's systems.

Besides, when it came down to it, even if we survived, would the difference in speed matter all that much? We'd be broadcasting continuously to Earth, and our transmissions would arrive home in nineteen years. What additional velocity we achieved would have negligible effect on the time of our rescue. Unless, of course, our broadcasts went unheard, which was quite possible given the vast interstellar clutter of background radiation and noise.

Well, nothing I could do about it, given our resources. I turned my attention to cargo. There, at least, we could have some effect. With our powered loading equipment a few men could easily empty the hold in days.

Challenger, like any ship, carried not only its own supplies, but freight bound for the colony it served. Admiralty would no doubt be incensed if I abandoned expensive and needed cargo, but there was little likelihood the material would ever reach Hope Nation even if *Challenger* were found, years hence.

On the other hand, assuming we were doomed to many years of sail, who could know what items we'd find useful?

I made a preliminary list, and as it happened, Walter Dakko was near when I asked Philip to review it. The middy merely acknowledged my order, but Dakko fidgeted and conveyed his unease until I glared and said, "Well?"

"I know it's not my place to interfere, but . . ."

"You're right, but out with it."

"Captain, have you considered the effect on the crew when you raise the issue?"

"What issue?"

"Having them toss overboard anything we might do without. It makes our abandonment seem so . . . final."

"You have objections to that?" I was prepared to put him in his place, and fast.

"No, I try to be a realist. But when some of the others see you acting in a way that suggests we have no real hope of res—"

Philip's tone was indignant. "Nonsense! When the Captain gives an order, the crew carries it out. There's no question of—"

"No, sir, of course not." Dakko hesitated. "But you see, you've been telling them a rescue ship will find us, and except for the Clinger and Andros crowd, that's been holding us together. If we're to be found and off-loaded, what does our velocity matter?"

"You'd have us sit here for years, waiting?" I waved it aside. "I'll decide what's best for the ship. The crew will do what they're told."

"I hope so, sir. Though I've heard it asked why you don't—"

"Enough!"

"—try to repair the fusion drive. Aye aye, sir." He fell silent.

I stood slowly, urging myself not to snarl. "Repair the drive? Impossible. Pass the word, Mr. Dakko: we couldn't begin to tackle that sort of job ourselves. Even at a Lunapolis shipyard . . ." Losing my struggle, I swore under my breath, with feeling.

If he heard me, he gave no sign.

Over the next days I struggled to decide what to jettison. Should we go so far as to strip the empty cabins of their gear? Of what possible use was the ship's launch, nineteen light-years from the nearest star? Its mass was considerable. Yet, I hesitated. Fusion drive or no, *Challenger* was a Naval vessel still. If I abandoned the launch, why not the laser cannon, or the console at which the crew practiced firing drills? Why keep the exercise machinery for the passengers' lounge?

In the end I made arbitrary decisions that satisfied no one, including myself. For the morale of the passengers I left the ship intact, including all its provisions, and jettisoned only some of the heaviest cargo: tool and die manufactories for Hope Nation's growing industry, stamped and molded alloys, and the like. If anyone objected, they were smart enough not to let me hear it.

I ordered two radio beacons put out, and waited an extra

day, monitoring to make sure they worked properly. Our rescue might depend on them. Later, we'd drop more.

When at last we were ready I called Dray and Philip to the bridge and set them to plotting our course with Kerren. At last everyone's figures agreed to several decimals. I entered our calculations on the screen.

Propulsive maneuvers were normally carried out by the Pilot, but we had no Pilot. As Captain I was assumed to have the necessary skills to maneuver a ship, yet I recalled with chagrin the ineptitude with which I'd handled docking drills as a middy. Now our lives depended on abilities I lacked.

"Dray, go below; report when you're ready." The Chief saluted and left, saying nothing, not even the customary "Aye aye, sir."

Finally the engine room sent the signal.

The power of our fusion engines, unusable for their primary purpose, was channeled to the pumps feeding our maneuvering jets at the stern and sides of the ship. "Mr. Tyre," I said stiffly, "I order you to advise me the moment you see me mishandle the ship. Don't hesitate."

"Aye aye, sir. I shall."

With that as encouragement I rested my hand on the thruster controls. "Declination, fifteen." Tiny squirts of propellant from the side thrusters brought the bow ever so slowly around. No need to waste precious fuel to line us toward home when a few extra minutes would accomplish the maneuver through inertia.

I corrected our declination and attitude, braking our rotation until we were lined up perfectly for Sol, nineteen light-years distant. I knew that as we accelerated I'd have to make numerous small adjustments; our rate of thrust would not be absolutely uniform while propellant spewed from our tubes; minute impurities in the hydrozine or corrosion of the thruster tubes would have some noticeable effect.

"Very well. I believe we're now set to accelerate. Correct, Mr. Tyre?"

"I think so, sir. Yes, sir."

"All ahead one quarter." My hand closed around the smooth round ball on the console. Slowly I slid it forward, my eyes glued to the screen that flashed our position and course. Carefully I brought us up to speed, occasionally tapping the side thrusters ever so gently to correct our course.

I maintained one-quarter propulsion for over an hour, until I was reasonably sure the thrusters were operating properly. Sometimes they'd been known to cough, and at docking, tragedy could result. For us, the danger was less immediate. We faced only the risk of hurtling helplessly wide of our course, our propellant tanks dry.

"Increasing thrust to one-half." Drenched with sweat, my arm aching from the tension of my grip, I eased the red ball forward. *Challenger* held true to her course. "Mr. Tyre!"

Philip leapt forward. "Yes, sir?"

"Call the engine room. Are the thrusters heating?" If I reached for the caller with my free hand, my concentration might waver.

I knew Dray would report any malfunction instantly, but I had grim memories of the terrible day the thrusters on *Hibernia*'s launch had exploded. *Hibernia* had lost her Captain and two lieutenants. The event had shaped the course of my life, had won Amanda and lost her forever, had made me brittle, lonely, and bitter.

"Temperature normal, sir."

"I'm going to three-quarters thrust." Each second we accelerated increased our velocity, until eventually we would reach nearly a quarter the speed of light. The sooner we achieved this velocity, the greater chance we had of seeing home. But our maneuvering jets weren't designed to operate at full thrust for long, and we would need to fire the thrusters for almost a month to achieve our maximum speed. I dared not bring us to full acceleration too quickly.

Our maneuver would have been impossible had not Captain Hasselbrad transferred much of *Portia*'s propellant to *Challenger* to ease his guilt in deserting us. Nonetheless, we would run out of propellant before we could achieve truly significant velocity. We would then face helpless years aboard an unmaneuverable vessel.

My wrist ached. I watched the numbers flash on our console, carried out to impossibly long decimals. The slightest variation from true course at the beginning of our trajectory would multiply into drastic and irremediable error as we progressed.

When we'd achieved three-quarters acceleration I pried my nearly numb hand from the ball. Now we could do nothing but wait, and be ever vigilant to jump to the side thrusters, to make any corrections Kerren did not. I wondered if I dared leave the bridge during the month to come.

There was at least one assist I could give to our morale. I picked up the caller. "Attention all hands and passengers. As you may have noticed if you looked out the portholes, we maneuvered the ship into position for acceleration. A short while ago I began firing our thrusters. We are on our way home. It will be a long, long voyage, but with the grace of Lord God we will, someday, see Terra again. That is all."

I replaced the caller and leaned back, the perspiration grown chill on my shirt. To my right Philip stood grinning with pleasure at our accomplishment.

Recalling his abuse of my prerogatives while I was disabled, I stared at him, expressionless, until his elation faded. "You may go, Mr. Tyre, until your watch."

He met my gaze, his eyes now bleak. "Aye aye, sir." He left.

Dray's relations with me were now coldly correct, absolutely unforgiving. He ran his engine room, carried out what responsibilities I assigned him, kept entirely to himself.

My relationship with Philip was virtually nonexistent. During the ten days since I'd left the wardroom in blind fury I'd avoided all casual contact with him, and spoken to him with icy formality when unavoidable.

Philip, Dray, and I had rotated watches for an endless week, relieving each other without conversation, at least, when I was present. I presumed the midshipman and the Chief were more congenial to each other than either was to me. I could imagine what they said about me in private.

Philip Tyre performed his duties with diligence and energy. He took an active hand in training our new recruits, and under his tutelage they began to take on the appearance and manner of Naval crewmen. Emmett Branstead and Mr. Dakko no longer spoke out of turn, and would have been reprimanded sharply if they had.

The transients who joined the crew formed their own subculture, until we dissolved it by merciless integration. They weren't allowed to eat together, bunk near each other, or pass free time in each other's company, but only among the other members of the crew. Resentful at first, they slowly began to adapt. Deke, who'd been beaten senseless by the deckhand Akkrit, now exiled to section four, was the last to respond, but after days of sullen withdrawal he too began to emerge from his shell.

Meanwhile, alone in my quarantine of the spirit, I sat brooding on the bridge.

Gregor Attani came to attention, all eager creases and backbone.

"Stand easy, Cadet."

"Yes, sir. Reporting as ordered, sir. We've apportioned all the remaining food into thirty-five lots and stowed each in a separate bin, labeled by weeks. Thirty-five weeks, sir. Less food in the later weeks' bins, as you ordered."

"Very well, Mr. Attani. Dismissed." I watched him go. A cadet reporting directly to the Captain; another cherished Navy tradition by the boards. A cadet was considered the lowest of the low, a trainee devoid of civil and personal rights, the ward of his superior officer. By custom a Captain did not deign to notice a cadet's presence, far less speak to him. He would certainly not assign a cadet to carry out important tasks. But Gregor, at eighteen, was five years older than the typical cadet, and in any event I had no one else.

I knew Gregor Attani was shaping up well, under Philip's guidance. Though only months younger than Philip, the cadet treated his senior midshipman with reverence bordering on awe. Recalling the brutality with which Tyre had tormented *Hibernia*, I couldn't fathom how he'd achieved such rapport with Gregor. I envied it, though I knew the hostility between us was of my own making.

Of course it helped that Gregor was not subject to a cadet's traditional merciless hazing. He was rather too old to benefit from it, and there was no one to haze him save Philip, whose energies were expended elsewhere. Despite Gregor's unwillingness to volunteer, he accepted ship's discipline and the constraints of his new role with good grace.

Still, all was not well with him. Earlier that day I'd gone

to the dining hall for a cup of coffee—thank heaven, our supply of that liquid was nearly unlimited. While I puttered unnoticed in the galley, Mr. Bree and Chris Dakko moved tables in the hall outside. Gregor arrived with a query from Philip; Mr. Bree scurried back to the storeroom, leaving Gregor and Chris Dakko alone.

"Hello, Chris." Gregor's manner was awkward. I groaned inwardly. As a prospective officer, he must keep his distance. Instead of making my presence known, I waited to hear out the conversation, uneasy at eavesdropping. Hadn't I just admonished Philip for doing the same?

Chris eyed Gregor's crisp gray uniform with contempt. "Do I know you, joey?"

"Funny."

"Not really. I'd call it pathetic."

"Call what?"

"How you sold out." Chris coolly contemplated his former friend. "I hear you're bunking with pretty boy Tyre. Have a good time together?"

I pursed my lips. To commissioned officers, a cadet was as nothing, but to a crewman like Chris, he was as any officer, and Naval courtesy was due.

"What's eating you?" Gregor's voice seethed.

"You heard me. You sold yourself to hardass Seafort and that cute middy. Why bother? In a couple of months we'll all be dead."

"What about you? Whose work shirt do you wear?"

"This?" Chris flicked his light blue shirt with scorn. "You know why. That trannie gorilla is waiting to beat the shit out of me and no one will stop him. Someday I'll kill him. I've already got it planned." A sneer. "But you don't just submit, you go along for the ride. Do they feed you better up there?"

"I think," Gregor said slowly, "I never really knew you."

"Don't worry about it, grode. You've got your new friends to suck up to, just like old daddy Walter."

"Remember who you're speaking to, Dakko."

"Yeah? Who?"

"An officer candidate. If the Captain heard, you'd be in all sorts of trouble."

"You gonna tell him, asslicker?"

Gregor took a deep breath. "Stand at attention."

"Oh, no. I take that crap from the gorilla, but not from you. Not unless you're man enough to make me."

"I am, but you're not worth the trouble I'd get in." He turned on his heel, stalked out. Chris muttered something derisive under his breath.

I waited until Mr. Bree had Chris's attention occupied and crept out unseen. Gregor had lost control of a crewman, but my stepping in would only make it worse. I filed it among my many unsolved problems.

Days crept by in dreary succession. I inched the thrusters to full power and kept them at maximum, poring over the readouts more anxiously than ever. They remained steady.

Our full attention turned to food production; everyone, including passengers, helped convert our unused cabins to urban farms. We had to ration sand, but we had plenty of water, thanks to Captain Hasselbrad. Tomato plants, lettuce, squash, legumes, even carrots began to sprout and were cherished like infants by our fervent gardeners.

Each meal we ate from our dwindling stores made us more aware of our desperate need to succeed in our gardening. Many of the passengers resented the food I sent daily to section four, the same rations we ourselves were given. I paid no heed, except to assure that the supplies arrived unmolested.

There was some altercation between Eddie Boss and Dray. I didn't know the details, and didn't want to ask. Eddie bore bruises for a week or so, until they faded, and thereafter treated all officers with increased deference. Dray didn't seem a match for the huge recruit, but he'd been around long enough to know a few tricks. And he ran an engine room, where rough joes were commonplace. Still, it was bad discipline for an officer to scuffle with a crewman. Because this was no time for me to interfere with Dray, I held my peace.

During these weeks I hardly saw my cabin during waking hours, though I yearned for its seclusion. What time I didn't spend on the bridge, anticipating with dread an alarm that would signal a deterioration in our course, I spent roving the ship.

I kept the recycler's mates taut with tension at my sudden

inspections. I constantly appeared at the hydro chambers and our improvised vegetable farms. I lost track of how often I passed through the launch berth lock and roamed the hold, hoping to find supplies or equipment I hadn't noticed on the manifest.

I'd retreated to my cabin late at night and was stripping off my clothes when the knock came. I don't know who I expected, but I was dumbfounded to find myself face-to-face with Philip Tyre.

"May I have a word, sir?"

"Is this an emergency?" I made my voice as cold as I could manage.

"No, sir."

"On the bridge, in the morning." I slapped the hatch shut. As I got ready for bed I seethed; Philip knew the Captain's cabin was inviolate. True, I'd told him he was free to knock. But that was before he ignored my orders about the mutineers. I snapped off the light, dropped my head on the pillow, waited for sleep.

Two hours later I turned the light on and, with a sigh of resignation, reached for the caller. "Mr. Tyre, to the Captain's cabin." I dressed myself, sat in the chair to wait. It wasn't long.

I regarded him coldly. "Well?"

He came to the at-ease position. "Sorry I bothered you at night, sir. I shouldn't have."

"But you did, so get on with it."

He squirmed, gave up the at-ease position, and studied the near bulkhead as if for flaws. "I, uh, came to apologize."

"Oh?"

"Yes, sir." Red-faced, he turned his gaze to me. "For my beh—my misbehavior in connection with the rebellion."

"You were wrong?"

"I—yes, sir. I was wrong. I'd be grateful if you'd forgive me."

"Why?" I felt no inclination to let him off the hook.

His eyes filled with sudden tears. "Because—damn!" He twisted away, thrusting his hands in his pockets.

At once I banished the triumph of revenge to some shabby recess of my mind. "Why, Philip?" I asked more gently.

"Because I need your respect," he whispered, his face

turned. "Because I'm so lonely, with only Gregor to talk to, and I can't stand . . . knowing you hate me again." He sucked in his breath.

Lord Christ, what had I done? I got to my feet. "I don't hate you, Philip. I never have."

"No?" He strove for calm. "I think you do, and I'm sorry for what I did to cause it. It's"—he faltered—"like the last time." His voice was low.

"I don't understand."

"On *Hibernia*, when everyone said I was hurting the midshipmen. I didn't understand, I never could; I just knew finally that something had gone terribly wrong. And now it's happening again."

With growing uneasiness I asked, "Why did you apologize, Philip?"

"I told you!"

"The truth, this time! Because you felt you were wrong?"

He whirled to face me, tears streaming. "Why do you make me say it? Isn't it enough that I apologize?"

"Only truth matters."

"The truth . . . No, sir, I don't think I was wrong, not deep inside. I wish I could, but I don't. I came because I need you not to hate me. Oh, God, let me be dismissed. I shouldn't have come!"

"Yes, you should!" I slammed my fist on the table, as a door flew open in my mind.

"Now I've made things worse . . ."

I shook my head decisively, not trusting myself to speak.

"Why not?"

"You were right!" I dropped into my chair and said again, more quietly, "Because you were right." The silence sat heavy between us. "That's why you felt no guilt, and why I've been miserable for the last month. God, I've wronged you."

He stood speechless.

"When you brigged the rebels, you were acting as Captain. My orders were irrelevant; you didn't even know yet if I'd recover. And, most important, my oath didn't bind you."

He whispered, "If that's true why didn't you say it before?"

I forced my eyes to meet his. "Because I resented your doing such a good job. I fuddled for five days and accomplished nothing; you took command and sorted out everything while I lay in a stupor. Maybe I did hate you a little, for that."

"That's not fair to yourself," he protested. "I got us into the mess, didn't I? I mean, by dropping my weapons so the rebels could get them. And you saved us by your unbelievable bravery. All I did was, well, housekeeping."

I smiled wryly. "Then you're a very fine housekeeper, Midshipman. Very good indeed."

He blushed with unexpected pleasure. "Really? You mean that?"

I nodded.

"I tried to think of everything. It was the only chance I've ever had to, well, run things."

"I know." Midshipmen were taught to follow orders; far between were the opportunities to give them.

"You called me a sea lawyer and said I was insolent—"

"I'm sorry."

"—and it was true, sir. I didn't try to explain to you; my pride got in the way."

"You shouldn't need to explain." I stood and began to pace. "You didn't know me when I was your age, Philip. When I was senior middy aboard *Hibernia*."

"They told me stories, Alexi and Derek."

"When Captain Malstrom died before commissioning a lieutenant, I pored over the regs, trying to find a way out. Vax Holser should have been appointed, and we both knew it."

Philip smiled bleakly. "He didn't think so. It's one of the few things he said about you."

"Well, I knew the regs. The Captain is in complete charge of the ship and everyone in it. There's no difference between Captain and acting Captain, as you were here on *Challenger*. I knew that then, and I knew it when I sent you from the bridge the day I relieved you. I was just so jealous."

"Of me?" he said in astonishment. "But why?"

"Christ, boy, look at you! You're young and handsome, and assured, and you're so competent. I'm not."

"Not assured?" he repeated in wonder. "On *Hibernia* I was terrified of you. You knew exactly what you wanted, and would settle for nothing less." He shook his head. "Not competent? Then what are you? How many times did you save *Hibernia*? Or *Challenger*?"

"I know my duty, but that doesn't mean I do it well. You have a knack."

"I'm glad you think so. I'd like a chance to command, someday." He wiped his sleeve across his face. "I'm sorry I burst in when you were getting ready for bed." He flashed a shy smile. "This time I really mean the apology."

I shook my head. "It isn't that easy for me, Philip. I've been treating you badly."

"No you haven't, sir," he blurted. I raised my eyebrow. "Not badly. You were very . . . polite. It was more that you weren't treating me at all."

"Even worse. I'm glad you still want my respect; you have it. I'll try to do better in the future."

"So will I." Awkwardly he pulled himself to attention. Ignoring that, I offered my hand. He took it. The warmth of his grip made it difficult to speak further.

After my reconciliation with Philip I bore my watches on the bridge with renewed vigor. To my amazement, *Challenger* was slowly returning to Naval standards, though Philip had his hands full training the streeters who'd joined the crew. His earnest and patient attempts to explain Navy methods didn't work; the transients either ignored him or laughed outright, which provoked him to retaliatory discipline that further antagonized them.

I felt some special obligation to the transients that I had difficulty defining. I was determined that they not be treated as second-class sailors, just as I had been determined that they not be second-class passengers. But how, for example, could we teach them to stand critically important watches in the comm room or the recycler chamber? Many were illiterate, all were essentially uneducated. How could I train them to man the lasers, or the radionics? Could they even understand the concepts involved?

I was distracted from that problem by another; the caller frantically paging me from section four. It was the deckhand Sykes, exiled with the rest of his unsavory comrades, able to communicate only with the bridge. "Mr. Clinger, he's hurt bad. Somebody do something, 'fore he dies in here!"

"What happened, Mr. Sykes?"

"Clinger and Andy, they been goin' at it, needlin' each other and all. Andy broke up a chair and took a piece of it, for a club . . . Clinger's lyin' on the deck, and I can't get him awake!"

I sighed. If I took Clinger to the infirmary he'd have to be guarded. And what about Andros? If I brigged him, would I be going back on my oath?

As if reading my thoughts, Sykes whimpered, "Please don' leave me alone with Andy, Captain. Not without Clinger here."

"Belay that, sailor. You got what you wanted." I paused. "I'll send a detail down for Clinger. They'll shoot to kill if you try anything."

I gave Walter Dakko the assignment; it seemed he had become our de facto master-at-arms. I decided to give him the title to match his role, and informed him when he answered my summons.

He seemed unaffected by his new appointment. I wondered how seriously he took any of our Naval traditions, in the privacy of his thoughts.

Shortly after Clinger was installed in the infirmary, and Dakko and Elena Bartel recalled to their medical efforts, Philip conveyed Eddie Boss's request to see me. That brought a smile; Eddie had learned from his previous attempt. "Very well, send him up."

The young sailor came to attention, if not smartly, then passably.

"Yes, Mr. Boss?"

"Cap'n, was thinkin' 'bout trannies. Crew trannies."

I waited. After a moment he continued, "Things you showin' me. You 'n boss boy."

"The midshipman. Mr. Tyre, to you."

"Okay, Tyre. Mist' Tyre." He checked for my approval before continuing. "He havin' trouble learnin' trannies. 'Bout jobs, 'n all. Dey don' listen good, 'n he get mad."

"No complaints about your superior officer, Mr. Boss."

"I ain' complainin'," he protested. "Jus' sayin'. I wan' ta help."

"How?"

He shifted uncomfortably. "I know I be dumb, Cap'n. Like learnin' read, know I don' think good. But I c'n try real hard. You an' ol boss bo—Mist' Tyre, if he show Eddie, I c'n teach trannies. Dey lis when I be talkin, not go laughin' like wid boss boy."

I drummed the console. It might work. Certainly the hulking sailor was motivated; he felt responsible for his compatriots. "Well, Mr. Boss, I'll—" I broke off as an idea struck. Could it work? It would solve another problem. But if it failed, I'd make things worse . . .

I thumbed the caller. "Mr. Tyre to the bridge. And Mr. Attani." I took a deep breath. "And Mr. Dakko. Junior."

A few moments later they all stood before me in the at-ease position. Chris Dakko's demeanor hinted of contempt, though with typical adolescent skill he avoided overt behavior for which I could reprimand him. No matter; I hadn't summoned him for a rebuke.

In a severe tone I said to Philip, "Mr. Tyre, how many transpops are on your watch roster for the recyclers?"

The midshipman shot me a surprised glance; we had discussed the matter only yesterday. "None, sir."

"And on the comm room watch?"

"None."

"I told you to train them to stand any watch."

"Yes, sir! I'll work on it immed—"

"Work on it with Mr. Attani. Perhaps he'll succeed where you failed."

Gregor radiated sullen anger at my attack on his mentor.

I turned sharply on Attani. "Cadet, you're now in charge of crew training. Teach the transients what they need to know to stand watch, or I'll make you sorry you were born. You're a cadet; you know what that means?"

"I think so, sir."

"You have no recourse, Mr. Attani. When I turn on you, I can do anything, and I will! So be prepared for months of misery, or get the transients trained now."

"Aye aye, sir."

"You're educated. Take a crewman who's had some schooling to help you teach Mr. Boss; he's got a way with the other transients. Show him what you want the rest of them to know, and he'll help you teach them. But if I catch you or the crewman slacking off . . ."

"Aye aye, sir!"

I said, as if in an afterthought, "Use Mr. Dakko here. He's been to school."

Chris opened his mouth to protest, thought better of it.

"You've something to say, Dakko?"

"No, sir," the boy said quickly.

"I hope not. Mr. Attani, as far as sailors are concerned, you're an officer. You have the right to have your orders obeyed. Mr. Tyre has dithered long enough; now get to work!"

"Aye aye, sir!"

"Dismissed, all of you. Mr. Tyre, you will remain." When the bridge had cleared I gestured to the console next to mine. Philip sat uneasily. I said nothing.

He let the silence continue as long as he could. Finally he said, hesitantly, "I didn't think I was doing that bad a job with the transpops, sir."

"Neither did I." My tone was gruff.

He studied me a long moment. "Then you weren't upset with me?"

"No. Just a show."

The tension drained from his body.

"I wanted to light a fire under Gregor and Chris."

"You did, sir. Did you see Gregor's face when he left?"

"It might solve a lot of problems at once. Gregor's relations with Chris Dakko. Give Gregor a taste of command. Maybe even straighten Chris around."

"Having Chris Dakko teach Eddie . . ." Philip winced. "I don't think either of them will like that."

"Or they might learn how to get along together." I spoke absently; my mind was already on the next problem.

The daily reports on fuel consumption were replaced by hourly, as our propellant dwindled. I was plagued by new doubts about shutting down the thrusters before the tanks ran bone dry. By continuing to increase our velocity we would cut almost four years off our return time.

On the other hand, did it matter? We were seventy-six years from home, at projected speed. Assuming our radio calls weren't intercepted, we'd have to endure a seven-decade voyage. After that long, what difference would forty-seven months make?

On the other hand, what reason was there to hold propellant in reserve? The chances of *Challenger* colliding with any object were minute, even in the distant future when she neared the Solar System.

But if we encountered the . . . fish. The aliens.

Interstellar space was vast, and it obviously didn't swarm with fish. Yet they seemed to be able to find our ships. *Telstar* had been attacked, *Portia*, *Challenger* . . . and other ships were missing.

I paced the bridge in growing frustration, trying to make a decision without enough data. What good would a few hundred gallons of propellant do us? We couldn't Fuse. We had laser armaments, but the crew was uneducated and unskilled in using them. If the fish attacked, our chances were negligible.

Yet . . . several times I was on the verge of recalculating our acceleration, to expend all our propellant now. Each time I withheld my hand. My indecision nagged like a broken tooth.

I kept to myself, meeting Philip or Dray as they relieved me, eating in my cabin or on the bridge. But one afternoon, seeking coffee, I ran into Gregor in the dining hall. He sported an unmistakable black eye. I pretended to ignore it, in the time-honored Naval tradition, but wondered what could have angered Philip so.

My head ached abominably; I was overtired, and brooding on Gregor's problems with Philip made me more uneasy yet. This was no time for niceties; I called Tyre to the bridge.

"It wasn't me, sir. Gregor and I get along fine."

"Well, then?"

"Have you noticed Chris Dakko lately?"

I hadn't. "An officer brawling with a crewman?" I cursed under my breath.

"Dakko was asking for trouble."

"Gregor knows the rules," I snapped. "He can't strike a crewman to enforce discipline." My head throbbed. Lord God, didn't the lad have any common sense? How then could he enforce his orders with a crewman bigger than he was?

"Yes, sir. I told him that. Perhaps, sir, if you didn't notice it this time . . ."

I didn't need a middy telling me my job. "No," I growled. "He'll learn the Navy way. Take the barrel down to the engine room, I'll be damned if I'll do it myself. Send the cadet to Dray." After a caning, he'd be more careful.

Philip said slowly, "Are you sure, sir? He's almost nineteen. I doubt he's ever been struck before."

My hand gripped the chair arm. I said coldly, "Consider yourself reprimanded, Midshipman Tyre."

Philip stared at me in shock. Then, stiffly, "Yes, sir."

"Leave the bridge."

"Aye aye, sir." He saluted, turned, and went.

I stood the watch, alone with my rage, on the verge of countermanding my orders, but watching the clock, delaying. I took a grim satisfaction in my stubbornness. Only when it was too late did I let myself recall Gregor, on the bridge, on the mattress near mine, pleased despite himself that I thought enough of him to make him an officer.

When I saw Philip the next morning I'd recovered enough aplomb to remark, "I won't put your reprimand in the Log."

"Very well, sir." He sounded indifferent.

"Just don't argue with me again."

"Aye aye, sir." He stared glumly at the simulscreen.

My irritation flared anew. "Is that all you have to say?"

He spun to face me. "What do you want me to say?" he shouted. "Just tell me, I'll say it!"

Stunned, I could only stare.

"You told me I was free to knock at your hatch, and you tore into me when I did. In your cabin you said you respect me, you even shook hands as if we were friends. Then you chewed me out in front of Gregor and Dray like I was a rank cadet!"

He hurled his ribbed cap at the chair. "Then you told me you weren't serious about chewing me out, except yesterday you reprimanded me, but now you tell me it won't go on the Log! How would I know what to say to you? Nothing makes sense!" Enraged, he met my glare.

A long time passed. Finally his eyes dropped; his face grew pink; at last he said in a small voice, "I'm very sorry, sir. Please forgive what I said."

My eyes bored into him. He fidgeted, blushed a deeper red, said humbly, "What would you like me to do, sir?"

Still I didn't speak.

Desperate, he blurted, "Should I go to my quarters, sir? Until you're ready to deal with me?"

"No. Stay." I could imagine how he thought I might deal with him. Summary dismissal from the Service. Confinement in the brig. At the least, the worst caning of his life. Any middy could expect similar consequences after such an outburst to his Captain, regardless of the provocation.

The trouble was that Philip was right. I stared blindly past the glittering lights of my console. When I'd been a midshipman on *Hibernia*, Captain Haag was remote, austere. Coming into his presence I felt a very young middy indeed, anxious not to call his notice to myself by some foolish lapse.

But *Hibernia* was a fully manned ship, where three lieutenants served between me and the Captain. My contacts were primarily with the lieutenants, and even they were objects of fear and respect. Captain Haag's confidants were his lieutenants or his friend the Chief Engineer, not a lowly middy.

On *Challenger* there were only Philip, Dray, and myself. Lonely, insecure, frightened, I'd come to rely too heavily on Philip Tyre, and then rebuffed the midshipman every time he responded to my demand for familiarity.

So now Philip had made a critical blunder, pushed over the edge by my contradictory demands. I'd whipsawed him until he lost control, and to punish him for it seemed morally wrong.

But not to punish him would confuse him all the more. How could I expect him to maintain the proper distance if I failed to react to even a gross violation of propriety?

"Well, now." Coolly I studied the offending middy. "What am I to do with you?"

He mumbled, "I don't know, sir."

"Neither do I. Eight demerits, for a start. Work them off within the week. And I withdraw my promise to you; if you exceed ten demerits you will be caned, like any other midshipman in any other ship."

"Yes, sir!"

"I'm sorry I confused you. We are the only officers aboard, except for Dray, so you may feel free to knock at my hatch. I may lash out at you, but that is my prerogative. Knock anyway."

A sheen of sweat dampened his forehead; he dared make no move to wipe it.

"Philip, I respect you, as I said before. Nonetheless, I am Captain and you are a midshipman, and you'll speak to me with courtesy. You will contain any further outbursts until you can deliver them to the bulkhead in the privacy of your wardroom. Is that quite clear?"

Philip nodded vigorously. "Very clear, sir."

"You're confined to the wardroom for the rest of the day. Reflect, if you will, on how lenient I've been. But I wonder if something else is bothering you, that caused you to lose control."

"No, sir, nothing. I—I didn't get much sleep last night, but that's no excuse."

"Why didn't you sleep?"

He colored. "Gregor, sir. He—I, uh, had a long talk with him."

"He was upset?"

Philip bit his lip before he answered frankly. "A closer word would be hysterical, sir. It took a while before I could get him to listen."

"And now?"

"I don't know. I think he'll be all right."

"Very well." It wasn't the time to explore that situation. "Dismissed." He fled the bridge.

16

Seaman Elron Clinger hovered near death, his skull fractured. I ordered his hands tied to the sides of his bed, and sent Elena Bartel about her duties with orders to check on him from time to time. I couldn't afford to spare a full-time nurse, and in his case I hadn't the inclination.

At my bidding Kerren conducted simulated laser drills at frequent intervals, for the crewmen training in the comm room. Deke, Eddie Boss, and Walter Dakko were among those chosen for training.

Mr. Tzee paced behind the consoles as the drills progressed, correcting the targeting on the trainees' screens. Deke showed no interest whatsoever until Walter Dakko leaned over and quietly explained that hitting imaginary targets with the imaginary laser was just like scoring points in Arcvid. I tried to imagine Walter Dakko pumping Unibucks into an Arcvid console. Perhaps he'd been out with Chris . . .

"Lord God, today is September 18, 2198, on the U.N.S. *Challenger*. We ask you to bless us, to bless our voyage, and to bring health and well-being to all aboard."

I waited for the murmured "Amen" of the assembled passengers and crew. I'd led the traditional evening prayer countless times, yet even now it brought a lump to my throat.

"Tonight I have an announcement," I said soberly. "In some three hours I shall cut the acceleration of our thrusters. We will have achieved the maximum speed we shall ever attain, and our course hereafter will be in the hands of Lord God."

"Are we out of fuel?" Old Mrs. Ovaugh, her fear evident.

"We have some reserves with which to maneuver, Mrs.

Ovaugh, in case it's necessary. Other than that, we have spent all our propellant."

"Could we increase our speed using it all?" It was the first time I'd heard Mr. Pierce speak.

"Yes. Every moment of acceleration increases our speed. But then we'd be entirely helpless to maneuver."

Someone said, "But we'd be going home faster."

I hadn't meant to initiate a policy review. "We began broadcasting our position over a month ago, and we've dropped radio beacons along our route. Our transmissions will reach Earth decades before we do."

Chris Dakko cautiously raised his hand. I nodded. "If the messages don't get through," he asked, "wouldn't the extra speed make a difference?"

I sighed, knowing I should have managed to avoid this discussion. "We might cut our travel time from seventy-six years to seventy-two with the remaining propellant," I said. "But I won't leave the ship entirely disabled. That," I said over rising murmurs of protest, "is already decided."

Elena Bartel raised her hand. I was grateful the crew knew better than to speak up without permission. "Sir, what good are our fuel reserves? What could we maneuver away from, without being able to Fuse?"

"Would you care to impact with an asteroid at one-quarter light-speed?" That silenced them for the moment. "The discussion is over," I said firmly. "Mr. Tyre, Mr. Attani, report to the bridge an hour after the meal." I sat.

Still the angry murmurs persisted. I tried to ignore them. As the stewards began to serve the meal Mr. Tzee approached my table with diffidence. "Sir, would you consider—"

I slammed the table so the silverware jumped, as did the two elderly passengers at my side. "I will not!" I roared. "Back to your place!" My outburst silenced the hall, and it was minutes before conversation began anew.

Our dinner consisted mostly of our dwindling stores; it would be many weeks before our laborious efforts at hydroponics resulted in edible crops. Daily I'd watched crewmen haul water and adjust the lighting in the plant chambers, and I'd set an example by helping.

Cautious buds had poked their heads above the sand and had begun to thrive. They shot upward with encouraging speed, tended by men whose very survival depended on their success. Embryonic tomatoes, cucumbers, and beans were visible if one looked closely.

I'd calculated, with Emmett Branstead's assistance, that our new crops would be ready for harvest just as our food stores dwindled to near nothing. For a time we would be on very short rations indeed, but we continued to expand our hydroponics efforts, so the food supply would gradually increase.

No one at my table spoke to me, perhaps not willing to risk another tirade. When the meal was ended, I hurried back to the bridge to relieve Dray. His salute was short of contemptuous, but not by much. He left without a word.

The readouts flashed on the console screen. Our thrusters had performed magnificently, never overheating. Still, I would be glad to power down.

Irritated at Dray's manner, I called up the day's laser firing drills while waiting for my officers. Two shifts of sailors had practiced today. Naturally, more than one work detail was trained for each of our critical tasks, in case crewmen were put out of action. I followed the book in that regard, though I saw little point in it. If comm room personnel were knocked out, for example, the ship was almost certainly lost. The aliens would inject their viruses, hurl the acid that ate through our hull.

Walter Dakko, Ms. Bartel, and Deke continually improved their scores, as expected. The other group—young Jonie, Mr. Kovaks, and a transpop called Ratchet—wasn't doing as well. I made note to have Mr. Tzee spend extra time with them, then remembered I'd just screamed at Mr. Tzee in front of the ship's company. Heaven knew what cooperation I would get from him henceforth.

A knock; I opened the hatch without looking to see who it was. Philip saluted stiffly. "Midshipman Tyre reporting, sir. Permission to—"

"Come in." I went back to my console. I'd noticed in the Log that Philip was slowly working off his demerits, dutifully logging each session in the exercise room. Since our confrontation four days earlier, he had retreated into stiff formality, but without sullenness. I matched his manner. "Would you care to sit, Mr. Tyre?"

"Thank you, sir." He took his place at his console, proper as a green young middy on his first watch. I wondered what I might say to relax him, then beat a hasty retreat. I had caused Philip enough problems.

A few minutes later another knock. "Let him in, Philip."

"Aye aye, sir." He jumped as if shot.

Gregor Attani came to attention in the corridor just outside the bridge. His salute was perfect, as if practiced for hours before a mirror. Perhaps it had been. "Permission to enter the bridge, sir."

"Granted."

"Thank you." The cadet's voice was icy, the words ejected as if through unwilling teeth.

"Stand here, Mr. Attani. Behind the console."

"Aye aye, sir."

I suppressed my annoyance at the frigid response. "I called you to the bridge to witness powering down the thrusters. Should our journey run its course, this will be remembered as the moment that changed *Challenger* from a powered ship to a missile. I thought you would like to be present." I took the caller. "Engine room, prepare for power-down."

Dray's response was immediate. "Power-down, aye aye." Knowing what was to come, the Chief must have been standing by the caller.

My hand hovered over the knob. I breathed deeply, slowly eased it upward along its track. I imagined I could hear the rumbling cease, though that was nonsense. From the bridge the vibration of the thrusters was imperceptible.

It was done. We hurtled through nothingness at some seventy-one thousand statute miles per second, and would continue for over seventy years. Our choice was made, and we had to live out the consequences. Unless our transmissions were received at home, I would emerge from *Challenger* as a doddering old man, if at all. A mere two generations would pass before our rescue.

"Lord God preserve us," I said, chastened.

"Amen." Philip seemed affected as well.

The moment passed. In a lighter tone I said, "Well, back to everyday problems. Mr. Tyre, have you reorganized the recycler's watch yet?"

"Yes, sir."

"And have you begun teaching the cadet navigation?" I nodded at Gregor.

"Yes, sir, just yesterday. Chapter One of *Lambert and Greeley.*" We'd all started with *The Elements of Astronavigation*, believing *L & G* impossible to master, learning with dismay that it was just the forerunner of more daunting texts.

"Very well." Instructing cadets and middies was the job of a senior lieutenant, but Philip was competent in navigation and our only available teacher.

I groped for some genial remark to offer Gregor, then decided he was letting his resentment show too clearly. Perhaps I'd overreacted in having him caned. Still, he ought to have the sense not to show his feelings. I was, after all, Captain.

"That's all."

"Thank you for having us, sir." Philip's tone was polite, his manner exemplary. He turned for the hatch. Gregor said nothing. His salute was perfunctory.

Beans and other vegetables had been planted, the new crew broken in, the rebellion crushed, the ship set under weigh for home. Our most pressing tasks accomplished, we settled into a dull shipboard routine.

Now we faced the demands of a daily struggle to survive: the drudgery of hauling water to the cabins in which our precious plants grew, tiring hours of laser practice by our new crewmen, the constant toil of laundry, food preparation, maintenance, and repairs.

Seaman Clinger lay in a coma for days. I assumed he would die; we could perform routine first aid but not brain surgery. To my surprise, he rallied. Elena Bartel, far too solicitous for my liking, tended his needs. As he became more alert he bitterly protested the straps that bound him.

Whenever the bridge was in other hands I roamed the ship, visiting the recycler chambers, the comm room, even the engine room, where Dray received me with scant courtesy. In the corridors the crewmen came to attention as I passed, the newer recruits imitating the ways of their experienced compatriots.

I was on my way to the galley when Walter Dakko made a curious gesture before coming to attention; his hand flicking out as if to stop me. Though he held attention, he didn't stand eyes front, but fastened his gaze on mine as if with urgency.

"What, Mr. Dakko?" I yearned for my waiting coffee.

"Might I make a suggestion, sir?"

Well, he hadn't approached me unbidden. Not quite. "Go on."

"The tomatoes are coming on strong. And some of the beans will be ready soon."

"So?"

"You've sealed the hydro chambers, haven't you? Only authorized crew can enter."

"Obviously. I don't have time for idle conver—"

"What about the cabins, sir? They're wide open."

I stopped short. Good heavens. Though our ripest vegetables had been started earlier in the hydro chambers, the majority of our crops were coming along in the cabins. "They're not ripe yet," I said.

"No, sir. But green tomatoes are edible. They might be very attractive to a man on short rations."

If a sailor was caught stealing food I'd have to deal with a riot, if not a lynching. A total breakdown of authority could follow. How could I have overlooked the obvious? I cursed under my breath. Daily I walked the ship, failing to see my duty.

"As you were, Mr. Dakko." As he relaxed I said, "This will earn you a promotion." His look was unfathomable. I realized how little that meant to an aristocrat who'd volunteered to save Rome from the barbarian hordes. "And my thanks," I added lamely.

That brought a faint smile. "You're welcome, sir."

"You're in charge of the food security detail. Requisition any supplies you need from Dray."

"Aye aye, sir." We parted.

* * *

I sat at a table with my steaming cup of coffee. Mr. Bree tried to ignore me as he puttered about the dining hall, but his nerves were frayed. In an effort to improve morale I'd asked him to make our meals as attractive as possible and to resume the custom of starched tablecloths at dinner. The crewmen who'd once been passengers saw nothing unusual in this, but I could imagine what our old hands thought, used to dinner in the utilitarian crew mess.

Bree and Chris Dakko, who'd become his assistant, were setting tables. Chris glanced at me, turned away, stone-faced. I took a tentative sip. "How are your lessons going, Mr. Dakko?"

"With the trannies?" Chris bridled at my obvious distaste. "They call themselves trannies," he said belligerently. "Why shouldn't I?"

"Because you're not one of them."

"At least I can be grateful for that!" He dumped a handful of silverware onto the table. *"Sir."* His tone belied the courtesy of the word.

I held my peace. Little would be gained were I to humiliate him. We had a long journey together. Perhaps, in time, he would come round. I took my coffee to the bridge.

When Philip settled in for his watch I went to my cabin, sat in my easy chair, one arm on the polished conference table, and tried to think of nothing. Disturbing thoughts intruded. I explored them, and realized to my surprise that I was frightened. Not of dying, as that immediate prospect had faded, but of seventy-six years imprisonment on this disabled ship, surrounded by well-deserved resentment, hostility, and contempt.

I'd made enemies with careless abandon and saw no way to extricate myself. I'd humiliated Gregor, made a nightmare of Chris Dakko's life, terrorized the Chief. I'd even been offensive to old Mrs. Reeves. Philip was the only one who stood by me, and that only from a sense of duty.

I sat miserable and alone until the dinner hour. Then I straightened my jacket and went to my duty.

In the morning I reviewed entries in the Log. Dray, I saw, had put young Deke on report. I called the engine room. "Why is Deke up for Mast?"

"Insubordination, as I wrote." That told me nothing.

"Why, Dray?"

A pause. "I'd rather come up to discuss it."

"Very well." A few moments later he arrived, breathing heavily from the two flights up the ladder. "Well?"

"He used insubordinate language to describe an officer," Dray said.

I waited for him to continue, realized he wouldn't. This burly, stolid man was embarrassed, unsure. "What did he call you?" I asked gently.

The Chief stared at me without expression. "Not me, Captain. You."

I bit back my surprise, but persisted. "Must I drag it out of you, Dray?"

"Scarface," he said. I couldn't help but flinch. "It's a name they have for you now, Captain. I wouldn't have that."

I fingered the ugly ruin of my cheek. "It's true."

"Still, he's a sailor." Dray's tone was uncompromising. I was intrigued by the divided loyalty of this complicated man, who could treat me with unconcealed insolence, yet send a man to Captain's Mast for doing the same.

I said hesitantly, "Dray, a lot has happened between us . . ."

"Yes." His tone was unbending.

"I would not do again what I chose to do to you. If there's any way it could be put behind us . . ."

"There is not." He spoke with finality.

"Very well. I'll deal with Deke without getting into specifics. You may go."

"Right." Without bothering to salute he turned and left.

Depressed, I waited out my watch. Toward the end of it, Ms. Bartel paged to tell me Seaman Clinger was begging to see me.

"Why?"

"I don't know, sir. He's rational now. We've been talking a lot. He keeps asking for you."

The last thing I wanted was to visit Clinger. "Very well. When Mr. Tyre relieves me." Some duties it was best to get over with. After my watch I went directly to the infirmary, sent away Ms. Bartel.

His head was still heavily bandaged, both hands taped securely to the bed rails. Near one wrist was a buzzer by which he could summon Ms. Bartel; she carried a caller that responded to it.

"Hullo, Captain."

My anger kindled. That was no way to speak to me. On the other hand, he couldn't very well salute. "What did you want?"

His tone was plaintive. "Do you think maybe you could untie one hand, just while we talk? Please, sir?" I shook my head; he added quickly, "I won't try anything. I'm still too dizzy to move much."

"All right." I unwrapped the tape from his right hand.

The moment it was free he scratched the side of his nose. "You know how hard it is not to be able to do that?" A weak smile.

I only grunted in response.

He said slowly, "Captain, I've fouled up good, I know that."

"Right."

"What could I do to earn another chance?"

"Are you kidding?"

"No, sir." He wiggled his toes under the sheets. "Andy was pumpin' me full of all sorts of ideas. When you brigged him, I got a little crazy."

"You mutinied."

He stared at his feet. "Yes. I did that."

"That's all there is to be said."

He spoke as if he hadn't heard me. "You know it was me got into the hold to get the food?"

"I presumed so. I didn't see your face."

"I'm from Liverpool, Cap'n. What about you?"

The question was bizarre. Despite myself, I answered, "Cardiff."

"Well, then." He spoke as if he'd proven a point. "You see, I got so bleedin' scared!" He turned his face away. "I dunno why I signed up on this frazzin' cruise. The bonus, I guess. I spent it all before I reported. We had some good times, me an' the other joes."

He took a couple of deep breaths, spoke more slowly. "But

I never figured on this. Bein' abandoned, like. I'm twenty-four, you know. Just twenty-four. I wanted so damn much to live!" He drew in a breath that was a sob.

"Easy, Mr. Clinger."

"That bastard Tremaine took all our food, as much as he could carry. They say it was Hasselbrad stopped him from gettin' the rest. So I knew we was goin' to starve, no matter what."

I said nothing.

"So we broke inna hold, me and Ibarez and Simmons. Just ta get some food. When I was a kid I saw a man once, starved to death after he been trapped in a chimney a week or two. All I could think of was lookin' like that."

"Nothing excuses mutiny, Mr. Clinger."

"An' when Ibarez got killed, I didn't know what ta do, I thought about it a few days, and got Andy out. 'Cause he'd tell me what to do."

I waited.

His tone held wonder. "It just kinda happened. I dunno why I listened to him. He said, get the guns while we got a chance, so I helped. And Simmons got hisself killed. So you got hold of the armory, and we was done for. So Andy said, take the engine room. It all seemed to make sense, the way he put it."

Exasperated, I snapped, "And now it doesn't? What do you want from me, Clinger?"

"I'm not wicked!" he shouted. His free hand pounded the bed, and he winced as it shook. "I'm dumb, God damn it, but no worse!" He took a shuddering breath. "Don't send me back to him. Please, Captain. Give me any kinda detail, I'll scrub the heads, I'll go on half rations, I'll do whatever you say. Let me make it right!"

"No." I took the roll of tape and grabbed his wrist. He resisted a moment, then was still. I taped him securely to the bed as quickly as I could.

"Please!"

"No." I walked out.

I went directly to my cabin. I examined my burns in the mirror. Scarface. Scarface Seafort. For an impossible moment

I imagined Amanda's soft hand on my shoulder. "It doesn't matter, Nick. I'm here."

But you aren't, Amanda. You never will be again.

"I loved you."

I swallowed. She had. But she was gone, and a retreat into fantasy wouldn't help. I lay on my bed, face pressed into the pillow. I tried not to cry, and failed.

That evening at dinner I was subdued, hoping no one would notice my reddened eyes. In any event, no one remarked on them.

That night I slept as if drugged, and roused myself with reluctance come morning. The day passed, followed by a dreary succession of others. Philip warned me one day of growing discontent.

"Mr. Dakko, sir. Senior. He passed me the word there's a lot of grumbling in the crew berth."

"What about?" I demanded. The bridge lights seemed unbearably bright.

"Trying to get home faster. There's talk again about repairing the fusion drive."

"That's nonsense!"

"I know, sir." The middy hesitated. "They feel so, well, helpless. A long cruise is hard enough when you know it'll end in a few months."

"Yes." And beyond the problem of morale lay another I dreaded to confront. How long would ship's discipline last once it became evident we wouldn't be rescued?

As Captain, I was a symbol of the U.N. Government. Once the crew and passengers realized we'd never again be subject to that Government, what would they do? Revolt? Demand free elections? I wasn't even certain I should oppose them.

I forced my mind back to the issue at hand. "The drive is irreparable, surely they know that. I'll run some more drills, to divert them."

"Aye aye, sir." Philip looked doubtful.

I glanced at my young midshipman and was overcome by gratitude for his loyalty. Though he might make mistakes, he strove unremittingly to please me, to carry out his duties. "Mr. Tyre . . ."

"Yes, sir?"

"Thank you for your efforts. Without you I'd—" I broke off. What was I doing? I cleared my throat. "Very good, Mr. Tyre," I said gruffly. "Keep your eye on the situation."

"Aye aye, sir." He was carefully formal.

"That's all, then." As the hatch closed behind him I beat my knee with my fist. How could I be so stupid? Could I expect Philip to maintain the right distance if I kept varying it? I would keep my feelings to myself. Damn it, I had to.

For the next three days I ran Battle Stations, General Quarters, and boarding drills at unexpected intervals. I succeeded in making the crew as irritable and jumpy as I; what effect it had on the scuttlebutt about repairing the drive, I had no idea.

Eventually I decided to take the bull by the horns, and so, in the late evening hours when most of the crew were off duty, I went to crew berth one. As I entered Seaman Kovaks roared, "Stand to!" and jumped to attention. Sailors in various states of undress formed lines in front of their bunks.

"As you were." I faced the ragged line. "I've heard," I said bluntly, "some foolishness about fixing the fusion drive. Who's spreading that goofjuice?"

No one spoke.

"Well?"

Elena Bartel said quietly, "Sir, why can't the drive be repaired?"

I scowled. "It's you?"

"No, sir." One hand went to her hip. "But there's been talk. Maybe if we heard the truth . . ."

"The drive is wrecked. When the aliens attacked, their acid melted through the shaft wall. You can see it through the transplex from the engine room."

"Everyone knows that," she said sharply. A sailor grinned; his smile vanished at my glare. "The issue, sir, is whether they can be repaired."

"The drive generates N-waves. You know that much, don't you? The N-waves are shaped as energy is fed down the shaft. The shape of the shaft wall determines the wavelength." I paused, trying to marshal my thoughts. "Now, it takes a shipyard months of trials to get the tolerances just right. If the curve of the wall is not perfect to the nearest millimeter, the energy isn't properly focused. Do you know what that means?"

I paced, waiting for an answer, but none came. "An unfocused beam could melt the shaft wall. And if not, there's still no way to aim the beam. We might Fuse, but to where? We could find ourselves heading out of the galaxy!"

"That's not what Sykes said," a deckhand muttered.

I rounded on him. "How much does Sykes know? Does he have his engineer's ticket?"

"I heard him talkin'," the man said stubbornly. "Before you locked him up. We could make new plates, weld 'em on—"

I shouted, "You can't weld steel plates to an alloy shaft wall! Don't you understand?"

A few faces retained a stubborn look I knew was irremovable. They would believe what they needed to believe; that somehow there was a way to sail home. "I'll have the Chief explain it again," I said, defeated. "Maybe you'll take his word for it."

The next morning I sent Dray to talk to them; he came away shaking his head. "Most of them are convinced," he reported. "That Walter Dakko, and the Bartel woman. Drucker and Tzee. But some of the others . . ." He descended to his engine room, still grumbling.

Everywhere I went I felt eyes, wondering and calculating. Nothing was said, but the doubts were evident, the yearning obvious. I'd put down rebellion once; I wondered when it would rise again. I fingered a stack of laser pistol recharge packs, still piled in a corner of the bridge. Would Dray stand with me this time? He stood watch, one shift out of three, on the bridge, where all our weapons were piled. Where he could seal the hatch, bar me from command . . .

I thrust aside my uneasiness. He would do what he would do. I had no choice but to trust him; I couldn't spend years sealed on the bridge in suspicion and terror.

Philip broke up a scuffle between Eddie Boss and Chris; they appeared at Captain's Mast while the new master-at-arms, Walter Dakko, stood by. Deke was on report as well; I dealt with him first.

"The Chief says you were insubordinate." I glowered at the young transient.

Deke shuffled his feet. "Dunno what it mean."

"Sir!" Philip Tyre roared. "You address the Captain as 'sir'!"

"Sir," the boy mumbled.

"It means refusing to obey orders or being disrespectful to lawful authority."

"He din' groo yo' joename."

"What?"

Eddie raised his hand cautiously. I nodded.

"Deke say'n, Chief din' like joename dey givin' you, Cap'n."

"Good God." Joename. Groo. Melissa Chong, come back to interpret for your young charges. I cut off that line of thought, too late. "Sailor, on every ship I've ever known, the Captain has a nickname. Usually not a fond one. What sailors call the Captain in private conversation is their own affair. The trick is not to use the, ah, joename in front of an officer."

I made a note in the Log. "Ten days punishment detail. Mr. Tyre, see to it."

"Aye aye, sir." Deke would be given extra chores, the less pleasant ones. He'd suffer no worse, nor should he.

"Mr. Boss is next, sir."

"I'll take him and Mr. Dakko Junior together. Come forward. Brawling, were you?"

Chris gave his messmate a look of pure hatred. "No, sir, Captain. The gorilla boy was shoving me around. I just defended myself."

My hand tightened on the console. What was the matter with young Dakko? He'd get nowhere by alienating me. His father's expression was noncommittal.

"I ain' shovin' no—"

I thundered, "Speak when you're spoken to!" Eddie recoiled. I swung to Chris. "You have one more chance to tell me your side."

"I was teaching the trann—the crewmen how to read gauges," Chris said hurriedly. "Jokko and Shay. They were laughing and pretending not to understand. I yelled at them. Then Eddie here came up and spun me around and started shouting I should teach him first, like you said. But he wasn't even in the room when I started, so how could I?" He paused for breath. "I was trying to get my arm loose, when the middy, I'm sorry, I mean Mr. Tyre, came around."

"Well, Mr. Boss?"

"Uppie yellin' at my fren," grumbled Eddie. "He don' know difference teachin' an' shoutin'. Not like you, Cap'n. Why doncha tellim," he appealed. "Like when you teach ol' Eddie read. You din' shout, get me more mixed up. Uppie boy, he jus' show off, thinkin' he's smarter."

"So you grabbed him?"

"A little, maybe. Din' hurt him."

"Very well." I made my note and snapped off the Log. "Ten days in the brig, both of you." Philip gaped. A stiff punishment for a minor scuffle, one that would have ended harmlessly and gone unnoticed if Philip hadn't been present to see it. I added, "In the same cell," and they blanched. "Master-at-arms, escort them to the brig."

"Aye aye, sir." Walter took his son's arm, steered him to the hatch. "Come along, Mr. Boss."

As they left I heard Eddie mutter, "Help'n run ship, he tol' us. What kinda helpin', dis? Like moppin' flo'?"

The incident didn't help morale. The civilian transpops, even Annie, pretended not to notice me when I passed, or worse, they exhibited outright hostility. The transients among the crew were more circumspect, but I sensed their anger as well.

On the other hand, Emmett Branstead, doing work he understood and liked, was affable and eager for my visits.

Not so Mr. Tzee; he seemed to retreat inward when I arrived, as if expecting criticism I never offered. Perhaps he took the failings of his trainees personally.

One night, as the ship lay quiet, I got up from my bed and padded to the bridge. I entered the code, let myself in. Dray, wide awake, glanced at me in surprise. "As you were," I said, though he'd made no move to stand.

I keyed the alarms. "Battle Stations! All hands to Battle Stations! This is no drill!" Sirens wailed and bells clanged throughout the ship.

"Jesus!" The Chief leapt to his feet. "What? Where?"

"Sit down, Dray, you're on watch. Kerren, record response times from all stations."

"No drill," he rasped, outraged. "No drill?"

"Why should response times differ between a drill and the real thing? We'll check."

Crewmen I'd routed from bed raced through *Challenger* to their stations, shutting airtight hatches behind them as they arrived. Philip Tyre dashed onto the bridge, clothing disheveled. Gregor Attani tagged behind; the cadet had no assigned duty station and followed his mentor.

One by one our stations reported. The comm room was first; Deke's excited voice in the engine room came last. "Chief ain' here, sir. Jus' me an' Ollie."

"Hold the bridge, Chief." I strode down the corridor to the comm room. "This is the Captain. Let me in." The hatch slid open. I walked past the row of consoles. Walter Dakko, Elena Bartel, and Jonie sat ready, eyes forward, hands at their firing controls. Ms. Bartel's clothes were awry. Neither she nor I paid any heed.

"Very well." I went next to the engine room.

An hour passed before I returned to the bridge. Philip, sleepy, shook himself awake as I entered.

"Go back to bed, both of you." I noted the results of the exercise in the Log, had the crew stand down, and went to my cabin, where I tossed and turned much of the night.

The next morning, short of sleep, I was sipping much-needed coffee when Philip brought Gregor to the bridge for a nav drill. Tyre seemed irritable, and the cadet was stiff and distant, as he'd been ever since I had him sent to Dray.

I thought to lessen the tension before the boy started his practice. "How go your lessons with the streeters, Mr. Attani?"

He said coolly, "As well as can be expected, *SIR*."

"What does that mean?"

The young man's aristocratic features betrayed his distaste. "They learn as fast as trannies can learn." Unwisely, he added, "I'll keep at it until you find something better for me to do, sir." It was staggering insolence.

I raised an eyebrow. "Do you have an attitude problem, Cadet?"

He said bitterly, "Not anymore, sir. Chief Kasavopolous saw to that."

My tone was even. "I think you do, Mr. Attani." I understood his resentment, but he was foolish to show it. If the boy pulled in his horns immediately, I would let it pass.

Sullen, he stared past me. "Then you must be right, sir." His contempt was no longer concealed.

Philip snarled, "Behave, Cadet!" Gregor was, after all, his responsibility.

As my glance strayed to the darkened screen, my gorge rose. Unless we were rescued, we might pass seventy years on this near-derelict vessel. Years with arrogant, half-trained, impudent children. With Dray's contempt, Chris Dakko's sullen insolence. With Eddie Boss and Elron Clinger. I slapped the console. "Mr. Attani, report to the Chief Engineer. Tell him he is to cane you for insolence."

Gregor looked at me, his gaze traveling with disdain from head to foot. He said distinctly, "You bastard!"

"Mr. Tyre." I barely got out the words. "Take the cadet to the engine room. See that he's given a lesson sufficient to guarantee good manners for the rest of the cruise. If Dray isn't adequate to the task, finish it yourself."

"Aye aye, sir." Philip, white-faced, spun toward the cadet. "Move!" He propelled Gregor toward the hatch. The boy scrambled to keep on his feet. The last I heard as the hatch slid shut was, "You fool!"

Left seething alone on the bridge, I called up the results of our most recent laser drill. I read the numbers several times before I gave up, snapped off the Log, and threw the holovid on the console.

"Is something wrong, sir?"

"No conversation, Kerren." I flung myself out of my seat and began to pace. The nerve of young Gregor. Aristocrat he may have been, but now he was a Naval officer in training. At this very moment he'd be learning his manners the hard way. He would give me no further trouble, I was sure. I'd seen Philip's outrage as he shoved Gregor into the corridor.

Well, so be it. Attani had made his bed; let him lie in it. Muttering, I paced until my adrenaline dissipated. Finally I resumed my seat. I took up the holovid, examined the drill again. The response times were faster than our previous drills, but not by much. I made notes where more practice was needed.

After a time Philip Tyre knocked. He came to attention. "The cadet has been disciplined, sir." His tone was somber.

"It's traditional," I said icily, "for him to report the fact himself."

"Yes, sir. I thought it best to take him back to the wardroom." Philip was pale.

"That bad?"

"I—it's no more than he deserved. I know that."

"I'm glad you do."

"Yes, sir." His manner was humble. "I should have had him under control. It's my fault."

"That's right." I recalled my own days as senior midshipman. Whatever trouble the middies in my wardroom had given me—and that was plenty—none would have dared abuse his Captain. Had there been question of that, I would have settled it, and fast.

"Dismissed, Mr. Tyre." I let my voice remain cold.

I busied myself conducting readiness drills for the engine room; it would do no good for Mr. Tzee's comm room crew to be standing by at their laser controls if the engine room didn't have firing power on-line.

With practice, I managed to cut the response time by almost two minutes, even with the Chief off duty, as he would be if he was standing watch on the bridge.

It was two days before I encountered Gregor Attani. Philip, called to the conn so I could go below to watch an engine room drill, brought the cadet along. Gregor's creases were immaculate, his hair carefully combed. He walked with great concentration, pain in his features.

I felt pity. Still, he'd called his Captain a bastard. I asked coldly, "Do you still have an attitude problem, Mr. Attani?"

An ember of pride flickered among the ashes of his misery. "I didn't think I had one, so I wouldn't know."

I couldn't fault his pluck, but courage was not at stake. "My compliments to the Chief Engineer, Gregor. And would he please cane you for insolence."

"Again!" The word was wrung out of him.

"Again. And the correct response is, 'Aye aye, sir.'"

Philip blurted, "Might I take him to the wardroom instead, sir? I assure you he'll—"

My voice was ice. "My compliments to the Chief, Mr. Tyre. For yourself as well."

The silence hung between us while Philip grappled with his calamity. "Aye aye, sir," he managed, crimson with shame. "Come along, Cadet."

"But—"

"Come along!" He yanked Gregor's arm. "Now!"

In half an hour they were back. Philip's hands pressed against the side of his pants. "The Chief Engineer's compliments, sir, and he requests that Midshipman Tyre's discipline be entered in the Log." His eyes were riveted to the deck.

"Very well." I made the notation.

Gregor shuffled forward. Only his reddened eyes betrayed that he had been crying. He was subdued, his manner without defiance. "The Chief's compliments, sir," he mumbled. "Would you please enter Cadet Attani's discipline in the Log."

I hated myself for it, but it was necessary to ask. "Do you still have an attitude problem, Mr. Attani?"

The proud young aristocrat's shoulders slumped. "No, sir," he whispered. "Not anymore." He stumbled over the words. "I won't be rude to you again."

"Very well." I made the entry. "Until the next time it's necessary." I stood. "You'll take the conn while I go below, Mr. Tyre. Don't let the cadet touch anything he shouldn't."

"Aye aye, sir." They remained at attention until I left.

On the way to the engine room I realized that I had become the monster every subordinate officer dreaded. Young Dakko in the brig, Clinger set to be returned to his prison, my two officers thrashed into submission. What next? Take off Dray's hand?

Grimly, I hurried on.

17

My brutality to Gregor and Philip quickly made the rounds. By morning no one, civilian or crew, chose to meet my eye or speak to me. I suspected that day's dinner was the last I'd share with my tablemates.

My surmise proved correct. I could have ordered passengers seated with me, of course. But a place at the Captain's table was an honor, not a duty. So it would remain, while I held command.

I took my seat at the empty table, and when all had arrived I stood to give the prayer. For a moment nobody stood with me. Then, reluctantly, they got to their feet for the traditional ritual. After, I signaled the steward. My table was served first, as always. The self-conscious steward progressed across the dining hall bearing his tray with only my portion on it. I appeared not to notice.

Days succeeded each other in monotonous activity. Responding to some inner need rather than any realistic requirement, I brought the ship to the highest state of readiness I could achieve, calling drills at frequent and random intervals. I ordered Philip and Dray to issue the crew demerits for the slightest infractions.

Ill will swirled around my feet as I stalked the corridors, ignoring sullen faces. Above, on the bridge, Philip and Gregor carefully masked their resentment. Our relations were formal, proper, and distant. As they should have been from the start, I realized. The Captain could allow no less.

One day I had Philip and Gregor haul our stock of weapons from the bridge back to the repaired arms locker. It made me uneasy, but if *Challenger* were to function at all like a ship of the line, we couldn't operate in constant fear.

I had a holovid sent to the brig with orders for Chris to

spend his time teaching Eddie, and for Eddie to spend his time learning. I acknowledged to myself the failure of that particular experiment, but determined to let it run the course of their brig time.

By the third night after I'd sent Philip and Gregor to Dray I wondered whether I'd fomented a revolution; wherever I turned, hostility was palpable. That night I strode into the dining hall through utter silence and took my place at my empty table. As I filled my water glass old Mrs. Reeves stood, whispered to her husband, hobbled slowly across the room on her cane.

"Might I be allowed to sit with you, Captain?" Blue orbs peered from the wrinkled folds of skin.

"You'd subject yourself to considerable displeasure." I waved at the rest of the hall.

"You should not dine alone." She made as if to sit, looked to me for permission. Recalling my manners I stood to help with her chair. Across the hall Mr. Reeves beckoned a steward and pointed, then shuffled slowly across the deck. He stared myopically in the general direction of my face. "Would like to join you," he rumbled. "With y'r permission."

I indicated a seat. "With pleasure, Mr. Reeves." He said nothing further for the remainder of the meal. As we ate I waited to see what Mrs. Reeves had in mind to tell me, but she made only small talk. Apparently her presence satisfied her purpose, and she bore no message of warning.

Days passed. When Chris Dakko and Eddie Boss were released from their cell, I had Chris brought directly to the bridge. I let him wait a moment at rigid attention. Then, "I've had enough trouble from you, sailor."

"Yes, sir."

"How long were you in the brig?"

"Ten days."

"Next time it'll be a hundred days. You have my oath."

"Yes, sir!"

"The time after will be a thousand days. You'll be twenty-one before you get out. Do you get my message?"

"Yes, sir!" A sheen of sweat gleamed on his forehead.

"Don't even dream of stepping out of line, Dakko."

"No, sir!"

"Very well. Your studies with Mr. Boss?"

He surprised me. "He's beginning to understand the graph curves, sir. Like the firing consoles show. We've been working on those. He's—" He bit it off.

"Go on."

"He's not so bad, when you get past his ways. I mean, he really tries to learn." Chris colored. "I'm sorry. I've given you a very hard time."

"Thank you. You may go below."

So one of my efforts was at last succeeding.

That night when I returned to my cabin I found a puddle outside my hatch. Who was on cleanup duty; Deke? How could he be so sloppy? I sniffed, realized it was urine. There was a residue on the hatch where it had dried.

I stepped over the puddle into my cabin, slung my jacket over the chair, dropped my cap on the polished table. I'd seen worse insults. At Academy, frustration and rage were sometimes expressed even more strongly. But the calculated affront was also a warning. I was pushing too hard, and respect for my rank had evaporated.

I brooded. We'd only just begun our interminable voyage. Discipline slackened now could never be reconstituted. That was my motive for the drills: to mold the crewmen into a cohesive unit, responsive to discipline. With a sense of duty, we might survive the years without sinking into the folly of anarchy.

I thought of cleaning up the puddle myself, decided to let it be. I need not notice it.

In the head adjoining my cabin I peered into the mirror, fingered my scar. My eyes were sunken in sallow skin. I was bone-tired from too many hours on watch, too many responsibilities. It would be decades before they ended, unless someone took them from me.

With obstinate determination I continued to drive myself and the crew. We turned the last of our sheet metal stock into a few more grow tanks, to extend our precious gardens another two cabins. Twice daily, I conducted laser-firing drills. Philip and Gregor, as exhausted as I, did their best. As days turned into weeks the pace of training remained hectic.

Philip, his mind on a nav drill, spilled coffee on my console. Furious, I issued five demerits. Protective of his chief, Gregor let his disapproval show. I sent him to the barrel. When he returned, humiliated and in pain, I made him review docking maneuvers for hours.

None dared speak to me.

An obscene drawing appeared on my hatch. I had Gregor scrub it off; he did so without protest. Then, for two days, all was ominously quiet. I waited, reminded of the oppressive calm before a Welsh storm.

It was Walter Dakko who approached. Saddened, I let him speak. I'd expected better of him.

He met my eye. "I'm the bearer of a petition."

"Oh." I was almost relieved. "For my removal?"

His look was curious. "No, sir, of course not." I couldn't tell if he meant that no one would sign such a petition, or that he wouldn't carry it. He handed it to me.

Before reading it I asked, "Have you signed?"

"No, sir."

"Then why involve yourself?"

He considered a long time before responding. "Because a lot of people are troubled and because it's very important to them. I don't know how their morale will hold up if you refuse."

I perused the laboriously written document, the scrawled signatures affixed below. "Repair the drive? You know that's impossible."

"I presume so, sir."

"Then what do you want of me?"

"Try to fix the drive, sir."

I studied him for a moment. "Since you're not insane, tell me what you're talking about."

A grim, momentary smile lightened his features. "Have you heard—"

"Come to my cabin and sit down."

"Aye aye, sir."

Before I'd taken two steps I realized I'd made a foolish mistake; I'd worked for weeks to maintain the proper distance from officers and crew, and I'd invited a sailor into my cabin.

About to countermand the order, I realized that doing so would be a worse mistake, and so, lips compressed, I said nothing.

Walter Dakko took a seat at the conference table, unawed by his surroundings.

"Go ahead, Mr. Dakko."

"I assume you have the facts right, sir, and that the drive is irreparable. But the situation is unacceptable to the crew."

"Is what?" I asked, unbelieving.

He said hurriedly, "I meant emotionally intolerable. Not everyone is as strong as you, sir. Most of the crew can't accept the notion that there's no way out, and would go glitched if they did. If we had no fusion drive they'd demand that you invent one, or teleport us to Lunapolis. Logic has nothing to do with their reaction."

"And?"

"If you'll excuse my saying so, you can continue acting in a logical fashion, which is your prerogative, or you can recognize their illogical needs."

"Get to the point, Mr. Dakko."

He shook his head. "I've gone about as far as I can, sir. I've read your regs and I have no desire to be hanged."

I grunted. He recognized, at least, the thinness of the ice on which he skated. The right of petition was not uniformly granted. On some ships it was not even to be considered. Presenting an appeal was one thing, but telling me what the crew demanded was quite another. He was quite sensible to stop where he had.

"I order you to tell me your thoughts, Mr. Dakko." If he'd read the regs, he'd know that I'd taken him off the hook. He could be hanged for refusing to obey, but if he spoke he couldn't be touched no matter what he said.

"Aye aye, sir. They need to believe the drive can be fixed. So, you might let them try to fix it. They can't possibly succeed, but it will keep them occupied and give them a goal."

"A false one."

"A necessary one, in my opinion. They need to believe in something."

"And when it doesn't work?"

"Some of them will begin to accept reality, and the others will keep trying. Let them. They can get mad at the drive, if need be. At least it won't be you."

I unfolded the petition. "Ms. Bartel signed this. I'm surprised."

"Yes, sir. I imagine she knows the drive isn't repairable. I think she signed to be one with the crew, sir. For her own reasons."

"Um." I perused the list; nearly everyone in the crew berth had signed. Except . . . "Chris's name isn't here."

"No, sir."

"Why not?"

A wary glance. "Are you ordering me to answer?"

"Yes."

"He wanted to sign. I took him into the head and told him I would beat the living hell out of him if he did, and he believed me."

I said after a moment, "You've changed, Mr. Dakko."

"Yes, sir. Six months ago I was too civilized to threaten him. I was too . . . sane. I was principled."

I smiled. "For all your telling him he was on his own, you still look after him."

"I wasn't sure how you'd react, sir. I'm still not. I don't want him hanged, no matter how unlovable he's become."

"Nobody will be hanged," I said with a long, tired sigh. It seemed I'd played the part of the tyrant all too well. "Tell your messmates their petition has been received, and I'm inclined to grant it. I'll work out the details with Dray. You understand, if they weld new plates over the hole, I'll allow low-power testing, but there's no possible way we'll fire an untuned drive, and the fusion drive will be untunable no matter what they do."

"Yes, sir. I don't intend to pass on your last remark."

I sent him back to the crew berth and remained in my cabin to mull over this latest development. The crew was fortunate to have a spokesman as prudent as Dakko. It occurred to me that he might have engineered his own selection, to present the matter in the least inflammatory manner.

Later, when I told Dray what I had in mind, he emphatically shook his head. "There's no way to repair the drive."

"Nonetheless, there's no harm in their trying. Drag the work out as long as you can. I don't look forward to dealing with their disappointment."

"I'll bet you don't."

I wanted to smash his face, to claw the smugness out of it. I swung my chair to face him. "Listen carefully."

"To another threat?" His tone was sour.

"A statement. If you want an apology for what I did, you may have one. In fact, here it is: I apologize. I regret I pretended to be insane and threatened to burn your fingers off. It was wrong of me to do it. I'm sorry for it."

He contemplated me. "It sounds like you have more to say."

"There is. Drop your contemptuous manner and speak to me with Naval protocol. The first time you don't, I'll toss you in section four with the rest of the mutineers and there you'll stay for the rest of the cruise. I so swear by Lord God's grace. You have until tomorrow to decide. That's all."

He studied my face intently. I met his gaze, expressionless. Grimly, he nodded and left.

Alone, I cursed my lack of self-control. If Dray chose to challenge me, I was bound by my soul to banish him, but I needed him. To whom else could I trust the engine room? Deke?

The enthusiasm with which the crew embraced the repair project astonished me. Virtually everyone asked to be assigned to the project in off-duty time. One of their first tasks was clambering outside the hull in magnetic-soled suits, measuring the hole in the drive shaft. I used it as an opportunity to give Gregor suit training; I bade Philip escort the cadet through the lock to the work area.

It was a long walk down the hull from the aft airlock on Level 2 to the drive shaft, at the very stern of the vessel. For each step Gregor must make and break magnetic contact with the hull, while Philip hovered near in his thrustersuit. I knew hull-walking could be exhausting to the novice, and was no great fun for the experienced sailor. But if Gregor misstepped and pushed himself off the hull, Philip would be there to bring him back. By custom, such a blunder by a cadet or middy was rewarded with enthusiastic hazing, but Gregor would be spared that.

They came aboard flushed and exhilarated. Gregor's elation didn't even dampen when I met them in the corridor near the lock, though his manner became more reserved and much more cautious.

"Well, Mr. Tyre, will the cadet become a spaceman?" I deliberately spoke to Philip rather than Gregor; I'd already parted with tradition too often.

"I think he'll manage, sir. If I can give him more practice."

"If it's practice he wants, make him a tool carrier. That should build up his leg muscles."

Both boys smiled at that. Gregor would be sent the length of the hull carrying instruments for the working party, perhaps several times each trip Outside. He'd soon get the hang of hull-walking. I grinned, recalling my own pleasure at the occasional opportunity to go Outside. Did all middies feel that way? Certainly all the ones I'd known.

"Very well." I added, "See that he has two hours of nav drill for every hour he's allowed out."

"Aye aye, sir." Maybe it was the oxygen; their exuberance was undiminished by the work I'd assigned. Feeling as decrepit as old Mr. Reeves I left them to their youthful pleasures.

I summoned Walter Dakko, issued him a stunner, and brought him to the infirmary. Seaman Clinger was well enough to be discharged. One look at the master-at-arms told Clinger all he needed to know, yet he begged piteously for a reprieve.

"No, I won't listen. Mr. Dakko, take him below."

"Please, sir, don't make me go back! Andy and me ... There's bad blood now. Twice he's hit me on the head, like to kill me. You put me back there, I gotta kill him or he kills me for sure, there's no other way."

"So be it, then."

He groaned. Walter Dakko took his arm. Clinger was too weak to offer any resistance, and didn't attempt any. I led them down to the section four hatch. The inside control was disabled so the men couldn't get out, and the outer control was sealed to my code. "Be ready to open fire, Mr. Dakko." I entered the code.

Clinger blurted, "Could I at least talk to Elena sometimes, sir? It wouldn't do no harm, if once in a while . . ."

"Elena? *Elena*?"

"Ms. Bartel, yes, sir. She got to talkin' with me a lot, back up there, and got me to thinkin'. If I can't get out of here . . ." He shuddered and went on quickly, "Could I talk to her once in a while? Please?"

"In!" I roared. He scuttled through the hatch. I slapped it closed.

Within a week I began to notice sailors skimping on their regular duties to make time for the repair project. Because we were so shorthanded, the men were already overworked trying to accomplish tasks necessary for our survival. Only by giving up all remaining idle time were they able to tend their project at all.

Now the recycler's mates short-checked the system gauges, rather than bleeding down the pipes to recalibrate the controls as the book required. I put the whole detail on report and banned them from working on the drive for a week. Despite the example I made, slackness increased.

Anxious to begin with, I had to watch helplessly from the bridge for endless hours as novice crewmen set out with more experienced sailors on dangerous hull duty. Their suits were constructed of tough fiber alloy, and the hull had no sharp edges, but some tools had points, oxygen tanks could run low, and there were myriads of ways my sailors could get themselves killed.

Any death would be a calamity, and from a cold-blooded perspective, I had no way to replace a man who died. I hated having to let them go out. I particularly could ill afford to lose any officer.

I gritted my teeth the first time Gregor lost contact with the hull. Every greenie floats at least once in his training; I wish I could forget the time I did it. Philip let him drift helpless a few minutes to learn his essential safety lesson, then I had him bring the cadet inside for the day.

Two days later I was enduring their idle chatter on the suit radios when it happened again.

"Whoops! Oh, damn!"

"Having a problem, Cadet?" Philip, with gentle malice.

"Could you get me down, Mr. Tyre? Please?" I knew the absolute dependence he felt was not pleasant.

"Perhaps later. I was thinking, the wardroom needs cleaning. The bunks taken down and the bulkheads scrubbed." Philip was doing his job: Gregor's carelessness could cost him his life, and a penalty was appropriate. But we didn't have time for hazing.

I keyed the caller. "Just bring him in, Mr. Tyre. Until he learns to be careful."

"Aye aye, sir. Let's go, Gregor. Stick out your arm. Watch it. Now let your heels settle to the deck. That's right. Now a step at a time. Walk, don't dance. You remind me of a girl I knew once. Okay, you're on your own."

A moment later Gregor yelped. "Oh, not again! I'm sorry, Mr. Tyre!"

"Take hold of him!" I roared. "Keep your hands on him until he's in the airlock!" Fuming, I left the bridge unattended and stomped down to the suiting room. Seeing me they immediately stiffened to attention. "Mr. Attani, my compliments to the Chief Engineer, and would he encourage you not to be such a clumsy dolt!"

Gregor swallowed, his look imploring my mercy. He found none. "Aye aye, sir," he murmured.

Philip said hurriedly, "He meant no harm, sir. I didn't make clear how important it—"

"Cadet, out!" As the boy scuttled to the corridor I rounded on Philip. "You're nineteen, Mr. Tyre. Six years you've been in the Service? You know better than to skylark Outside, and you certainly know better than to argue with me. Do you think a midshipman may countermand a Captain's orders?"

"No, sir. I wasn't countermanding—"

"You're arguing. Most nineteen-year-olds aren't caned, as you well know. They know their duty, and their place."

"Yes, sir." Philip was pale.

"Report to the Chief. Tell him I said to put you over the barrel. Remind him this is the second time you've argued with orders and I intend it to be the last time."

"Aye aye, sir!" He dashed to the hatch.

"If you behave no better than a cadet, you'll be treated

like one!" A cheap parting shot, at a target who couldn't fight back, but I thrust down any hint of remorse.

A short while later Philip and Gregor, chastened, reported to the bridge. For the first time in the years I'd known him, Philip Tyre seemed sullen. I didn't dare call him on it, for fear of plumbing its depths. If I'd finally broken his irrepressible goodwill, the consequences on my prison ship would be grim indeed.

I had no doubt whatsoever about Gregor's disposition. It was brooding and ominous. He reported civilly enough, saluting properly and requesting his discipline be entered into the Log. But I had the sense that if I pushed him one iota further he would turn on me and lash out, perhaps kill me.

I knew I couldn't allow that. If I were not to fear him from now onward, I had to confront his behavior. "Philip, to your quarters."

"Aye aye, sir." He saluted, wheeled, and marched out, the performance marred only by his stilted gait.

"You have something to say, Mr. Attani?"

"No, sir." Gregor's eyes were fastened on the deck.

"I find your manner unpleasant. Change it."

"What do you want me to do, sir?"

I slapped him. He recoiled in dismay.

"Do you know a cadet's legal status, Mr. Attani?"

"I guess so."

I slapped him harder. His fists clenched, but thank Lord God he didn't raise his hand. Had he done so I'd have been bound to execute him. "A cadet is the legal ward of his Captain. He has no personal rights. He is as a child to a parent. How many times would you like your face slapped, Mr. Attani?"

"Please, sir!"

I shouted, "Answer me!"

"No times! I don't want you to hit me, sir!" His eyes brimmed.

I slapped him again. "Look at your hand, Mr. Attani. It's a fist!"

He stared at his fingers, his eyes widening. Slowly he opened them.

"Please," he whispered. "Let me go down to the crew berth with the others."

"No. You're a cadet. Go to the wardroom."

He blurted, "I'm not a child. It tears me to shreds when you treat me as one!" He took several breaths in an effort to control himself. Then the dam burst; he rushed on, "I went to the engine room like you ordered and lay across that barrel, and Christ, he hurt me! I tried to hold still, I know I'm supposed to, but I couldn't anymore, my rear was on fire and Mr. Tyre had to grab my arms and hold me while I yelled, and please, sir, I don't understand why! By Lord God's grace, let me go back to the crew!"

"No. You're an officer in training and I'll have you behave like one. Do you want to be hit again?"

He spoke so softly I could hardly hear. "No, sir." He slumped in abject defeat.

"Do you want to be sent to the Chief?"

"God, no, sir, please!"

"Behave as I expect, and neither of those things will happen. Go to the wardroom."

Standing helplessly, hands pressed to his sides, he began to cry, choking sobs that racked his body. He made no move to cover his face or wipe the streaming tears.

I dropped heavily into my chair, swung it the other way. I waited a few moments before I said, "You may go to your quarters, Gregor."

It took a moment for his discipline to reassemble itself, but it held. "Aye aye, sir." I didn't turn for his salute. As he left I breathed a heartfelt sigh of relief.

I had broken him. He would do his duty. I had left him nothing else.

I slept that night, but not well. In the morning I forced myself out of bed to face another day. In the head I stepped under the shower, still half asleep, turned on the welcome biting spray of hot water.

A second later I came stumbling out, my squawk echoing from the bulkheads. I rubbed myself vigorously with the towel.

It was the coldest water I'd ever encountered, short of a block of ice.

I let the water run. If anything, it got colder. Cursing a blue streak I wriggled into my pants, flung my jacket over my bare shoulders, charged out into the corridor.

Chris Dakko didn't duck out of my way in time; I bounced off him and resumed course for the ladder. Moments later I was down to Level 3, heading for the engine room.

"Jeez, it's the Captain!" Blurred figures came to attention as I whirled past, coattails flying. I pounded at the engine room hatch in blind frustration until my fist accidentally hit the control panel and the hatch flew open.

I snarled. "What in God's blue blazes do—"

Deke glanced up from the pipe he held in place.

"Don't move it, you silly pup!" Dray roared. Jokko, making himself unnoticed in the corner, flinched.

I took in the puddles of water, the dank steamy atmosphere. "What happened?"

Dray grunted. "These damnfool joeykids took their eyes off the gauges." He wrenched at the pipe. "Let the steam pressure build up, they did. Blew the main feed valve." He glanced at me, added heavily, "Sir."

"The water in my shower—"

"Cold, I'll bet." His mouth turned up but his eyes held no humor. "The pipes are drained dry now, sir. If I'd gotten here a few minutes later they'd probably have frozen solid. And if they'd burst . . ."

"What were these—people doing?"

He gestured at the stores compartment. "Helping Eddie look for a plate the right size, sir." My mind on the puzzle, I nonetheless noticed his careful courtesy.

I groped. "A plate?" Then I swung to Deke. "For the damned fusion drive? You neglected your watch for *that*?"

Deke opened his mouth, thought better of it. He hunched over as if afraid I would physically attack him. I'd have liked to. My eye strayed to the barrel mounted in the corner; I wished I could send them to it. Unfortunately I could not. Young officers were subject to corporal punishment, but not ordinary sailors. For them I had recourse only to punishment details or the brig. A wise provision; otherwise a tyrannical Captain would provoke rebellion by crewmen whose manhood couldn't stand physical abuse. Of all the enlisted men on a Naval vessel, only the ship's boy, still a minor, could be beaten, and rarely was.

A trickle of water ran down my nose, as a thought crystallized.

My eyes slowly turned from the barrel to Deke. "How old are you, sailor?"

The young transient shrugged. "Dunno, sir. Dey tellin' me sixteen, seventeen, some'pin like dat."

"Well, now. And Jokko is eighteen. Both of you short of majority." I gestured to the barrel. "Chief, do you need help, or can you handle it yourself?"

"You mean, cane them like middies?" His face darkened. "It would be a pleasure. But I need their help to clean up this mess first."

"I'll be in my cabin. Tell me when I have water for a shower. When I do, discipline your children!" With what dignity I could muster I padded barefoot back to the ladder.

I eventually got my shower, and soon put the incident out of my mind. But the next day Walter Dakko stopped me in the corridor. He was terse. "We'd better talk privately."

By now I knew he would bother me only for something important. "On the bridge, in half an hour. Make sure nobody sees you." I wondered if Dakko knew how dangerous was his role of informer.

I waited impatiently. When he knocked I sealed the hatch behind us. "Now, then."

"Again, sir, I'm not suggesting how you should run your ship."

"I know," I said impatiently. "Belay that. I order you to bring me information you think I ought to have. Remind me if I take offense."

"Aye aye, sir. I think you ought to go armed for a while."

I drew in my breath. "It's that bad?"

"I think so. It didn't help any when Dray brought the transients back, wailing and carrying on."

"This is about caning Deke and Jokko?" I said, unbelievingly.

"It's about physically abusing enlisted men." His tone was sharp.

"But I have the right—they're legally children! How dare you call it abuse!"

"I didn't say I did. It's what the crew berth calls it."

"What do you call it, Mr. Dakko?"

He shrugged. "It's a fitter punishment than mopping already clean decks for a week," he said. "Probably no more than they deserved. At times I wish I'd done the same to Chris."

"He wouldn't have stood for it. He wasn't in the Navy then."

"I know, sir." A sigh. "In any event, there's some wild talk."

"Mutiny?" My voice was hard.

"Wild talk," he repeated. "That's all it may come to. After they—"

"Who?" I interrupted.

His eyes closed. "I knew it might come to this," he muttered. "When I chose to warn you."

"Answer me. Who?"

"Please withdraw the order, Captain." His tone was flat.

I sneered, "You're afraid you wouldn't obey it?"

"No, sir." He sounded tired. "I'm afraid I would." He held my eye until I was forced to look away.

"I'm sorry, Mr. Dakko." My voice was quiet. "I withdraw my question. While it's just talk, you need not tell me. But if they make a move . . ."

"I'm still a Roman citizen," he said with a small smile. "And the walls are still under siege."

After I sent him below I wondered how to save myself from the disaster I'd caused. Perhaps it would be better to do nothing, to let a mutiny form and run its course.

After an afternoon sulking on the bridge I went directly to dinner. I'd grown used to a general hostility; now it was blatant and almost universal. I met cold silence from the moment I entered the room until I'd finished the prayer.

Mrs. Reeves eased herself into her seat. "Is there any way I can help?" she asked.

"No."

She accepted the rebuff. "The talent of leadership is not to get too far ahead of the populace." She spoke offhandedly, as if in answer to a question. "You can only lead people where they are willing to go."

"*Challenger* is not a democracy," I snapped.

The old blue eyes gazed myopically. "You're angry?"

"Not especially. I'm trying to do my duty."

"I'm worried for you."

I could find nothing to say to that.

I stared at the beans and mixed vegetables, all I'd see on my plate for years to come. I tried to concentrate on my food and block out the rising babble from other tables.

China crashed to the deck. "Stinkin' trannie!" Seaman Kovaks was on his feet, fists bunched. Across the table, Deke and Jonie lunged. Mr. Tzee ducked, guarded his plate.

I scrambled to my feet as Jonie shrieked a challenge to the maddened seaman. She charged into the fray.

"STAND TO, ALL OF YOU!" My bellow stopped her, but just barely. *"ATTENTION!"* Kovaks, white-faced, paid no heed. Savagely I shoved him aside. "Stand to, this instant!"

For a riotous moment my authority teetered on the balance, before their discipline asserted itself. "Mr. Kovaks, out of the hall. Go to crew berth two."

Rage suffused his features. "But they—"

"SHUT UP!" It made my throat hurt. He blanched. I snarled, "Leave!"

"Aye aye, sir." He stalked out.

"You two, go to crew berth one."

"No way," Jonie spat. "Not afta—"

"Master-at-arms! Chief petty officer!" Walter Dakko and Eddie Boss came at a run. "Escort these sailors to the brig."

"Aye aye, sir." Walter Dakko took Jonie's arm. The young transpop twisted free.

"Knockidoff, Jonie," growled Eddie. "Go widda man!" From behind, he slammed his palms into Deke's shoulder blades; the younger boy skidded toward the exit. "You too, Dekeboy. Call yaself a sailor, huh? I be showin' ya!"

I waited in silence until they were gone, rounded on Mr. Tzee. "What was that all about?"

"Mr. Kovaks had a comment about Deke's welding, sir." His face showed no expression.

"Welding?"

"The plates." He sounded reluctant. "For the fusion drive."

For a moment I couldn't speak. "That project, again?"

"Yes, sir."

I turned on my heel, stalked back to my table. Tempers were running high; I'd have to be careful not to overreact and set them—

No, by God. I would not. I strode to the center of the room. "All hands, form a line. Officers in front."

I waited, hands on hips, until all complied. Philip pushed Gregor to an officer's place, five feet in front of the assembled men. The passengers remained in their places, all eyes fastened on mine.

"Attention, all of you." I spoke very quietly, battling to contain my rage. "Mr. Tyre, straighten the line."

"Aye aye, sir." He broke ranks, turned smartly. "You, forward. Back, Mr. Bree." In a moment he had them standing properly, and returned to his place.

"At ease."

With commendable precision the crew moved into the at-ease position, hands clasped.

"I won't have slack discipline on my ship." I stopped in front of Philip. "All work on the drive shaft is suspended."

A murmur of discontent.

"Pardon?" I raised an eyebrow. A wall of silence. "The work is halted until I order otherwise. Which won't happen until I find your conduct acceptable."

"Christ!"

I whirled. "Who spoke?"

Stony silence.

"Well?"

"I did." Drucker, the hydroponicist's mate.

"Two days in the brig for insolence and blasphemy. Report there. Stand at attention outside the hatch until someone comes to take you in."

His indecision lasted only a couple of seconds. "Aye aye, sir." His voice was sullen, but he walked out as bidden.

"I won't tolerate insubordination," I snapped. "Or sloppy drills, or fighting. When I'm satisfied in all respects, we'll see about the fusion drive."

"Excuse me, sir."

I glared at Ms. Bartel. "Yes?"

"We're ready to start testing, sir. Can we at least do that?"

"No." No one spoke, but their resentment was unmistakable. I knew it was suicidal to push them farther, but I wasn't sure I cared. "Remain where you stand until I finish my meal. Then you'll return to quarters." Without a further glance I strode back to my table.

I had already eaten most of my meager serving but for effect, I toyed with the vegetables a few moments longer. I topped off my coffee from the pot on the table, sipped at it. When I felt I'd made my point I said evenly, "Mr. Tyre, dismiss the men to quarters. Mr. Dakko, go to the brig and put Mr. Drucker into a cell."

I stared unseeing into my coffee cup until they were gone. Mrs. Reeves said nothing.

When I had no excuse to remain I said, "If you will excuse me," and left my place. I went to the bridge.

Dray let me in. I told him what I'd done.

The look he gave was carefully neutral. As I'd demanded, he'd eliminated any hint of insubordination from his manner. Now there was nothing. "It only delays the inevitable," he finally said.

"I suppose." I assumed he meant my overthrow.

"The drive won't work no matter what they try. I can't answer for their actions when they find that out."

"I know." I was glad I'd misread him. I left him to his watch.

Morale continued to plummet. I sensed the inevitable outcome, and hardly cared. I released Deke and Jonie from the brig with a stern admonition to behave. The next day I did the same with Mr. Drucker.

Hours later Drucker was back before me, seething with sullen hatred. Philip Tyre glared accusingly. "Insubordination, sir!"

"Just tell me what happened," I repeated, my tone weary.

"Mr. Branstead said we had to check the nutrient baths more often because the tomatoes were getting leaf wilt. When I gave Mr. Drucker the order he, uh, told me what I could do with the tomatoes."

"Which was?"

"Please, I—"

"Answer!"

"Aye, aye, sir. He said I should shove them up your, uh, arse, sir." Philip's face was red, with suppressed anger or mirth I couldn't tell.

I rounded on the seaman with unconcealed fury. "Anything to say, Mr. Drucker?"

"No." He glared back.

"Two months imprisonment. Midshipman, escort him to the brig."

Philip returned to the bridge a few minutes later. "He's brigged, sir." His tone was stiff, his eyes on the simulscreen so as not to meet mine.

"Very well." I was in no mood to probe his petulance.

"We'll need to replace Mr. Drucker on the hydro watch schedule," Philip prompted.

"I know."

"There's no one left to—"

"Dismissed."

He snapped a salute, left at once. Knowing what I had to do, I quelled my distaste. "Master-at-arms to the bridge."

When Dakko arrived I handed him a pistol, bade him follow me below. I stopped at the section four hatch. "Cover me."

"What are we doing, sir?"

"Retrieving Mr. Clinger." Dakko's eyebrow rose measurably, but he said nothing. I punched in the code; the hatch slid open. "Clinger!"

A slovenly Seaman Akkrit drifted out of a cabin to regard me with indifference. "Think he's in the lounge or somethin'."

"Get him." I waited, prey to my misgivings. A few moments later Clinger appeared, haggard, unshaven, eyes ringed by black circles. He eyed me uncertainly.

"Did you mean what you said?"

"Huh?" He stared, mouth working.

"About another chance."

"Oh, Jesus God. Please." He sank to his knees. "Please."

"Come." I backed through the hatchway. After an unbelieving moment he followed. "You're dropped to apprentice seaman. No seniority. No ratings."

"Yes, sir!"

"Understand this: you get one chance, no more. Disobey

an order, violate any regulation, and I'll execute you on the spot."

"I got it, sir! I won't give you any more trouble, honest. I'll—"

"You'll replace Mr. Drucker in hydroponics. Mr. Dakko, go to stores and issue him his personal gear, then have him report for duty."

"Aye aye, sir."

As they departed I mulled over my latest feat. I'd brigged a conscientious but frustrated sailor and replaced him with an unscrupulous rebel who'd tried to take over the ship.

All in the name of discipline.

18

"Commence firing!" I watched the simulscreen as *Challenger*'s forward lasers found their target: scrap metal released from the forward lock. Within seconds the metal glowed red.

"Better," I acknowledged. "All right, switch to simulation drill." I keyed the safeties on, making actual laser fire impossible.

On most ships laser drills took aim at computer-generated imaginary targets. But once, on the Training Station over Farside, Sarge had let us cadets fire at real scrap that otherwise would have been hauled back to base. I still remembered the thrill when at last the target glowed and sputtered and disappeared from the screens. On my own ships I used real targets from time to time, and been pleased by the improved results.

Still, enough was enough. Every target had to be released from the lock, and it was time consuming. "Kerren, simulated firing, random targets fore and aft, retained from three to twelve seconds. Visual confirmation on the laser screens."

"Aye aye, sir," said the imperturbable puter. The screen flashed.

I keyed the caller. "This drill is scored for destruction, not accuracy. Demolish all targets." In an accuracy drill missed shots counted against the gunners; in a destruction drill hits scored favorably and misses didn't count. However, each target remained on screen a random time; if it disappeared before being hit the gunners' scores were penalized.

"Begin!"

The gunners' voices crackled on the speaker. Two crewmen sat at each laser emplacement. One controlled the targeting, his mate regulated the duration and intensity of fire. A puter could direct our fire more accurately, of course. But only a man could be trusted to know at what to fire. After a century of dispute, the Navy had at last learned to trust crewmen over machines.

"Target oh seven five, closing!"

"Go! I got 'im."

"Target one nine oh! Target two one four."

"Fire!"

"Get the other one!"

Kerren duplicated on our bridge simulscreen the targets he gave my gunners; the darkness of space glowed with hostile points of light. Realistic flares indicated hits. Many targets abruptly disappeared, untouched.

After fifteen minutes I called a halt. "Gunnery crews stand down." A few moments later Mr. Tzee appeared in the hatchway, hopeful. I shook my head. "Not good enough."

"But—yes, sir."

"What's their problem?"

"None of them were originally trained as gunners, sir. And they have to learn to work closer together."

"They've had plenty of time for that." I waved a dismissal. After an hour reviewing the Log I picked up the caller and flicked the alarms. "GENERAL QUARTERS! ALL HANDS TO GENERAL QUARTERS!" Sirens wailed.

"Kerren, simulated laser drill, as before. Tabulate scores for each laser team. Forty minutes of continuous targets."

As a middy I'd conducted laser drill; an officer was supposed to be familiar with every station on his ship. I remembered continuous fire practice as nerve-wracking, the more so the longer the drill.

"Comm room reporting ready, sir!"

"Engine room ready, sir!"

"Gunners, commence firing!"

I paced irritably, eyes on the simulscreen where Kerren displayed the scores. After the first few minutes they began to rise as our gunners found their marks. Then, slowly, accuracy began to fall, as they tired. After an endless interval, they began to climb again, as if grudgingly, until they surpassed the previous test.

The screen abruptly darkened. "Exercise completed, sir."

"Thank you, Kerren." I keyed the caller. "Gunners stand down."

For three days I'd sounded General Quarters, Repel Boarders, and decompression alerts until the crew was thoroughly disgusted. I ran snap inspections, citing every violation I found. The crew's hostility was masked by only the thinnest veneer of discipline.

Philip Tyre was no longer sullen. Instead, he seemed almost apathetic. In a way, that was worse. Any effort I made to cheer him was met with indifference. I became increasingly uneasy. Finally, in desperation, I took him to the officers' mess for coffee. He stared into his steaming cup.

I sat, but stood again almost immediately to pace a few steps and examine the texture of the bulkhead. "Mr. Tyre—" That sounded too formal. "Philip. You're next in line to command should anything happen to me." My voice was husky.

He stared, suddenly worried. "Yes, sir."

I blurted, "We're all going to die here. I know that."

He sat stunned at the voicing of his own fears.

"Philip, I have no answers. I don't know how to act nobly. I don't know what to do."

He stirred. "Sir, I—"

"Let me finish. There's a chance some of us will survive, but not a great one. I assume I'll end my life on board *Challenger*. Perhaps very soon." He sucked in his breath. "I don't mean suicide; that's mortal sin. But the crew—" I gestured. "They won't take much more."

"Sir, if you explain to them—"

"There's nothing to explain." I stared at the silent bulkhead. "I don't have solutions. All I have is my oath. I swore to uphold Naval regulations; *Challenger* is a Naval vessel and I haven't been relieved. So I'll follow the regs. It's the only course I know."

He said nothing, scrutinizing me intensely.

"The regs require military etiquette, so I'll enforce it. They require that we be prepared for emergencies, so I'll continue to train the crew." I smiled bleakly. "I know it seems useless, but it's all I know to do."

He swallowed. "I haven't been much help lately, sir. I'm sorry."

"You've been an immense help. If you know a better course, suggest it. Or relieve me and follow it yourself." His glance was shocked. "I don't think you'll have to answer to Admiralty."

"I will never relieve you." He spoke with finality.

"You may go down with me, Philip."

He stood. "So be it." A moment's silence, while he mustered his courage. Then, "It is a privilege to serve under you, sir."

My chest tightened and I couldn't speak. I gestured to the hatch. He saluted formally and left.

"FIRE IN THE COMM ROOM! FIRE IN THE COMM ROOM!"

Feet pounded on the treads of the ladder as fire control parties raced to their duty stations, spurred by wailing alarms.

"Engine room reporting full water pressure!"

"Damage control ready!"

"Comm room controls shifted to bridge!"

In the corridor outside the comm room I keyed my stopwatch. "Three and a half minutes." Panting crewmen waited, hoses in hand. "Very well, Mr. Tyre. We'll try for better next time." I ignored the glowers my remark earned. "Have the crew stand down." I returned to my cabin.

It was four in the morning.

The next afternoon I ran laser drills and decompression drills. After the evening meal I called an inspection and toured the ship while the exhausted crew stood by at their stations.

After trudging what seemed like miles I returned to the bridge and gratefully sank into my seat. Philip and Gregor waited attentively; they'd accompanied me on my inspection, stopping first at the wardroom where I sternly checked the bunks and gear stowed neatly in the duffels. I found no irregularities, and expected none. Philip was a seasoned officer, and would have seen to it that Gregor's gear was in order as well as his own.

"Pass the word," I said. "The crew may resume work on

the drive project, so long as drill scores remain high." Though I foresaw nothing but problems when the repair project failed, I had to concede that the crew met my expectations. Their hostility was manifest, but their state of readiness was acceptable.

When I went back to my cabin to wash for dinner I found outside my hatch a crude rag doll, stuffed with old torn sheets, made to look like the Captain. Its head had been cut off.

The next morning work parties went Outside for a final inspection of the welds on the drive shaft. I ordered Gregor to accompany them. He did so with reluctance, no doubt recalling my fury at his previous escapade, and its humiliating consequences. This time he was careful not to lose contact with the hull.

By midafternoon Walter Dakko conveyed a request to allow low-power testing to begin. The Chief reassured me once more that at low power we'd do the shaft no damage. Sighing, I gave my consent.

I took the bridge, with Philip at my side for moral support. The Chief remained below in the engine room, at his usual station for Fusion. I knew a knot of crewmen from the project committee would be peering anxiously over his shoulder.

"Bridge to engine room, prepare to Fuse." I cleared my throat. "Rather, prepare for fusion drive test."

The Chief's flat voice responded almost immediately. "Engine room ready for test, sir."

"Very well, stand by." I looked up to the screen. "Kerren, nominal Fusion coordinates, please."

"Aye aye, sir." Kerren flashed the coordinates for home on the screen. I felt a lump in my throat. If only we could use them.

"Very well." No point in manually rechecking the coordinates. We weren't going anywhere. "Go ahead, Chief."

"Aye aye, sir. Fusion drive is . . . on." Automatically I glanced at the screens as if expecting them to go blank. The cold pale points of light remained.

Alarms shrieked. Kerren exploded into life. "Fusion drive malfunction! Coordinates not attained. Improper power settings! Fusion drive failure! Emergency shutdown achieved!"

"Captain, we've lost power to the fusion drive!"

"I know, Chief!" I muttered a curse as I slapped off the

alarms. "Kerren, we're running low-power tests. No Fusion is expected."

Kerren hesitated a full second. "Low-power testing is a dockyard maneuver, Captain. I have no program to accomplish it under weigh."

"We're running the tests manually, Kerren. Disconnect your alarms."

"Alarms are operative at all times, Captain."

"Override."

He paused. "Alarms are overridden as per Captain's order. Override entered in Log."

"Monitor N-wave output and graph it to the screen against expected wave output at similar power."

"Aye aye, sir," he said doubtfully. "That will replicate the engine room monitor displays."

"Yes." I waited but the puter had no further objections. "Disengage your supervision of engine room controls, Kerren."

"That violates my directives, Captain. My function is to assure the safety—"

"Override. It's part of the test."

"Overridden," he said after a moment. "Engine room power is reactivated."

"Engine room, resume testing."

"Aye aye, sir."

"Apply power."

A jagged line pulsed on the screen as power reached the drive. A moment later the smooth line representing normal N-wave generation appeared as well. The wave we generated bore no resemblance to the sleek curve of a proper N-wave.

We watched in silence.

On my console the gauges fluctuated wildly. Below, in the engine room, the Chief tried without success to modulate the wave. After a few minutes he muttered into the caller, "No use. Maybe if we adjust the baffles . . ."

"Very well. Shut it off."

The jagged line faded from the simulscreen. "When do you want to try again, Chief?"

"Does it matter? There's no point in—I dunno. Tomorrow I can rig up something."

Beside me Philip Tyre said, "I knew it couldn't work, but still I was hoping . . ."

"So was I," I said shortly. I stood. "I'm going below."

Dray regarded me dourly from the engine room hatchway. "Well?"

He was blunt. "Hopeless."

"You're sure?"

"Of course!" he snapped. "What do you think I've trained in for thirty years?" He pulled himself back. "Sorry, sir. Bartel and Clinger and the others, they watched me like I was a doc trying to save their baby. It got on my nerves."

"Yes." I added cautiously, "It would be best to keep testing, if there's any possibility of improvement."

He glanced at me, knowing. "Yes, sir. I don't want to think about when they're finally convinced it won't work. Tomorrow I'll try to make finer adjustments on the baffles, and see if varying the wave strength has any result."

"Thank you."

He gave me an odd look. "You're welcome, sir."

The next afternoon we began another series of tests. Again the wave we produced was a jagged, uncontrollable line on the screen. Off-duty crewmen crowded into the engine room to observe. Our machinists fabricated new controls for the baffles in repeated efforts to overcome the problem.

By day's end everyone was short-tempered, including me. Elena Bartel asked for permission to speak with me, and I had her brought to the bridge.

"There's one thing we haven't tried, sir."

"And that is?"

"More power."

"I'm no engineer, Ms. Bartel, but even I know how dangerous that would be."

"The wave front might straighten."

"And it might melt the shaft wall." Pensively I tapped the console. "We may not be generating true N-waves, but we're putting out energy in the attempt. If we overheat the shaft—"

"The sensors will—"

"Don't interrupt!" She drew back, startled. "You're a sailor speaking with an officer, Ms. Bartel, and don't forget it!"

"Aye aye, sir." She sounded reluctant.

"If we melt the shaft the energy could turn back on us and we could destroy the ship." I stood. "I've gone along with this charade, and I'm willing to let it continue, up to a point. You may test again only if we can do it without further endangering *Challenger*." I glowered. "Dismissed!"

She saluted, turned on her heel, and left.

Philip brought me the word the next morning. "Walter Dakko, sir. I was walking down the corridor and he hauled me into the lounge. He actually yanked my arm, sir, as if he didn't care that I'm an officer. Said he had to talk to you immediately."

I felt my arms prickle with a cold sweat. "Right now, then." I thumbed the caller. "Master-at-arms to the bridge!"

Moments later Dakko had joined us. "Things are getting out of hand."

"Be specific."

"The crew berth, a lot of wild talk. You won't allow testing at high power because you don't want us to go home. You know the drive can be made to work but—"

"Goofjuice!"

"Yes, sir. But it's real to them. They're getting, ah, rather worked up."

"Still only talk?"

"For the moment. But they're—" He swallowed. I waited. "There's talk about running tests without your permission, sir."

"How could they? I'd have Kerren override the fusion drive circuits."

"If you're in control." He met my eye without flinching.

"Break out arms, Mr. Dakko. For you, me, Mr. Tyre, and the Chief."

"Aye aye, sir. And one other thing—"

"Yes?"

"Chris. I want to keep him out of harm's way."

"How?"

"Lock him in a cabin, if I must. I don't want him involved."

"Denied. He's a sailor. He knows his duty and the consequences of rebellion. Go break out the arms."

"No. You owe me that much." He held my gaze, not defiantly but steadily.

"You too, Mr. Dakko?"

"If that's how you must have it."

I clapped my jaw shut before I made it worse. He had, after all, repeatedly risked his life to bring me essential information. I changed tack as smoothly as I could. "Mr. Dakko, Chris is seconded to you for special duties until the emergency is over. Break out the arms."

"Aye aye, sir. Thank you." He left at once.

Philip said hesitantly, "If we go armed, sir, we'll show the crew we know what they're thinking."

"Yes. It's time we all knew where we stand."

Half an hour later Walter Dakko was back with a load of laser pistols and stunners. I took a pistol, sounded the alarm. "All hands to General Quarters!" The sirens wailed.

One by one the stations reported. When the last voice crackled in the speaker I said, "All hands remain at General Quarters until inspection."

We made the rounds, Philip, Walter Dakko, and I. At each station I checked readiness, on the alert for misplaced gear or other violations. Our last stop was the engine room, where Deke and Jokko stood by with the Chief.

I paused at the hatch. "Dray, how high can we set fusion drive power without overheating the shaft?"

Perhaps he'd heard the scuttlebutt; at any rate he made no comment about the futility of our testing. "I'm not entirely sure. Somewhere near fifty percent, I'd think."

"If you increase power slowly will your monitors warn us of overheating in time to shut down?"

"Aye, sir."

"Very well." I took the caller. "All hands stand down!" I made my way back to the bridge, Philip dutifully at my side.

"Now what, sir?" he asked.

"Fire drill." I reached for the caller.

"Right after GQ?"

By way of answer, I hit the alarm.

During the afternoon I ran two more alerts and a laser drill. The crewmen were brooding and sullen, but my orders were carried out. At dinner, immediately after the prayer, I made an announcement. "Fusion drive testing may resume under the Chief's supervision. He will decide what power settings do not imperil the ship's safety."

Before the echo of my last words had died Elena Bartel was on her feet. "Does that mean we can start tonight?" Her tone was truculent.

"Sir!"

"Sir. May we start tonight?"

I thought of delaying until tomorrow, in response to her bad manners, but that would be altogether too petty. "Very well."

The ragged line flickered across the screen. Rarely did it intersect for more than a moment the smooth curve of the theoretical N-wave. As the Chief increased power the strength of the wave grew but it remained obstinately erratic. I yawned.

Philip spoke suddenly, startling me. "If that were music it would be some weird kind of jazz." His eyes too were riveted on the simulscreen.

I grunted. Through the speaker I could hear the Chief growl at his crew of eager and determined assistants while they wrestled with the new, unfamiliar baffle controls they'd rigged.

I yawned again. It had been a long day and the drills and inspection had left me exhausted. I glanced at the temperature readouts. The shaft wall was not overheating. I yearned for my bed, decided abruptly that there was no reason for me not to be in it. "Watch the readouts, Mr. Tyre. Shut down if we overheat."

"Aye aye, sir."

"You have the conn." I left the bridge.

In my cabin I unbuttoned my jacket, hung it neatly over the chair. I had to tend to my own clothes; *Challenger*, half abandoned, had no ship's boy to bring the Captain's breakfast and hang up his jacket. Of course, I was not so long removed from the wardroom that I minded.

I loosened my belt and yanked off my tie, which as always made me feel better. I wondered for the hundredth time why we still wore the adornments. Naval dress was so rigidly obsolete.

Something tapped at my hatch. A strange sound, definitely not a knock. It sounded again. I froze, my heart pounding, afraid but not sure why.

The tapping came again. Too tired for melodrama, I slapped open the hatch.

Mrs. Reeves had her cane raised, to tap once more.

"What do *YOU* want?" I coursed with adrenaline.

"To talk—"

"You're not allowed here." The extent of my rudeness punctured my fury. I said more civilly, "Passengers aren't allowed in the officers' section, Mrs. Reeves."

"I know that," she said tartly. "But this is where you are, and I need to speak with you."

"In the morning, then. I'm quite—"

"Captain, do an old woman a courtesy and stay awake a few moments longer. You're young enough. It won't hurt you."

Aching to slam the hatch in her face I nodded reluctant agreement. "Come in, then."

She hobbled into my cabin, glancing at the sparse furnishings. I indicated a chair at the conference table; she sat carefully, mind turned inward to the mechanics of lowering herself.

"There." She settled into the chair. "You don't know how fortunate you are, young man, to have a body you can trust."

I waited pointedly. Recognizing the tactic, she smiled, not at all put out. She waved her cane in the general direction of the engine room. "That fussing with the motors. Will it work?"

"They're still testing, Mrs. Reeves. I can't—"

Her shrewd blue eyes pierced my equivocations. "Will it work?"

"No. It won't."

She let the silence continue, very much in control. For a moment I recalled Father, reviewing my lessons at the rickety kitchen table. "You've made a great mistake, Captain," she said at last. "And I don't know if you have time to correct it."

"Allowing the tests? I had to show them that—"

"No, not that."

My anger rose; I wasn't used to interruptions.

She said, "If the drive won't run, you'll spend at least a generation on this ship. I won't be with you, thank heaven. I've had my time in the sun, as it were." Her crinkled eyes found mine. "Those people can't live their whole lives under military discipline, Captain."

"Those are matters you're not—"

She overrode me yet again. "I'm talking to you while I may, Mr. Seafort. If I wait much longer you won't be Captain."

"I don't know that I care," I said bluntly, astonished I could say such to her.

"It may cost your life."

"I don't know that I care," I echoed. I had to look away.

"Care, boy!" Her cane rapped on the edge of the table, startling me. "Life in its fullness is all too short. And you have a duty to these people. Who else could lead them? The Chief Engineer, who would drink his way out of his dilemma? The midshipman whom everyone treats as a boy because he feels himself one? A committee of untrained passengers?"

"I'm doing what I know to do." My voice was hoarse.

"Bells ringing at all hours, people racing to and fro. What is it all for?"

"They're readiness drills."

"Readiness for what?" she demanded. "Crew and passengers have to learn to live together, to cooperate. Not to respond like robots to some archaic military drill they'll never use again."

"This is a military vessel."

"Was." The word had a finality that shook me.

"We haven't been decommissioned. *Challenger* is not abandoned and she's heading home."

"At a speed that makes the issue academic." She leaned forward. "Don't you understand? We have to create a society that will work under such bizarre conditions. We have to ameliorate their stress and anxiety. Your way only increases it."

"My job, Mrs. Reeves, isn't to create a society. It's to maintain law and order on board this vessel." I wondered if I sounded as fatuous as I thought.

"And are you doing that?" she asked unexpectedly.

"Yes. I think so."

"Then why were you carrying guns today, you and the boy? Since when has that been your custom?"

"There's been tension. I was afraid—"

"Ah."

My fingers drummed the edge of the table in growing anger. "I understand your concern, ma'am, but you have no right to challenge me."

Mrs. Reeves raised her eyebrows. "Good heavens, young man. Whatever I'm doing, it's not meant as that. I want you to see the outcome of your efforts."

"And that is?"

"They'll overthrow you or kill you, and create a form of society they can live with." Her words were stark in the silence of my cabin. For a while I could hear nothing but our breathing.

After a time she continued. "A leader can only lead where the people will follow. Surely you know that."

"What were you?" I asked curiously. "A historian?"

"A psychologist, actually." A mischievous grin. "So I'm supposed to know how to manipulate you. I'm not doing a very good job."

I warmed to her smile. "But you make me think." As some of our tension dissipated I leaned back. "You say my choices are limited by the crew's unwillingness to lead a military life indefinitely. That may be, but I'm also bound by my oath. I am not free to create a social order amenable to all of us. I am subject to the Naval Code of Conduct, and by the oath I've sworn to my Government."

"An oath is a fine thing, but the spirit of your regulations is to keep the ship in order. You can't do that if you're dead or deposed."

"I can't determine whether I live. I can only determine whether I'm true to my oath."

"Young man, you take a narrow view that does not encompass our circumstances."

"That's as must be."

"And what of the people?" She leaned forward on her cane. "Understand, you're not speaking only of fidelity to your oath. You're talking about the needs and miseries of all the others on board. Some of them, the children, might live through this to our eventual rescue."

I closed my eyes in despair. "What would you have me do?"

"Relax your Naval discipline. Ease the distinctions between crew and passengers. Eliminate the ridiculous drills and inspections. Stop using coercion and punishments."

"And what will that accomplish?"

"Don't you know?" Her rheumy eyes searched mine. "This life aboard ship is all that many of us will have before we die. Let us live it in peace."

I stared at the deck. Behind me, Amanda softly touched my shoulder, and faded. I said bitterly, "Peace. I don't know what that is. I've seen it, but never held it in my hands."

"It's fragile," Mrs. Reeves admitted. We fell silent.

I brooded, lost within myself. She was right, of course. My efforts to maintain military discipline were making our lives miserable. I could ease the drills, the inspections. I could be more friendly. I wondered if, eventually, I could permit an elected government and somehow square it with my oath.

I met her eye again and smiled shyly. "I'm glad you came," I said. "I'll try—"

The siren shrieked. Alarms reverberated in the corridors. Philip Tyre's frightened voice cut over the cacophony. "Captain to the bridge, flank! All hands to General Quarters!"

Mrs. Reeves struggled to her feet with surprising agility. "I'll go back—"

I snatched my jacket. "No, the corridor hatches will seal in a moment. Stay here!" I dashed to the bridge, my steps resounding to the unforgiving clang of the alarms. Crewmen careened past on their way to duty stations.

The bridge hatch was sealed, the camera eye swiveling back and forth. The hatch slid open as I raised my hand to pound on it. I scrambled through and it slid shut immediately. I shouted, "Turn off those bloody alarms!"

Philip's hand flicked over the keys. Silence echoed. He pointed at the simulscreen.

"Oh, Lord God." I snatched the caller, bellowing over the incoming reports. "Battle Stations! Comm room, prepare for laser fire. All passengers and crew stand by your pressure suits. Stand by to repel boarders!" I took a deep breath.

"Engine room, shut down the drive! Full power to all lasers! Power up maneuvering jets!"

The fish were back.

Two of them, one off the bow on the port side, the other amidships to starboard.

They were some kilometers off. With Kerren's screens on maximum magnification, the fish seemed unnervingly close. The digits flashing below the screen showed them on a closing course.

"We'll intercept the forward one first," said Philip unnecessarily.

"I know." I called the comm room. "Get a lock on the forward target!"

"Aye aye, sir." Mr. Tzee. "I think they're out of effective range yet."

"I can see that," I growled.

The speaker crackled. "Power to maneuvering jets, sir!"

"Very well, engine room."

"I was watching the N-wave line," Philip blurted. "One minute everything was fine, then they were there!"

"Be silent, Middy!"

"Aye aye, sir," he whispered.

The range closed. I checked the readouts on the thrusters, cursing the propellant I'd recklessly expended to increase our speed.

"Sorry, Philip," I said presently. "Nerves."

"Thank you, sir." His voice was unsteady, his face white.

"Easy, Midshipman." For his benefit, I made my tone calm.

"Approaching firing range!" The puter.

"Thank you, Kerren." I flicked the caller. "Comm room, commence firing when I activate." My hand hovered over the laser lock.

"Maximum range achieved!"

Still, I hesitated. "They'll swerve when we hit them. If we wait 'til they're closer, we might burn through with the first shot."

Kerren's sensors followed the fish that approached our bow. A tentacle began to separate from the globular mass. Lazily the stringlike appendage began to rotate. I jabbed the switch. "Fire!"

Though there was nothing to watch, I searched the screen anxiously for the invisible beam of light from our laser.

Voices murmured in the speaker; our caller was set to comm room frequency.

"Full pulse. I've got a lock!" Walter Dakko, his voice rising.

The fish jerked, propellant misting from a vent.

"Follow him!"

"Gottim!" Deke, tense with excitement. My arm ached; I found my knuckles white from squeezing the armrest. I flexed my wrist.

Beams from three lasers centered on the fish off our bow. It was almost too easy. The goldfish bucked once; colors swirled in the undifferentiated mass of its outer skin, then it was still. Fluid or gas spurted from within.

"We gottim! We gottim!" Cheers erupted, shushed by Mr. Tzee. As we drifted alongside the inert fish I realized how much smaller it was than the one that had menaced *Hibernia* eons past.

"Target closing oh eight four, sir." Kerren was brisk.

"Lock on!" I said with growing confidence. If it was to be this easy . . .

Philip gasped as the alarms shrieked again. He waved weakly at the simulscreen.

Three more aliens.

Even as I watched, a fourth fish burst onto the screen. Then another, appearing from nowhere. Kerren erupted with angry vehemence. "Target aft, bearing oh two oh, range two hundred meters! Target amidships port! Target—"

"Fire at will!" I bellowed. "All lasers, individual fire!"

A fish loomed, amidships. A tentacle twirled, about to break off in a deadly spiral. An icicle stabbed my spine.

The Lord is my shepherd.

"Lock on target three!"

I shall not want.

"Burn the sumbitch!"

"BEHIND THE DRIVE SHAFT! TWO OF THEM!"

He maketh me to lie down in green pastures.

"I see 'em!" Alongside us a fish leapt convulsively.

He leadeth me beside the still waters.

"Bridge, engine room here. One of them's closing fast on us; another's close behind."

He restoreth my soul.

"I see them, Dray."

Admiral Tremaine had taken several of our laser mounts for *Portia*. Few of the remaining lasers pointed aft. I goaded my numbed brain into action. "Maneuvering jets! Oh nine oh, two jets!" Squirting propellant frantically, I swung the ship in a ponderous turn so our lasers could bear.

He leadeth me in the paths of righteousness for his name's sake.

"Get a lock on him!"

A fish blossomed and seemed to crumple. A wild cheer.

Yea, though I walk through the valley of the shadow of death, I will fear no evil.

"Watch them other two!" As *Challenger* rotated, the nearest fish detached a spiraling arm. It sailed lazily across the few meters that separated us. Thanks to our turn the mass would hit forward of the disks, in the hold. Had I not come about, it would have caught us astern, perhaps on the drive shaft.

For thou art with me.

New alarms rang loud. *"HULL IS BREACHED! HOLD PENETRATED!"*

Thy rod and thy staff they comfort me.

"Look out for the two amidships!"

"I'm swinging round!" I braked our spin with a reckless burst of propellant.

Thou preparest a table before me in the presence of mine enemies.

The mottled skin of the nearest fish seemed to swirl. As in a dream I watched the rotating mass expand. A lump grew on the fish's skin. Then the figure was through, and launched itself at *Challenger*.

"Lasers, get that outrider!" I hit the sirens. "All hands repel boarders! Decontamination imminent! Suit up!"

Thou anointest my head with oil.

"I've got a lock on the son of a bitch!" A new voice; Elena Bartel. Her laser found the floating figure. It flared and wilted just before it passed within our circle of fire, where our lasers wouldn't depress far enough to hit it.

My cup runneth over.

"There's another!"

Surely goodness and mercy shall follow me all the days of my life.

"I gottim! I gottim!"

"Steady, Deke. Wait for range." Walter Dakko.

And I will dwell in the house of the Lord for ever.

"Gottim!"

"Good boy!"

"LOOKATIM PLODE!"

Amen.

And there was silence.

19

My unsteady hand shut off the last of the alarms. Slumped in my armchair, a stranger called for damage reports. He seemed to have something caught in his throat.

"Engine room reporting, no damage. Full power on-line, but we're damn near out of propellant."

"I know, but we had to maneuver." I spoke as if from a great distance.

"Hydroponics, no damage, sir."

"Comm room, no damage, sir."

Beside me, Philip Tyre sat frozen at his console, fingers gripping the sides of his chair.

"Recyclers, no damage, sir," said the speaker.

A tear ran unchecked down the boy's face.

"Galley is undamaged, sir."

The midshipman caught his breath.

"Kerren, status report!"

"All systems within normal parameters," the puter intoned. "All compartments airtight except the hold. Hold is breached portside, thirty point three meters forward of the launch berth. Hold is decompressed."

Philip straightened his shoulders, leaned back, took a deep shuddering breath. His hands remained fastened on the armrests.

"What happened to the projectile that beast threw?" Pointedly, I ignored the middy.

"It dissolved the portside hull plating in the hold," said Kerren. "Sensor lines are destroyed and dislodged cargo is blocking my camera view. I cannot estimate the size of the breach."

I frowned. Beside me Philip attempted a smile. He shouldn't have. His face crumpled. He threw up his hands and his shoulders shook.

I cleared my throat. "Inspect the corridor, Mr. Tyre. Check

the wardroom for damage. Then find the cadet and see he's all right."

"Aye aye, sir." Gratefully Philip fled.

It wasn't much, but it was all I could think of on the spur of the moment. At least it allowed him the privacy of the wardroom.

I'd wanted to meet in the officer's mess, where we could gather at the informal breakfast table, but I no longer dared leave the bridge untended, even for a moment. So Philip Tyre and I sat at our consoles, seats swung round to face the chairs from the lounge occupied by the Chief and Gregor Attani.

I asked simply, "What do we do?"

Silence hung heavy, punctuated only by the muttering of Kerren's monitors and sensors. I'd allowed the crew to stand down from Battle Stations only after we'd passed several tense hours without encountering more fish.

The Chief cleared his throat. "Is there really a decision to make, sir? What options do we have other than to do what we're doing?"

"You think our situation unchanged?" I sounded more acid than I'd intended.

Gregor, saying nothing, stared at the screen.

Dray held his ground. "Essentially, yes." He waved toward the hold. "Kovaks and Clinger will have the breach sealed in a couple of hours. Then we're in the same situation as before."

"Except that we're virtually out of propellant. And the hold may be contaminated. It's where our remaining food supplies are stored."

I'd given Philip and Dray permission to interrupt freely, so Philip's interjection was not impertinent. "We rigged Class A decontamination gear in the launch berth," he said. "And all the stores of food are sealed. We should be able to get to them safely." He bit his lip. "Will we need to go back to the hold later for anything else?"

"We'll go through full decontamination whenever we do," I growled. Vacuum or no, I would take no chances.

They waited for my lead. "So we go on as before?" I was unsatisfied.

The Chief said again, "What else can we do?"
"Is there any chance whatsoever we can get the drive working?" Philip, to Dray.
Gregor stirred. "Sir, I—"
Philip swung on him in fury. "You're here by sufferance, Cadet! Open your mouth again and you'll wish you'd been born without one!" Gregor recoiled from his senior's anger.
"No chance of doing anything with the drive," Dray said gruffly. The Chief stared into the intermediate distance, about ten meters beyond the hull. "We're testing right now, and I suppose we'd better keep on. It's the only hope we can offer the crew."
I asked, "How long can you string it out?"
"A long time, if necessary."
I sighed. "We may not need long. Kerren, replay the tape." I looked at the screen where Kerren displayed the ragged N-wave produced by our damaged drive.
"Aye aye, sir." The first alien appeared abruptly in what had been empty space.
"Again, in slomo."
Kerren cut to the beginning of the recording, at very low speed. I still couldn't detect an interval between the time we saw nothing, and the moment a fish floated off our bow.
"How did it find us?" Philip muttered. Over his head, the scene continued to replay.
"Remember, they found *Challenger* before." My eyes were on the screen. "When Admiral Tremaine had her. All we've done since is fire the thrusters."
In replay, one by one the fish on the screens fell to our laser fire, except the last survivor, which pulsed and abruptly disappeared as the lasers found its range.
It blipped out of existence as fast as the first fish had appeared.
"They could come back any moment." I was reluctant to say it aloud.
"But why?" Philip cried. "Why do they keep coming?"
Gregor Attani said, "Sir—"
"You don't have permission to speak," Philip snapped.
I felt sorry for Tyre, doing his best to hide his fear, unaware

that it revealed itself as savagery toward his charge. I stepped carefully. "I would be willing to hear him, if you give permission," I said with delicacy.

Philip turned scarlet. "Aye aye, sir." He nodded to Gregor. "Go ahead."

Gregor swallowed. "How do they get here, sir?" he asked.

I shrugged. "That's one of the many things we don't know."

"I watched a holovid once, back home." Attani shifted awkwardly. "About inventing the fusion drive. They showed a ship Fusing. It looked a lot like the way that fish disappeared."

"The fish are alive," I said. "They don't have fusion drives."

"Birds don't have airplane engines," he said.

I was speechless a long moment. "Organic fusion?" I sputtered. "How?"

The cadet shrugged. "I don't know, sir. What else could it be?"

The Chief shook his head. "I don't see how it's possible. An N-wave couldn't be generated organically."

"Bats navigate by generating sound waves," Philip remarked.

I waved him down. "That's all beside the point. The issue is why they seek us out, not how."

"Sir, if you'll permit—"

I glared at Gregor. "You've had your say. We don't have time to speculate where they're from." I turned to the Chief, my tone glum. "I suppose you'd best continue drive tests as long as—"

Gregor shot to his feet, gripped the back of his chair with both hands. His face was pale. "Listen to me."

Philip and the Chief exchanged glances, astonished at the cadet's impertinence. We all rounded on Gregor.

"Ten demerits!" snapped Philip. "You're confined—"

"I'll teach that youngster—"

"They hear our N-waves!" Gregor's voice was sharp over the babble.

"—to behave—"

"After all I've taught—"

We fell silent, gaping. The cadet appealed, "I'm sorry to

interrupt, sir, but can't you see?" He gestured at the screen, where the jagged line wavered. "If they travel by N-wave, they must be able to sense them. Hear them."

I said slowly, "How can we be sure—" My mind reeled. Did they hear us travel in Fusion, or only when we Fused or Defused? Were ships attacked while actually in Fusion? If so, would we ever learn of it?

"Lord God." I don't know which of us said it.

"We've used the fusion drive for over a century," I demanded. "Why didn't they hear us before?"

"Maybe they've come a long, long way," Gregor Attani said. I felt a chill.

"Let's assume they hear us Fuse and Defuse," I said slowly. "That would explain why they attacked our ships at nav checkpoints."

"How could you hear an N-wave?" the Chief wondered. His glance traveled up to the simulscreen, where the jagged line pulsed. "And what about that wave we're producing. That—caterwauling."

I wasn't listening; I'd already swung to the console and slapped the power lever to "Off." The jagged line vanished from the screen. "Kerren, reset emergency override on the engine room! Disconnect power to the drive!"

"Aye aye, sir. Override reestablished."

I stared at the simulscreen, terrified of what might appear. Nothing came. After long moments I forced my muscles to unknot and swung my chair back to the waiting officers. "There's no proof you're right," I said to Gregor. "But we'll proceed on the assumption you are, until we learn otherwise."

"Yes, sir."

"Anything else?"

"No, sir." He looked as if he wanted to make himself invisible.

"Then take your seat."

He did, quickly. We had little left to discuss and the conference ground to a gloomy halt. I told the Chief to explain to Ms. Bartel and the others why we'd stopped testing. "If there's any grumbling, send them to me. And keep standby power to the lasers at all times."

I took up the caller. "Mr. Tzee, summon the first laser

firing detail. They and Group B will rotate watches for the next week." Hard on them, but I couldn't risk less.

"I'll take the next watch," I said, blinking back exhaustion. We'd been up through the night, time unnoticed, and it was already near end of morning watch. "I'll go change my shirt first. Chief, you have the conn 'til I'm back. Philip, get some rest. You too, Cadet."

Wearily I trudged to my cabin, wondering what had become of Mrs. Reeves. I had my finger on my hatch panel when the alarms sounded again.

I scrambled back to the bridge. I only needed one glance at the simulscreen. "Chief, go below!"

"Right!" He moved fast for a big man.

This time, there were eight.

In a moment the departments began reporting. Philip Tyre, his duty station on the bridge, dashed in, coat awry.

"Lasers have power!"

"Seek targets!"

I gripped the thruster controls. There was little to do but watch.

"Target bearing one five four, range five hundred meters!" Elena Bartel.

"Kill it!"

"He's getting ready to throw!"

Deke shouted, "Big'un behin' us, Cap'n!"

I saw. A copious squirt of the port thruster, and *Challenger* responded with an unbearably slow turn.

"Amidships! Jesus, he's close!"

"Got a lock!"

Kerren's monotone was continuous. "Encroachment oh five oh, declination three five, range five hundred meters. Encroachment two six one, declination oh eight four, range one hundred meters. Encroachment—"

"Watch the one above us! He's settling!"

"Power line overheat! Switching to alternate!"

There were too many, too close. *Save us, Lord God.* "Philip, all passengers stand by to don suits. See to it."

"Aye aye, sir."

A whirling tentacle broke free, sailed toward us in the deadly silence of vacuum. "Damn! Get it!" Walter Dakko.

"I'm tryin'! It's movin' too fast!" Deke.

"Inside our circle!"

"It's comin' at the launch berth!"

I was already at the thrusters. *Challenger* turned her broadside from the swirling mass, not enough to avoid it, but enough so it struck the hull forward of the launch berth.

"Propellant reserves at minimum," Kerren said calmly. "Two minutes maneuvering left, Captain."

"God damn them!" My blasphemy went unremarked.

"At the stern," shouted Dakko. "The shaft!"

A big fish drifted aft, colors pulsating against the black night. As I watched horrified, a blowhole opened, squirted. The fish floated toward the drive shaft wall, below the engine room.

Reluctantly I squirted another precious blast of propellant. We swung away from the danger. The fish followed. A patch in its skin began to swirl and change colors. One of its outriders began to emerge.

"Stand by to repel boarders!"

Not one, but three of the figures launched themselves from the fish alongside the engine room. They sailed to the hull surrounding the drive shaft.

"Got the sumbitch!" Ahead a fish wilted, its innards spurting into the night.

"Engine room reporting. Alien boarding party on hull outside the drive shield." Somehow, Dray made it sound like a routine status report.

"Master-at-arms, repel boarders at engine room! Dray, get your people suited!"

A fish forward of the disk pulsed rhythmically, disappeared.

"Look! The bastard Fused when he got hot!" Elena Bartel.

"We're already suited, sir," said Dray. "Uh, the fish is closing fast."

On the simulscreen, I watched catastrophe approach. My eyes flicked to the readouts. We had propellant for barely one more maneuver.

"Jesus, Lord Christ!" Philip rose from his chair. Aghast, I started at the screen.

About three hundred meters off our starboard side a fish had appeared, the largest I'd ever seen.

Kerren intoned, "Encroachment oh nine three, declination zero, range three hundred meters and closing."

Propellant puffed from a blowhole. Already a tentacle was forming on the exterior. The fish drifted closer.

"The fish at the stern is just off our shield, Captain!" Dray's voice was ragged. Nothing but a plastalloy drive shield separated the engine room from the vacuum. When the fish dissolved the shield, the engine room would decompress. And my suited men would be in the compartment with those—beasts.

"Is Dakko there?"

"Here, sir! Engine room."

"Can you fight them off?"

"There's three of the outriders Outside. If they eat through, we'll burn them. But the fish itself—" He left the rest unsaid. Dakko's puny weapons could do naught against the might of the looming fish.

We were under attack from all sides, but the most immediate danger came from two fish: the one releasing invaders to the engine room, and the immense creature looming amidships.

I glanced at the screen. The aft fish was within meters of the drive shaft. If it hurled its acid projectiles at the hull . . . I recalled the deaths of *Hibernia*'s crewmen. Walter Dakko and his party were helpless against the acid.

All was lost. "We have to abandon the engine room," I said, the taste of defeat so bitter I paused before issuing the command.

"No!" Philip leaped to his feet.

"There's no choice—"

"We'll lose power to the lasers!"

"Unless we get our men out they'll be killed!" I gestured helplessly. "We can't save the engine room!"

The huge fish amidships let go a projectile. It spun lazily toward the hull.

"We can!" Philip insisted.

"No lasers fire far enough inward to cover the drive shaft."

Dray's voice, edged with panic. "The fish will make contact any second!"

"The launch." Philip was pale. "Let me take it."

"It's unarmed."

"It's got hot propellant and it can ram."

Dumbfounded, I stared.

He waved at the simulscreen. "What difference does it make? Look at them!" Still I said nothing. "Sir, let me go. Maybe I can scare that thing off."

I found my voice. "No."

"What else am I good for?" His young features contorted.

"No!"

"Then we'll die for nothing!" He hesitated, then ran to the hatch. "Maybe I can sear the fish with our exhaust." The hatch slid open. He paused a microsecond. "Permission to leave the bridge, sir!"

I had to try twice before I made the word audible. "Granted."

The midshipman flipped a perfunctory salute and ran down the corridor out of sight.

I swung to the screen. Our fire had neutralized the projectile from the midships fish, but the alien had formed another glob, already swirling toward us.

In less than a minute the console lights blinked, warning me the launch berth was occupied and depressurizing.

The midships projectile sailed untouched through our fire.

"Sombitch!" screamed Eddie Boss in the comm room, blasting my eardrums. "My gun! He got my gun!"

"Midships laser malfunction!" Kerren.

The launch shot from its berth.

"Shut down power to midships laser!"

"Power is down."

"Captain, it's gonna throw at the engine room right now!" The Chief, his voice taut.

I swallowed. "Abandon eng—"

"Hang on, Dray, I'm almost there," Philip Tyre's voice was steady. "Get in the shop compartment, you'll have another bulkhead between you and the acid."

"Do that, Chief." My hand gripped the console.

"Aye aye, sir."

Mr. Tzee's voice cut across the babble. "Look at the screen, sir."

The huge fish amidships was growing three more projectiles.

"Fire on him!"

"They've knocked out all our guns that bear at this angle, sir. I need a bow-on shot."

"I'll come round!" I squirted propellant. Our nose drifted ever so slowly toward the fish.

Kerren's camera picked up the launch. Philip maneuvered the stern of his tiny vessel toward the fish at our shaft. He kicked a jet of propellant at it, causing the launch to shoot away from the fish. The fish quivered, random dots of color swirling in its skin, but it remained still.

"Go, you bastard!" Philip's voice was savage. He swung his craft close for another try.

A cry of dismay from Mr. Tzee. "Captain, they've got our bow laser."

"Can you bring anything to bear?"

"We've nothing big enough to hurt them, sir."

If the Admiral had left us more of our lasers . . . "Very well."

Philip squirted a blast of propellant at the aft fish, without effect.

It wasn't working. I rested my head in my hands.

"Engine room decompression! Captain, they're through the hull!"

"Keep away from the acid! Burn the outriders as they poke through!"

"I'm going to ram," said Midshipman Philip Tyre.

"No, Philip!"

"It's our only chance. The impact may drive him away. I'll try to eject before contact." I knew that was impossible, as did he.

"Mr. Tyre—"

He swung his little ship about, spending propellant with reckless abandon. About a hundred meters distant he matched velocities and aimed his prow at the bow of the fish.

"Mr. Tyre!"

"I'm glad I served with you, sir. If you see Alexi, tell him I'm sorry." He jammed his throttle to full. The launch spurted forward.

If his aim was true he would lance the fish head on. "Sir, Godspeed—"

I snatched up the caller. "Kerren, record! Mr. Tyre! I, Captain Nicholas Seafort, do commission and appoint Midshipman Philip Tyre a Lieutenant in the Naval Service of the Government of the United Nations, by the Grace—"

The radio crackled and went dead—

"Of God!"

Challenger's launch tore into the bow of the fish, accelerating still as it clawed through the alien tissue. The fish bucked. It appeared to ripple. Viscous material spewed from the gaping hole. The momentum of the launch tore the fish from our hull. Inert, it drifted out of sight behind *Challenger*, our launch imbedded within.

"Penetration in the hold!"

Lord God, I repent my sins.

"DECOMPRESSION LEVEL 2, SECTION SIX!"

"Captain, east hydros are decompressed!"

Pray forgive my trespasses.

"Engine room!" I expected no answer.

"Here, sir! Only two of the outriders got through, and we fried 'em both. Clinger, get that patch in place!"

"Full power to the thrusters, Chief. Give me all remaining propellant."

"You've got it! We've less than a minute's burn, sir."

Lord, I beg Thee, take me unto Yourself.

"I know."

Challenger had swung almost nose-on to the midships beast that still threw its projectiles. I glanced at the screens; other fish maneuvered alongside. There was no way to avoid them all.

"Kerren, ramming course!"

"Course true! Relative oh oh oh!"

I'm coming, Amanda.

My hand jabbed at the red ball of the thruster control. *Challenger* drifted forward almost imperceptibly.

I cried, "Christ, is that all we've got?"

"Acceleration is cumulative," said Kerren, as if that explained everything. Perhaps it did.

Our motion was more evident now. As we neared, the huge fish squirted propellant and began to float aside. I slammed the port thruster to full to correct course, and five seconds later ran out of burn.

"All passengers and crew suit up, flank!" My eyes were locked to the simulscreen. Foolishly I braced myself as we approached. The bridge was in the disk, halfway down the length of the pencil that was our ship. The view on my simulscreen was from Kerren's camera forward. It, not I, would make first contact.

"Wait for us, you bastard!" My teeth clenched, I slurred the words.

In seconds we would skewer the fish with our pointed prow.

The fish began to pulse rhythmically.

"Wait for us . . ."

The fish pulsed. If it disappeared now . . .

"WAIT, YOU THING OF SATAN!"

Contact.

Kerren shrilled warnings. "Prow disintegrating! Forward sensors inoperative! Hull collapsing forward of the disk! The hold is—"

The screen went black.

I was on my feet, braced for an impact I couldn't feel. "Kerren?"

No answer.

"Kerren?" I waited for the power to dim. If Kerren was destroyed—

The lights remained steady.

"Kerren!"

"Fusion is successful, sir," the puter said calmly. "Please provide course for my data calculations."

"What?"

"Fusion drive is on, sir." The puter's tone was patient. "As you Fused manually, I do not have the calculations to—"

"DRAY!"

"Engine room, sir."

"Is the drive on?"

He snorted. "Of course not."

"Oh, Lord God!" I stared at the screen, willing the stars to reappear.

"What is it?" Dray asked.

"The fish. It tried to Fuse just as we hit."

"Yes, sir?" He waited.

"It . . ." I stumbled for words. "It took us with it."

20

We came together in the Level 2 corridor, Dray, Walter Dakko, Gregor and myself. Seconds had dripped into hours, while the screens remained blank.

Kerren insisted we were in Fusion, and I didn't dare examine the rents in our hull to find out. When we were Fused, any object thrust Outside would cease to exist. A body too near a hull opening would be caught up in the stresses of the field, and would suffer molecular collapse and oblivion.

"Now what?" I'd dropped all pretense of military formality. It was all I could do to keep from trembling.

"We're alive," Dray said gruffly.

"For the moment."

"Where are we?" Walter Dakko's voice was a husk.

I shrugged. "In purgatory, perhaps." Dakko raised an eyebrow, said nothing.

"What's going to happen?" Gregor.

I stated the obvious. "We'll die."

Gregor winced, gathered himself. "When, sir?"

"Soon. When the fish Defuses or digests the ship. Or when the food runs—"

"Digests?" blurted Dakko.

I said, "Just before the alien, uh, Fused, Kerren reported the prow was disintegrating and the hull collapsing where it pierced the fish. Now he says all his hold sensors are inoperative. We don't dare open the hatch from the launch berth to the hold because of radiation and the danger of viral contamination. When whatever's dissolving the hull eats as far as the hatchway, we're through."

"How long will that take?" Gregor, again.

"How the hell should I know!" My rage drove him back a step. "Don't ask stupid questions!"

"Sorry, sir! Aye aye, sir." He held himself at near attention.

The mood changed subtly. Walter Dakko asked, "What do we do now, sir?" They waited for my response.

I had an urge to say, "Whatever you damn well please," and stalk to my cabin, leaving them standing in the corridor. What more did they want of me? I had no miracles to bestow.

I sighed. "Engine room status, Chief?"

"We got the hull patched before Fusion, sir, so the engine room's inhabitable. One of the power output lines was hit but the other one's all right."

"You mean after all this we still have power?" I couldn't believe it.

"Enough for lights and heat, yes, sir. I might be able to patch the second power line too. Anyway, we don't need power to the thruster pumps; we're out of propellant. And the lasers were wiped out, so . . ."

My mind spun slowly. We were imbedded in the body of a fish in Fusion. The engine room, aft, was in good shape, the disks where we all lived were airtight, while our hold forward of the disks was being eaten away.

"What else do we know?" I labored through a fog. The Chief's report seemed an annoying distraction.

Dakko said, "The recycler chamber is undamaged, but some of the feeder lines are out of commission and the fluids in them are lost. East hydros—"

"They're gone," said the Chief. "Decompressed. I don't think we should try to open the hatch. We'd have to pump out section eight to get in there, and anyway the plants are dead."

"West?"

"West hydros weren't damaged, but we never got them fully operational again."

"Between east hydros and section eight, we've lost about half our food supply." Dakko grimaced.

"Have Mr. Branstead take a look. Can we repair the lines to the recyclers?"

"Probably most of them, sir. If we can scrounge up enough materials without going into the hold." Dray waited expectantly.

I kept my irritation in check. "Get on it, then."

"Aye aye, sir. The chemicals that were in the lines—I have no way to replace them now that we've lost the hold. The recyclers will just barely keep up."

"Do what you can." They waited for more orders; I forced myself to think anew. "Where else are we decompressed?"

"Level 2, sections four and five, sir," said Dakko. The rebel prisoners were gone, then. Except for Mr. Clinger, saved by the providence of Mr. Drucker's ill temper.

"Oxygen reserves?"

Dray answered that one. "Just sufficient to re-air the ship, sir, but after that it's going to be tight on recycling."

"It won't matter after a while," I said. I turned to Gregor. "Mr. Attani, see who's survived among the passengers and crew. Bring me a list. I'll be in my cabin."

"Aye aye, sir."

"Chief, do what you can to clean up. Mr. Dakko, look to the needs of the crew as best you can."

"Aye aye, sir."

I headed for my cabin, concerned no longer about manning the bridge; my work there was done. We would live until the hatch gave out, or the food, or the air.

Then it would be over.

At the top of the ladder I met Mrs. Reeves, hobbling heavily on her cane. She eyed me with a curious smile. I waited.

"So you were right after all, young man."

"Right?" I tried to recall our conversation.

"About your military discipline."

"It didn't save the ship."

"We live."

"Not for long," I replied.

"That's not for you to say," she rejoined tartly, and continued on her way.

I lay on my bunk in a daze. Lord, how I'd wanted *Challenger*, before she was snatched from me. But I'd entered her in disgrace, assuming that I was to die on her. It seemed fitting. But never in my strangest dreams had I imagined such a prelude to death.

After a time, not knowing what else to do, I got up and

sat at my immaculate, polished, useless table. How does one wait for death, certain of its inevitability but not knowing when it will arrive?

"One lives," said Father, almost aloud, so near I almost jumped. "Our deaths are all in the hands of Lord God. Nothing changes that."

"Easy for you to say," I muttered. "You're not aboard." I sensed his disapproval and ignored it, but knew he was right. One lives, as long and as well as one can. One does his duty.

A soft knock at the hatch; I went to open it. Gregor Attani saluted, offered me a paper. "You said to bring this, sir."

"What?"

"The list. Casualties."

"How many?"

"Only two passengers, sir. They were caught without suits when the Level 3 corridor decompressed."

They were the lucky ones. "Have Mr. Tyre arrange stowage of the bodies." My tone was weary.

His look was strange. "Mr. Tyre is dead, sir. The launch. He—"

I sagged against the bulkhead, unable to speak.

"Sir, are you all—"

"Get out!"

When he was gone I thought of going to my bunk but it seemed easier to remain where I was, propped against the bulkhead.

I'm sorry, Philip. But how can you blame me for losing track? I've killed so many of you. Amanda. Nate. Crewmen. Passengers. Uppies and trannies. So many.

After a time I wiped my face and went out to the corridor, where all was quiet and still. I could sense, if not hear, the steady imperturbable throbbing of the engines below.

Level 1 seemed abandoned. I passed the hatch to the launch berth. On the far side of the berth was the hatch to our hold. I poked my head into the bridge. The instruments hummed silently, recording pointless data.

I had a craving for coffee. On the way to the officers' mess I passed the Level 1 passengers' lounge. On impulse I stopped and looked inside.

Walter Dakko sat across from his son. He held Chris's

hands in his own. The two glanced up wordlessly. I mumbled something and backed out of the hatchway.

The boy was crying.

I wasn't sure about the father.

I made the coffee hot and strong, the way I liked it. I sipped greedily, hunched over the long wooden table, waiting for the caffeine to jog my system.

"Sir, is there anything you'd like me to do?"

I whirled, spilling hot coffee down my shirt. Gregor waited.

"Don't sneak up on me, Cadet!"

"I—no, sir! I mean, aye aye, sir."

I regarded him balefully. "What should I have you do, Mr. Attani?"

"I don't—I didn't mean—I'm sorry, sir."

"Just leave me be," I growled.

He hurried to the hatch.

"Mr. Attani!" He stopped. "I'm . . . sorry." I swallowed my ire. "For my manners."

"Yes, sir."

"Do as you wish. See if you can help Mr. Dakko or the Chief. I'll page if I need you."

"Aye aye, sir." He seemed grateful for the directions.

I was left alone.

As I washed the cup to put it away I glanced at the small mirror hanging alongside the galley sink. My jagged scar flamed vividly, as if in reproach. Get hold of yourself, I ordered. You were prepared to die. So now you're doing it. Even now, there is duty.

As penance I walked the habitable areas of the ship. Everywhere I was greeted with pathetic welcome. The crew hung on my words and scurried to do my bidding, as if my orders could extricate us from our calamity. Those passengers I met contrived to have a word with me, some even going so far as to shake my hand.

Detouring around the sealed-off sections of Level 2 that would never be reopened, I finally completed my tour. Eager for isolation, I approached the bridge with unaccustomed eagerness and sank thankfully into my chair.

"What can you tell me about the hold, Kerren?"

It was the wrong question. "The hold is two hundred thirty

meters in length, averaging twenty-four meters across, tapered at a ratio—"

"Cancel. Tell me about the current condition of the hold."

"I have very little information about the state of the ship forward of the launch berth," Kerren said, his voice stiff. "If you would Defuse long enough to—"

"Tell me what you *DO* know, you burned out pile of chips!"

A shocked silence. "Last sensor reports," he said primly, "indicated prow disintegration and collapse of the hull in the forwardmost twenty meters of the hold. That was at 0911 hours. At 0942 the midships hold sensors became inoperative. I can only conclude that the progressive damage reached that point."

"What sensors still work?"

"You are referring to the hold, Captain?"

"Yes." I heard my teeth gnash, willed my jaw open.

"Adequate references would facilitate our conversation," he said sweetly. "To answer you, only one. The internal port sensor is still operative. We had a starboard sensor too, but the line was cut when the hold was first punctured. The operative sensor is mounted on the hull above the catwalk, twenty meters forward of the launch berth hatch."

"Thank you."

"You're quite welcome, Captain." He spoke with his typical courtesy, so I couldn't be certain of his sarcasm. "The fact that the sensor is operative suggests the hull retains structural integrity to that point."

"Thank you," I said again.

"You're welcome," he repeated.

I brooded a moment. "Kerren, can your sensors indicate anything about the exterior of the ship or our location?"

"Not while the fusion drive is operating," he said. "Certainly you must know that."

"Kerren, we're not Fused."

"But we are, Captain."

"Kerren, monitor status of fusion drive."

His pause was infinitesimal. "The drive registers as off, Captain."

"So you—"

"But external registers confirm we are Fused. Therefore the drive monitors are inoperative and their data is ignored."

I sighed. Kerren's programming didn't allow him to accept the possibility of Fusion other than by our drive. I wasn't sure my own did, either. Perhaps the puter could be reprogrammed, but I saw no point in trying.

We'd lost well over half our food plants, and the remaining food stored in the hold was inaccessible. Though three crewmen, our four prisoners, and two passengers were dead, that still left us facing certain starvation. Our recyclers labored to keep breathable air circulating through the ship. Until the feeder lines could be repaired, they barely functioned.

In the meantime we were in Fusion or some analogous state, hurtling toward an unknown destination, entangled with a deadly and hostile alien.

And I was hungry. Should we ration the remaining food? Would we live long enough for it to matter? How long could we make it last, even with rationing?

I thumbed the caller. "Mr. Attani, Mr. Branstead, Mr. Dakko Junior to the bridge."

Emmett Branstead arrived first, looking surprisingly trim and fit. He'd lost about eight kilos since taking the oath, and with it some of his ruddy complexion. True to his word, he'd obeyed orders with dogged determination from the moment of his enlistment.

Moments later the cadet and Chris Dakko entered.

"I need an immediate survey. Our current food production and stores graphed against consumption at half rations and at one-third rations. Determine whether we can survive until we bring more crops on-line. Make your calculations and report back in two hours. Mr. Attani, you're in charge, of course. Avail yourself of Mr. Branstead's expertise regarding production. Mr. Dakko, make yourself useful."

Only after they left did I realize it was the first time the cadet had been allowed to lead a work detail. I worried for a moment before remembering it didn't matter.

". . . We ask you to bless us, to bless our voyage, and to bring health and well-being to all aboard."

The prayer done, I looked from Mr. and Mrs. Reeves to Mrs. Ovaugh and Mr. Fedez, all seated at my table. I looked beyond them to the tables occupied by the other passengers, the subdued groups of crewmen huddled together for comfort. I said, "I will not deceive you about the gravity of our situation. It is hopeless." There was an audible sigh.

"We will almost certainly run out of food before we can grow enough to replace what we lost. At one-third rations, we can last perhaps ninety days. It is barely possible that with conservation and intensive plantings, we can survive until enough crops mature to sustain us. Mr. Branstead's best estimate is that to stretch the food so long we would have to reduce our rations to the point where many of us would die nonetheless."

Elena Bartel raised a hand. I nodded. "What about the—the bodies?" she asked.

To my shame, I'd considered it. "We will not prolong our lives by resorting to cannibalism." My tone was firm. "The bodies have been moved to the engine room for cremation."

"They could sustain life!"

"At the cost of our humanity. I will not allow it." I glanced around the hall. "That decision has already been taken and is not a subject for discussion." I held her eye until she reluctantly sat.

"In any event we are unlikely to live long enough to starve. When we emerge from Fusion, or more likely before, the ship will be consumed." I looked beyond the crew tables, to the far bulkhead. "It is my decision that *Challenger* will go to one-third rations as of our next meal, so as not to foreclose the possibility of extending our lives. We shall continue to function as best we may, until the end. May Lord God bless you all."

I sat to a stunned silence and fixed my eyes on my plate.

The day was followed in dreary succession by another, then a third. Our tension subsided, and an eerie simulation of normal life resumed. The whole ship's company nursed seedlings in a desperate effort to replenish our food supply. But as Gregor Attani's task force had calculated, we had no way to stretch our available stores to sustain us until the new plantings matured. Deke muttered about letting some starve so others could live, but I chose not to understand him.

As the days dragged on, I sat on the deadened bridge, staring at blankened screens, reviewing the Log, contemplating the succession of follies that had led us to this pass. If only the Admiral . . . If Captain Hasselbrad had just . . . If I had refused command and let them hang me . . .

Twelve days into our grim vigil I woke from a doze at my console to hear Kerren's voice, behind a blinking warning light. "The remaining sensor in the hold has failed, sir."

"Failed?" I asked stupidly. "What? How?"

"It showed a rise of thirteen degrees Celsius during the hour just before failure, Captain. Then nothing. I have no way to determine if the line was cut, a connection loosened, or the sensor became inoperative."

"What is the condition of the hull inside the hold?"

"I infer hull status from the sensor data, Captain Seafort. I now have no way to determine the status of the hull forward of the launch berth."

"Very well." I stared at the console. "The hatch from Level 1 to the launch berth is secure?"

"That is correct."

"And the hatch on the other side of the launch berth to the hold?"

"Sensor data says it's functional, sir."

"Very well," I said again. I wanted to confer with Dray, but there was nothing he, or any of us, could do.

Ten more days passed. Though I'd lost only a couple of kilos, my cheeks were sunken, and the scar on my cheek was more noticeable.

Elena Bartel asked through Mr. Attani to see me. I allowed her onto the bridge.

"Elron—Mr. Clinger and I—we would like to be married."

I stared in openmouthed astonishment until she blushed with embarrassment.

"You want to marry Elron Clinger?" Not one of my more astute remarks.

"Yes, sir."

Marriage among crewmen was unusual, but not unprecedented. Sailors needed the Captain's permission to marry, and in our case I was the only one aboard authorized to perform a marriage. The couple would maintain separate bunks in the crew berth, of course, but there were always the crew privacy rooms.

"Well, er, I suppose . . ." I had no reason to deny permission. "Are you quite sure . . . about Mr. Clinger, that is?"

"Quite, sir. Mr. Clinger has thought a great deal about his former life."

"Very well," I said. "You have permission. When would you like the ceremony performed?"

"As soon as possible. We're not—sure how much time we'll have together."

"This evening? Tomorrow?"

"This evening would be fine, sir." She blushed again. "Thank you."

After the ceremony I reflected on the irony. She was at least ten years older than he. Clinger must have indulged in the usual life portside; she'd once admitted to me she'd never had so much as a boyfriend. Ms. Bartel upheld the proprieties; he was a rebel who'd tried to seize the ship.

Perhaps they'd know happiness. More than Amanda and I.

Whether it was the wedding ritual and unspoken thoughts of its aftermath, or some other cause, I felt urgent desire that night, for the first time since Amanda had died. I tossed and turned restlessly and was glad when morning came.

A full month had passed since we'd embedded ourselves in the alien. We relied on shipboard routines to carry us through the gray remorseless days. Gregor Attani lived alone in the wardroom, eagerly performing what chores I found for him. Taking pity, I put aside the tradition that a Captain didn't deign to notice a cadet and made sure to chat with him every day. I also noticed him conversing with Chris Dakko, who seemed miserable and depressed.

Dray spent most of his time in the engine room. I wondered if he'd rebuilt his still, but I saw no evidence of it and didn't choose to investigate. One day I decided to play chess with Kerren, and it gave me so much pleasure I made it a daily routine: one game in the morning, another in the afternoon.

After I lashed out at Gregor, the cadet learned not to disturb me at these times.

Kerren did not play as well as Darla. Or Danny.

On the thirty-fifth day Dray brought word that Eddie Boss sought to speak with me. To avoid the formality of the bridge I called him to the officers' mess, where I waited with a cup of coffee. Thank Lord God for our unabated supply; the hot liquid soothed my nearly constant pangs of hunger and sated my addiction.

Eddie seemed reluctant to tell me why he'd come. I waited as patiently as I could. I even had him sit; it didn't seem to help. His fingers drummed the table as he stared into his lap.

I tried to jar him out of his funk. "Why ol' Eddie be 'fraid talkin' ta da man, hey? Big Eddie, he be chickenshit tella Cap'n boudit?"

That brought a reluctant smile. "You ain' no trannie, sir. Like I tole you once."

"Maybe I'm learning to be."

His smile faded. "You wouldn' wanna be one." His fist tightened. "No way to live, dat. Noway." He stared moodily at the deck. "Funny you sayin' dat. It's what I wan' talkin'—talk to you 'bout."

I waited.

He appealed to me. "Bout bein' a trannie. Don' go laughin' at ol' Eddie, Cap'n, ifn it funny." His fists knotted. "I knows—I know it don' matter none, but you teachin' me read, n' all . . ."

With a flash of insight I guessed what might be coming. I said carefully, "Go ahead, Mr. Boss."

He blurted, "Could you teachin'—teach me, not actin' like trannie? Not talkin' trannie?"

"How do you want to act?" I asked.

"Not like dem Uppies!" he said emphatically. "Not Mr. Tyre, or dat Chris Dakko. Maybe . . ." He flushed. "More like you." He kept his eyes carefully on the table. "I know it don' matter, we gonna die 'n all, but I just be wantin', before den—" He lapsed into embarrassed silence.

An image rose unbidden, of the passenger lounge in *Portia*, Eddie hunched over the table, struggling to learn his letters from Amanda.

"Before then," I said. "Not 'den': then."

His eyes rose to an unforeseen miracle. "Before then," he said with great care.

"Two hours in the morning with Walter Dakko," I said. "Two hours in the afternoon with me. Every day."

He swallowed several times before daring to speak. "Thank you," he whispered.

Later, when I discussed the project with Walter Dakko, he nodded as if it were the most ordinary request in the world. "It's more than just how he talks," he remarked. "His mannerisms. His walk. He doesn't stride, he shambles."

"He's determined to learn."

"Better to have pride in who he is than to learn to be someone he's not."

I glanced up sharply at the rebuke but saw none intended. "It's what he wants more than anything, Mr. Dakko, and I'm inclined to give it to him." I did not mention my reasons.

"Of course, sir." He smiled wryly. "Actually, it will be a challenge. Perhaps I can teach him to behave better than Chris."

"Perhaps." I was noncommittal. After a moment I availed myself of the opportunity. "How's Chris doing?"

"We're—reconciled," was all he said. I didn't press it further. Several times over the next few days I noticed them together.

Dray had to shut down our overburdened recyclers for repair. For an anxious half day we went to canned air. Even afterward, the recyclers were unable to keep up. Our atmosphere was going bad, slowly enough that the effect wouldn't be noticeable for a while yet. Perhaps our food would run out first.

Still, we carried on day to day as if the end were not clearly in sight.

We'd just sat down to our evening meal when the alarms sounded. I scrambled from my seat and dashed to the bridge.

Kerren spoke endlessly in his urgent warning tone. "Launch berth hatch to the hold has failed! Launch berth depressurized!" Now the width of the launch berth was all that separated us from the end. I switched off the alarms.

* * *

It was the fortieth day.

It wouldn't be much longer.

Gregor Attani, gaunt and hollow-eyed, stood before me, hands twisting anxiously. Eager for the conversational scraps I threw to him, he'd never dared initiate a conversation. Until today.

"Sir, do you think . . ." He swallowed, then rushed on. "Is there a chance I could make midshipman, sir, before—before . . ." He faltered.

I looked gently at the misery in his eyes. "Will I be needing midshipmen, do you think, Mr. Attani?"

He blushed. "No, sir. I'm sorry."

I cursed myself under my breath. What had I done? I regarded him somberly while I considered. "Do you want me to give it to you?" I asked at last. "Or do you want to earn it?"

"Earn it," he replied without hesitation.

"Philip—Mr. Tyre was teaching you navigation, wasn't he?"

"Yes, sir. I've been looking at the books on my own now, trying to make sense of them." With a sudden pang I thought of Derek Carr doing likewise.

"Your conduct is exemplary, Mr. Attani. I am satisfied you now have the maturity to be an officer. Study your navigation. I'll try to help, though in truth it wasn't my strongest subject. I'll set up drills for you with Kerren. Spend two hours a day with the Chief to learn the fusion drives. You're relieved of all other duties until your studies are completed."

"Thank you, sir." With a salute worthy of Academy he turned and marched out. Well, it was little enough to give him. Admiralty would never know, and I no longer cared whether they'd approve.

My days were busy now; astronavigation with Gregor in the mornings, sessions with Eddie Boss in the afternoons, sandwiching my chess games between. Sometimes, after our meager, pitiful dinner I would go to the passengers' lounge and chat, with Annie, Jonie, Mr. and Mrs. Reeves. I discovered to my surprise that I was almost content. Annie, in particular, seemed a nice girl, though her streeter ways put me off.

The mood of completion seemed to be catching; people brought their diaries up-to-date, studied ancient languages, watched holos they'd always meant to view. The activities diverted our thoughts from hunger. Our impending end was, by common consent, not mentioned. I'd decided that if the launch berth hatch showed signs of blowing, there was no point to going to suit air for whatever few hours it would extend our lives. So, with patience that surprised me, I waited for the next and final act of dissolution.

In the meantime, Eddie Boss learned to take a long moment's pause before he spoke, to marshal his grammar and overcome his crude dialect. He practiced new forms of etiquette with Walter Dakko. Whatever humor his transpop associates saw in the situation they swiftly learned to hide, for his temper was as fierce as ever.

Out of pity I did my best to keep Chris Dakko busy, assigning him to work details and inconsequential projects. He had retreated into a dazed docility, his terror betrayed only by an occasional unguarded expression.

"He's very afraid of dying," his father said.

"Yes." I knew of no comfort I could give. One night, sitting in the corner of the lounge, Chris suddenly and unexpectedly began to cry. We—his father, the other passengers, and myself—froze in awkward embarrassment. It was young Jonie who went to him, boldly took his head into her bosom, and eventually led him off to private comfort. I silently begged Lord God's blessing on her.

"Maneuvering jets, please, sir."

"Aye aye, power up," responded Dray from the engine room.

Gregor sat stiffly at the watch officer's console while I sat by, with the ritual obligatory scowl. I'd taken Alexi Tamarov, Derek Carr, Philip Tyre, and Rafe Treadwell through these maneuvers, and was an old hand at being an ogre.

Gregor licked his lips. "Steer oh five eight degrees, ahead two-thirds."

"Two-thirds, aye aye." The monitors duly indicated the increase in engine power. All simulated, of course. We were no longer a powered vessel.

"Declination fifteen degrees."

"Fifteen degrees, aye aye."

Gregor was maneuvering the ship into position to Fuse, in hypothetical interstellar space far from any obstacles. A midshipman had ample time to learn the finer points of piloting. My object was merely to see if Gregor grasped the principles of navigation.

"Ship positioned for Fuse, sir." He looked at me expectantly, only a fine sheen on his forehead betraying his anxiety.

"Satisfactory, Cadet," I said gruffly. I snapped off the simulation and the stars faded from the screen. Then I unbent. "Very good, Gregor." He shot me a pleased smile before reassuming the stiff dignity of his station.

That afternoon I beat Kerren twice at chess. He conceded the second game before I could see clearly that I'd won.

It was the fifty-third day.

During the quiet times between Eddie's and Gregor's lessons and my games of chess, I busied myself keeping the Log up-to-date, in case *Challenger*'s remains should ever be found. I wasn't sure why I bothered; I had no idea whether we'd even emerge in our own galaxy.

Seven more days passed. Mrs. Ovaugh died in her sleep; malnutrition certainly was a factor.

Even vast amounts of coffee didn't help my exhaustion. I lost three more kilos, and my appearance was grotesque.

I was asleep in my cabin when the caller snapped me awake. "Captain to the bridge, please." Disoriented for a moment, I couldn't place the voice. Then I realized it was Kerren, but the alarms hadn't sounded. Puzzled, I dressed quickly and hurried to the bridge.

"Please advise if the current condition requires alarms," he said. "My hatch sensor shows abnormal temperature readings in the launch berth."

"Abnormal?"

"Higher than might be expected, sir. They've been climbing very slowly for several days—"

"Then why did you wake me now?" I demanded.

"And the launch berth temperature is up a full degree in the last hour."

"Oh." I found it necessary to sit. My heart was racing.

"If you would Defuse, sir, we might determine the cause."

"I can't Defuse, Kerren."

"One Defuses by turning the fusion drive off."

"Try it," I invited.

"You know I'm unable," he said reproachfully. "The monitors don't respond. They show the drive switched off."

"That's because it *IS* off."

"Refusal to recognize reality indicates an aberrant mental state, sir."

"Thank you."

"You're welcome, sir."

I could have the launch berth hatch reinforced, but if the acid was nearing our disk, it might penetrate the bulkhead anywhere, not necessarily at the hatch.

"How much hotter than this did the hold sensor register before it failed?"

"Eight degrees, sir."

I decided that was comforting. Then I decided it wasn't.

"Sound the alarms when the temperature is five degrees higher than at present."

"Aye aye, sir. What shall I sound? Battle Stations?"

"General Quarters and decompression alert." We had no weapons with which to do battle, and no one to fight.

"Very well, sir. Have a good night."

I slapped the bridge hatch control with extra force and went to my cabin, my hand stinging.

Have a good night. If only he were a midshipman.

21

Three more days passed without incident. Then Walter Dakko approached me, face grim. I took him to my cabin without ceremony. "I'm the bearer of a petition, sir."

"Again."

"Yes." His terseness warned me of trouble.

"Go on, then."

"Everyone agrees our situation is desperate. Many of the crew want you to try turning on the drive."

"What?" I rose from my chair.

"Ignite the drive and see if that will kick us back into normal space."

"Good God."

He said nothing.

I sighed. "Who's behind it?"

"I'm not sure where the idea started. Just about everyone's behind it now except me, Chris, and Eddie Boss."

"You threatened Chris again?"

He smiled tightly. "No, sir, this time he reached the conclusion on his own."

"What conclusion is that?"

"That trying to Fuse will destroy us."

"Or catapult us into another galaxy. We can't Fuse blind, even if we could Fuse at all!"

"Yes, sir."

"Let's talk to Dray." We headed below to the engine room. The Chief listened impassively, shook his head. "No. One of the globs they threw during the last attack melted the drive shaft wall. There's no possible way to generate an N-wave, even a skewed one. All we'd accomplish is to overheat the shaft and most likely blow out the engines. That's if we were lucky."

"You're sure?"

"I'm sure." He regarded me almost angrily. "I'll give you ignition, if and when you give me a written order. I don't expect we'll discuss the results afterward."

"I have no intention of turning on the drive, Dray. Meet me in crew berth one in an hour. Mr. Dakko, gather the crew."

An impatient hour later I faced them. "Chief, tell them what would happen."

"We'd vaporize the drive shaft walls, for one thing. We'll overheat the engines. As it is, we've barely enough power to sustain our internal systems. As to the navigational effect, I have no idea, and neither does anyone else."

I said harshly, "Any questions?"

As I might have expected, it was Elena Bartel who stepped forward. "What's going to happen to us if we don't ignite the engines, sir?"

I was forced to answer. "We'll die."

"When, sir?"

"We don't know that. We'll begin starving in earnest in about two weeks. If the ship remains intact."

"Does anyone know whether the fish could stay in Fusion if we turned on the engines?"

I said bluntly, "I don't know if the fish would continue to exist if we turned on the engines. The energy we'd put out would bear no resemblance to N-waves."

"But it might force the fish to Defuse."

"You don't know that, Ms. Bartel. There's no way to guess the likelihood."

"What do we have to lose?" Behind her, crewmen nodded agreement. I noticed Elron Clinger gazing at her sorrowfully, making no effort to intervene.

"Our lives, immediately."

"We think it's worth the risk." She spoke with defiance.

"I don't. It's not your decision to make."

"I didn't say it's my decision," she said coolly. "That's why we petitioned rather than demanded."

I concentrated on her words rather than her tone of voice. "Very well. The meeting is concluded. Chief, Cadet, come along." I left with as much dignity as I could muster.

Soon after, we consumed the last of our canned foods and had only our meager crops to sustain us. They were not enough.

On the fifty-seventh day Gregor Attani offered his dinner to Mr. Reeves, who refused it. My mood snappish, I ordered the cadet in no uncertain terms to eat every bite of the food he was given. It was little enough; we were reduced to weak soup and boiled vegetables, a few spoonfuls apiece.

That night in my cabin I prayed to Lord God not to prolong our misery.

All day long, I could think of little but food. Our meals, mostly boiled water with weak dilutions of sustenance, failed to satisfy in any respect. The crew's discipline began to dissipate, and there were fights. There would have been more, but for the lassitude of starvation.

I retreated to the bridge and endless games of chess. I played the game openings over and over, trying minute variations after the sixth or seventh move. It seemed as if there was something I could do with the Queen's Bishop's Pawn, if only I could work out the permutations. But I was so tired, so hungry.

I was deep in thought when the speaker crackled. "Bridge, engine room reporting. We have, um, a situation here." Dray's voice was stiff with tension.

Wearily I tore my attention away from the board. "What now, Chief?"

A new voice gave the answer. Elena Bartel. "We're going to ignite the drive."

I bolted from my seat. "What? You can't!"

"We have to, Captain. I'm sorry. It's our only chance."

"Dray, throw her out of there!"

"He can't do that," she said calmly.

"Dray!"

"Yes, sir. My hands are tied behind me. She coldcocked me, sir, with some kind of pipe. And she's got a big knife."

I said, "You can't fire the drive. The bridge override is set."

"I've direct-wired it, Captain. At least, I think I have."

I tried to slow the pounding of my heart. "What is it you want, Ms. Bartel?"

"Nothing. I'm going to turn on the drive. I wanted you to be ready when we come out of Fusion."

"Wait."

Her tone was inflexible. "There's no point in waiting, sir."

I stumbled for words. "Yes, there is. Don't just fire up the drive; make sure the baffles are set properly! You want full power on the first try; I don't think you'll get another."

"Dray can show me how."

"No!" I roared. "It's my ship! I'll show you!"

A laugh of derision. "No, Captain Seafort. I'm not that stupid. You have a well-earned reputation for ingenious trickery."

"I won't trick you." I fumbled at the safe, holding the caller between my neck and shoulder.

"That's right, sir. You won't get the chance."

I said slowly and clearly, "Do not fire the engine before we set the baffle. That is imperative."

No answer.

I took a deep breath. "Elena, I want to go down and supervise. I give you my oath before Lord God Himself: I will attempt no trickery, I will do you no harm, I will in no way interfere, and I pardon you your acts. I so swear, by Lord God's grace. I understand your desperation. Perhaps it's the best way."

"You really understand, sir?" She sounded wistful.

"I do. Please let me come down." I shut the safe.

"All right. But remember the knife at Dray's throat. I'll use it if you try anything."

"You already have my oath not to interfere," I snapped.

A pause. "All right."

Gregor Attani came bounding up the ladder as I started down. "You heard, sir? What she—"

"Yes."

"What are you going—"

"Be silent, Cadet."

His mouth shut with a snap. "Aye aye, sir."

"Wait on the bridge in case I need you."

"Aye aye, sir." I left him behind.

Walter Dakko waited at the foot of the ladder. "I'm sorry, sir. I should have known—"

"It's done." I gave him a fleeting smile as we walked toward the engine room. "Who else is involved?"

"Kovaks and Jokko helped her take the engine room, sir. But she insisted on being the only one inside."

"Where are the others now?"

He looked grim. "In the brig. I had help. Chris, Eddie Boss, Emmett Branstead. Mostly Eddie."

"Very well."

"Sir, we could hear you on the corridor caller."

"Very well."

"Sir, your oath. Are you going to let—"

"Mr. Dakko, I order you to be silent."

"Aye aye, sir." His obedience was instant, for which I was grateful.

"Wait here, around the bend from the engine room hatch."

"Aye aye, sir."

I rounded the corridor bend. Only a few crewmen were afoot, among them Elron Clinger, who shifted miserably from one foot to the other, like a joeyboy who needed to relieve himself.

"I'm sorry, Captain. I tole her, honest, I tole her not to! She wouldn' listen to me!"

"Out of my way."

"I tole her it was wrong, after you trusted us an' all! I'm sorry!"

"Move!" I shoved him aside.

"I'm sorry what she done!" He needed me to know, and to acknowledge.

"I understand, Clinger," I said wearily. "Stand aside."

"Aye aye, sir. Please don' be angry with her. She don' know, it's not like with me, I was crew a long time."

I ignored him, pounded on the hatch. "Ms. Bartel, it's me. Open up."

"What are you going to do?" she asked. Her tone was suspicious.

"Nothing. You have my oath. No tricks. I'll just help set the baffles. I'm alone and unarmed."

"Very well." The hatch slid open.

Dray sat heavily on a bench, hands trussed behind him. "Sorry, sir," he mumbled.

Elena Bartel held the knife near his throat. "Close the hatch and seal it, please." Her thin, bony figure was stiff from tension.

I did so. "Shall we get at it, then?"

She gazed at me, reflecting, and nodded. "I'm sorry, I really am, but somebody had to do something." She looked at me with forlorn appeal.

I nodded. "Mutiny wasn't the answer."

"Perhaps there was none," Elena said. "But we had to try. Can you understand?"

"I understand," I said.

"I don't suppose you'll forgive me?" she asked wistfully.

"No," I said shortly. "But I'll pardon you." I gestured. "Let's get on with it."

Elena lowered the knife. "The baffles are over here, sir."

"I know." I pulled the laser pistol from my back pocket and fired into her heart. Elena spun and fell. Dray screamed.

The knife clattered to the deck. I picked it up and waited for a dizziness to pass before I hacked at the cords binding Dray's wrists.

I tossed the knife onto the table. "Have her body disposed of." I turned to the hatch, stepping over a puddle of Elena Bartel's blood.

Dray was ashen. "Sir—you—I mean, you said—" He stumbled to a halt.

"Have you a problem, Chief Engineer?"

"No, sir! None, sir! I—please forgive me."

"Very well." I slapped open the hatch.

Elron Clinger slouched against the far bulkhead on the opposite side of the corridor. He glanced into the engine room and froze in shock. His face crumpled. I started for the ladder.

"I tole her!" he wailed, beating his thigh with his fist. "Oh, Lor' God, I tole her not to!" His chest heaved in a sob. "Elena! Whadda I do now, honey? Whadda I do without you!" He ran after me, gibbering. "Captain, what'm I gonna do? She loved me! She wassa only person loved me, ever! What about me, now?"

Mercifully Walter Dakko appeared. Clinger's grief faded into the background. I proceeded up the ladder. I passed the bridge and continued to my cabin. I took off my jacket and hung it on a hanger. I washed my face. I dried myself with the towel. I looked into the mirror with loathing.

I sealed the hatch and turned off the lights. I lay down on the bunk.

It was the sixty-third day.

On the sixty-fifth day I sat at my console, staring at the darkened screen.

"Will you have some tea, sir?" Gregor Attani asked. His voice was hoarse.

"No."

"I could get you a cup of coffee."

"No." I felt very tired, very weak. But for Walter Dakko, I'd have remained in my bunk until the end. For two days he periodically knocked at my hatch. I never answered. He finally put his mouth to the hatch and announced that if I didn't open he would get a torch and cut his way in.

I'd let him steer me from my cabin to the officers' mess, and drank the cup of near broth he gave me. Then I combed my hair and went to the bridge.

Every day I found myself straightening my tie, adjusting my jacket, wanting to wash my hands and face. Over and again.

Gregor hovered like a mother hen. I paid no attention. Even his barely concealed misery didn't move me. I tried to invent an errand that would send him elsewhere, but it seemed too much trouble.

I checked the Log to see that its entries were current. I was meticulous about that. Everything must be shipshape now, everything ready.

I remembered something left undone. "Cadet."

"Yes, sir?"

"Stand at attention."

"Aye aye, sir." He did so at once, worry evident.

"I've been examining the Log."

It called for no answer but he said, "Yes, sir."

"You've completed the engineering course with Dray."

"Yes, sir."

"And you have studied navigation to my satisfaction."

"Thank you, sir."

"Though your conduct was not always laudable, especially at first, I am satisfied that you now understand what is required of you and will do your duty."

"Thank you, sir."

"Kerren, record. Therefore, I, Captain Nicholas Seafort, do appoint Cadet Gregor Attani as Midshipman in the Naval Service of the Government of the United Nations, by the grace of God."

"Thank you, sir!" His face was red but he held himself rigid.

"As you were." He relaxed and his gaunt face broke into a slow grin. I couldn't leave it at that. "Congratulations, Midshipman."

"Thank you very much, sir."

My answering smile was brief. "You won't mind if we dispense with the tradition of Last Night, cad—uh, Midshipman Attani. We suffer enough trials that additional hazing wouldn't be tolerable." I paused. "Get the purser's key from Mr. Dakko and find a proper uniform. A midshipman wears blue, not gray."

"Aye aye, sir!" His salute was magnificent. He wheeled and left the bridge.

I relapsed into my stupor. Hours passed.

"Would you like to play chess, sir?" Kerren inquired.

"No."

"Is something wrong?"

"Mind your own business!"

"Aye aye, sir," he said sadly.

Brooding, I realized how much I missed *Portia*'s puter, Danny. Kerren's officious manner put me off, while Danny's naive impudence attracted as well as irritated.

"Do puters have souls, Kerren?" I asked suddenly.

There was a pause of at least a second. "The question has no referent, sir."

"Have you read the Bible?"

"I contain several versions of it, Captain. I have applied analysis to them without productive result."

"Humph."

There was a longish pause. "Do you have a soul?" he asked.

"Yes. I've damned it."

"How so?"

"I foreswore my oath. I gave my oath for the purpose of deceit, knowing I intended to foreswear it."

"I am not equipped to discuss your theology, sir."

"That's a relief."

"What?"

"Nothing."

"I've decided that I do not have a soul as you probably define the term, sir."

"Thank you." I stood. "I'll be in my cabin. Summon me when necessary."

"Aye aye, Captain Seafort. Incidentally, the hatch temperature has risen another two degrees."

I swallowed. "You know where to find me."

I fell on my bunk. Chills alternated with drowsiness and sweaty tossing.

I lay in bed the remainder of the day and into the next. Walter Dakko brought Gregor and Annie to tend me. I tried to push them away.

"Let me, Mista Dakko. I make him eat." Annie proffered the spoon. I turned away, but she forced liquid through my lips, and it was easier to swallow than fight her. After a few moments I slurped greedily at the hot broth, stronger than I'd had in weeks. Then I turned and slept. When I woke, I was alone.

Time passed. Gregor brought me more broth, which I accepted without protest. While he waited, I tottered to the table and was spooning the last of it when the General Quarters alarm sounded.

Our eyes met. "This is it, then." My voice was dull.

Gregor turned away with a whimper, then straightened himself. "Sorry, sir."

"Help me into my jacket. I'll go to the bridge."

"Will you suit up, sir?"

"No. I prefer not."

Eons later the hatch slid open and I made my way to my

console, hot and feverish, alarms still shrilling in my ears. I slapped the switches and they subsided into silence.

"Report, Kerren."

"Engine room has Defused, sir. There seemed to be no one on watch."

"What?"

"We are Defused and in normal space. If you will permit me, you really should have a word with the Chief Engineer, sir. It's most irresponsible to Defuse without—"

"Shut up!" I reached for the caller. "Chief?"

Dray responded. "Aye, sir. I'm here."

"What's happening?"

"Nothing down here, sir. We haven't touched anything."

"Kerren, what do your outside monitors show?"

"Sensors aft show we are in normal space. No sign of the aliens. As I have no reference coordinates it will take some time to determine our location. Sensors forward are nonfunctional."

"Would forward sensors help determine our location?"

"Yes, Captain. Or you could turn the ship."

"No, we can't; propellant tanks are bone dry. Midshipman, you've never been Outside on your own."

"No, sir."

"Go below, find someone in the original crew who's been Out. The two of you suit up, exit by the aft lock, and dismount the wide-band sensor portside aft, remount it forward of the disk."

"Aye aye, sir."

"Keep your suit radios on at all times."

Half an hour later they were clambering along the hull with the aft sensor. I waited impatiently. "Look forward, Gregor. Can you see anything?"

"Not beyond the disk, sir. The disk obscures the bow. I'll be there in a minute."

"Bridge, comm room reporting."

"What is it, Mr. Tzee?"

"It's—I think you ought to listen to this, sir."

"Listen to what?" My voice was irritable.

"We're picking up something odd."

"Oh, my God!" Gregor.

"What is it, Midshipman?"

"A fish. The hull. The whole front of the ship."

"Bow."

"I mean bow. Oh, Lord God!"

My fingernails drummed the console. I muttered, "One of you had better tell me what's going on." My tone was ominous.

Mr. Tzee said, "Captain, you won't believe—"

The simulscreen sprang to life as the new sensor came online. I gasped. Gregor had mounted the camera at the bow end of Level 1, aiming forward. The screen was filled with the pulsing mass of the fish we'd rammed. The remains of our hull, melted and fused, disappeared into its side. A mass of inert protoplasm surrounded the hull, walling it off. It reminded me, I realized, of a scab. The fish's skin looked gray, unhealthy.

A tentacle began to form, ever so slowly, while I watched mesmerized.

I found my voice. "Get away from that, Gregor!"

"You better believe it, sir!" I made a note to rebuke him later, then realized my foolishness.

Kerren rotated the camera in all possible directions. The screen swung dizzily.

"Hey!"

"Sorry, sir. Data input." When the puter was finished he refocused the camera on the fish.

The tentacle had stopped growing. Dots and circles of protoplasm in the fish's skin seemed to flow away from the scabbed hole in its side. Then, while we watched, it stopped moving altogether.

The pulsing ceased. Some essential element seemed to be gone.

"Captain, please let me put this on the speaker!"

"Huh? Oh, go ahead, Mr. Tzee."

Kerren said over the speaker's blare, "I have confirmation of our location, sir. It went faster than expected because for obvious reasons the data was stored first on my retrieval disk. We're—"

I turned to the speaker. My mouth worked. "Good Christ!"

The six o'clock news.

"—home," announced Kerren. "Just outside Jupiter's orbit, about forty-five degrees off elliptical."

I lay back in my chair, the sounds and lights dimming. I shut my eyes. Philip swam before me, then Amanda, holding Nate.

Lord God, please don't let me live.

Please don't make me live.

After a time I stirred myself. "Mr. Tzee."

"Yes, sir?"

"Broadcast this message on all Naval frequencies and emergency rescue channels. Message follows: U.N.S. *Challenger*, returned to Solar System, requests immediate assistance. Dead, injured, and starving aboard. Must have immediate food supplies and medical aid. Class A decontamination procedures must be observed entering and leaving *Challenger*. Alert Naval Intelligence. We have with us the nearly intact body of an alien. Extreme caution advised regarding viral contamination. Suggest the remains be examined to determine means of organic Fusion employed by aliens."

I wiped my hand across my face, discovered my cheeks were wet. "End of message. Add our coordinates. Broadcast continuously until answered."

"Aye aye, sir!" Mr. Tzee's joy was unconcealed.

After a time Gregor appeared at my side.

"Well, boy, enjoy your walk?"

"As much as anything," he said casually. Unbidden he sat at the watch officer's console, an offense for which a middy would commonly be caned. "Sir, why home? Of all the places in the galaxy?" He shook his head. "The odds against that are . . ." He fell silent.

"Who knows? We were already heading that way at a quarter light-speed. Maybe it knew. Our Fusion coordinates were set for home; perhaps it heard that. Or maybe it was following the Fusion tracks of our other ships leaving Earthport Station."

"You agree that's what they do, then?"

"Probably."

"But why, sir?"

I shrugged. "Why do moths seek the flame, Mr. Attani? It is a thing we may never know."

22

"The Admiral will see you now, Commander Seafort." In the comfortable office within Lunapolis Base, the young ensign held open the hatch.

"Thank you." I tucked at my jacket and ran my hand through my hair, again a nervous young middy summoned to the awesome heights of the bridge.

I came to attention before Admiral Brentley's desk. I held my salute just a moment longer than necessary, taking in his appearance. He'd aged greatly in the year and a half since I'd seen him. And he'd shrunk. Before, he was an old lion. Now he was just old.

"As you were." He shot me an appraising glance. "You're looking more fit than the last time I saw you, Nick."

"Thank you, sir."

His glance was shrewd. "You don't remember, do you?"

"Truthfully, no, sir. I wasn't all that well."

"You were about two days from starving to death, my medics say."

"Perhaps. I wouldn't know."

"Sit down, then. Forgive me, I should have suggested it sooner."

"I'm all right, sir." But I sat anyway, gratefully.

He settled in the comfortable sofa next to my straight chair. For a long moment he gazed at me, saying nothing. Then, "Hell of a cruise."

I nodded agreement.

"I'm so sorry, Nick. About your family."

"Thank you." I spoke with stiff dignity, holding it at a distance.

I'd been debriefed weeks before. Interviewed and reinterviewed, interrogated and challenged. Heedless of the consequences, I'd answered every question as truthfully as I could. *Challenger*'s Log, from her initial sailing, and the copy of *Portia*'s Log, through the time of my removal, verified what I told them.

They held their investigations shipboard and here at Lunapolis Base. I suspected that though we were examined minutely and believed free of contamination, no one wanted to risk sending us groundside just yet.

The Board of Inquiry found me not culpable in *Challenger*'s destruction.

Dray testified vehemently on my behalf. I said as little as decently possible. When it was over I went back to the quarters they provided me in Lunapolis and saw no one, while I slowly regained my strength.

Brentley said, "You're becoming fit again, Commander. Would you like shoreside duty or another ship?"

"If I'm not to be cashiered, I'd like a ship, sir. I don't want to go ashore."

"Cashiered?" he echoed. "Is that what you deserve?"

"I've twice foresworn my oath, sir. I have no honor." Nor any hope of salvation.

His lip curled in a smile. "How? When you perpetrated a ruse against that madwoman?"

"When I swore no harm would come to her, intending to shoot her."

"A legitimate ruse of war, Commander."

"I don't see it that way, sir."

"Absolutely necessary to save your ship."

"Yes, of course." It made no difference. An oath is an oath. It is what I am. Now I am nothing.

He shrugged. "What was the other time?"

I was tired of his toying with me. "I believe you already know, sir."

"Perhaps I do. What was the other time, Seafort?"

I accepted the implied rebuke. "While Admiral Tremaine was transferring passengers from *Portia* to *Challenger*. He gave me a lawful order to accept them. I refused, in violation of my oath of loyalty and obedience."

His hand slapped against the arm of the sofa. "Tremaine,

yes. There's another story." He stared at the bulkhead, brooding. Eventually he looked up again. "I'm sorry, Nick. About him. He—" The Admiral lapsed silent and turned away. "He isn't my doing," he said finally. "That's all I can tell you. He's—I had no choice in the matter."

"He was my legitimate superior officer."

There was anger in Admiral Brentley's voice. "He started as that, yes."

"And should have ended that way."

"Nick, what he did was unforgivable."

"Abandoning us? There was no room on *Portia* for everyone."

"Then he should have sent your ship on ahead, and waited. Or, at most, transferred his flag to *Portia*."

"It's what I would have done, perhaps. But it's not my prerogative to second-guess my superiors."

He nodded agreement. "Up to a point, his actions were defensible. But look at the whole and you see his cowardice." Again he brooded. "Bringing as many passengers as possible onto *Portia* was legitimate. But taking your food, even your lasers . . ." He shook his head before resuming fiercely, "And off-loading passengers he didn't like, to leave them drifting interstellar. Despicable!"

"He was selecting the most useful passengers, sir. As he did with the crew."

"That wasn't his judgment to make!" the old man said fiercely. He shook his head in sorrow. "Abandoning children in space!" He put his hand over his eyes, but not before I saw them glisten. "Nicky, I'm ashamed."

"Ashamed?" I echoed.

"For what he did to you in the name of our Service." He stared into the bulkhead and his mouth became grim. "He's a disgrace. As I said, you could justify many of his actions. But put them together—stealing your ship in the first place, interfering with your internal discipline, deceiving you into approaching his vessel rather than issuing a straightforward command, off-loading the transients, taking *Challenger*'s lasers, leaving her without a doctor . . ." He shook his head. "He'll be court-martialed, of course. And convicted. No board of captains could stand for that."

We sat in silence. He said, "I've studied your reports. Minutely and repeatedly, I might add."

"Thank you, sir." I was aware his remark was ambiguous.

"That boy who didn't do so well on *Hibernia* last time, he turned out to be a good officer, eh?"

"Lieutenant Tyre died doing his duty, sir. I will miss him."

"I'm glad of that." He got up heavily and went to his desk to get something from a drawer. "This is for you."

I untied the leatherette folder and opened it. I stared dumbly at the contents. Before embarking, every officer was required as a matter of course to dispose of his property in the event of his death. I'd left mine to Amanda, or to Father.

Philip had left his to me.

There was a receipt for his duffel, now in storage, and his few personal things. A couple of letters. The stubs from his uncollected pay.

I began to cry.

Admiral Brentley waited, saying nothing. When I was able to collect myself he smiled gently.

"So much blood," I whispered. "So much death."

"Yes. You've seen more than your share." He looked pensive. "The information you brought us is invaluable. The body itself—the xenobiologists have gone wild. And Naval Intelligence is spooked out of its collective mind at the thought those beasts have reached our home system."

He smiled briefly. "Our physicists are muttering incomprehensibly about augmented N-waves. Those fish of yours travel faster than we do, Nick. They must, if you were able to get back in sixty-odd days from where it took you seven months to sail."

He stood and began to pace. I wondered if he saw himself on a bridge, far interstellar. He said, "I imagine there'll be some new devices coming out of the labs that will considerably shorten the distances between colonies. And so the world changes again."

He sat heavily. "But I won't be here to see it." I looked up in surprise. "I'm retiring, Nick. As you can see, I'm not well, and I want—" He broke off. "My daughters are buried on Vega Two," he resumed after a moment. "Been a long time since I've seen them, though I talk to them at night. I want to be with them, when my time comes. If the war heats up I won't be able . . . well, it's time for an old man to move on." His eyes misted.

I dared say nothing. Eventually he cleared his throat and tried a tentative smile. "So this is the last I'll be able to help you, Nicholas Seafort. After this you're on your own."

"You've done more than enough for me already, sir."

"Probably. But I'll do more. I told you I'd put you back to Captain after your next voyage. You're still younger than I anticipated, as you got back earlier than expected. But as of today you hold full Captain's rank in the U.N.N.S."

"Thank you, sir," I said, trying to simulate the elation I knew he'd expect.

"Doesn't mean much, eh? Well, you've had a rough time. Are you up to taking out a ship?"

"Yes." I would have long hours in Fusion when there'd be nothing required of me but to sit in my cabin. Days and weeks of blessed nothingness.

"I've got two possibilities for you. *Churchill* will leave for Arcadia in about four weeks. And I've got a ship just come in from Caledonia, that we're sending on to Hope Nation."

"I'll take her." I'd spent most of my career trying to get to and from Hope Nation. Perhaps I'd reach it this time. There were always the Ventura Mountains. Perhaps I could sit overlooking the cliffs with my memories of Amanda.

"She's *Hibernia*, Nick."

The folder slid from my lap. My heard pounded. *Hibernia*! I'd come to Captain her by tragic accident, and managed to guide her safely back to Earth. A full ship of the line, but more. A familiar ship. A home.

"My seniority, sir," I stammered. "I—she—I'm way down the list for a ship so large."

"Yes, ordinarily you would be." He leaned forward, arm on his knee. "But I'm Admiral Commanding of Fleet Ops, and she's mine to give. We owe you for what you've gone through, and besides . . ." He trailed off.

"Yes, sir?" My curiosity was piqued despite my lassitude.

"There's something about you, Seafort. You have luck,

intuition, integrity"—I snorted in derision—"and you always seem to be in the right place at the right time. And you do the right things."

My fist knotted. "I've fouled up about as badly as a Commander can. Why do you keep rewarding me?"

"You brought *Hibernia* back against all odds. You did the same for *Challenger*."

"I didn't bring her back, the fish did!" I cried. "Can't you see? It wasn't me, it was fortune!"

"Or Providence," he rejoined. He shook his head in wonderment. "Captain Von Walther. A legend, when I entered the Service fifty years ago. There's never been another like him." Nor would there be. Hugo Von Walther, Commander of the search vessel *Armstrong*, who'd found the remains of *Celestina*, opened two colonies to settlement, fought a duel with the infamous Governor of Hastings Colony, and been appointed Admiral of the Fleet before serving as Secretary-General.

The old Admiral touched my knee awkwardly. "Son, sometimes I see another Von Walther in you. Or more."

"Goofjuice!" I said with vehemence, entirely forgetting my place.

"Oh, you may think so. But you're not far into your twenties, and look what you've already done.

"By God, Seafort, if you're not another Von Walther, then what are you?"

"Accursed," I said bitterly. "In both senses. People around me die. I wish—" I bit it off. I only wished I could die as well.

"Someday soon, when I'm in my dotage, I'll tell them I knew you. No one will believe me, of course, but I'll know it was true."

"That's nonsense," I said with force.

"One of us is right." He stood carefully, hands on knees to help himself straighten. "*Hibernia*'s leaving in two days. It won't give you any time to go down." Groundside, he meant.

"I have no need." Something occurred to me. "Sir, Admiral Tremaine relieved me before. When I get to Hope Nation, he may want to do so again."

"He might. But you'll carry orders for his dismissal. That's the last thing I'll be able to do for you, boy. When you get back I'll be gone."

"Sir, I swore to kill him."

"Your duel?"

"Yes, sir."

He shrugged. "So be it. I'll shed no tears. Once he's relieved, the dueling code is operative. You'd save us the trouble of a court-martial." He looked at me closely. "Choice of weapons is his, you know."

"I'm aware."

"He's quite good with archaic powder-fired handguns. He may well kill you."

"I won't mind," I said truthfully.

He studied me. "You've been through a lot, boy. I'm sorry." He stood. "I'll have my staff brief you tomorrow on the technical details. But I'll tell you now, our strategists believe the fish hear our ships Fuse or Defuse rather than the Fusion itself. So orders are to make one long jump, as close to Hope Nation as you can."

"That makes sense." It was the opposite of Admiral Tremaine's orders, of course.

"Some of your older passengers are still too ill to travel, but the Reeves couple in particular asked if you'd be going back to Hope Nation and requested whatever ship you'd be on." I shook my head in wonderment. People could be mystifying.

He went on without a pause. "Your, uh, crew. We've offered remission of enlistment. Some have accepted. Two asked to travel to Hope Nation as crew, with permission to resign at the end of the voyage."

"Who?"

"The Dakkos, father and son. Would you mind having them aboard?"

"No, sir."

"And a few of the transpops elected to remain in the Service. It's probably a better life than they'd have otherwise. They're not what we'd like in the Navy, but under the circumstances I can't very well refuse them."

"All right."

"The rest of the transients." He eyed me, then looked away.

"I expect that relocation program will be shut down. It was ill-advised to begin with, as we all knew. But everyone feels it best that the transients not be politically exploited back home, so we're sending the pilot group on to Detour, as originally planned. Would you mind having them aboard?"

"No, sir."

"I didn't think so. You seem to be a sort of Pied Piper to young passengers and crew. It'll be crowded, but we'll make room for them."

I stirred. "How many to a cabin, sir?"

"I don't know," he said testily. "As before, I imagine. Six."

I took a deep breath. "No."

"We're hard-pressed for room these days, Seafort. We've lost several ships, and despite the dangers there's more traffic than ever. Anyway, they're used to it by now."

"No."

"I beg your pardon?"

"I won't bunk them more to a cabin than any other passengers. I consented once to Admiral Tremaine's abominations, and I will not do so again."

The old lion stirred within his gaunt frame. "Captain Seafort, I remind you that you're speaking to the Admiral Commanding."

"I understand, sir."

"I'm giving you an order to ship those passengers."

I got to my feet. "No, sir, I will not."

He snorted with anger, retreating to the formality of his desk. "Captain, you will obey orders!" We glared at each other. "If you want *Hibernia* you will take those passengers."

"I'm sorry," I said. "I would have liked *Hibernia* again."

"I'll have you court-martialed!"

"That's your prerogative, sir." He tried to stare me down. I met his glare as best I could.

The Admiral gave me an odd look. "You really don't care, do you, Nicholas?"

"The truth, sir?" He nodded. "No, sir. I do not."

He came out from behind the desk. "Four, then. That's humane. I'll off-load some regular passengers."

"No, sir." I spoke with finality.

"You stubborn young whelp! After all I've done for you!"

"They are human beings, sir. I've been taught that the Navy has but one class of passengers."

"Yes, but this is different. We're at war, and they're used to it. Three."

"No, sir."

"You'd give up your career for them? Truly?"

"If you force me."

"Two, then." I shook my head but he persisted, "It's no worse than married couples are given! Think!"

I capitulated. "Two, then." He was right. "But in the larger cabins."

"You're dangerous, boy," he growled. "Because you don't care what's done to you. It's well I'm getting you out of home system."

We both smiled, glad to end our confrontation. "A couple of other things," he said. "First, the, ah, mediamen have been clamoring for weeks to get at you. A number of them are gathered outside in the amphitheater."

"Me?" I gawked.

"Yes, you. I kept them away after your last trip, and that's only made them wilder. Your picture is all over the holos and on every photozine. You'll have to let them at you this time."

"But, why me?"

You're world-famous, Nick." He looked at me oddly. "Didn't you know?" I shook my head. This was ridiculous. I felt a growing anger.

He gestured toward my cheek. "That, ah, burn scar. Would you like to do something about it?"

"Not particularly."

"Um. Well, it's your choice. Parents all over the world will hate you."

He saw my puzzlement. "The fashion you'll set," he explained. He opened the old-fashioned hatch. French doors, really. Onto the sublunar chamber.

We walked together through the outer offices, to the corridor that led through the amphitheater back to Old Lunapolis. As we reached the amphitheater entrance I remembered. "What was the other thing you were going to tell me, sir?"

There was no time for an answer. A roar of sound, and I

was blinded by a hundred piercing lights. They came at me, microphones thrust forward, questions screaming in my ear. I froze in shock, my jaw hanging foolishly.

"How did it feel to meet the aliens again, Captain?"

"Do you have any proposals for Naval strategy?"

"How do you feel about—"

"Your wife?"

"All the crewmen who died—"

"Did your family—"

I clutched the Admiral's shoulder. "*GET ME OUT OF HERE!*" One glance at my face and he swept forward, smiling and waving, guiding me through the frenzied horde.

Minutes later I sat, head between my knees, trying to control my trembling. We were in some compartment off the main corridor, still in Naval territory.

"I'm sorry, son. I didn't realize they'd come at you like wolves."

I mumbled something. Then, "I apologize, sir. I'll be all right."

"Good." He shifted awkwardly from one foot to the other. "What I was going to tell you earlier—maybe I shouldn't just now—"

"Go ahead."

"You have a visitor. Your father."

I stumbled to my feet. "Father? Here, on Luna?"

"Yes. He cabled us when the news of your return hit the holos to ask if you'd be going down. We told him it was unlikely, if you accepted another ship, and he said of course you would, so he asked permission to come here. I saw no reason to refuse."

Father on Luna? Impossible. That dour old man who'd rarely left Cardiff except to take me to Academy, enduring the peculiarities of one-sixth gravity just to see me?

My head spun. "Where is he?"

"Waiting for you, son. Down the corridor." Admiral Brentley had the grace to look embarrassed. "Shall I take you?"

"I'd rather go myself, please. Where?"

"West corridor, toward the end. There's a waiting room outside the offices."

"If you'll excuse me, sir?"

"Yes." He hesitated. "I probably won't see you again, Nick, before you go. Or . . . after." Almost shyly he offered his hand. "Good luck, Captain Seafort. And Godspeed."

"Thank you, sir." I roused myself to give a passable imitation of an Academy salute. It was what he would appreciate.

I hurried down the corridor.

The Naval station occupied a separate wing of the teeming new city built onto Old Lunapolis. Two main corridors penetrated its warren of cubbyholes, offices, dormitories, and quarters. After all, Lunapolis held the second biggest Naval Station in existence. The largest was Lunar Farside Academy, halfway around the planet. The Terrestrial Academy base at Dover was tiny by comparison.

I trudged the length of the main corridor, past the regulation suit lockers every twenty meters, absently taking and returning salutes. Midshipmen and lieutenants, respectful of my rank, stepped aside as I passed. In a daze, I stopped to answer civil questions of fellow Captains, until I realized they were making excuses to speak with me. They shook my hand, flocked around me, touched me.

Eventually I made my way to the cluster of offices and waiting rooms at the corridor's end.

I went into the outer office. "Pardon me, is there a Mr.—"

He stood. Creased, older than I remembered.

"Father?" I whispered.

"Nicholas." He walked with the careful tread of a newcomer, still half fearing to lose contact with the floor. He raised his hand gently, touched my cheek. "You're sore hurt."

"Aye." I fell into the old speech.

"They told me. And in other ways. I'm sorry for your family. Your pretty young wife, and the baby I never met. May He cherish them."

"Thank you, Father."

"I've read about you," he said with a thin ghost of a smile. "Something every day. Much of it made up, I warrant."

"Most of it, I'd imagine."

We perused each other, strangers. "You're all grown now," he said at length, almost in wonderment.

"Aye."

He glanced at his watch. "I'll have to go back soon, tonight. I only had a three-day ticket."

"It can be changed—"

"No, there's no need. I've seen you, and I'll say what I've come to tell. Nicholas, you've done your duty. Through all the fantasies of the mediamen, I can read that. You're hurt, but you've carried on. I just wanted you to know that I know it."

"You came all the way to Lunapolis to tell me?"

"I might not be here when next you return; His ways are unfathomable. I wanted you to know."

"Thank you, sir," I said, overwhelmed.

He shrugged. "And now I can go. These places, He made them, but not for me."

I blurted, "Father, I've foresworn my oath."

"Oh, Nicholas!" He bowed his head from the pain. "You're damned."

"I know."

We stood in terrible silence. Fleeting memories crowded one another aside: me, still a boy, crying in Captain Forbee's office on Hope Nation, because my oath wouldn't allow me to set down the burden of Captaincy. My first subtle misstep, when I perverted Admiral Tremaine's orders to cane Philip. The awful descent that has destined me irrevocably to Hell.

"Tell me how it came to be."

And so I told him, haltingly, of *Portia*'s voyage and of *Challenger*'s. I made no excuses, but neither did I look for ways to blame myself as Amanda often rightly accused me of doing.

When I finished we stood in grim silence, aware of the enormity of my folly. Then he astonished me.

"Your oath is your compact with Lord God Himself. Once shattered, you cannot repair it. I taught you that." I nodded. "You are damned irretrievably to Hell everlasting."

"I knew that when I chose to foreswear my oath, Father."

"Yes. I taught you well; how could you think otherwise?" He shook his head in sorrow. "I must adjudge you damned, for so we are taught. But it may be, son, that in His infinite wisdom He has greater mercy than ever I can comprehend. Perhaps He has it in Him to forgive you. Truly I hope so."

He clasped my shoulders in his hands. "Good-bye, Nicholas." He turned and went.

Overcome, unable to speak, I watched him go. Thus I watched him half a lifetime ago, after we crossed the field to the Academy gates, my duffel heavy on my shoulder, aching for the comfort of his kindness, knowing I was not to receive it. After, he gently pushed me toward the gate, and I entered it, and turned to see him striding away, step firm, never looking back.

"Father!" It need not be so again.

He paused at the hatch. "Yes?"

"Father, do you love me?"

A long silence, while he tasted the word, strange to his palate. He shook his head in wonderment. "Love, Nicholas?" He considered. "Love of your fellow man is transient, surely you know that. Only His love endures. Only His love is worth considering. Were I to say I love you, I would be turning your head with inconsequential fancy. But, though it may have damned you, you've done your duty as you understood it. I respect you for that, Nicholas. Know then that you have my respect." And he turned and was gone.

With a pang of longing I knew that it wasn't enough. It never would be.

But it was all I would get.

It was more than I'd ever had before.

Epilogue

We sailed into the deep night, that great ship full of fallible souls, her anguished Captain at the helm.

The pair of frantic days before our departure was consumed in briefings, introductions, sad reunions. Much of *Hibernia*'s crew had been reassigned, but Chief McAndrews still manned the engine room with unabated force, Machinist's Mate Herney still walked belowdecks, and affable Mr. Chantir was now first lieutenant. Enough other old hands remained so that my arrival was preceded by a crackle of excited gossip: "Captain Kid's back!"

My ghastly appearance discouraged any overt welcome from the crew, though Chief McAndrews seemed at least outwardly unperturbed. I had just time, when I found he would be aboard, to scout Old Lunapolis for one of those strange shops where anything might be procured, and return with a securely wrapped package of his smoking weed. I put it in my cabin safe for days that might come later in the cruise.

I prepared for castoff amid a jumble of new, anxious faces: astoundingly young midshipmen, stiffly formal lieutenants, a green ship's boy stumbling over himself in eagerness to please.

And the transients. Eddie Boss had elected to remain a crewman. He performed well, a seasoned hand now, though his discipline was marred by a broad smile whenever he saw me. My scowl failed to inhibit it.

We cast off from Lunapolis Station, fired our thrusters for thousands of kilometers to a safe distance, took our bearings, and Fused.

We would be fifteen months en route.

Captains have prerogatives even in the cost-conscious Navy, and I'd used mine to have all the furniture in my old cabin replaced, so that nothing I'd shared with Amanda would remain. I couldn't have borne that.

I settled into the familiar yet unfamiliar cabin, unused at first to the luxury of a fully trained, ample crew. I haunted the bridge until our puter Darla asked why I never seemed to sleep as much as I used to. Then I realized my foolishness, and left the officers to their work.

I sat alone in my cabin, sometimes reading, sometimes communing with Nate and Amanda, who never seemed far away. I opened the present that Admiral Brentley sent before we cast off; inside the finely carved, worn mahogany box were two ancient pistols and a supply of powder and shot. Intrigued despite myself, from time to time I practiced with them, sighting on a cushioned target against a launch berth bulkhead.

I took my meals in the dining hall, sitting with the passengers the purser assigned to my table, making occasional courteous small talk, fleeing afterward to the welcome solitude of my cabin. I watched the training of the midshipmen without interest.

Life held no pleasure, nor did I expect any.

One day Eddie Boss asked permission to see me on the bridge, and to my surprise brought Annie with him. I waited for him to speak, but apparently his role was to provide moral support; he pushed Annie forward and gestured toward me. Blushing furiously, she stammered something unintelligible.

"Mr. Boss, what is it you want?" I asked with impatience.

Eddie said carefully, "Annie wants t'ask you somethin', sir."

Despite myself I smiled at his conscientious diction. "Ask, then. Why is she mumbling and twisting her skirt?"

Annie stamped her foot in frustration. "Stop talkin' 'bout me like I ain' here!" she cried. "I already tolya what I'm askin'!"

"Tell me again," I said more gently. "I couldn't understand a word of it."

"That's what I been sayin'" she said indignantly. "I wanna talk like—like Cap'n make Eddie do!"

"You mean, speech lessons?" I was flabbergasted.

"Not jus' dat, alla other stuff. Like you showin' Eddie,

walkin' ri, talk like other people." She sniffed. "Like dem Uppies."

"What's wrong with being who you are?" I asked quietly.

Hey eyes fell to the deck. "Miz Captain, she said I c'n be what I wan'," she said. "When she showed me doin' my hair 'n all."

I had no answer to that.

I should have refused at once. But I assented, for reasons I did not understand then and have not since.

We met in my cabin regularly each day. With excruciating patience, Amanda's example before me, I gently corrected Annie's speech, helped her practice social graces, tried to teach her civilized ways.

The more I saw of her, the more I thought of Amanda. I missed not only her companionship, but her body. Her warmth at night, her tender caress, the delight of our coupling.

As time passed I relaxed somewhat with Annie and spoke of these things to her. She seemed to understand, and became my confidante as no other had been. I found she had in her a strength, a resilience that I came to respect and prize.

Walter Dakko, *Hibernia*'s master-at-arms, helped teach her as he had Eddie. After two months of nerve-wracking work, I was delighted with Annie's progress and told her so.

"Thank you, Captain."

I smiled. A month before, it would have been, "Gras, Cap'n."

"You'll be a lady to respect, Annie. Amanda would have been proud of you."

Instead of pleasing her, my remark caused her to stamp her foot with petulance. "Amanda, Amanda! Wid you it always be her!"

"*With* you."

"Wid, with, who care! I always be hearing about Amanda!"

"I'm sorry," I said stiffly. "I miss her. I won't mention her again."

"I miss her too!" she cried. "She was good lady, yeah! She done my hair, she helpin'—she helped Eddie when no one else would! But what about me? Amanda dead, Captain! Amanda dead, an' Annie live!" She threw her hands over her face and wept. Astonished, I could not think how to comfort her, until eventually, awkwardly, I drew her head against my shoulder.

For a long time she lay against me, swaying as we stood. "Don' you need let her go?" she finally asked. "Don' you have needs? Man needs?"

"Needs?" I said hoarsely, stepping away from her. "Look at me! Do you see my needs?"

Her eyes darted down, then back. A mischievous smile flitted across her features. "I c'n fix dat, Cap'n. Let ol' Annie be fixin' yo' needs."

"Don't talk that way!" I cried, unsure as to whether I meant her grammar or her coarseness. "There's been no one," I added, embarrassed. "Not since Amanda."

"Den it be time," she said simply, and came to me, and wisely said no more.

The days and weeks passed. We sailed on, the darkness Outside banished, lit within by the glow of our bodies, rising and falling as if to the waves, sliding, flowing, grasping at each other, floating together, as the great silent ship sailed ever onward through the void.

THE SEAFORT SAGA

Look out for these magnificent adventures:

Midshipman's HOPE

A hideous accident kills the senior officers of UNS *Hibernia* – leaving a terrified young officer in command of a damaged ship with no chance of rescue or reinforcement . . .

Prisoner's HOPE

To save the world, Nicholas Seafort must forsake his vows – and commit an unthinkable, suicidal act of high treason . . .

Fisherman's HOPE

Alone at the centre of a cosmic apocalypse, Nick Seafort faces his final battle . . .

Voices of HOPE

For Nicholas Seafort, the race to save mankind from destroying itself has become personal – for to save his son, he must save the world . . .

THE SEAFORT SAGA

The science fiction adventure of a lifetime

Published by Orbit

THE STILL

David Feintuch

An epic fantasy adventure from the author of the hugely popular Seafort Saga.

Prince Rodrigo was born to rule, but the spoiled young heir of Caledon has paid little attention to duty, compassion or the power that will be his. And when the death of his mother forces him into exile, Rodrigo, now a hunted outlaw, desperately needs allies to claim his throne. To win them, he must learn to rule. To rule, he must command the Still, the ancient power of Caledon.

But first he must rule himself. For to become king, Rodrigo must first become a man.